Chasing Aquila

by
James Hume

Chasing Aquila

Editing by Kerry Barrett

Cover Design by Victoria Bushby

Book Design by JMPL

Thanks to Alastair Dinsmor at Glasgow Police Museum

First JMPL electronic publication: 20 May, 2019

English Edition
ISBN No: 9781099428913
Published in the UK by Jim McCallum Publishing, 2019.

For

SANDRA

The real-life one

My soulmate!

Chapter 1. Tommy

They'd just cleared away the dinner dishes when the phone rang. Jane picked up the receiver, 'Hello?'

'Jane? It's Grandpa Thomson here. How are things over there in Nuremberg?'

He didn't seem his usual cheerful self, she thought. 'They're fine. That's two weeks since the trial started and it's . . .well . . . a bit harrowing at times to interpret and translate.'

'I'm sure it must be. And how are my boys? Looking forward to Christmas?'

She sensed a choke in his voice and wondered why.

'Yes, only three weeks to go now. It all starts here tomorrow night when they put a shoe out for St Nicholas to leave treats if they've been good.'

'And have they been good?'

She smiled. 'Yes, they have. They've settled in well at the international school, and even speak some German already. So with a bit of luck, they'll also be bilingual. They're asleep now or you could have spoken to them.'

'Yeah, sorry to call so late, but I have some . . . sad news for you. Tommy was found dead on Saturday morning.'

'Oh, my God.' Her hand went to her mouth. 'What happened?'

'He drowned in the River Clyde at Dalmarnock Power Station. The police have investigated and confirmed he was very drunk on Friday night – even more than usual. It seems he staggered past his close, went down the side of Dalmarnock Bridge towards the river, banged his head on the bridge, and fell into the water. The police say it was an accidental death under extreme intoxication.'

'Oh, I'm so sorry. How's Grandma Thomson?'

'She's very upset, and just wishes she could give the kids a hug.'

'Oh, please tell her I'm so sorry. He didn't deserve to end like that.'

'I know. But he'd been unhappy for a long time now. I know you've had your differences with him in the past few years, but I hope, when you tell the boys, they'll remember their dad for his good points and not for his bad points.'

'I will. I'll make sure of that.'

'Thanks. Grandma will try to call and talk to the boys later in the week.'

'Okay. We'll talk again then.'

She hung up and turned to her mother. To her surprise, she felt a tear in her eye. She told her mother about the call, speaking in Czech, their mother tongue.

Her mother didn't comment. Jane knew her mother had never liked Tommy, so she just focused her thoughts on the happy early years of their marriage, rather than the loveless husk she'd walked away from a couple of years ago in '43.

***

Every Wednesday, Commander Sir Jonathan Porritt, head of the British delegation at the Nuremberg War Trials, had lunch with his translator group. The huge volume of work meant they'd had to find a new faster way of coping. He'd proposed the use of simultaneous interpretation, where the translators listened to the speaker on a headset, interpreted what they said, and spoke their translation into a microphone. It demanded much more from the translators compared to their usual roles, where they translated each phrase separately.

Porritt knew some of his translators struggled to keep up the pace and avoid errors to ensure justice was done. The evidence would also become more harrowing as the trial progressed, so he wanted to keep close to the group and ensure they were kept as calm and comfortable as possible.

After lunch, as the group broke up, Jane Thomson, one of his senior German-English interpreters came over and sat beside him. They'd worked together for years.

'I just wanted a word, sir. I had a call from my father-in-law in Glasgow last night. My ex-husband was found dead on Saturday morning, drowned in the River Clyde.' She gave him the details.

'Oh, I'm sorry to hear that, though I know you didn't have much of a marriage in the last few years.'

'Yeah. After the Aquila incident, we never got together again.'

'Are you okay to carry on here?'

'Of course, sir. I just wanted to keep you up to date.'

'Well, remember, if you need any help, particularly with the children, just let me know.'

'Will do, sir. And thanks.' She got up and moved away.

He watched her go, and thought back to the night they'd rescued her from Aquila. The spy gang had disguised her appearance, and he'd been struck by her resemblance to the actress Rita Hayworth, but with more prominent cheekbones. Since then, she'd retained that hairstyle and make-up, and the vague likeness still stuck with him.

Within a few minutes, Porritt rose and headed back to his office. From his background in Admiralty intelligence and the Special Branch, he always suspected anything that seemed a little out of the ordinary. Jane's comment on the Aquila incident triggered a memory he wanted to check out.

He picked up the phone and eventually got through to the right person.

'Maxwell'.

'Sandra, it's Jonathan Porritt here. How're you today?'

'I'm very well, sir. What can I do for you?'

'Do you remember the Aquila incident, about two and a half years ago?'

'Of course, sir.'

'Well, I've just talked with Jane over here in Nuremberg.' He took Sandra through the conversation. 'Now, why would her ex-husband stagger drunk from the pub, pass the entry to his flat – a route he must have followed hundreds of times – go down to the river and accidentally fall in? It just doesn't feel right.'

'Suicide, sir?'

Porritt screwed up his face. 'No, from what I've heard, he wasn't the type. Let me run something past you, Sandra.'

'Okay.'

'Maybe I'm just a suspicious old bugger, but I've always had a question mark over the death of the Aquila spy, Brenner. I never realised how important he was to the Germans until after he died. The info he carried was like manna from heaven for them. Yet no one from Germany has ever asked about him, not even via the Red Cross. I find that *very* strange.

'We wiped out Aquila in the UK, but now the war's over, maybe there's a last vestige of it somewhere that now wants to know what happened to Brenner? We kept it very quiet. We made no official statement. So, if someone from Aquila – or even from the man's family – wanted to find out what happened to him, where would he start?

'I think he'd first talk to some of the Aquila gang still in prison, and he'd find out from them that Brenner was alone with Jane when he disappeared. The searcher would then have to find Jane. Someone may remember her contact details from Station 19 that gave her address in Glasgow. So, he goes there, but finds she's moved. What would he do?'

'Ask her husband, because he's still there?'

'Exactly right, Sandra. So, you're on the spot over there in Glasgow. How would you like to check if there's anything suspicious about Tommy Thomson's death, from the point of view that someone targeted him for information on Jane, but he didn't cooperate. It's a long shot, but I'd really appreciate it if you could cast your gimlet-eye over this for me. I want to know if I need to protect Jane.'

'Right, sir. Leave it with me. I'll get back to you as soon as I can.'

He rang off. Maybe it was nothing, but his guts said maybe not.

Chapter 2. Sandra Maxwell

Sandra Maxwell, head of Special Branch for the West of Scotland, hung up the receiver. She'd last met Porritt a few months ago when he'd brought his SB regional heads together to announce his new challenge in Nuremberg, and pass the baton for Special Branch over to Dave Burnett, the head of SB in Yorkshire. Burnett had given an inspired talk on SB's future in peacetime, and most of them agreed he was the right choice as the new leader. But Porritt was extra special. She'd do anything for him.

She went to her office door and signalled for Tom Hamilton, one of her best Inspectors, to join her. 'Remember the translator girl, Jane Thomson, we rescued in '43?'she asked.

'Of course. The Aquila case.'

'That's right. I've just had Commander Porritt on the phone from Nuremberg. She's working with him over there on the Nazi War Trials, and she's just told him her ex-husband was fished out of the Clyde at Dalmarnock on Saturday morning. An accident while drunk, according to our local police.'

His eyebrows raised. 'Blimey.'

'Could you do two things for me, please, Tom. Find out who's the senior officer on the case – presumably it's Eastern Division – and see if we can visit him later today.' She glanced at the clock. 'Say around five. And would you also get the files on the Aquila case up from the archive? I've got to finish a report for the chief, but when the files arrive, come in and we'll check through them.'

'Right, ma'am. Will do.'

Ten minutes later, the porter arrived with two large cardboard boxes of files. Tom came into her office. 'Did you find the SIO?' she asked.

'Yes, ma'am. It's Inspector Jack Bruce, and he'll see us at five.'

'Good. Don't think I've ever met him.'

'Oh, you'd remember if you had, ma'am.'

'Why's that?'

'He's got a reputation as a hard man and makes sure everyone knows it. He made his name as the one who broke the Bridgeton gangs in the thirties.'

'Do I sense a 'but' coming?'

'Well, there was always a rumour he got too close to one of the gang leaders.'

'Who was that?'

'Dan McFadden.'

'Mmm. Nasty piece of work. Well, let's just guard what we say to Bruce in case he's a blabbermouth to the wrong people. Right, let's get started.'

'What's the story, Ma'am?'

'The Commander's suspicious about Thomson's death.' She went on to give him Porritt's concerns. 'He wants us to check whether someone's targeted Thomson.'

'Right, ma'am. So, where do we start?'

'Let's find Jane's original contact info from Station 19. Try Box One.'

They searched the box files. 'Got it, ma'am.'

Sandra opened the box file and flipped through the documents. 'Here it is.'

Thomson, Jane. Date of Birth, 18 May 1918. Place of Birth, Prague, Czechoslovakia. Address, 811 Dalmarnock Road, Glasgow SE. Next of Kin, Thomas Thomson (Husband), Date of Birth, 14 March 1918, Married 26 September 1936. Contact Number, Home:

Nil, Work: Rutherglen 2000 (Stewarts & Lloyds). Dependants, Stephen (Son), Date of Birth, 29 April 1937, George (Son), Date of Birth, 11 October 1938.

She passed it over to Tom. 'So, who in the Aquila organisation might remember her address? Obviously, the two guards at Station 19, Brown and Henry, who copied that info in the first place. And the wife of John Kay, the Aquila spymaster in Yorkshire. And of course, the two spies here in Glasgow. So they're the five people most likely to remember her address and pass it on. And they're all still in prison. So, if the Commander's right, someone must have visited one of them – and then contacted the husband.

'Now, after trial, they went to Lincoln prison. So, let's see where they went then.' She picked up the phone. 'Can you get me the governor at Lincoln prison please, Gillian?'

A few minutes later her phone rang. 'Governor Collins, ma'am.'

'Governor, I'm Superintendent Maxwell of the Special Branch in Glasgow. We're looking into a death up here that may be the result of contacts with people you held in your special segregation unit about eighteen months ago. We have possibly five prisoners involved, and we'd like to know where they are now, and if they've had any visitors in the last few months – say since the end of the war. Could you help us, please?'

'Well, I'll certainly do my best. Give me the names and we'll see what we can do.'

She read out the names.

'Right. Well, we only have a small special unit here, but we do still have Brown and Henry. We want to move them to Manchester, but they want moved to Belfast, and their appeal has dragged on far too long. So, give me a few minutes and I'll get back to you.'

'Thanks, governor. Really appreciate your help.'

Sandra and Tom pulled out the rest of the box files and sorted them into sequence. Then her phone rang again.

'It's Governor Collins, ma'am.'

He came on the line. 'Brown's the only one who's had visitors in the last six months. Three weeks ago, he had two together, for about an hour. His lawyer, George Slavin from Belfast, and his cousin, Aidan Connor, also from Belfast. I've got their addresses.' He read them out. 'Now, one other thing. We photograph all visitors in and out the special seg unit. So, we've got photos of these men as well, if you want.'

'Do visitors know they're photographed?'

'Well, we state, on our Visitor Terms and Conditions, that we keep an appropriate record of their visit for safety and security reasons, but we don't spell out the details. And it's not obvious, so they may not realise it.'

'Okay. Can you radio telegraph these photos up to me please?'

'We'll need to do that from from the central police station in Lincoln. It'll take about twenty minutes or so.'

'Which photo's which, by the way?'

'We're not sure. We think the older dark-haired man is the lawyer, and the younger fair-haired man the cousin.'

'Many thanks for your help, governor. We appreciate it.'

'No problem, ma'am.' He rang off.

'Well, well, well. How about that?' she said. 'Tom, could you make sure our people get the photos to us as soon as they arrive, please?'

Sandra thumbed through the Aquila papers. It had been a huge task to put the case together with a team of officers from across the country, but a great result. The files brought it all back. She smiled with satisfaction, then picked up the phone.

'Could you get me CS McGowan in Belfast, please, Gillian?'

A few minutes later she heard his warm Belfast tones. 'A pleasure to talk to you, Sandra, so it is. And what can I do for you?'

He'd also been involved in the Aquila case and knew the background. She explained Porritt's call and gave him the names and addresses of Brown's two visitors. 'I'm told Slavin's a lawyer and Connor's a cousin of Brown. Could you check them out, please, Alan? Just to make sure they're kosher? I'll send you over their photographs in about half an hour.'

'Sure, Sandra. Call you back later.'

***

Sandra took an instant dislike to DI Bruce. She usually got on well with most people, but he'd irritated her from the start.

He was a big man – well over six feet – with a bullet head and permanent sneer. He welcomed her with, 'You want to know about the Thomson death, ma'am? You here to check up on us?' said with a smirk.

Why would he say that? she asked herself. Maybe it was just a misplaced sense of humour. But, as the highest-ranked woman in the Scottish police force by far, some of her male colleagues seemed to regard her as an alien. Yet another over-sensitive gorilla officer, which they still had too many of in the force.

'Not at all, Inspector. This man Thomson was on the fringe of one of our major cases a few years ago that involved national security.'

Both Bruce and his young assistant, DC Orr, seated alongside him, registered surprise.

She went on, 'We'd therefore like to review your evidence and talk to your witnesses to see if someone targeted Thomson for certain information.'

'What sort of information?' Bruce asked.

'I'm not at liberty to say.'

'Uh-huh. Well, of course, ma'am, we're happy to help where we can. Unfortunately, I'm due at an urgent meeting with my CS right now, so I've got to go. I suggest DC Orr, who did all the ground work on the case anyway, helps you as much as possible, and if necessary, I'll come back later and fill in any blanks. Okay?'

Sandra nodded. 'Certainly. That's fine.'

Bruce stood up, leaned over the table and shook hands. 'Ma'am. Inspector.' He then turned to his assistant. 'Give them as much help as you can, Dougie. It'll do you good to see how other people work.' He left the room.

Sandra sighed with relief. 'Right, DC Orr, take us through the case as you see it? Then we'll look through the case file, go out to the scene and talk to your witnesses. Okay?'

'Yes, ma'am.'

'On you go then.' Tom prepared to take notes.

Orr opened his notebook. 'We got a call from the Chief Engineer of Dalmarnock Power Station at 08.12 last Saturday. His team had found a body at their inlet screens. They pump in river water for their cooling systems through screens and filters to remove river debris. They clear them twice a day. They say they find two or three bodies a year on their screens.

'We went out with a forensic team and examined the body. He had a severe bruise on the right temple, but died from drowning. The power station is adjacent to

Dalmarnock Bridge. On the underside of the bridge, across the road from the power station, the team found blood and skin where Thomson had banged his head. His glasses lay on the ground at that point. The PM report indicated severe intoxication.

'We interviewed his parents, employer, next-door neighbour, and the barmaid and two customers of the Boundary Bar, on the next corner down Dalmarnock Road, where Thomson spent Friday night. In fact, he drank there almost every night. They all said much the same thing. He used to be a cheerful bloke – the life and soul of the party, but got depressed when the RAF turned him down at the start of the war because of poor eyesight. And when his wife left him a couple of years ago to work down south, he got even more depressed. We don't know where the wife went, but the barmaid knew Thomson quite well, told us where his parents live in Cambuslang, and his father identified the body.

'We concluded Thomson left the pub on Friday night, severely depressed and drunk, staggered past his close entry, and clambered down the bank of the river to commit suicide. We believe he banged his head on the side of the bridge, and rolled down part of the bank, fell in the river and got caught by the strong flow into the inlet screens. We've recorded it as an accidental death while intoxicated. We regard the case as closed, subject to inquest.'

Sandra nodded. 'Thank you, DC Orr. Now, can I see the case file, please?'

'Of course.' He pushed the file across the table to her.

She scanned through the documents, and passed them to Tom. The post-mortem report showed a high level of intoxication. The witness statements backed up Orr's summary.

'Right, let's go and have a look. Do you want to ride with us?' she asked Orr.

***

The car dropped them in Birkwood Street outside the Boundary Bar. Sandra looked around. 'Let's walk up to the bridge and have a look. Then we can come back here.'

Thirty yards along Dalmarnock Road, they came to the close entry at number 811.

'Thomson lived here, ma'am. One floor up.'

Sandra nodded, but kept quiet about her previous visit to Thomson's flat, when she accompanied his wife Jane. She remembered Thomson; not a pretty sight.

They walked another thirty yards to the bridge, and Orr pointed out where Thomson had hit his head as he clambered down the bank at the side.

'Do we have to scramble down there too?' she asked.

'No, ma'am,' Orr replied. 'Let's cross the road. There's a wide set of steps down to the pathway – they're part of the power station complex.'

'So, why didn't Thomson use these steps?' she asked.

'We asked ourselves the same question, ma'am. We think he wanted to stay on that side of the road so neighbours couldn't see him, whereas they could easily see these steps.'

She glanced back and nodded. They had a look under the bridge and then walked back along the path beside the power station until it became a metal walkway and they could see the inlet screens below them – a series of vertical metal bars about a couple of inches apart. The water fast flowed through them into the power station. At this time of day, bits of wood and bracken already blocked the bars.

'That's where we found the body, ma'am.'

She looked down at the water flow, with the hum of the pumps in the background. 'Hell of a place to die, huh?' The others nodded.

They made their way back to the steps, crossed the road, and entered the close entry at number 811. Orr rang the bell at the house next door to Thomson's.

The door opened and Orr put on a big smile. 'Hello, Mrs McGregor. It's DC Orr again, and my colleagues, Superintendent Maxwell and Inspector Hamilton.' They all showed their warrant cards. 'May we come in for a moment, please?'

She opened the door wider. 'Aye, come in.'

Sandra entered the flat – a living room / kitchen, a bedroom, and a small bathroom between the two. Mrs McGregor, a small, grey-haired lady wearing a flowered pinny, led them into the living room.

Orr opened up. 'Mrs McGregor, the Superintendent would like to ask you a few questions about Mr Thomson. Okay?'

Mrs McGregor shrugged. 'Aye, it's okay, but I told you all I know at the weekend, son.' She turned to Sandra. 'I did some shopping for Tommy, but he never got over being rejected by the RAF. And then his wife left him.'

'Do you know where she went?' Sandra asked.

Mrs McGregor shook her head. 'No. She'd some important job down south. Don't know where. I don't think he knew either, or maybe he just didn't care.'

'Did he ever have any visitors?'

'No. Well, apart from his mates from the pub. They'd sometimes come back with him and play cards and have a few beers, but I never saw him with anyone else.'

'Did you ever see anyone at his door?'

'Ach, there's always people at the door – selling insurance or other rubbish.' She stopped. 'But, now you mention it, there *was* a man at his door last week. I thought someone had knocked at *my* door, and opened it, but he'd knocked at Tommy's door. He asked about Tommy. I told him he worked overtime till eight, then would probably go to the pub. "The one on the corner?" he asked, and I said yes. He was a friend of a friend of Tommy's, and in Glasgow for a few days. He'd promised to pass on his friend's regards.'

Sandra's heart leaped, but she kept her face straight. 'Could you describe this man?'

Mrs McGregor thought for a moment. 'About the same height as him,' she indicated DC Orr, 'but broader. Pleasant face, nice smile, but he spoke funny – like a foreigner. And he didn't know what Tommy looked like. I had to describe Tommy so he'd know him in the pub, because, as a pal of a pal, he'd never met Tommy.'

'Can you remember when that was, Mrs McGregor?'

She shook her head. 'Wednesday or Thursday last week. Maybe Wednesday, round about half seven, I think.'

'Good. Now, I'd like to show you some photos. Could you have a look at them and let me know if one of them is the man you spoke to last week?'

Sandra went into her bag and pulled out the photos from Lincoln. She passed over the one with the dark-haired man.

Mrs McGregor studied the picture, then shook her head. 'No, it's not him.'

Sandra passed over the other picture. Mrs McGregor glanced at it and said, ‘That’s him. He’s definitely the man at Tommy’s door last week. Who is he?’

Sandra glanced over at Tom and smiled. DC Orr’s jaw had dropped. ‘I’m afraid I can’t say, but thanks for your help, Mrs McGregor. We really appreciate your time.’ She handed over a card. ’Just call me if you remember anything else.’

Mrs McGreagor smiled and looked pleased. ‘Oh, you’re welcome. Glad I could help.’

Sandra put the photos in her bag, and stood up. As they left, Sandra asked Orr if he had the keys to Thomson’s flat.

‘Yes, ma’am, got them here.’

She turned to Mrs McGregor. ‘We’ll just have a look at Tommy’s flat for a few minutes, Mrs McGregor.’

‘Oh, okay,’ she replied, and closed her door.

They went into the hallway, a double bedroom to the left, then a long bathroom, then at the end on the left, the kitchen / living room, which had a bed recess in it. The hallway then led to the right into a large front room with an oriole window, at more or less the same height as the top deck of passing trams. Sandra looked across to the power station and the bridge over to the left. A bed recess in this room had a couple of teddy bears on the bed.

She turned to the others. ‘I want to go to the car and make a phone call. Could you look around the flat and see what booze Thomson had here? He got tanked up on Friday night, and I want to know if he came back here after he left the pub.’

‘Right, ma’am. Will do,’ said Tom.

Sandra left the flat, went back to the car and picked up the radio phone. She got connected in a few seconds.

‘Doctor Paterson.’

'Colin, it's Sandra Maxwell here.'

'Hi Sandra. What can I do for you?'

'You know the PM report on the body fished out of the river on Saturday?'

'You mean Thomson?'

'Right. He'd a very high alcohol level. Could it get that high on beer or would he have had spirits as well?'

'Oh, beer's as weak as water these days, Sandra. He'd have drunk spirits.'

'How much, roughly?'

'I'd say he drank about half a bottle of whisky before he drowned.'

'Thanks, Colin. Appreciate your help as always.'

She went back to Thomson's flat and found Tom and DC Orr in the kitchen.

'What did you find?' she asked.

'Just a few bottles of beer in the cupboard, ma'am, and a couple of empties in the bin.'

'Right. Well, I've just spoken to the pathologist. He reckons Thomson drank a half bottle of whisky before he drowned. Hence the high alcohol reading. So, if there's no whisky here, then either he bought it himself or someone gave it to him. Let's get down to the pub and see what we find there.'

Orr shook his head. 'Jesus, I'm sorry we missed all this, ma'am.'

'Oh, don't beat yourself up, DC Orr. You started with a body and worked your way back. We've started from a different point you couldn't know about.'

They walked into the saloon of the Boundary Bar. It was very quiet, with only a couple of men sat in the far corner. It sounded busier in the adjacent public bar. The barmaid looked up as they approached. A busty, blowsy woman in her late twenties, with big hair, big eyes, big mouth and a big smile. Typical barmaid, thought Sandra

– attractive enough to lure the punters and hard enough to deal with them. DC Orr did the introductions again, and the barmaid, Peggy McLeod, indicated a quiet part of the saloon where they could sit.

Sandra opened up. 'I just wanted to ask you a few questions about Tommy Thomson.'

Peggy nodded and looked down at her hands in her lap. *Was there a hint of a tear in her eye?* Sandra wondered.

'How well did you know him?' Sandra asked. Good barmaids often knew lots of private stuff about their regulars.

Peggy looked down at her lap again for a few moments. Then looked up at Sandra. 'Well, we were in the same class at primary school in Cambuslang, so I've known him twenty-odd years.' She went quiet for a moment 'And okay, we had a bit of a fling. Has somebody blabbed? Is that why you're back?'

'Well, it's not, actually. But now you've mentioned it, could you tell us about it? How long did it last?' Both Tom and DC Orr wrote in their notebooks.

Peggy sighed. 'Oh, maybe two and a half years ago now? His wife had left him to work down south. He was already depressed because he couldn't get into the RAF, and his kids lived with his parents in Cambuslang. I don't think he got on too well with them either. So, he just sank lower. I tried to sympathise and one thing led to another. Moved in with him for a while, but it didn't work, and I moved out after a couple of weeks.'

'What went wrong?'

She sighed again. 'Tommy was bright and cheerful, always up for a laugh, sometimes even the life and soul of the party here in the pub. But at home, he became cynical and sarcastic, and difficult to live with. I'd already had my fair share of that type of man, so I bailed out. And the sex wasn't great either. It just didn't work, sadly.'

It had always surprised Sandra how some working-class women in Glasgow talked openly about sex, and often described practices she herself found unimaginable. Her own limited experience of sex with the love of her life, before he'd been killed ten years ago, had been gentle and tender and loving, and she initially assumed it was like that for everyone. But clearly not. At least this woman spared them the details.

'So, how did you moving out affect him?'

Peggy thought for a moment. 'It didn't help, obviously. But sometimes you take daft decisions on the spur of the moment and then pay the price. What do they say – marry in haste, repent at leisure? It was kind of like that. I regret it now.'

'Well, thanks for being so open. Do you know what happened to his wife?'

'She came back to Glasgow after the war, but she never got back with Tommy again. I think she lived with her parents in the West End somewhere. But she's just taken the kids and gone off abroad this time. She'd to let him know her address and phone number, but she hasn't. And he got depressed again.'

'So, he didn't know where she went, then?'

'Oh, he knows the town. He told me, but I can't remember. Something burg, I think.'

'Did he say what she went there for?'

She shook her head.'No. I don't know.'

'Okay. Can I turn to last Friday night? I understand Tommy came in here most nights and was a heavy drinker. Is that right'

'Yeah, he did come in most nights. We'd cook up a simple meal for him when he arrived. Jeanie's a wiz with powdered egg. But he wasn't really a heavy drinker. Maybe a couple of pints midweek and a bit more on a Friday and Saturday.'

'Did he ever take spirits?'

She shook her head. 'I've never known Tommy to have spirits – not even at New Year. Whisky's too expensive for this area.'

'So, what about Friday, then? Was he more depressed than usual?'

She thought for a moment and frowned. 'No, I don't think so. He'd a new audience last week. If anything, he seemed perkier than usual.'

'What do you mean – a new audience?'

'Well, the regulars here get a bit fed up with Tommy's recycled jokes and funny stories – they regard him as a bit of a bore. But there was a stranger in here last week. He gave Tommy a new audience for his jokes. That's what I mean.'

'When did this stranger come in? And could you tell me about him?'

She paused and thought. 'He came in last Wednesday – a week ago tonight – maybe a bit later than this? Sat at the bar and chatted. Really nice lad. A bit of a charmer, to be honest. Mid-twenties, maybe? An engineer from Amsterdam. He spoke good English, though. He worked with boiler controls, and was here for a few days at the power station.'

'Do you know his name?'

'Yeah, it's a funny name. I'll write it for you.'

Tom turned over a page in his notebook, and passed it to her. She wrote on it and passed it to Sandra. She'd written, 'Pieter van der Huizen'.

Sandra looked up at her. 'How did you get this?'

'Because when he told me his name, I thought he said "housing" and I said, "That's a great name. Can you get me a house?" I mean, me and my boy still live with my mother in a room and kitchen. It's not easy. So he wrote his name down for me.'

'What did he write it on?'

'On a newspaper. It was lying on the bar.'

'Do you still have it here?'

'No, it went out with the rubbish. It's long gone.'

'And did Tommy meet Pieter that night?'

'Yeah. Tommy came in about his usual time – around quarter past eight – saw me talking to Pieter, and kind of butted in. I think Tommy feels – well, felt – something still between us. Anyway, I introduced them and they started to chat, so I left them to it.'

'What did Pieter drink?'

'Half pints of beer.'

'Do you know where he stayed?'

'He said a small hotel near Queen's Park. I mean, there's no hotels east of Glasgow Cross, so he'd have to stay somewhere else.'

'Did Pieter stay till closing time?'

'No. He left about nine. Said he'd some work to do, but he'd see us the next night.'

'And did he come back on the Thursday night?'

She nodded. 'Yeah, it was like a re-run of the Wednesday night.'

'Did he ever ask about Tommy's wife at all? Ask where she is?'

She frowned. 'Tommy's wife?' She shook her head. 'No. Well, it might have come up at one point. But as I said, I don't know where she is.'

'Okay, so about Friday night? What happened then?'

'They met up again, this time with Billy and Jackie, two of Tommy's mates. The four of them sat in the corner over there and played dominoes, with lots of shouts and laughter. I threw them all out at ten with the rest of the punters.'

'Apart from Pieter, were they regular mates of Tommy?'

'Yeah. Usually four of them met every Friday. Haven't seen the other one, Davy Wilson, for a while, though. Got injured at work. Tommy looked after Davy quite a bit.'

'How do you mean?'

'Well, Davy had problems with life in general. He didn't really read or write, and so Tommy tried to help him as much as possible. Treated him more like a brother.'

'I see. So, back to Friday night. Pieter stayed till closing time?'

'Yeah.'

'Did you see where they went afterwards?'

'Well, as I closed the doors at ten past ten, I heard singing outside. Now, that's a no-no in Glasgow pubs, so I went out and found it was Tommy and Pieter. You know the song, *My Lily of the Lamplight*? Well, Birkwood Street still has gas lamps, and that must have inspired them. I told them to shut up and bugger off. Pieter said something like "Right. I've got to go and pack. Got a train in the morning," He waved to everybody and walked across to the tram stop to go into the city.'

'Did you see him get on a tram?'

'No, I came inside to help clear up.'

'And Tommy? Where did he go?'

She looked across at DC Orr. 'As far as I know, Billy and Jackie said they saw Tommy walk up Dalmarnock Road towards his close.'

DC Orr cut in. 'They actually said he staggered up the road, but they went the other way along Birkwood Street.'

'Right, so the last known sighting of Tommy was around ten past ten on Friday night?'

'That's correct, ma'am.'

Sandra turned to Peggy. 'Thanks for your help so far, Peggy. I've only a couple more points. Okay?'

Peggy nodded. 'Yeah, of course.'

'Thank you. Now, I'd like to show you two photographs. Would you look at each of them and let me know if one of them is the man you know as Pieter?'

Sandra passed Tom's notebook back to him, pulled the photos from her bag, and showed her the one of the dark-haired man.

Peggy looked at it and shook her head. 'No.'

'How about this one?' Sandra passed over the one of the fair-haired man.

Peggy looked at it for a long moment, then looked up at Sandra. 'That's him. How did you know? Who is he?'

'We don't know yet. But with your help, we'll find out. Now, one last point. On Friday night did either Tommy or Pieter buy any whisky here – like a bottle or a half bottle?'

'No, they didn't. But they wouldn't buy it from here anyway. They'd get it from the Off Sales counter, on the other side of the public bar. You'd need to ask Edith. She serves in the Off Sales as well as the public bar.'

'Could we speak to her?'

'Yeah. Hold on a minute and I'll see if I can get her.' Peggy disappeared behind the bar.

DC Orr shook his head. 'Jesus, ma'am. I don't believe what's happened here.'

Sandra nodded. 'I know. But it's only the start.'

Peggy came back with another girl. 'Here's Edith. She can answer your question.'

Sandra smiled at Edith. 'Do you know Tommy Thomson, who died at the weekend?'

Edith nodded. 'Yeah, everyone here knows him – knew him.'

'Did Tommy buy a bottle or a half bottle of whisky on Friday night from the Off Sales?'

Edith shook her head. 'No.'

'Okay. Now I've got a photo here of a man. Could you tell us if *he* bought a bottle or a half bottle of whisky on Friday night?' She passed over the picture.

Edith nodded. 'Yeah, he bought a half bottle of Johnnie Walker. Around half past seven? We don't sell much whisky, so you tend to remember it.'

Sandra took the photo back. 'Thanks, Edith.'

'You're welcome.' She went back behind the bar.

Peggy asked, 'Did that man, Pieter, have anything to do with Tommy's death?'

Sandra pursed her lips. Tears welled up in Peggy's eyes and her face began to crumble. It took five seconds for the tears to flow. 'Bastard. Bastard. Bastard!' she shouted, and banged her fist down on the table. She sobbed her heart out. 'Bastard,' she said weakly.

Sandra got up, sat on the arm of Peggy's chair and gave her a hug. She just had to let Peggy cry her grief out. Tom gave her a handkerchief and she dried her eyes.

Sandra knelt in front of her and held her hands. 'Peggy, will you listen to me, please?'

Peggy nodded, still with tears in her eyes.

'Will you promise me you'll never say that again to anyone – about Pieter and Tommy? All our evidence says Tommy had an unfortunate accident. We don't know if this man Pieter's involved or not. *We* can't say – and *you* can't say. Promise?'

Peggy nodded tearfully. 'I promise.'

Sandra squeezed Peggy's hands in appreciation and resumed her seat. 'Now, we'd like to stay here for a few minutes to pull our thoughts together. Will you be okay?'

Peggy had regained her composure. 'Yeah, I'll be fine. I won't say anything.'

'Good. If you want to talk to me at any time, just call me.' Sandra gave Peggy her card and she went back behind the bar.

Sandra looked at DC Orr. 'Can I see your case file again, please?'

'Certainly.' He pulled it from his briefcase and passed it across the table.

She thumbed through it. 'There's no mention of this Davy Wilson here?'

Orr shrugged. 'His name never came up, ma'am.'

'The other person not mentioned here is this man Pieter?'

'Well, again, his name didn't come up in the same way as tonight. To Billy and Jackie, he was just a man in the pub, called Pete. We didn't have a second name, or a photo. The witness Jackie saw Pete get on a tram to the city, and so that took him out of the picture with Thomson still around. We concluded he wasn't relevant to Thomson's death. It allowed us to close the case quickly. We're under pressure on clear-up rates, ma'am.'

'Uh-huh. Aren't we all?'

Sandra passed the case notes back to Orr and closed her bag. 'Can we see these other two witnesses, Billy and Jackie? Where do they live?'

'Just round the corner, ma'am, in Woddrop Street. They're neighbours.'

They found both of them in, and the five of them gathered in Billy's kitchen. Sandra explained they wanted to know a bit more about Tommy.

'Oh, a great guy,' said Billy. 'One of the best.'

Jackie nodded. 'Yeah, one of the best.'

'We also want to find out more about this man,' Sandra showed them Huizen's picture.

Billy looked at it. 'Oh, Pete? Hell of a nice lad.'

Jackie nodded again. 'Yeah, real nice bloke.'

'Did you just meet Pete for the first time on Friday night?'

Billy nodded. 'Yeah, but I think Tommy knew him from before.'

'Did he ask you about Tommy's wife? Where she'd gone?'

Billy thought for a moment. 'Yeah, I think he did. But I don't know where she is. Someplace burg, I think.'

Jackie cut in. 'Aye, but you told him she was away on trial.'

Billy shook his head and sneered. 'Jackie, that's shite.'

'You did.'

Sandra cut in. 'I'd like to know if you mentioned a trial at all.'

Billy shrugged. 'Well, he says I did, but I don't remember it.'

She turned to Jackie. 'You told DC Orr here, you saw Pete get on a tram to Glasgow after closing time. Is that right?'

'Yeah. That's right.'

'You sure?'

He frowned. 'Well, yeah. I mean, he wasn't at the stop when the tram moved off, so he must have got on it.'

She pursed her lips. He didn't sound a hundred percent certain now, but she wouldn't get any more from them. Time to go. 'Well, thanks for your help, both of you.'

Back on the pavement, she turned to the others. 'Shall we just complete the picture?'

They walked round to the gatehouse of the power station, introduced themselves, and asked to meet the head of the maintenance department. It quickly became clear they'd had no checks done on their boiler controls last week, and had never seen the man in the photo.

They left the gatehouse, stood on the bridge, and looked down on the river and the pathway alongside the power station. Sandra turned to DC Orr. 'Where's the next bridge across the river if we walk along the pathway?'

He thought for a moment. 'Rutherglen Bridge, about a mile and a half from here.'

'Mmm. A half hour walk. Let's assume our man Pieter does the dirty deed on Tommy under this bridge – thumps him, fills him with whisky to get him to talk, then pushes him into the river. Would he really take another half hour to walk to the next bridge, or would he just get a tram or bus from here? What do you think, lads?'

Tom and DC Orr glanced at each other. Tom said, 'For me, ma'am, it would take Pieter at least half an hour to bash Tommy's head against the bridge, pour whisky into him, give it time to absorb, question him about his wife, then push him in the river, maybe even longer. So, we're then close to eleven o'clock. I wouldn't fancy that pathway in the dark. You'd never know what lurked behind the next bush. I'd say he'd come back up onto this bridge, but not walk past the tenement or the pub, where people could see him. I think he'd walk the other way, over the bridge, and get a tram or bus from there.'

'What do you think, DC Orr?'

Orr nodded. ‘I agree with Tom, ma’am. Makes sense to me.’

‘And to me.’ Sandra turned to Tom. ‘Right, Tom, will you organise three things, please? First, a team to find and interview every conductor on a tram or bus that passed here on Friday night between say half ten and half eleven. Let’s find out where Pieter went.

‘Second, a team to check every hotel and B&B in the city to see if our man stayed with them last week. He’s an experienced liar, so his Queen’s Park remark is probably false. I’d start with hotels on the north side of the city rather than the south side.

‘And third, a team to drag the river under the bridge here to find the half bottle of whisky. I’m sure he’d just throw it in the river, and it could have his prints on it.’

Tom asked, ‘Wouldn’t the river wash off fingerprints, ma’am?’

Sandra shook her head. ‘Doc Roberts once told me if prints are sebaceous, if they’re oily from having previously touched hair, skin, blood or other oily substances, then his people can pick them off glass or metal even after weeks under water. So, we can but hope.’ She turned to Orr. ‘Do you want to be part of this, DC Orr?’

‘Yes, please, ma’am.’

‘Well, if DI Bruce agrees, join Tom in his office first thing tomorrow.’

‘Will do, ma’am.’

‘Now, Tom and I need to make another call. Can you make your own way back?’

Orr nodded and smiled. ‘Yes, ma’am. No problem.’ He headed off to catch a tram.

‘Where are we going, ma’am?’ Tom asked.

'Out to Cambuslang to see Tommy's parents and tie up a couple of loose ends. I also want to check if this lad Pieter has contacted them.'

***

Mr Thomson opened the door to them. They introduced themselves, showed their warrant cards, and Mr Thomson showed them in. 'I've met you before,' he said to Sandra. 'You came out here with Jane the night her brother died.'

'That's right,' Sandra replied. 'Another sad occasion. We're sorry to hear about Tommy. Sorry for your loss.'

'Thank you,' he murmured.

They went into the front room. Mrs Thomson looked up from her easy chair next to the fire and put her knitting into her lap as her husband introduced them.

'Do you still see Jane?' he asked.

'No, I haven't seen her since then. But I wanted to ask you about your telephone call to her last night. How did you get Jane's number?'

Mrs Thomson looked surprised. 'When they first arrived in Nuremberg, the children wanted to call us and tell us all about it. We got the number then.'

'I see. And did you pass the number on to Tommy?'

She frowned. 'Tommy? No, we haven't talked to Tommy for a long time now. Probably about four months.' She shrugged.

Sandra thought there seemed hidden tensions in the family. 'Okay. Now, can I ask if you've seen this man?' She passed over the photo of the fair-haired man.

Mrs Thomson looked at the photo, passed it to her husband and shook her head. 'No, haven't seen him.'

Mr Thomson said, 'Nor me. Who is he?'

'We don't know yet. He met Tommy last week, and we're following it up.'

Mr Thomson snorted. 'I knew it. I bloody knew it. Stupid bugger got himself mixed up with shady characters. Is this man involved in Tommy's death?'

'We can't say, Mr Thomson. The police report on Tommy states he had an unfortunate accident. Why do you think he got involved with others?'

Mrs Thomson cut in. 'Well, after Jane left him I think he found things a bit tight, and he borrowed money from us. Then about four months ago he paid it all back. Said he'd got a promotion at work, but he seemed to have a lot more cash. We just wondered about it.'

'Mmm. He worked at Stewarts & Lloyds. Right?'

She nodded. 'Yes, he served his time and was a draughtsman there.'

Mr Thomson said, 'You're secret service. Is this man involved in something?'

'We're Special Branch, sir. At the moment we don't know exactly what this man's involved in. So, if you should see him at all, please call me.' Sandra passed him a card.

She and Tom stood up. 'Thank you so much for your time. And again, sorry for your loss.' They left the house and got into their car.

'What do you think of that?'

Tom pursed his lips. 'I think there's maybe more to Tommy than meets the eye.'

'I agree. Let's just check.'

As they headed back towards Glasgow, they pulled up at the Stewarts & Lloyds factory in Rutherglen. They went into the gatehouse and introduced themselves. 'Is there anyone still here who can tell us about Tommy Thomson, one of your draughtsmen?'

The gateman nodded. 'Yeah, I think the drawing office is working late tonight. Let's see.' He got on the phone and a couple of minutes later said, 'Tony Smith's on his way over. He's one of the senior men. Pretty sad about Tommy, though, huh?'

Sandra nodded. Sad seemed the universal word to describe Tommy's passing. A few minutes later, a fresh-faced man in his forties appeared and shook hands. 'Hello, I'm Tony Smith, deputy chief draughtsman. Let's go in here.' They entered a meeting room.

Sandra said, 'We'd just like to know a bit more about Tommy Thomson. I understand he'd worked here for some time and had recently got a promotion. We just wanted to fill in some gaps in his background.'

Smith nodded. 'Well, we were all sorry to hear about Tommy's death. But he left here about six months ago. Jumped before he was pushed, to be honest. And he certainly never received a promotion. His coat was on a very shaky nail for a long time. He was far too cynical and sarcastic, and upset the wrong people here. Sorry, I don't mean to speak ill of the dead, but you might as well know the truth.'

'Do you know where he went after he left here?'

'I don't. He mentioned to a workmate he'd grabbed a once-in-a-lifetime opportunity with both hands. But he didn't say what. Most of us just thought it his usual big talk.'

'And when did he leave, exactly?'

He pulled out a diary. 'A few weeks after VE Day – I'd say the end of May. I'll check when I go back, and if it's different, I'll give you a call.'

'So, he didn't work any notice, then?'

He shook his head. 'No, we were glad to see the back of him.'

'Mmm. What sort of pay rate would he get here?'

'I'd need to check, but typically, with overtime, he'd get over five pounds a week.'

'Okay, thanks. Have you had any other police visits to ask about Mr Thomson?'

Smith thought for a moment. 'Yeah. A detective came here on Monday. A big fellow. Talked with Mr Harding, our chief draughtsman.'

'Could I speak to Mr Harding?'

'I'm sorry, he's not here right now.'

'Could I speak to him on the phone?'

'Oh, I see. Let me try and get him for you.' He picked up the phone and asked for a number. 'Hello, Alan? It's Tony here. I have the police with me asking about Tommy Thomson. They'd like a word with you.' He passed the phone to Sandra.

'Mr Harding. I'm Superintendent Maxwell. I understand you had one of my colleagues visit you on Monday. Can you remember his name?'

'Em, Inspector . . .. Bruce, I think. His card's in my top left drawer. Tony can check it for you, if you want. A very tall man, rather blunt spoken.'

'Oh, yes. Did you tell DI Bruce that Thomson had left your employ six months ago?'

'Of course. I told him. We don't know who or where, but he seemed to be doing well. Appeared to be quite prosperous.'

'And what did DI Bruce say?'

'He didn't say anything. He just wanted me to confirm Thomson was depressed and a heavy drinker. I confirmed it, and DI Bruce seemed happy.'

'Thank you very much, Mr Harding. Sorry to have bothered you.'

'No problem, Superintendent. Glad to help.

She handed the phone back to Smith, stood up, and gave him a card. 'Thank you very much for your help. Call me if you think of anything else.'

He nodded and showed them out.

They stood beside their car. Sandra shook her head. 'Well, well. A man with a secret, huh? Everybody thinks Thomson still works here, but he doesn't. So, what was he doing? And why do the witness statements from the family and the employer, not mention more cash or changing jobs? Were they deliberately excluded? Why would the SIO do that? Just to get the case closed quickly, or what? Let's check Thomson's flat again. I wonder if Mrs McGregor has a key?'

They drove down the road, across the bridge past the City of Glasgow sign, and parked opposite Tommy's tenement building.

As they went up the stairs, Tom said, 'Do we need a warrant, ma'am?'

Sandra shrugged. 'No. We suspect him of a possible serious crime; we've got an urgent timeline and we've already been in there tonight; and he's not around to give permission anyway.' They rang Mrs McGregor's doorbell.

Mrs McGregor had a key. 'You might as well keep it,' she said. 'I don't need it now.'

Sandra and Tom entered Tommy's flat and put on fine gloves. They checked the first bedroom on the left. Under the bed, they found a small suitcase that looked new. Empty, except for keys in the bottom.

They then checked the bathroom next door, the kitchen / living room, the chest of drawers at the top of the hall, the hall cupboard, and the front room. Tom checked a writing bureau against the right-hand wall near the oriole window. All clear.

But that triggered off a memory for Sandra. 'When we prepared the Aquila case, Malcolm Craig from London told us a story of how the safecracker on his team found a secret compartment in a writing bureau. Let's have a look and see if there's one here.'

She followed the sequence Malcolm had described, and discovered a secret compartment behind the three upper drawers. She smiled at Tom. 'How about that?'

'Blimey,' Tom exclaimed. 'Well done, ma'am.'

The compartment contained an ID card; a passport; a small black notebook; two plastic bags, with foreign words printed on the outside and full of small white pills; eight small plastic bags, each with a thin red reseal strip, and five of the same pills; and several stashes of five and one pound notes, all neatly bundled in elastic bands. Sandra lifted out the ID card and the passport, both in the name David Wilson. The ID card gave his address as 15, Ardenlea Street, Glasgow, SE, and a date of birth of 11 April, 1916. The passport showed Mr Wilson had entered Holland through Schiphol Airport three times in the last four months, the first on 23rd July. The photograph in the passport was Tommy Thomson.

She gently lifted out the plastic bags. 'Wonder what these are?' she murmured, 'and how did he get them here? Tom, could you get the suitcase from the bedroom, please?'

She lifted out the cash and estimated more than three hundred pounds. So, whatever Tommy had been doing, presumably selling these pills, had been very lucrative. She glanced through the notebook – full of names and numbers. She'd need time to study it.

Tom came back with the case and Sandra examined the inside. She estimated distances with a pencil. 'I think there's a false top and bottom in this case – maybe an inch gap in each? Big enough to hold these pills. I'll bet that's how he brings them in.'

She sat down on the arm of a sofa and pondered. 'Tommy must sell these pills for big money. Yet, he's dead five days and no one seems interested. Now, it can't last. I think we need to do two things – check on this David Wilson, and set up a camera here to see who comes to call. Let's go. Have you got an evidence bag? We'll take this lot into safe custody.'

He pulled out a large paper bag from his inside pocket. 'Got one here, ma'am.'

'Right, let's get this lot into the car. We'll take the suitcase too.'

They closed the bureau, locked the flat, and put the bag and case in the car boot.

'Can you find out where Ardenlea Street is, Tom, while I make a call?'

The phone connected. 'Roberts.'

'Alex, it's Sandra Maxwell here. Remember the cat camera you set up in Shawlands last year? Do you still have it? I'd like to use it in a house in Dalmarnock Road.'

'Well, it's on a table next to me here, but I'd need to check if the Selenium cell still works and put a new battery and film into it. When do you need it?'

'Now, if possible.'

'Right, I'll check it out, and if it's okay, I'll drop it off on my way home. Be about forty-five minutes. What's the number?'

'811. One up left. Name of Thomson.'

'Okay. See you then, Sandra.'

She got out of the car. 'Have you found Ardenlea Street?' she asked Tom.

'Yes, ma'am. Just along Birkwood Street, two streets over.'

'Okay, let's keep a low profile and walk over.' She told the driver that if Doc Roberts appeared before they came back, ask him to wait.

***

They rang the doorbell and waited. Sandra could hear shuffling and bumping behind the door and glanced at Tom. After a few minutes the door opened and a man peered at them through his glasses. He leaned on a crutch. 'Mr Wilson?'

The man nodded.

They introduced themselves, and asked if they could come in. The man struggled behind the door and they then realised he had two crutches, and a plaster cast on his right foot.

'What you here for?' he asked, abruptly.

'We're sorry to bother you, but we're following up on the death of Tommy Thomson, and wondered if you could tell us about him.'

Mr Wilson's head dropped onto his chest. 'I can't believe it. I can't get over it. Just the best mate any man could have. Christ, they sure take the good ones first.'

'How well did you know him?'

'I feel I've known him all my life, but it's only since he came to live here just before the war. He kept me right. I don't read or write very well. Tommy got me a wee bank account, and slipped me a few quid now and then. Got me a lawyer to sue the company over this.' He indicated his foot. 'I don't know what I'll do now. I mean, these letters up there,' he pointed to the mantelpiece. 'Christ, what do I do?' he pleaded.

'Can I have a look?'

'Yeah, go ahead.'

Sandra stood up and got the letters. 'There's two from the Clydesdale Bank and one from an insurance company. Do you want me to open them?'

He nodded. 'Aye, if you would.'

She took a pencil from her bag and slit the three envelopes. 'The first letter from the bank gives changes to the Terms and Conditions of your account. The second asks you to go and see them to discuss possible investments.'

He shook his head. 'I don't even know what any of that means.'

'Well, why don't I go in and see them for you, and get them to help you.'

He nodded. 'Thanks.'

'And you should pass this other letter from the insurance company to your lawyer. Do you have his name and address?'

It's on the table over there. His name's Wallace.'

Sandra looked at the few letters lying open on the table and found one from the lawyer. She noted no letters from the bank amongst them. 'Right, I've got it here. Why don't I go and see him as well for you and sort this out too?'

He nodded again. 'Yeah, thanks.'

Sandra put the letters in her bag. 'I'll do it tomorrow. What's your date of birth?'

'Eleven four sixteen.'

'Okay. When did you last see Tommy?

'Last Thursday, when he brought me back from the hospital. He usually came round two or three times a week.'

Sandra nodded. 'One last point.' She pulled the photo of the fair-haired man from her bag. 'Have you seen this man at all? Has he been at your door?'

He looked at the picture and shook his head. 'No, I've never seen him.'

'Okay.' She wouldn't get anything else useful here. Tommy had obviously used Wilson's ID without his knowledge. 'Well, thank you for your time, Mr Wilson.' She picked up her bag, and she and Tom left, making sure the door closed behind her.

Sandra glanced at Tom. 'What a situation, huh?'

Tom nodded. 'Poor bugger. Can hardly move, and can't read or write. We don't know when we're well off.'

They got back to their car just as Doc Roberts drove up. They shook hands and Sandra led the way up to the flat. Sandra pointed to the chest of drawers in the hall. 'I thought we might put it on here, looking down the hall to the front door.'

'Okay,' said Roberts, pulled the ornament out of his bag, and placed it on the unit.

'Blimey,' Tom said. 'It just looks like any cat ornament. How does it work then?'

Roberts smiled. 'The Selenium cell in this eye is light sensitive. It triggers when the light changes, up or down, and in turn, triggers the Minox camera behind this eye. So, if we close the side doors from the hall, then whoever comes in the front door will put on the hall light and the cat will take his picture. It's a bit crude, but it works. At least, it did last year. I'll come in every morning to see if it has triggered and let you know.'

Tom laughed. 'Brilliant.'

'Right, if you two leave first, I'll set the camera and join you outside.'

On the way into the office, Sandra and Tom discussed the three tasks agreed earlier. Tom said, 'I'll get the night shift started on the first two to give us a head start.'

Sandra nodded. She just wanted to get to her desk and think through the events of the day. And she needed to call Porritt back as well.

A note on her desk said CS McGowan had called her. Would she call him back, please? Let's get this out of the way first, she thought, and picked up the phone.

'Alan, sorry I missed your call.'

'Just to give you an update, Sandra.'

'Great. What have you got?'

'Right, George Slavin, the lawyer, is kosher. He got approached by a Mr John Coyle, Sergeant Brown's father, to see if he could get Brown transferred to Northern Ireland. You might remember Sergeant Brown had a false ID. His real name's Charles Coyle.'

'I do remember.'

'So, John Coyle introduced Aidan Connor to Slavin as a relative. We asked John Coyle about Connor, and he admitted Connor's not a relative. He'd approached Coyle out of the blue, wanted to talk to Sergeant Brown, and offered Coyle a lot of money – and would pay the lawyer's fees on top. Coyle went for it.

'If he has to contact Connor for any reason, he writes to him at the address you gave me, which turns out to be a 'convenience' address.'

'Oh? What's that?'

'I think you know over here we have two very separate communities – the Unionists and the Nationalists – protestants and catholics.'

'Yeah.'

'Well, most people think the two never meet. But in fact, there are lots of relationships across the divide that need to communicate with each other in a safe and private way. So, way back in the early thirties, a very enterprising man, who owned a small newspaper shop in the city centre, started a sort of club. For a small fee, you could have your secret mail delivered to the shop address. When you went in to buy your paper and ciggies, you gave your name and your four-digit access code, and if you had fully paid, you got your mail as well. I believe he started it to help a mate out and it just mushroomed from there. In fact, our lads saw the postman arrive with a small sack of mail, and he gets that twice a day. The current fee's a shilling a week, so he has a good sideline there.

'Anyway, the man admitted he had an Aiden Connor as a member, and recognised the picture, but he didn't come in very often, and the name's probably false. He reckons most of his members use false names. It doesn't matter to him.'

'Jesus. Is that legal, Alan?'

She could sense him shrug at the other end. 'Don't think it's illegal, Sandra. Not unless someone uses the name and address as an official ID. Anyway, bottom line, we don't know who Connor is. We'll check out any Aiden Connors we have on the voters' roll, but I wouldn't hold out much hope. Sorry, Sandra.'

'Oh, don't be sorry, Alan. A great piece of work so quickly. Thanks.'

'Right, well, if anything else breaks, I'll get back to you.'

***

Sandra put the evidence bag in her safe, the suitcase in her cupboard, and locked both. She then sketched out what she'd say to the Commander, and asked for the number.

'Porritt,' came the familiar voice.

'Good evening, sir. Sorry to call so late, but I thought you'd like to know your suspicions over Thomson's death were justified.'

'Really? Tell me about it.'

She took him through her findings of the visitor to Brown in prison who then appeared in Glasgow and befriended Tommy. She outlined her thoughts about what happened, and concluded, 'We don't know whether Thomson's death was deliberate or accidental, but they must have fought because Thomson wouldn't give Huizen any info on Jane. I think the most Huizen probably got from his visit, was Thomson's wife could be in a place called something 'burg', and maybe has something to do with a trial. Could he work out from that where she is? I don't know. But on balance, I think he might turn up in your area soon.

'At the moment, I can't prove what happened. But I'm certain Thomson did not commit suicide or fall in the river by himself while drunk. That conclusion doesn't even fit the basic evidence, without our wider background. Makes me suspicious of the SIO.

'I'll send you over Huizen's picture and details, sir, if you give me the number, and I'll let you know tomorrow what else we find.'

'Brilliant, Sandra.' He gave her the number. 'Appreciate your quick work.'

'No problem, sir. However, the case has become complicated, because I've just found out Tommy Thomson was also a drug dealer, and so he might have been targeted for that. But, for the moment, I'm sticking with Huizen, aka Connor, as the guilty party.'

She hung up the phone. Enough for one day. It would start all over again in the morning. She headed for home to relax.

***

Her phone rang just as she got into bed.

'Sorry for calling so late, ma'am.'

'Okay, Tom. What have you got?'

'I've just had DC Orr on the phone, ma'am. All Eastern Division staff have been pulled off our job. They had a possible murder tonight.'

'Well, that's understandable.'

'Guess who the victim was, ma'am?'

'Who?'

'David Wilson.'

Sandra sat on the bed, and stared at the wall. Jesus. This could get very messy. She had knowledge about the victim no one else had. She pursed her lips. 'Shit.'

'That's what I thought, ma'am.'

'Okay, let's sit on it for the moment, and see what happens in the morning.'

'Right, ma'am. Good night.'

Two minutes ago, she couldn't wait to get to sleep. Now her brain raced. She stood up and put her dressing gown back on. How the hell would she handle this?

Chapter 3. Cian

Cian gritted his teeth. A third night in this grotty pub, with its grotty people, grotty barmaid and grotty beer, and he still hadn't got the information he wanted.

He'd used all his charm and best Dutch accent, but every time he raised the subject of his wife, Tommy just backed off. The barmaid couldn't remember – somewhere abroad – something burg. Now, with his last chance, these two numbskulls, Billy and Jackie.

Tommy had gone for a pee and another chat with the barmaid. He leaned forward and spoke quietly to the two. 'I thought Tommy had a wife. Does she ever come in here?'

Billy scoffed. 'No chance, mate. She's buggered off and took the kids.'

He lifted his eyebrows. 'Jeez, really? Where did she go?'

'Christ knows. Someplace burg. To do wi' a trial, I think.'

Jackie cackled. 'Aye, it's Pissburg.'

Billy scowled at him. 'No, it's no' Pittsburgh.' He paused. 'Hamburg?'

Jackie cackled again. 'Ham an' egg burg. Do you think we'll ever see them again?'

'Shut up, I'm thinking.'

Cian glanced over at Tommy, still deep in conversation, and then leaned towards Billy. 'Oh, it's okay, Billy. Forget it.' He wouldn't get anything useful from these two dodos.

Tommy came back to the table with a round of drinks. 'Come on, Billy. Get the dominoes out. I thought you'd have them ready by now.'

Jackie screwed up his face. 'Hey, Tommy. Where did your wife go again?'

Cian grimaced. *Shit*, he hadn't wanted that mentioned.

Tommy didn't even look up. 'Bloody nowhere. Who the hell cares? I don't. She can rot in hell wherever she is. Come on, let's get on with the dominoes.'

Cian played dominoes with them, and laughed at their stupid banter. He planned to have a nightcap with Tommy and get him drunk on whisky to loosen his tongue.

The bell rang at ten o'clock, and everyone had to leave the pub. He noticed the gas-lamps in the street. 'Hey, they remind me of the song, you know, *Underneath the lantern, By the barrack gate, Darling I remember, the way you used to wait*'. Tommy came over and joined in, linking shoulders.

Then Peggy appeared and told them to shut up and bugger off.

Cian turned to the others. 'I've got to catch an early train in the morning. Good night, everybody.' He waved, and crossed the main road to the tram stop. He watched Tommy stagger along the other side of the road and enter his close mouth. Give him a couple of minutes to get up to his flat and then he'd join him for that nightcap.

A tram came along from the left and stopped because of a tram already at Dalmarnock terminus. The new tram blocked his view of the pub, and more importantly, blocked their view of him. Another tram came from the right across the bridge and stopped alongside the terminus tram. He'd never have a better chance to cross the road unseen. He hurried up his side of the road as the terminus tram moved onto the crossover. Now completely blocked from view, he nipped across the road and entered the close at 811. He stopped to get his breath and then moved towards the stairs.

He'd just reached them when he sensed a movement out of the shadows on the right, and suddenly Tommy appeared, grabbed him by the throat, thrust a gun against his neck, and pushed him back against the wall. Tommy's strong glasses, an inch from his face, seemed more sinister in the flickering gaslight.

Tommy snarled at him. 'What the hell do you want, ya creepy bastard?' Tommy rammed the gun harder into his neck, and pulled his tie upwards, choking him. Cian's body shivered with fear, and he felt warm fluid running down his legs. 'Why're you so bloody interested in where my wife is, eh?' Tommy thrust the gun into his neck again and pulled the tie tighter. 'Come on, talk, ya bastard. D'ye think I'm stupid or something?'

He tried to speak, but could only croak. Then a door banged somewhere upstairs and they heard someone coming down.

Tommy pulled the tie back harder, pushed him through the close into the back court, and rammed him up against the wall in the darkness with the gun at his neck again. 'Come on, move!' Tommy pushed him along the wall to the end of the building, then across ten yards of grass towards the bridge. Cian trembled, afraid of what might happen.

He got pushed down the grassy slope at the side of the bridge. Shit, Tommy was going to shoot him and dump him in the river. Then they both lost their footing and tumbled down the slope to the river bank under the bridge. Tommy dropped the gun, and the stranglehold on

Cian's tie eased. It was the fraction of a second he needed to grab Tommy's hair and bang his head against the underside of the bridge, and then bang it again to make sure. Tommy slumped to the ground, his glasses landing nearby.

Cian bent down and pulled Tommy fully under the bridge. He noticed the gun lying on the ground and kicked it into the river. That made it more even, he thought. Tommy moaned and tried to sit up. He pulled the half bottle of whisky from his pocket, opened it, held Tommy's nose closed and poured the whisky into Tommy's mouth. Tommy spluttered as he swallowed. He gave him more whisky the same way.

He leaned over Tommy. 'Where's your wife? Where's she gone? Tell me and I'll let you go.' He shook Tommy's head. 'Tell me.'

He held Tommy's nose again and poured more whisky into his open mouth. Tommy spluttered and opened his eyes.

'Tell me. Where's your wife?'

Tommy snarled, 'Bugger off.'

He held Tommy's nose and gave him more whisky. Only a few drops left now. 'Where's your wife?'

Suddenly Tommy's hands came up around his neck, though not as tight as before. He punched Tommy in the face, which pushed him further down the bank. Tommy's head lay only an inch from the flowing water. He stretched out and grabbed Tommy's neck. 'Where's your wife?'

Tommy tried to punch him in the face, but the movement changed Tommy's body position and it slid down the bank into the river. Cian reached over, tried to grab Tommy and hold him back from going under, but couldn't get a proper grip, and Tommy gently slipped under the surface. Bubbles came up from his mouth.

Cian watched in dismay as Tommy floated slowly away. He pushed the whisky bottle into the river and got onto his knees. Then he clambered up, leaned against one of the bridge supports and tried to calm himself,. His whole body shook and shivered with the emotion and effort he'd put into saving himself.

He stood for a while in the darkness, recovering, then scrambled up the grassy bank to the road and staggered over the bridge to a bus and tram stop. A few minutes later a bus came along going to Glasgow. He signalled it and got on.

He brushed dirt off his coat with his hands and fixed his tie. All that effort and time wasted. Shit, what would he do now? And he'd have to tell G he'd failed. This spying business was harder and more dangerous than he thought.

***

He staggered into the hotel, after a long walk out the Great Western Road from the city centre. He hadn't dared take a taxi in his condition.

Annika jumped out of her seat as he entered the room, came rushing over to him and threw her arms around his neck. 'I've been worried sick.' She stepped back and looked at him. 'Oh, *mijn God*. Let's get your coat off.' She helped him struggle out of his coat. 'This'll need a good brushing. What happened?'

'I was in a fight.'

'With who?'

'A man called Tommy.'

'Is this the man you want to find his wife?'

'Yeah. And I still don't know where she is. Someplace called burg – and it might have to do with a trial. It's all I've got. And G won't be happy. He's spent all this money to find her, and I've failed.'

'Don't get too downhearted. Burg sounds German. Let's check it out tomorrow. What happened to the man, Tommy?'

'He drowned – in the river.'

She stared at him with her mouth open. 'What?'

He nodded. 'Yeah.'

She looked at the floor, and choked. 'Oh, *Jezus Christus*.'

'Well, it was either him or me. Kill or be killed. He attacked me with a gun.'

'So, you defended yourself. Did anyone see this?'

He shook his head. 'No. And self-defence would be difficult to prove.'

'Is he still in the river?'

'Yeah, I suppose so.'

'Well, he won't be found until it's light. Eight o'clock at the earliest. We'll get out of here early. Catch the first train to London. We can sort out where we go from there.'

'Right.'

He began to realise the enormity of what had happened and his stomach leaped. He dashed into the bathroom, knelt in front of the toilet bowl and spewed his guts into it. After a few minutes he scrambled to his feet and took a drink of water, then staggered back to the room, slumped into an easy chair, put his head back, and fell asleep within minutes.

***

He sat in the middle of a long row of seats in the middle of Central Station. Everything seemed normal. The noises of the station echoed around him. The men on a high platform updated the destination boards. The seven o'clock train to London Euston was indicated for Platform One.

He could see Annika at the ticket window, her bright blonde hair a startling contrast to those around her. As usual, she wore her new *Kleppermantel*, a long, hooded, rubber-lined German raincoat with a shiny grey cotton surface that shimmered and rippled as she walked, such a contrast to the short, dull utility clothes around her. She looked super-attractive, and several men turned and admired her as she walked past. He just wished, this morning, she'd have been a bit less conspicuous.

She sat next to him, and the man on her other side got up and left a newspaper behind. She picked it up and held it towards him, *The Glasgow Herald*. 'Do you want this?'

He shook his head. He couldn't concentrate on anything except to get away from here.

She started to flick through the paper, then stopped and read an article on page three. She leaned over to him and murmured, 'You need to read this,' and passed him the paper folded at the relevant article.

'Hess Says Loss Of Memory Was Hoax

Pretence Adopted for "Tactical" Reasons

Prepared Statement Read to Nuremberg Court

Nuremberg, Friday

The War Crimes Tribunal this evening heard an extraordinary declaration from Rudolf Hess that his loss of memory had been simulated for "tactical" reasons, and that, together with his comrades, he wished to face the verdict of the court.

Lord Justice Lawrence, the President, with an astonished glance at his fellow Judges, hastily adjourned the Court until tomorrow.'

The article went on to give details of the events, including the reactions of prosecuting counsel for Britain, the United States and Russia.

She leaned over to him again. ‘Didn’t you say she translated German to English?’

He nodded. ‘Yeah. That’s what Brown said.’

‘Well, there must be a hell of a lot of translation required there. I think that’s where we should head.’

Chapter 4. Porritt

By the time Porritt arrived in his office on Thursday morning, he'd more or less worked out what to do. He picked up the phone and asked for the number.

'Ja. Direktor Wolff.'

'Hans, it's Jonathan Porritt at the Palace of Justice. How are you today?'

Silence for a moment. 'Ah, Jonathan. Good to hear from you. What can I do for you?'

'I'm looking for some police help, and would like to talk to you about it.'

'Do you mean *real* police help?'

'Yes, I do.'

'*Mein Gott*. Of course. Anything to get me out of this crazy limbo.'

Porritt knew lots of Germans felt the same way about the Occupation – stoic tolerance at best. He wondered how he'd feel in the same situation. 'Good. Do you want to come over here or should I come to you?'

'What is it you say? It would set too many rabbits running if you came here. I'll come to you. In about twenty minutes or so?'

'Thanks, Hans. See you then.'

Porritt liked Hans Wolff, head of KriPo, the detective branch of the State Police in the Nuremberg area; a broad-shouldered man with a round face, ready smile and twinkly eyes that belied his profession. He'd met him a couple of times at receptions. They had a lot in common, swapped stories of real cases, and treated each other as equals. Porritt thought he could trust him and get his support if he told his story the right way. Anyway, he couldn't bring his own people over from

Britain because of the language problem. So, he didn't have much choice. He *had* to make it work. He also thought it a lot more exciting than his rather false job in Nuremberg.

He'd had to organise everything from translators and stenographers to food, transport, accommodation and security for the British judges and lawyers at the Trial. But he also had to work alongside his equivalents from the other occupying countries, and that wasn't easy. He breathed a huge sigh of relief when the first Trial – the International Military Tribunal for major war criminals – had started on 20th November.

Porritt felt his own little world in Nuremberg mirrored the national picture. After the German surrender in May, the Allies had divided Germany into four military occupation zones, where each of the Allied countries – France in the southwest, the UK in the northwest, the USA in the south, and the Soviet Union in the east – had full sovereign authority in their respective zone. The German people had no say on any matter.

Porritt asked himself how the hell Germany could possibly recover from such a defeat? He answered, from his experience so far, their best chance was to exploit the fact the victors couldn't speak with one voice.

The overall direction for Germany was set by the Allied Control Council, in which senior members of each occupying country acted together to deal with nationwide problems. But while *they* issued a series of laws and directives, the *real* power rested within each zone, which had its own separate agenda, and often limited the Control Council's actions. The French wanted to grind Germany down so it would never reappear. The Americans thought this crazy, because Europe could never survive economically with a hole the size of Germany at its heart. The Brits, as usual, were somewhere in the middle. And the Russians only wanted control of everything east of Hamburg.

In Nuremberg, Porritt was the main driving force to get things done. But he wasn't a natural diplomat, and got frustrated at the separate agendas of his equivalents. Once he realised Jed Baker, the tall, laid-back Texan who headed the US group, had a natural flair for convincing the others, the two of them joined forces and drove through much-needed changes. Provided Sergei, their Russian equivalent, could have more than the Americans, and set the rules, he was happy. In much the same way, if Pascal, their equivalent from France, could veto any power to any German, and ignore any rules set by Sergei, he was happy. That way they all reached a consensus.

The next big battle Porritt and Baker faced was over transport. Each of the groups had a fleet of Mercedes cars, and they all turned up in the main courtyard in front of the Palace, morning and evening. The whole place became totally grid-locked, and Porritt needed a strong, multi-language figure to impose a solution. But he or she could not be French or German, because neither would take orders from the other, and so he'd proposed they find a Dutch or Swedish person for the role, as they would be acceptable to everyone. But his recommendation got bogged down in trivial arguments about access – everyone wanted set down or picked up at the front door – and Porritt wished the others would all just go away and leave him to get on with it. Then he got the call Polizeidirektor Hans Wolff had arrived, and so he now had to focus on this meeting.

Wolff shook hands and exchanged pleasantries. 'So, Jonathan, how's the Trial going, now you've got started?'

Porritt thought for a moment. 'Maybe a bit slow to start. Everyone has to find their feet. But I think it's now going well. What do you think? What's the word out there?'

Wolff pursed his lips and shrugged. 'It's *your* show, Jonathan. Our views don't matter.'

'Well, I'd still like to know what you think.'

Wolff paused for a moment. 'There's a view out there the Trial's just a very fancy and very expensive lynching party.'

Porritt knew Wolff had worked for a while in Chicago between the wars and it showed in his English. 'Oh, I don't think that's fair. We examine all the evidence of war crimes rather than just opinion. So, it's not a lynching party.'

Wolff pointed out the window. 'Evidence? Have a look over there. Just to the left of the steeple. That's *our* evidence of a war crime.'

Porritt looked out the window and frowned. 'I don't see what you mean.'

'Exactly. There's nothing there now. Used to be our historic old town, full of bars and restaurants, where people went to enjoy themselves. And now obliterated by *your* bombers. Thousands killed. That's what *we* call a war crime, Jonathan.'

Porritt nodded and sighed. 'I know, Hans. It's the same in our country. Cities flattened, thousands of our people killed by *your* bombers. And neither of them were right. They didn't progress the war one iota, except maybe our people became more determined to fight.'

'And that was the difference, Jonathan. Your people in Britain and America had a free press. They knew the big picture – how the pieces all fitted. We haven't had a free press for over ten years. Our people only knew what the Nazis wanted them to know – how great we were –

blah, blah. They didn't know the truth. These things coming out at the Trial – concentration camps – gas ovens – we never knew about them. You obliterated our beautiful old town. We knew about *that*. But why? What had *we* done wrong? Baffled and confused. We couldn't make sense of it all.

'But,' he shrugged, 'at the end of the day, we're just policemen, Jonathan. We uphold the law and help people as much as we can. Hence why I'm here. How can I help you?'

'I understand, Hans. I'd probably feel the same in your shoes. But, to business. I have a problem, and I'd really like your help with it. I believe one of my girl translators here could be targeted by a man because of information she has about an incident during the war. I'd like you and your team to help me catch him. Here's his photo.' He passed over a copy of the picture Sandra had sent from Glasgow.

Wolff studied it for a moment. 'Sure, but what makes you think that?'

'Her ex-husband drowned in Glasgow, Scotland, on Friday night, and we think it was part of an attempt to find out where she now lives.'

'Can you give me some background?'

'One morning, about two and a half years ago, at the height of the war, we found a man unconscious on a beach in England. He carried German ID papers.'

Wolff's eyebrows raised.

'We took him to hospital and I got called in to find out more about him. The man spoke only in German, so I used Jane, one of our translator girls, to help with the interrogation. To cut a long story short, the man escaped from our custody, but took the girl translator with him under duress, because he fancied her.

Wolff guffawed. 'Jeez! How stupid was that?'

'Yeah, right. Anyway, during their journey, the man had an accident and died, and the girl alerted the authorities.

'We recovered his body, and he turned out to be part of an undercover spy group that used Irish people with German sympathies.

'So, now the war's over, I think someone from the group – or maybe from the man's family – wants to find out what happened to him, and the only way he can do that is to talk to the girl. I'd like your help to find him.'

Wolff stroked his chin. 'Right. So, let me just clarify this. You don't really want to protect the girl as such, you want to find out who's behind this threat?'

'Well, I want to protect the girl, of course, though I'm pretty sure she's not in danger. I think whoever's behind it wants to find the person who ultimately caused the death of the man and destroyed their carefully built undercover organisation in the UK.'

'And who's that?'

'Me.'

'You? So, you want to use this girl as a lure to put yourself in danger?'

'Well, I don't want put in danger, but essentially, you're right.'

Wolff shook his head. 'You're a brave man, Jonathan.'

'You mean brave or stupid, you don't know which.'

Wolff snorted. 'Right. Tell me about the girl.'

'She's Jane Thomson, one of my senior translators. She's over here with her mother and two kids. They have a local nanny during the week. She has an apartment in the new town.'

'Does she have a car?'

'She has the use of a pool car and driver.'

'Okay, so what do you say if we replace the driver with one of our men to act as a sort of bodyguard, and have a team of two follow her as well? And we also put a team of two to follow the kids – they could be a vulnerable target. A total team of six, including me. What do you think?'

'Sounds fine.'

'Will you pay separately, or just want billed through your organisation?'

'I'm happy to pay separately.'

'Do you mean in Reichsmarks or the new Allied Occupation Marks?'

'Which would you prefer?'

'To be honest, neither. Reichsmarks aren't worth the paper they're printed on, and the Occupation Marks are a joke.'

'Okay, what would you suggest?'

'We have lots of problems out there you never see, Jonathan. Our adult food ration is less than half what you give your British soldier, and that's not much. And now it's winter, we can't keep ourselves warm. There's no coal, and everybody scrabbles around to find firewood. If you could pay us in food and fuel, it would be a godsend.'

'Okay. Tell me what you'd like, and I'll see if I can do it. I might even get the Americans to help, since we're in their zone.'

'Great, Jonathan. When do you want it set up?'

'As soon as possible.'

'Will do. I'll get back to you in a couple of hours.'

'Fine.' They stood up and shook hands.

Two hours later, Wolff called back.

'Jonathan, how about this? Our six men, who would work on this job, have twenty-five direct dependants between them, including themselves, wives and children, parents and siblings. How about if you provided the equivalent ration you'd give one of your British soldiers to each of these twenty-five, plus enough firewood per day to heat six houses? Plus some fuel for three cars. What do you think?'

Porritt thought for a few minutes. He'd already talked with Jed on the American side, who had agreed to help. In the circumstances, the barter economy made sense. He could probably negotiate it down a bit, but hell, let's leave the man with some dignity. And the proposal seemed reasonable. 'Okay, Hans, I agree, provided we put a time limit on it – say until we catch him – or until the end of March, whichever comes first.'

'Of course. Makes sense, Jonathan. Right, I'll bring the team over to meet you at two o'clock. Josef will be the girl's permanent driver, and he's a good bodyguard. Can you clear it with your car people? And, if you send me the details, I'll line up the tracking teams for the girl and the kids to start this afternoon.'

'And if you get the names and addresses of you and your team over to me, I'll start the deliveries this evening.'

'Brilliant, Jonathan. Really appreciate this.'

'No problem, Hans. Look forward to working with you.'

***

Porritt looked up at the knock on the door. Jane said, 'You wanted to see me, sir?'

He waved her in. 'Yes, Jane. Please, come in. Have a seat.' He went round the desk and closed the door, then sat down beside her.

'I want a word with you about what you told me after lunch yesterday – about the death of your ex-husband in Glasgow.'

Her eyes widened. 'Oh?'

'It triggered off a memory of the Aquila incident that has always intrigued me.'

She sat on the edge of her seat, and stared at him, hardly breathing.

'Most people think, during the war, there were no communications between Britain and Germany, but it's not true. Lots of official diplomatic communications went via the Swiss embassy, and even more semi-official communications via the Red Cross, mainly about prisoners of war, and missing soldiers and airmen.

'Now, the spy, Brenner, must have been very important to the Germans. The info he carried was of incredible value to them. We did well to close Aquila down. But to my surprise, we never had a question about him from the Germans after his death. I'd expected to see some sort of enquiry about someone that important who had disappeared. It made me wonder about Aquila and how it fitted into the overall German spy networks.

'Then, when you told me yesterday about your ex-husband's death, in what I thought were dubious circumstances, I wondered whether it was because someone wanted to find out where *you* are, because you're the only person who really knows what happened to Brenner.'

He could see her eyes moisten and hoped she wouldn't cry.

'So, I asked Sandra Maxwell in Glasgow – you remember her?' Jane nodded. 'I asked Sandra to look into your husband's death to see if he'd been targeted, rather than just fell into the river. And she's come back and told me, in her opinion, he *was* targeted.'

Her hand went to her mouth. 'Oh, my God. Am I in danger, sir? What about my kids?'

He saw tears in her eyes and spoke quickly. 'I don't think so. And I'll tell you why.'

She seemed to calm down a bit.

'At one end of the scale, the searcher could be someone from Brenner's family who wants closure, and that's understandable. We buried Brenner in an unmarked grave near Belfast, but I have all the details of the location and would be happy to help them recover his body.

'At the other end of the scale, he could be someone from the remnants of Aquila, who wants to know what happened to their agent and how their organisation disappeared in one night. And I'm happy to tell them that too. So, I don't think you're in danger as such. I think you're just one step in the road they're following to flush out the ultimate decision maker – me – and get closure on Brenner.'

She thought for a moment. 'But why target Tommy, sir?'

'Because, when you think about it, only two people in the Aquila group knew you were alone with Brenner when he disappeared – the guards Brown and Henry. And they might remember your Glasgow address off your contact card at Station 19. But then the searcher finds you're not in Glasgow now, so he tries to find out where you've gone from Tommy. But Sandra thinks Tommy didn't tell him, and suffered as a result. But he may have got enough hints from others, so she thinks he may turn up here.'

'Does she know who targeted Tommy?'

He leaned over and lifted the photo from his desk. 'She thinks it's this man. He visited Brown in prison and then spent a few days in Glasgow befriending Tommy.'

She studied the picture. 'So, who is he?'

'We don't know. He used a Northern Irish ID when he visited Brown, and a Dutch ID in Glasgow. We've got to stay alert. So, I've organised the local police to look after you. They'll provide a permanent driver and bodyguard for you. We'll also have two tailing teams, one for you and one for your children. So, just be aware, Jane, if a stranger approaches you out of the blue, stall him and call security, and we'll get the police on to him.'

She nodded, but looked worried.

Sophie Silverman, his personal assistant, popped her head round the door. 'Direktor Wolff and his team now in Conference Room B, sir.'

'Thanks, Sophie.' He turned to Jane. 'Would you like to come and meet them now?'

She sat and looked at him as though she didn't know what to think, then nodded. 'Yes, let's do that.'

They walked along the corridor to the Conference Room. The men in the room turned as they entered. Porritt guided Jane over towards Wolff and introduced them. 'Jane, this is Direktor Wolff, Head of the local Police Detectives. Hans, this is Mrs Jane Thomson. Would you like to introduce your team, please?'

Wolff smiled at Jane and bowed his head slightly. 'I'm pleased to meet you, ma'am, and we're very honoured to be asked to protect you and your family, and try to catch this man. Let me introduce my team.' He led the way and introduced each of his team in turn. Porritt noted Josef, Jane's driver and bodyguard, was the youngest of the team, maybe in his late twenties, with very blue eyes. They looked an experienced bunch, though.

After the handshakes, Porritt stood beside Jane, facing the six detectives. He was surprised at her poise.

She looked at Wolff. 'Thank you, Direktor. I already feel much safer.'

Wolff smiled and nodded. She turned to the others and repeated her words in German. They all then smiled and nodded. Porritt thought that a clever touch from Jane. She did surprise him at times.

She turned to him. 'What now, sir?'

He looked at Wolff. 'Hans? Any questions?'

Wolff nodded. 'Two points, ma'am. What time do your children finish school?'

'Three-thirty.'

'How many children do you have?'

'Two boys. Stephen is eight and George is seven.'

'And who picks them up'

'The nanny. A local girl, Frieda Beck. Sometimes my mother goes too.'

'May I suggest, ma'am, that today, we leave here just after three, and Josef drives you to the school and you greet your children – as though you just happened to be passing. Gives us the chance to identify them and get an idea of the route they take back to your apartment.'

She looked at Porritt. 'Okay, sir?'

He nodded. 'Yes, of course.'

Wolff explained in German to his team what they'd just agreed to do. They all nodded. He turned back to Jane. 'Second point, ma'am. Where and when do you get picked up in the evening from here?'

'About ten past five from the main front door, though it's usually a bit chaotic to find the car. Everyone leaves at the same time.' She glanced at Porritt with a smile.

He grimaced. 'We're working on it.'

She went on. 'However, once or twice a week, like tonight, I'm on duty at a VIP reception in the Garden Room, at the back of the building.' She pointed over behind her. 'And then I get picked up at the North Door, usually around ten past six.'

Wolff translated for his team. 'That's fine, ma'am. Now, we have some matters to discuss with Commander Porritt. You're welcome to stay if you want, but it's not necessary if you have other work to do.'

'Well, I'll leave you to it, then. Thank you, Direktor.'

'You're welcome, ma'am. We'll see you about three. Where's your office?'

'It's Room Sixteen on the ground floor. The interpreters' room.'

'Fine. Thanks.'

She smiled at them, and left the room.

Wolff and his team had a discussion in German for a few minutes. Then Wolff turned to Porritt and held up the photo of Huizen. 'Would this man have a photo of Jane?'

Porritt pursed his lips. 'I don't know. But I don't think he got much information in Glasgow. On balance, I'd say he doesn't.'

The team had another discussion. Josef seemed to make a strong point.

Wolff turned to Porritt again. 'Josef asks, if the man doesn't have a photo of Jane, how does he find her when he gets here? Who would he ask?'

Porritt thought for a moment. 'Good question. I suppose he could ask for her at the main Enquiry Desk. I think it's unlikely, but I'll alert Gisela Schwartz, Head of Admin here, for her staff to stall any enquirer, call security and then you.'

Wolff asked, 'Would Jane be known to any of the lawyers or reporters here?'

Porritt shook his head. 'I don't think so. She'd be known within the interpreters group, but not outside it. A good point, though, and I'll alert Andreas Schaeffer, the head of the group, in the same way. Of course, if someone asked a lawyer or reporter about her, it wouldn't be difficult for them to find her.'

Wolff and his team discussed these points in German. 'Can we see where she works?'

Porritt nodded. 'Sure. She usually works in the Courtroom. Let's go and have a look.'

They left the Conference Room and walked along several corridors and around corners until they reached two doors guarded by US Marines.

Porritt stopped, and the detectives gathered around him. 'We're not allowed to talk in the Courtroom. So, let me tell you what you'll see. We're going into the Public Gallery. We'll be at one end of the Courtroom looking down on the length of the room.

'Along the right-hand wall, high above the court floor, sit the main judges. In front of them, we have the prosecuting lawyers and their staff. As we move left across the court floor, we then have the defence lawyers and their staff. Then we have the two rows of defendants, and behind them, standing along the left wall, we have a row of US Army Military Police, who guard the defendants. Below us, we have the international press corps.

'Now, if you look at the left of the far wall, beyond the defendants and the row of MPs, you'll see four desks behind glass panels, two in front and two behind. Each desk has three people. They're the interpreters on duty. The English desk is the one to the right in the front row, and the three people there interpret from Russian, French and German into English. Jane usually sits at the right-hand side of that group. The Russian, French and German desks operate in the same way. To the right of these desks, you'll see four people who monitor the output in each language to pick up any errors, and correct the transcript. To their right, you'll see the witness stand. Anyone in the courtroom can listen through headphones to the proceedings in their chosen language. Okay?' Wolff had translated each phrase to his team. They all nodded.

Porritt moved forward, showed the Marine his pass, and entered the Courtroom with the group. They stood at the back of the Gallery. Porritt still got a thrill in the Courtroom, his eyes drawn to the two rows of defendants. As usual, Rudolf Hess looked uncomfortable. Hell mend them, he thought. It had taken a huge amount of effort to get it started, but now we had justice in action. After a few minutes, they made their way back to the Conference Room.

Wolff had a discussion with his team and then turned to Porritt. 'I think we're okay, Jonathan. Let's collect Jane and get going.'

They went downstairs. Four of the team headed for the front door. Wolff and Josef collected Jane from Room Sixteen.

Porritt watched them leave the building. He'd now done what he could to safeguard Jane and her family, and went off to find Gisela and Andreas to tie up the loose ends.

Chapter 5. Lister

His distempered roof had become a huge black hemisphere, sparkling with thousands of stars and speared with shooting stars. He held the girl under his arm by her tiny waist and leaped up to catch the fleeting beams. Each time he leaped, the girl squealed and giggled, her laughter echoing like a glockenspiel. They floated for over a minute before they landed again. He wanted to show her the beautiful garden, with the red and yellow flowers, and the bright green mattresses on the sunbeds. As he leaped in the cool air, he saw it in the distance on the other side of the railway tracks, bright, shining, like an oasis of light in the darkness. He needed to make love to the girl on a green mattress. She laughed languorously, taunting him to take her. He showed her the shining garden, and leapt over the tracks . . . .

***

CI Trevor Gault looked up from the post mortem report as ACC Lister entered the mortuary room. 'Jesus Christ, Trev, what have we here?'

'Another one, sir. It's like an epidemic. The fourth in two weeks in this part of Surrey. All caused by these bloody methamphetamine tablets.' He held up a small plastic envelope with a red resealing strip and four tablets in it.

'Are we sure of that?'

'Yeah. Doc says a mixture of methamphetamine and alcohol, probably champagne. Witnesses say he leaped about on his own, like a jester, straight on to the level crossing, and bang. No chance. We've got to do something, sir. These men all worked in London, and must have got the tablets up there. Apparently, they're not illegal. But Christ almighty, sir, they're causing carnage here and probably elsewhere. And we just shrug and sweep it under the carpet? It's not good enough, sir.'

'Mmm. Why call me on this one, Trev?'

'Big political connections, sir. Relative of the Home Secretary. This one needs a diplomat way above my pay grade.'

'Oh, shit. Anyone told him yet?'

'No, sir.'

Lister stood and pondered the mess on the slab. 'Okay, Trev. I'll do it. And I'll pass on the message. On this one, let's emphasise champagne rather than tablets, eh?'

'Right, sir.'

Chapter 6. Stukas

Sandra Maxwell sat at her desk on the Thursday morning, wrestling with her dilemma. She looked up as Tom knocked her open door and came in. He closed the door behind him. 'Have you seen the morning paper, ma'am?'

She shook her head. 'No. What does it say?'

Tom turned to an inside page. 'There's a short piece about Wilson's death. DI Bruce is quoted as saying the death might be suspicious. They're making extensive door-to-door enquiries, and would like to talk to two men seen in the area around ten o'clock, and a couple seen earlier in the evening.' He looked up. 'I guess that's us, ma'am. What do we do?'

She pursed her lips. 'Well, let's not panic. We searched Thomson's place and met Wilson as a logical and legitimate part of our enquiry into Thomson's death, and his double life as a drug dealer using Wilson's ID.

'With Wilson's death, some criminal must be coming from the drug user direction, working back towards the dealer, who they think is Wilson. At some point, they'll realise Wilson's *not* the drug dealer, and someone else used his ID. But how would they find out it was Thomson? If they don't know what *we* know, they'll *never* make that link.

'Now, the police will almost certainly find Thomson's fingerprints in Wilson's flat, and investigate the link. So, I'd expect the police to visit Thomson's flat to check. But I'm suspicious of the SIO. Why's the Thomson case file so bland? And why did he close the case so quickly? Is it because he *knows* Thomson dealt drugs and wants to keep it for himself, or is he in cahoots with criminals?

'So, if *criminals* visit Thomson's flat, it tells us two things. They can only know the link because the police told them. But it would also tell us who's behind Wilson's murder. So, I want to wait and see what our cat camera shows up.'

Tom nodded. 'So, how long do we have, ma'am?'

Sandra thought for a moment. 'Not long. I'd say, if we don't find something today, I go to the chief first thing tomorrow.'

She saw Doc Roberts heading across the office towards her door and waved him in. 'Good morning, people,' he said. 'I'm here to make your day even more exciting.' He sat down with a big self-satisfied smile.

Sandra smiled back. His shock of white hair, ready smile and breezy manner, always gave her a lift. 'I take it you have a result.'

'I do indeed, ma'am.' He went into his bag and pulled out an envelope. 'Our cat camera's been busy this morning. At 06.12 it took this picture.' He pulled a photo from the envelope and passed it to Sandra. It showed DI Bruce and another man entering the hall of Tommy's flat. 'The camera next triggered at 06.43, when they left the property and put the hall light off. So we can assume they spent thirty one minutes searching the flat – quite a long time when you think about it.'

Sandra looked up at him. 'Who's this other man? One of his team?'

Roberts shrugged. 'I assume so.'

'Mmm.' She studied the photo. Was he a cop? Heavy coat and hat? She passed it to Tom. 'Do you know him?'

Tom shook his head. 'No, ma'am.'

'Okay, then what?'

'The camera then recorded two more visitors at 07.06, and here they are.' He pulled another photo from the envelope.

Sandra didn't recognise them and passed it to Tom. He shook his head. 'Who are they?'

'Ah, dear boy. Two fine examples of Glasgow's criminal elite. The one in front is Sam McFadden, second son and presumptive heir to the Dan McFadden criminal empire. The one behind, his right-hand man, Johnny Bailey, a very effective enforcer for Sam and the group. They're well known to our Eastern Division colleagues, though neither has ever appeared in court. They spent a total of twenty six minutes in the flat. And, if you look very carefully, you'll see Mr McFadden has a key in his hand. Now, where do you think he'd get that?' He smiled at each of them in turn.

'I arrived at 08.15 and found the place a mess, with every drawer pulled out and its contents on the floor. They'd made a very thorough search for something. Of course, sadly, we don't know if they found anything.'

'Brilliant, Alex. Well done to cat camera. Now I'll need to think through what it all means, though. Could you do some other checks while you're here?'

'Certainly, ma'am, if I can.'

She went to her safe and got the two bags of pills. 'Could you find out what these are?'

He glanced at the bags. 'I know immediately, ma'am. They're methamphetamine hydrochloride tablets, manufactured in Germany, and used extensively by the German army and air force during the early part of the war.

'They have two huge effects on the human body. They give a tremendous feeling of euphoria and energy, people think they can fly and feel totally invincible, and they have a very strong aphrodisiac effect, to the point some people can maintain sexual stamina for several days. These pills had such a powerful effect the German pilots nicknamed them Stukas, after the Stuka dive-bomber, because they could fly so high and then dive down, release their sexual bombs, and keep repeating it.'

Sandra's jaw dropped. 'Wow.'

'They were first produced just before the war, and I'm told the owner of the company was very close to the German High Command, and some of *them*, including Hitler, became addicted to these tablets. They then issued the tablets to all of their forces, and it's said the hugely effective drives by the German army in 1940, westwards into France and the Low Countries, and eastwards into Russia, were fuelled by these tablets. The army called them Hermann Goering pills, after the senior Nazi who authorised them. However, when the soldiers stopped taking the tablets, they had severe withdrawal symptoms and became like sleepwalkers for a few days. Not a great attribute in an occupying army.

'By 1942, the German Health Leader decided the upside wasn't worth the downside, re-categorised the pills under their Opium Law, which made them illegal, and closed the factory in Berlin. But the genie was out of the bottle. The factory relocated to keep the supply going to Hitler and other senior people, and to feed the growing black market among soldiers that eventually spilled over into the wider population as a recreational drug. It became a large organised drug supply network.'

Sandra gasped. 'Jesus, Alex. How do you know these things?'

He smiled. 'Because, ma'am, two weeks ago, on a busy Saturday afternoon, a man got knocked down and killed by a bus in the Saltmarket. Several witnesses said he shouted he was flying, as he ran onto the road in front of the bus.

'Now, the man was a low-level gangster called Willie Milne, renowned as having been at the front of the queue when the good looks were handed out, but at the back of the queue when the brains were handed out. Handsome, but dumb. And to make it more interesting, he was married to the sister of that man's wife.' He pointed to the picture of Sam McFadden..

Sandra's jaw dropped again.

'And when we dealt with Milne's body, we found a packet with four of these tablets in an inside pocket. At the time, I didn't know what they were, so I called a pal in the Met who specialises in these matters, and he told me all about them. He'd got loads of info from a friendly German medic in a POW camp in Hampshire.

'In fact, since the end of the war, these Stukas have now appeared in many of our major British cities. I'd suggest, ma'am, this looks like a local drug dealer's stash.'

'Jesus.' Sandra glanced over at Tom, who looked stunned.

Roberts went on. 'Now, it's not illegal to possess these pills in *this* country, ma'am, and the tablets we found on Milne were handed to his family with the rest of his things. So, I'd hazard a guess this man, Sam McFadden, has had an earwigging from his wife, to find the man who supplied the tablets to her sister's husband and effectively killed him. And Sam has decided either to exact retribution on the supplier or take over a lucrative business. These tablets sell on the street for two pounds a pop. Whatever his motives, I'd say he's trying to find the dealer and his supply. So, the question is, how does he end up at Tommy Thomson's door with a key in his hand?'

'Good question, Alex. So, you reckon these packs are worth a total of two thousand pounds on the street? I think we need to look after them *very* carefully.'

'What else do you want checked, ma'am?' Roberts asked.

She went to her safe again, and came back with the little black notebook and the suitcase. 'Could you photograph this notebook for me, Alex? How long would it take?'

He thumbed through the book. 'About fifteen minutes tops.'

'Great. And could you check this case for me, please? I think from measurements, there are hidden sections in the case, top and bottom, but when you look from the inside it seems solid. Could you confirm that for me one way or the other? '

'Sure.' He got up and left the room.

Sandra looked at Tom. 'What do you think?'

Tom sighed. 'Well, I think the Doc's question's bang on. From your earlier analysis you said a criminal could only get that lead from the police. What do we do about it, ma'am?'

Sandra leaned back in her chair with her hands behind her head. 'Right. I'll arrange to see our Chief Constable later this morning and give him the evidence as I see it. I can't take any other direct action, and it's up to him to deal with his officers. I'll also contact Burnett. This could get very messy, and I'll need all the support I can get.

'Put the evidence bag and case into our SB evidence vault, Tom. It means no one can then access it without my permission. Make sure everything's recorded. And then chase up the three teams we set up last night, re Huizen. Let's meet at four for an update unless something breaks earlier.'

Tom stood up. 'Will do, ma'am. Talk later.' He left the room.

She picked up the phone and got a slot to see the chief in two hours time. Then called Burnett. She took him through the sequence of events that had started with the call from Porritt. Burnett also had a lead role on Aquila and understood the background.

'However,' he said, 'Once you heard about the possible second murder last night, and you knew the second victim's name and address had been falsely used for drug dealing by the first victim, you should have told the SIO. Now, I know why you didn't, because you don't trust him, which has now been confirmed with your hidden camera. So, to that extent, your delay's justified. But, I think you need to take your local CC into your confidence now. Show him your evidence, the photos, the gaps in the case file, and let him sort out the problem with the SIO. Don't waffle, keep calm, and give him the facts.

'As for the drugs, unless you think they've anything to do with the Aquila backwash, then agree with the CC what to do with them. As far as we know, they're not illegal, so by right, you should return them to the first victim's family as part of his assets.

'Now, I'll back you, Sandra, if you need it, but I think you've got to get back to tracing the mysterious Dutchman. That's what Porritt wants – and needs.

'Thank you, sir. '

'No problem, Sandra. Let me know how it goes with your CC.' He rang off.

She sat and pondered the conversation. Her instincts told her the situation was more complex than Burnett appreciated. But he was right. If she couldn't link the drugs to Aquila, she shouldn't get distracted by them. First things first. She'd need to handle the CC very carefully, and began to work out what to say. She glanced at the clock. Just one hour to go.

***

Ten minutes later, she sensed a commotion in the outer office and looked up to see Assistant Chief Constable Douglas marching towards her room accompanied by another officer in the uniform of a Chief Superintendent. Uh, oh. This looked like trouble with a capital T. Douglas was always a cold fish, but ice-cold towards her. She took little consolation from the fact he'd been the same with her predecessor.

He slammed her door closed and barked, 'What do you think you're playing at, Superintendent?'

She stood up and tried to stay calm. 'In what context, sir?'

'In the context of our possible murder scene last night.'

She held up a hand. 'Just one moment, sir.' She went to her door and signalled over to Tom to join her. She needed a witness here. Then she remembered she had a recording machine on her conference table. Tom came in and she indicated they should all sit round the table. 'For the avoidance of future doubt, I suggest we record this, sir.'

His eyes narrowed and he gritted his teeth.

She started the recorder. 'Meeting at Glasgow Police HQ on Thursday 6th December, 1945. Officers attending, ACC Douglas, CS . . .' She looked over and waited.

'CS Taylor of Renfrewshire Police,' the officer said.

'Superintendent Maxwell, and Inspector Hamilton. Time 10.43 am,' she went on. 'Right, sir, would you care to begin?'

Douglas's lips tightened and he glared at her. 'This meeting relates to events last night and this morning in relation to the suspicious death of David Wilson at his home around ten pm last night. Do you know about this death, Superintendent?'

'Yes, sir.'

'When did you know about it?'

'Just after eleven o'clock last night.'

'I see. And you didn't think to tell any of my officers you'd been in the flat? Why was that? You know the first hours are vital. So why didn't you tell us? My officers spent hours trying to trace a rogue fingerprint lifted from a side table, before finding it was yours, Superintendent. It's now almost twelve hours since you knew about this death, and you still haven't told us why you were there.'

'It was part of our legitimate enquiries into the death of Tommy Thomson last weekend, sir. Wilson's name came up as a close associate of Thomson, and so we visited him last night just before eight o'clock to ask him about Thomson.'

'So, why didn't you just call us?'

'Because Wilson's death had a potential impact on my investigations, and I wanted to see how it played out.'

'What impact?'

'I'm afraid I can't say at this moment, sir.'

'You can't, or you won't?'

'It's the latter, sir.'

'Oh, I see. So, to hell with the fact we have a potential murder on our hands, your case takes priority. Is that it?'

Sandra didn't reply.

He raised his eyebrows. 'Well, there's nothing you've said so far that explains this critical delay. Are you going to tell me now?'

'No, sir.' She swallowed. She'd now gone out on a limb.

'Really? Well, as far as I'm concerned, that's a gross dereliction of duty, and I'm going to recommend to Commander Burnett you're suspended pending an investigation. If you were mine, I'd have you out on your ear in a heartbeat.

'It was all very well for Porritt to take control of Special Branch nationally during the war, but now the war's over, I think you and your lot should revert back to local control. We can't have you clod-hopping around our work. Therefore, you will not meet or talk with any of my officers on any subject without CS Taylor, as an independent witness, being present. Do you understand?'

'Yes, sir.'

'I dare say we'll talk again later.' He got up and marched out the door.

Sandra spoke into the recorder, 'Interview ended, 11.04 am,' and switched off.

CS Taylor cleared his throat. 'I want to make clear, I'm not here to interfere with your work. In any case, I don't have the right security clearance for what you do. So, if you point me at a desk, I'll get on with my own work. Let me know when you're meeting with any of ACC Douglas's staff, and I'll join you.'

'Right, sir.' She pointed to a desk in the far left-hand corner of the outer office. 'You can use that desk, sir. It's free at the moment.'

'Fine, Superintendent.' He left her room.

Sandra turned to Tom. 'You come with me to see the chief in ten minutes, and bring the recorder with you.'

'Will do, ma'am.'

***

Sandra and Tom waited in the secretary's office. The chief was running late. Then his door opened and ACC Douglas emerged. He glanced at them and stopped in surprise for a moment, then continued to march out of the room.

The chief appeared at the door. 'Sandra, please come in. Sorry to have kept you.' He frowned 'Is Inspector Hamilton joining us as well?'

Sandra nodded. 'Yes, sir. If that's okay?'

'Sure.' He showed them into his room. 'I've just had ACC Douglas in here fuming about your behaviour, and your refusal to explain your actions. Do I get the feeling you're about to tell me?'

'Yes, sir.'

He looked at the recorder. 'And you want to record this?'

'Yes, sir. For the avoidance of future doubt on a sensitive matter.'

He pursed his lips and went to the door. 'Christine, could you ask ACC Clarke to step in here right away, please?'

Clarke was okay, Sandra thought. Head of Admin.

'Right, let's get set up around this table.' Clarke came in and shook hands with Sandra and Tom. Sandra gave the introductions on the recorder.

She then took the chief through her actions in investigating Thomson's death, and her findings. When she finished, the chief sat back and studied her. 'Are you alleging collusion between one of my officers and known gangsters, Superintendent?'

'I'm presenting the evidence, sir. It's up to you to draw the relevant conclusions.'

He sat with his chin resting on pointed hands, looking at the photos. He passed the photos to Clarke. 'Who's that with DI Bruce? One of his team?'

Sandra watched Clarke examine the photo. She'd like to know too.

Clarke studied the picture, then shook his head. 'Don't recognise him, sir.'

'Really? Well, well.' The chief sat in silence for a minute. 'And where are the drugs now?' he asked Sandra.

'I have them in safe custody, sir, in my secure evidence vault. We're still checking on whether there's any connection between the drugs and Aquila. Doc Roberts tells me the drugs are not illegal in this country, and so we'll offer to return them to Thomson's family as part of his assets when our investigations are complete.'

'I see.' He sat and thought for several minutes. 'Thank you for bringing this matter to my attention, Superintendent. We now have a difficult decision to make. I'd like you to keep this matter strictly confidential, please.'

'Will do, sir, though I'll need to brief Commander Burnett on this meeting. We would also appreciate it if you kept the reason behind Thomson's death confidential.'

'Yes, of course. And I can tell you I will not support ACC Douglas's request to have you suspended, and will remove the oversight role of CS Taylor with immediate effect.'

'Thank you, sir.'

***

Sandra updated Commander Burnett when she got back to her office

'Right,' he said. 'Let's leave it to your CC to solve his own problems. You stick to your line. Present the evidence, and don't give an opinion one way or the other.'

'Will do, sir.'

'I was interested in your drug findings, though, and talked to a pal in the Met who knows about these things. He got very excited about the evidence you picked up at Thomson's flat, and he's now got me involved in a high-level meeting this afternoon. Apparently, the Home Secretary's very concerned at the rapid spread of these drugs and wants to know what we can do about it. Although it's not our area, if it turns out there's an overseas connection, then we'll get dragged in anyway. I'll let you know what happens.'

'Sounds exciting.'

He snorted. 'No such thing as an exciting Home Office meeting, Sandra. These people have an uncanny ability to turn every initiative into a bureaucratic maze that, once you're in, it's difficult to find your way out.'

She laughed. 'Well, I look forward to hearing about it anyway.'

'Okay, talk later.' He rang off.

She smiled as she hung up the phone. Burnett was good to work with. He gave clear and direct instructions once and then moved on. And he also saw the bigger picture. Just right for that level.

She looked up as Tom knocked the door and came in. 'Got a minute, ma'am?'

'Sure.' She indicated for him to take a seat.

'I've just had an update. All three teams have got results.'

'Already? Christ, that was quick.'

'Good people, ma'am.'

'So, what's the news?'

'First, we found the bus conductor from Friday night. He recognised Huizen's picture. A hundred percent positive. Huizen got on a seventy-one bus coming in from East Kilbride at Dalmarnock Bridge around five past eleven. The conductor said he looked dishevelled. His coat was dirty, like he'd been in a fight. He sat in a daze the whole way into Glasgow.'

'So, our theory was right, then?'

'Looks like it, ma'am. Huizen stumbled off the bus at Killermont Street Bus Station and staggered away.'

'Right. Do we know where he went then?'

'We do, ma'am. Your idea of the north-side hotels paid off. We found a Mr and Mrs Huizen stayed at a small private hotel out the Great Western Road near Anniesland Cross from Wednesday to Saturday last week. Again a hundred percent positive ID on the photo. We've got the prints boys out there now, though the room's been cleaned in the meantime, hopefully not too well.'

'Brilliant. What do we know about them?'

He checked his notes. 'Pleasant couple. Showed a photo ID on arrival. She's an attractive blonde. Kept to themselves. Out during the day. She always wore a long, grey raincoat. He had business meetings in the evenings, and came back very late on Friday night. The owner heard him arrive around one o'clock and shortly after, being violently sick in the bathroom. They ordered a taxi for six o'clock on Saturday morning to take them to Central Station, paid their bill in full and disappeared. That's it so far, ma'am.'

'Good stuff. Can we get a police artist picture of the wife, please?'

'Yeah. Will do, ma'am.' He took a note.

'Can we find out where they went?'

'We'll try, ma'am, but it's a long shot. I'd guess, with Thomson's death, they'd want to clear the country pronto, and that means London and across the Channel on Saturday.'

'Yeah, you're probably right. But let's check anyway.'

'Right, ma'am. Next, our diving team retrieved an empty half bottle of Johnnie Walker from the river.'

She laughed. 'Hey, excellent news.'

'And, within two feet of the bottle, they found a gun, ma'am, fully loaded and active. They're now with Doc Roberts' people.'

'Jesus Christ. A gun? Serious stuff, then. Be interested to see which one it belongs to – Huizen or Thomson.' She shrugged. 'Of course, it might have nothing to do with either of them. Well done to all the teams, Tom. Make sure that gets passed on.'

'Will do, ma'am.' He stood up to leave. 'Still want to meet later?'

She nodded. 'Yeah. Four to five – ish. Particularly if we get a prints match between the bottle and the hotel room.'

'Okay, see you then, ma'am.' Tom left the room.

Sandra opened the envelope Doc Roberts had left earlier. It contained a pile of photos of Thomson's notebook. A note said, 'Copied only pages with a written entry. Also, two papers folded in back cover. Case more of a problem. Need more time for that. Alex.'

She remembered the notebook had a series of indented pages with letters of the alphabet in sequence. The first photo was one of the B pages. The list read –

BNDR G 08020540 09130540 10250540

Then a gap –

BNHB N 08030540 09072020 10052020 11022020

Then a gap –
BPGC N 08170540 10050540

All in very neat printing. Just like a draughtsman would use, she thought. The other photos had a similar pattern, some with more entries, some with less.

The last page read –
CD NKFLFKS 440847 PRD BPGVJC ICP3053
072320012
091050010
1112100008

She examined the photos of the two separate papers. One was a newspaper cutting of a classified advert. 'DISTRIBUTOR for new product. Glasgow area. Potential high earnings. Legal. Must be comfortable dealing with men of 30+ in sociable situations, eg pubs. Experience of direct selling an advantage but not essential. Full training provided. Give age, background, and two photos, headshot and full length. 2103, Herald Office'

This must be the opportunity the employer mentioned. She called the newspaper. The advertiser was a company called GT Pharma Ltd, with an address in Hampstead, London.

The other document was a single page, headed, GT PHARMA DISTRIBUTOR, followed by David Wilson's name and address, with the code number GB06. It detailed six steps in what seemed a job contract.

1. After completing the GT Training Programme, you have been allocated the franchise to sell GT Pharma products in Glasgow.
2. This franchise renews annually, provided you reach and maintain your sales target of one tablet per month per thousand population. Failure to reach and maintain this target as

agreed, will result in this franchise being voided and re-allocated.

3. The costs of GT Pharma products to you are set annually by GT Pharma Ltd. Your minimum selling prices and volume discounts are set by your Principal Regional Distributor (PRD), to provide a satisfactory income and fairness between adjacent franchises. You must maintain that price structure and limit the use of free samples to one per customer.
4. You must call your PRD each Monday with your sales results for the previous week. Failure to do so will result in this franchise being voided and re-allocated.
5. You will be responsible for collecting new supplies of products from Central Distribution (CD), giving one week's notice. After collection, you will be solely responsible for the security and safety of your supplies. We recommend you use the GT Suitcase and GT Writing Bureau, both of which have proved effective. GT Pharma has no responsibility for your personal security or safety at any time.
6. Amendments may be made to this contract by GT Pharma from time to time to reflect changes in organisation.

This contract meant Thomson had a target of about one thousand tablets per month, given the Glasgow population of around one million. It sounded pretty substantial, she thought, although it probably reflected reality somewhere. She also noted the requirement to call in every Monday. Thomson had failed on that one, so what would happen to the contract now? Would it be re-allocated? If so, how would they do it? Would they call the second placed candidate from the advert or re-run it? She'd keep an eye out for it. Maybe a chance to worm her way in without alerting them.

She went back to the page entries. Clearly, Thomson had applied a code to the names, but the numbers seemed to follow a pattern. The first two numbers looked like the month, followed by the next two numbers as the date. Then what?

On the indented pages, the lists must refer to his sales – the names and numbers of tablets sold. So, the fifth and sixth digits could be the number of tablets, and the last two digits could be the price. Alex had said the tablets sold at two pounds each, or forty shillings, so the last two digits could be the price per tablet in shillings.

If this was right, then the first person listed on the B page had bought five tablets at two pounds each on 2nd August, and then repeated the purchase every six weeks, presumably for his own use. On the other hand, the second person listed had bought five tablets on 3rd August, and then twenty tablets at a pound each every four weeks. He looked like he supplied others. So that's how Tommy built up his business. And he probably gave each customer a free trial tablet up front to get them hooked.

The last page must show his purchases. He'd bought two hundred tablets at twelve shillings each on 23rd July, then five hundred tablets at ten shillings each on 10th September, then a thousand tablets at eight shillings each on 12th November. Each date coincided with a trip to Amsterdam. The name and number above these entries could be his contact in Amsterdam at Central Distribution. So, even with a few giveaways, Tommy had more than doubled his money. A very lucrative business indeed.

She now had two problems – who did he sell to – and where? All the sales dates were either a Thursday,

Friday or Saturday. So, where did Tommy go on these dates? It could be anywhere people gathered to have a good time. But the tablets were expensive, and the advert indicated the target market was men over thirty. So, it sounded like up-market pubs would be the place to sell. How could she find out where?

And the purchaser's names were coded. How could she break that code? She had a sudden thought. It couldn't be, could it?

She picked up the phone. 'Get me CS Malcolm Craig at SB London, please, Gillian?'

A few minutes later her phone rang. 'Hey, Sandra. Long time no speak. What can I do for you?'

'Hi, Malcolm. I'm on to pick your brains again.'

'Again? When did you do it the first time?'

'Oh, sorry. Yesterday I came across a writing bureau, and I remembered you told us, when we were all together on the Aquila job, how you watched your safecracker find a secret drawer in a bureau. I followed the same procedure and – voila – found a secret drawer.'

'Christ, you must have a great memory, Sandra.'

'I also remember you told us how the whole Aquila job kicked off when you picked up a coded message. The Bletchley Park boys said it was a simple code used by German agents in the field so they didn't have to carry a code book. But you thought it quite clever. Can you remember it now?'

'Oh, jeez, Sandra. Give me a minute to think. Erm, each letter in a word moved forward in the alphabet by its position in the word. So the first letter moved forward by one, the second by two, and so on. So, your name, Sandra, would appear as T-C-Q-H-W-G. Get it?'

She worked it out on her pad. 'Yeah, I think so.'

'And the numbers work the same way. So, the number 1122 would appear as 2-3-5-6.'

'Right, okay. Just let me try this.' She looked at the B page in front of her and worked out the coded names. BNDR became A-L-A-N; BNHB, A-L-E-X; and BPGC, A-N-D-Y. 'Right, that works, Malcolm. Just one last check.'

She wrote on her pad WILLIE M, the name of Sam McFadden's brother-in-law, who had been killed by a bus in the Saltmarket. She coded it as XKOPNK N. She turned to the X page in the photos – and there it was. He'd bought five tablets on 10th November, the day he died. Wow, the code worked.

'Malcolm, you're brilliant.'

'Nice to hear. What're you doing?'

'I've just decoded the names in a drug dealer's notebook.'

'Bloody hell, Sandra. That's some coincidence.'

'How do you mean?'

'A drug dealer uses the same code as Aquila? Is he part of a network?'

She hesitated. 'Yeah, it looks like it. I've got a copy of a contract for the distributor here in Glasgow. So, I assume there must be others elsewhere. Let me just check this with you. There's a mention in the contract of a Principal Regional Distributor, with a coded name and number. Let me just decode it.' She worked out the number on the last page. 'It would appear to be Andrew at a number HAM 2829.'

'That's a London number, Sandra. Hampstead 2829. Let me check the subscriber for you. It'll only take a couple of minutes. Do you want to hold on?'

'Yeah, I'll hold.'

Within two minutes, he came back on the line. 'You've hit gold, Sandra.'

Her heart leaped. 'How do you mean?'

'The subscriber at the Hampstead number is a Mr Andrew Lyall. I don't know if you remember, but the spymaster who ran Aquila in London and the south of the country was a Mr Roger Lyall. They're definitely back in business, Sandra, but this time Aquila's a drug network, not a spy network.'

Her heart pounded. This was the connection she needed. 'Jesus, Malcolm. Can we keep this between ourselves, please, until I talk to the boss?'

'Of course.'

'He's in a meeting this afternoon with the Home Secretary on the spread of these drugs across British cities. This'll change the whole picture. Thanks so much for your help.'

'No problem. Let's have dinner the next time you're in London. On me.'

'Will do. Bye.'

She hung up and stared at the pages. The whole story of how to develop a drug network lay in front of her. She turned to the last page again and looked at the name and number, CD NKFLFKS 440847. This must be the Central Distribution contact in Amsterdam, where Thomson got his supplies from. She decoded the name on to her pad. M-I-C-H-A-E-L. Then decoded the number 3-2-7-4-9-1.

Could she do it? Validate the number? She could act as a close friend of Tommy Thomson, aka Davy Wilson, who wanted to get into the same business, but Davy had said they wouldn't use a woman. But, because she insisted, he'd given her this number to check. Hence the call.

She'd worked undercover before and knew she had to be totally credible in the undercover character. She began to calm down as she thought of her false self. She'd use the character she used a few years ago, Sarah

Miller, and dug through her desk to find her papers and ID card. It all flooded back to her, and she relaxed into her new role. She now wanted to start her own business in a different town. It would have to be big enough to support this type of business. Let's say Paisley. She picked up the phone. 'Could you get me the International Operator, please, Gillian? I'll hold on.'

'International. What number, please?'

'I'd like Amsterdam 440847, please.' Let's try the number as listed first, she thought.

'One moment, caller.' There was a delay. 'I'm sorry, caller, there's no such number.'

'Oh, I'm sorry. My mistake. Could I have Amsterdam 327491, please?'

'One moment, please.' Silence, then, 'Go ahead, caller.'

'Ja?' A woman's voice.

'Oh, hello. Could I speak to Michael, please?'

'Nee. Erm, sorry. No. He will be one hour.'

'Okay, thanks. I'll call back. Bye.'

'Erm. Okay.'

She hung up. The number was valid for Michael. And she hadn't had to pretend, thank goodness. Now what should she do?

She needed to talk to Porritt and update him, but she needed to wait for Huizen's prints first. She also needed to update Burnett, but he'd still be at the meeting with the Home Secretary. Shit. Patience didn't come easy to her.

She looked up as Tom knocked her door. She waved him in. 'What have you got?'

'Well, Doc Roberts has pulled out the stops for us. We've got prints off the whisky bottle, and they match a set of prints lifted off the back of the toilet bowl in the hotel room. The same man. No doubt about it.'

'Brilliant, Tom. Can you get me a set of prints and I'll send it over to Porritt?'

'Will do, ma'am. The other big news? We got a set of prints off the gun. Tommy Thomson's, ma'am.'

'Wow. So, Thomson had the gun, and presumably threatened Huizen with it.'

'Yep. That's what it looks like, ma'am. And then something happened, and it all went tits up for Thomson.'

'Jesus. Must have been quite a fight down by the river.'

'Yeah. And that's why Huizen sat in a daze on the bus. It didn't go as he expected.' He handed over an envelope. 'Here's the artist's impression of Huizen's wife, ma'am, from the owner of the hotel.'

She pulled out the sketch. A pretty enough girl with blonde hair. Nothing distinctive. You could find a hundred girls in Glasgow who'd match it. 'I'll send it over to Porritt as well. What else can we do?'

He shrugged. 'I think that's it, ma'am. We'll check, but I'm sure Huizen and his wife will have scarpered out of the country. And they'll have travelled under another name, so we'll never trace them.'

Her phone rang. She picked up the receiver. 'Maxwell.'

'Desk Sergeant, ma'am. We've a woman here to see you. A Mrs Peggy McLeod. She's pretty hysterical, ma'am.'

'Okay. Put her in a meeting room, sergeant. We'll be right down.' She stood up to put her jacket on. Tom looked over to her in surprise. 'Come on,' she said. 'Peggy McLeod's turned up hysterical. Let's go down and see her.'

They entered the meeting room. Peggy jumped up from her seat, rushed over to her, and dissolved into tears.

'Oh, ma'am. I'm so sorry,' she sobbed. 'I tried to keep my promise to you, but I couldn't. They threatened my boy.'

Sandra took her by the arm, led her back to her seat and sat beside her holding her hand. 'Now, just start at the beginning, Peggy. Tell me what happened.'

Peggy took a few minutes to recover. 'They got me just as I left the bar after lunch today, and forced me into a car.'

'Who did, Peggy. Do you know them?'

She shook her head and started to bubble again. 'No. Three of them. All smiles, but scary. They wanted to know what I told you last night.'

'About?'

'About the photograph. They showed me the same photo you had last night. Of Pieter. They wanted to know his name. But I'd promised you I wouldn't talk about it to anyone, so I didn't say. But then they threatened if I didn't talk, my boy would get hurt. And they really meant it.' She sniffled with tears again. 'And so I told them the man's name – I'd to write it down for them – and he was from Amsterdam, and had stayed in a hotel near Queen's Park. I'm really sorry, but I had no choice, ma'am.'

Sandra patted her arm. 'I know. You had no choice.' She turned to Tom. 'Could you get the photos Doc Roberts showed us this morning, please, Tom?'

'Sure.' He left the room.

Sandra turned back to Peggy and held her hand. 'Now, it's okay. It's not easy to come in and tell me this, Peggy. So, thanks for that. I'll do my best to make sure you and your boy stay safe. So please try not to worry, though I know it's difficult.'

Tom came back into the room and passed the pictures to Sandra, face down.

'Now, Peggy. I want you to look at this picture and tell me if they're the men who threatened you today.' She passed her the picture of McFadden and Bailey.

Peggy dissolved into tears. 'That's two of them. The other one's older. Late forties.'

Sandra folded the other photo to show only the man behind DI Bruce, and held it up to Peggy. 'How about this man?'

Peggy's eyes widened. 'Yes, that's him. You always have pictures of these men. What's going on?'

'It's a complicated story, Peggy. Can I just check? Would you go to court because they threatened you?'

She shook her head, and looked scared. 'Oh, no way. They'd hurt me and my boy.'

Sandra patted Peggy's hand. 'That's okay. I believe they only wanted that information, so you should be okay now.'

Peggy looked up at her. 'Do you think so?'

Sandra nodded. 'I'm pretty certain. But you know you can call me at any time.'

'Thank you.'

'Let me show you out.' She helped Peggy to her feet, and guided her back to the desk.

She came back into the meeting room and plumped down in her chair again. 'These bastards.' She shook her head. 'Why the hell would Bruce be stupid enough to visit Thomson's flat with a criminal? What sort of hold do these people have over him? What does he give in return? And why would McFadden threaten Peggy? Why couldn't he get Huizen's name from Bruce?'

Tom pondered the question. ‘I don’t think Huizen’s name was mentioned at the pub, ma’am. Peggy wrote the name in my notebook and passed it to you. But DC Orr never saw it, so he couldn’t put it in his report to DI Bruce, who couldn’t then leak it to McFadden. They couldn’t ask us for it. They had to get it from Peggy direct.’

Sandra nodded. ‘You’re right. So, if McFadden wants Huizen’s exact name, then he must want to track him down. He must think Huizen has something to do with Tommy’s drug business. And he doesn’t. It’s probably not even his real name.

‘So what will McFadden do now?’ she mused. ‘Will he go to Amsterdam? I don’t think so. But I assume these gangsters have some sort of network, so he’ll pay an associate in Amsterdam to find out for him. And Bruce just turns a blind eye to it all. I hope the CC nails the corrupt bastard sooner rather than later.’

Tom pursed his lips. ‘Yeah, I agree. But it would make a big difference to McFadden if he got a copy of Tommy’s notebook and his contacts. I wonder if Bruce knew about that?’ He stopped and thought for a moment. ‘Maybe he does, and wants to keep it all to himself. Either way, ma’am, you need to alert the CC about who’s in that photo.’

She snorted. ‘Yeah, I really need to keep him onside.’ She didn’t mention Tommy’s notebook might be difficult to unravel for someone without her insider knowledge.

***

Sandra called Porritt mid-afternoon. ‘I’ll send over a full set of prints for Huizen, sir. We picked them up from his hotel room. We also got his prints from the whisky bottle. Hundred percent match.'

'Great. Well done, Sandra.'

'I'll also send over an artist's impression of Huizen's wife, sir. A pretty, blonde girl, but nothing distinctive.'

'Okay, thanks. I've already set up protection for Jane from the local police, so we'll keep an eye out for her as well.'

'Right, sir. The situation over here with Thomson has got even messier in the last twenty-four hours.'

'How do you mean?'

'In three areas, sir. First, with Huizen. We discovered a loaded gun, with Thomson's prints, in the river. So, we think they'd quite a fight, probably because Thomson didn't give Huizen any info on Jane.

'Second, with Thomson and his drugs. He used a false ID – the name and address of a pal – and that pal was found dead last night, murdered we think by local gangsters trying to muscle in on Thomson's drug business. They also turned up at Thomson's flat looking for the drugs. And they *did* get Huizen's name as the person responsible for Thomson's death. I think they've linked that with the drugs business, and so they've probably sent a team out to nail Huizen if they can find him.'

'You're right, it *is* getting messy.'

'And lastly, sir. I've just analysed Thomson's notebook that details his drug dealings and contacts. They're all in code. I remembered Malcolm Craig talking about a code Aquila used, and surprise, surprise, it's exactly the same code, sir. And to crown all, the Regional Distributor of the drug network is a Mr Andrew Lyall of Hampstead, the same name as the man who ran Aquila in London. Malcolm and I think this is

Aquila reincarnated as a drug network and not a spy network.'

'Bloody hell, Sandra.' There was silence for a minute. 'And do you think Huizen's coming in from the spy end or the drugs end?'

'From the spy end, sir. He visited Brown in prison before he appeared in Glasgow. But he now could have a bunch of gangsters on his tail who think he's part of a drug network.'

'Okay, Sandra, we'll keep our eyes open here. Keep me informed.'

'Will do, sir. Bye.'

***

Just after five, Sandra's phone rang. 'It's Commander Burnett for you, ma'am.'

He came on the line. 'Hey, Sandra. What's happening your end?'

'Plenty, sir.' She gave him an update much as she'd covered with Porritt, with the additional information that, after she decoded Thomson's notebook, she'd verified the number in Amsterdam for Michael, Thomson's drug supplier.

'Wow. The same code? Aquila reincarnated? Great work, Sandra. Just what we need.'

'How do you mean, sir?'

'Well, the Home Secretary wants to make an impact, and take action on this drug menace before it really gets started. So, he's putting together a top-notch two-person team to dig out the facts and present a quick report on what we can do. He's selected one of his top Home Office chaps to be part of it, who looks pretty reasonable. But the HS also wants a good cop to work alongside him. So I volunteered you, assuming you'd like to do it, of course.'

'Me?' She grimaced. 'Why me, sir?'

'For a number of reasons. First, we need someone with top-notch analytical skills, and you fit the bill. You've also got evidence that no one else in the country has, and we need to use it to make an impact. So, it would be good for your career. It would also get you out of the toxic atmosphere in Glasgow while the CC takes appropriate action with his staff. And last but not least, you'd immediately move up to CS, which you deserve, and it's the right level for this job. So, what do you think?'

She was stunned. 'Is the CS permanent, or just for this job?'

'Permanent. As I say, you deserve it, Sandra.'

'And what would happen here?'

'Move your best Inspector up to CI, pro tem. It's only for a few weeks. The HS wants your report by the end of January, and we can both keep an eye on him.'

'And would I come back here?'

'That's the plan, Sandra. You might have to oversee some on-going action, depending on what you recommend, but you could do that from Glasgow.'

'Okay, sir. I'll do it. What's the next steps?'

'The Home Office fellow's Bill Franklin. Here's his number.' She noted it. 'Give him a call tomorrow and arrange to get started. The HS had a private meeting with Franklin and myself afterwards, and made it clear, while officially you're doing a review, unofficially he wants this drugs menace closed down. You're free to bend the law as much as you like, just don't break it. If you're going undercover or need help, let me know, so we can put the necessary links in place for you. And give me a weekly update when you can.'

‘Right, sir. Will do.’

She hung up and took a deep breath. What an opportunity. Her brain buzzed with ideas, but she just had to calm down and take time to think. She noticed Tom with his hat and coat on ready to leave, went to the door and called him.

‘Tom, the boss has asked me to do a special job for the Home Office for the next few weeks, and we’d like you to step up and run this unit while I’m away. You’ll get a temporary CI, so it’s good for your career. Will you do it?’

‘Blimey, that’s a surprise, ma’am. Thank you. I’m happy to do it. What’s the job?’

‘It’s a special review of this new drug menace spreading across the country. Both Burnett and I will help you if you need it at any time. So don’t hesitate to call. Okay?’

He nodded. ‘Sure, ma’am. ‘

‘Good. See you in the morning.’ She saw Doc Roberts coming across the outer office with the suitcase. ‘Hang on a sec, Tom. Let’s hear what Alex has to say.’

‘Good evening, people. Glad I caught you. Just to let you know, on the evidence of this suitcase, the people you’re dealing with are *very* clever. In my opinion, you should not underestimate them.’

Sandra smiled. ‘Really? What have you got?’

‘Let me demonstrate, ma’am.’ He put the suitcase on her desk and opened it. ‘I agree with your assessment. Measurement indicates about a one inch gap top and bottom, but it’s taken us most of the day to figure out how to get into it. Let me show you.

‘The top and bottom are identical, so let’s unzip the satin liner from the bottom.’ He did so and folded it to the back of the case. ‘You see now we have a complete leather base covering the bottom, and smoothed right round the edge under this rim, so it appears part of the case shell. And it doesn't come out.' He tried to lift it out.

'Now, we know there's a gap underneath, so how do we get to it? We thought it must have something to do with these buttons.' He pointed out four leather buttons on the base, each around two inches diameter and located close to each corner. 'We pulled the buttons out.' He got a penknife from his pocket, and gently eased off one of the buttons to reveal a plastic disc with a large slot across it. 'We first wondered if it was a screw, but when you turn it,' he got a shilling from his pocket, put it into the slot and turned it, 'nothing happens. It just rotates. Now, it obviously does something, but what?' He smiled at each of them in turn.

Sandra opted to keep quiet and let him get on with it.

'Then we had a breakthrough,' he went on. 'By chance, we had left one of the discs aligned vertically to the case, like this.' He turned the disc.' And one of our team noticed the leather liner seemed looser at that point. So we aligned all the discs the same way,' he turned the other three discs, 'and voila, the leather liner lifts out.' He lifted the liner out to reveal a fine steel frame built inside the case shell, and surrounding a hidden space.'

Sandra smiled. 'So, how does it work, then?'

'If you look under here,' he turned the leather liner over, 'you see these four steel pods are connected together with this fine metal frame, which matches the frame in the case outer. So, if I take this paper clip,' he lifted a paper clip from her desk, 'and put it against the base of the pod, you see it just falls off. But if I turn this slot 180 degrees and put the paper clip on now, it sticks. The pod has become magnetised. And if we do the same with the three other pods, the whole frame becomes magnetised and sticks to the frame in the case shell.

'These pods are in effect magnetic switches. When they're on, you can't lift the leather liner out. But when they're off, you *can* lift it out and access the hidden space. Neat, huh? And *very* clever. We've never seen anything like it before. It looks like a neat piece of German design, and *very* effective.'

Sandra thought, no wonder the GT Pharma company want their people to use this suitcase. It's doubtful anyone would ever find the hidden compartments with a casual search. 'Brilliant, Alex. We'll hold on to it for the moment. Could you put the case into our evidence vault on your way out, please, Tom?'

'Yes, ma'am.' Alex put the case back together and Tom left with it.

'Anything else I can do for you, Sandra?'

She shook her head. 'No thanks, Alex. I've got to figure out how I use all this info now.'

'No problem, Sandra. Give me a shout if you need me.' He left the room.

Sandra remembered Porritt outlining his analysis of Aquila at that time. He definitely had not underestimated them, and she wouldn't either.

***

She'd just put out her bedside light when the phone rang. She sighed. Not again. She picked up. 'Two-five-six-seven?'

'Watch your back, you interfering bitch.' He rang off.

She sighed again. A local accent. It must be Sam McFadden or one of his team, with their sense of entitlement that they should get whatever they wanted at the threat of violence. As though a stupid phone call would somehow get her to cooperate. How dumb were these people? Plenty dumb, she thought, on the evidence of Davy Wilson. And how would they follow up, if at all?

Now she had to follow procedure. She called the Duty Inspector and reported it. He'd put a uniformed cop on her front door overnight. Like most senior police officers, she already used different routes to and from the office each day, but now she'd have to move her mother to her sister's home in Ayr for a while. Bastards.

Maybe the boss was right. She should get out of this toxic atmosphere for a while. She picked up her book again and tried to read her way to sleep.

Chapter 7. Sam

Sam lay in the hotel bathrobe and watched the girl walk naked round the end of the bed and head for the bathroom. He caught a glimpse of her large wobbling breasts in the wall mirror, and admired her neat ass as she disappeared through the door. Slim and petite, and a bloody good ride. Worth every penny. But he needed more. His skin seemed to ripple all over. He padded through to the lounge, and picked up the phone.

'Reception?' He asked for the number.

A few clicks later, 'Yep?'

'It's me. Need another one. You know what I like.'

'Okay.'

'How long?'

'An hour, tops?'

'Good. Thanks.'

'No problem, boss.'

He went back to the bedroom just as she reappeared. 'Right, toots. Time to go.'

'Aw, Sammy. I thought we might have longer.'

'We've had the whole bloody night.'

She stretched up on tip toes and put her arm round his neck. 'But you were so good, Sammy. Will I see you again?'

'Yeah.' He playfully slapped her bum. 'Now, get dressed and get going. I've got things to do.' He lifted his wallet and pulled out two five-pound notes. 'Here's a wee bonus for you. Now, bugger off.'

'Okay, Sammy. See you again.' Within minutes she'd gone.

He had a quick shave and shower. Still semi-erect, even after a night of frantic love making. Christ, that pill was magic. No doubt about it. He relaxed in the bathrobe, clear thinking, alert, and with his senses fine tuned. He'd never felt this good before.

He thought back to Sunday at the mortuary. His wife, Helen had taken a tearful Marion out the room after she'd identified Willie's body. The mortuary attendant gave Sam an open-topped box with Willie's clothes in it. Sam noticed the little plastic bag, with four pills. 'What are these?' he asked.

The attendant shrugged. 'Don't know, mate. The doc says they give you a hard on for three days. But, they're not illegal, so you get them back.'

Sam frowned, 'Really?' and slipped them into his pocket.

He'd fretted over the pills for two days. Where the hell had Willie got them? He'd had one of his best men, Eddie Frame, on Willie's tail for nearly two weeks because he didn't trust Willie any more. He reckoned Willie had leaked information to a rival.

That night, Eddie got into Sam's car. Eddie had a valuable role in the organisation, but always kept in the background. He'd been an actor in his younger days, and could disguise his appearance and accent. He could ferret information useful to the family, like no one else. 'Hi, Sam. Something up?'

'Yeah. You know how you said Willie ran around the Saltmarket like an aeroplane before he got hit by the bus on Saturday? I found he had some strange pills. He must have got them that morning. Did you see him buy them from somebody?'

Eddie shook his head. 'I didn't Sam. He was in the Horseshoe Bar on Saturday lunchtime and it was packed. I had a good view of him at the bar, though, and I'm pretty sure he didn't get any pills there. But he stopped to talk to a lad at a table on the way to the loo. I couldn't get a clear view, so he might have got them then. I think it's the only possibility, Sam.'

'Do you know this lad?'

'I don't, but Willie knew him. He spoke to him the previous Saturday as well. I didn't notice anything suspicious then either.'

'Could you find out about him?'

'Yeah, I'll do what I can, Sammy.'

'Good man. Let me know at the weekend how you get on.'

Now, a couple of days later, Sam sat and admired the hotel gardens. His whole body craved action. He'd lasted one more day, before he booked a suite at his favourite south-side hotel to check out these pills. At least he wouldn't run under a bus here. He'd told Helen he'd to go to Edinburgh for a couple of days on urgent business.

There was a knock at the door. He got up and opened it. Christ, Johnny had chosen well. Even bigger tits than the last one. She smiled. 'Sam? I'm Tracey.'

He opened the door wide. 'Come in, Tracey. Good to see you.' His loins had stirred already. A good day ahead.

***

The following Saturday night, he met Eddie at the same location. 'How did you get on?'

'Oh, he's a slippery bugger, Sam. He sat in the Horseshoe Bar for three hours. Once you know what you're looking for, you can bloody see it. He had a succession of men sat beside him. All greeted like old pals. But he deals under the table. I reckon he got two fivers for a small bag of pills – with maybe five in it?'

'Jesus Christ.' Two quid each, thought Sam. But bloody worth it when you know the effect they have. 'Then what?'

'He left the bar at half two, and jumped on a tram heading down Union Street. I caught the one behind it. He then jumped off in Bridge Street, and went into the Underground station. I caught up with him on the platform. He stood at the far end, waiting on an Inner Circle train back into the city. I stood halfway down and got on the next train. He got on as well, but just as the gates closed, he stepped off onto the platform, and walked over to get an Outer Circle train. That was it. Lost him within five minutes. He used the 'last on, last off' ploy. Makes him very difficult to follow, Sammy.'

'Did he know you were on his tail?'

Eddie shook his head. 'No, it's just the way he operates.'

Sam thought for a moment. 'He's obviously a sharp cookie. I want him, Eddie. I want his business. We already control cocaine and heroin in this city. We don't want some amateur coming in with a new drug just as good and not illegal. It would put us out of business.'

'Is it that good?'

'It's bloody good, Eddie. I snaffled the pills Willie had, and tried one. Gave me a hard on for two days and the energy to use it. Never felt anything like it before.'

'Jesus Christ.'

'So, I want him, Eddie. How do we catch him?'

'Well, we've got to start from what we know. And that's not much. Looks like he spends three hours every Saturday lunchtime in the Horseshoe Bar. Why don't we bundle him into a car when he leaves? Make him an offer he can't refuse.'

Sam nodded. 'Yeah. Let's do it.'

***

They stood at the bar, wearing football scarves to blend in. Sam glanced at the table five yards away, with the 'Reserved' sign on it, but no one sitting there. 'Where the hell is he?'

The barman stopped in front of them to wash some glasses. Eddie leaned forward. 'Excuse me. Do you know if this guy's coming in today?' He pointed at the table.

The barman frowned. 'Oh, Davy Wilson?' He glanced up at the clock. 'Yeah, he's usually here by now. Maybe got held up, eh?' He moved away to serve someone.

Eddie murmured. 'Just got to wait. But at least we've got a name.'

By two o'clock the table was still empty. Sam silently screamed with frustration.

Eddie turned to him. 'Sam, just think about it. They've got a 'Reserved' sign on the table. It means they've organised it. Davy must pay them off. Let's try something.'

The bar was now quieter, and the barman again stopped in front of them. Eddie leaned over. 'Excuse me.'

The barman looked up. 'What can I get you?'

Eddie said, 'We'd like some information.' He went into his wallet, pulled out a five pound note, and folded it in his hand. 'Do you know where Davy lives?'

The barman shook his head. 'No, sorry, I don't.'

Eddie leaned forward again. 'You've got a great bar. Well run. Good crowd. We'd like to do a bit of business here as well.'

The barman glanced at Sam, and then back to Eddie. 'On or under the table?'

'Under.'

'Legit or illegit?'

'Legit.'

'You need to see the bar manager, Benny Dougan. He deals with that side of things. He could probably tell you more about Davy as well.'

'Is he here?'

'No, he's away this weekend. A wedding down south. He'll be back on Wednesday.'

'Anyone else we could talk to today?'

The barman grimaced. 'No. Come in after seven on Wednesday, and see Benny. You really don't want to talk to anyone else.'

Eddie nodded. 'Thanks, mate.' He stretched out to shake hands and passed the fiver over in the process. 'Appreciate it.'

They finished their beers and left to get into the two cars outside.

***

On the Wednesday night, Sam entered the bar with Eddie and Johnny. The barman saw Eddie, held up a finger, and went to a phone behind the bar. A few moments later he came over to them. 'Benny's on his way. Can I get you anything?'

Eddie shook his head. 'No, we're fine, thanks.'

A couple of minutes later, a heavy built, florid faced man approached, with a big smile, but wary piggy eyes. 'Hello, gentlemen. Benny Dougan.' He held out a hand.

Eddie shook hands. 'I'm Eddie. This is Sam and Johnny.' They shook hands.

'Come on up to the office, gentlemen.' Dougan led the way up a couple of flights of stairs. Sam thought 'office' a grand title for the small, dull room, with a too-big desk. Dougan went round the desk to the matching too-big chair. Eddie and Sam sat at the desk. Dougan waved Johnny to a sofa. 'Just move some of these boxes and have a seat.'

'No, I'm alright here.' Johnny leaned against the wall, two paces from the desk. Dougan glanced at Johnny, unhappy with his position, but turned to Eddie with a smile.

'I understand from Joe you want to do some under the table business with us. We're always interested, provided it's legit. Five pounds an hour, cash up front. Booze extra.'

Eddie nodded. He turned to Sam. 'Yeah, sounds good. What do you think?'

Sam nodded. A *very* expensive rate. This guy was smarter than he looked.

'Great.' Dougan smiled at the two of them. 'When do you want to start?'

Eddie thought for a moment. 'We're not quite ready to go. Maybe a couple of weeks?'

'No problem. Just let me know, and we'll set it up for you.'

'Good.' Edde went into his wallet and drew out two five pound notes. Sam saw the piggy eyes glint at the money. It's all the bastard's interested in. Eddie went on, 'We'd like some information as well.'

'About what?'

'You know Davy Wilson?'

'Yeah.'

'We think Davy's got a good thing going, and we'd like to help him. We're part of a big organisation, and we'd make sure you get a share.' The piggy eyes gleamed. 'I mean, Sam's dad has fantastic connections. You may have heard of him, Dan McFadden,'

Dougan's face blanched. His piggy eyes looked scared. Good. Dad's name still carried a punch in these circles, thought Sam.

Eddie continued. 'We'd like to talk to Davy about this, but we don't have his address. Could you give us it?'

Dougan glanced at the money in Eddie's hand. He reached towards his desk drawer and thumbed through a notebook. '15, Ardenlea Street, Glasgow SE.'

'Do you have a phone number?'

'No, he's not on the phone.'

Eddie stood up. 'Good. Enjoyed doing business with you, Benny. We'll see you again in a couple of weeks, huh?' They shook hands and the money transferred over.

Dougan shook hands with Sam and Johnny with a forced smile. He didn't look too happy, thought Sam, but bugger him, they'd got what they wanted.

They got into the car, and Johnny drove off towards Renfield Street. Sam turned to Eddie in the back seat. 'Thanks a lot, Eddie. You've got to get back, right?'

Eddie nodded. 'Yeah, sorry Sam. We've got family over tonight.'

'No problem. We'll drop you off.'

'Thanks. What will you do?'

'We'll go and see Davy. Give him an offer he can't refuse.' Sam sat back. He needed a magic pill. But only had three left. He had to find this fellow and get his stash. Tonight.

***

Sam pressed a gloved finger against the doorbell. He heard the faint sound of a radio from somewhere, then shuffling on the other side of the door. 'Who is it?'

Sam called, 'It's me, Davy.'

The door unlocked and slowly opened. Johnny pushed hard against it and knocked Davy back against the wall. They quickly entered and closed the door.

Sam realised Davy had two crutches and helped him upright again. 'What happened to you, Davy?' he asked, pointing to his foot.

'Broke my ankle. Who are you?'

Sam guided Davy into the kitchen. 'We're here to help you, Davy.'

'To do what?'

'To become even more successful. You just need to tell us, Davy, where are the pills, and where do you get them from?'

Davy looked from one to the other. 'What pills?'

'Now, Davy, we want to be nice about this. We want to work with you, but you need to help us too. Where are the pills you sell in the pub?'

Davy shook his head. 'I don't know what you're talking about. The only pills I have are for the pain in my ankle.'

Sam tightened his lips. What a knucklehead. 'Last time, Davy. Don't be stupid about it. Where are the bloody pills?'

'It's no' me being stupid about it.'

Sam lost his temper and pushed Davy down into an armchair. He snarled, 'Now, don't bloody move.' He turned to Johnny. 'You take this room, I'll go through to the other one.'

They'd agreed to look for some plastic bags with white pills, and some record of where Davy got them. They might find some cash around as well, but they'd just leave it.

Sam went into the bedroom, and checked the pillows, bedclothes and mattress. Nothing. He emptied a couple of boxes from under the bed, then the wardrobe, a cupboard, and a chest of drawers. Nothing anywhere. He checked the cistern in a small toilet between he rooms, then went back into the kitchen.

Johnny had emptied two cupboards and tipped the contents of all the packets and tins on the floor. Nothing. Sam took out a large penknife and slashed the cushions and fabric of the sofa. The only place left to check was the armchair Davy sat on.

'Come on, get up.' He grabbed Davy by the arm and pulled him to his feet, and then slashed the cushions and frame of the chair. Nothing.

Davy shouted, 'Bastards'. Sam looked up to see him swing one of his crutches at him. Sam dodged it and Davy overbalanced, and collapsed into the fireplace with a crash.

Sam stared at Davy, blood now seeping out of his head into the hearth. 'Come on, let's get out of here.'

They dashed to the door, and rushed downstairs. They raced round the corner, into their car, and Johnny drove off.

Sam fumed at the way the visit had turned out. 'Stupid bastard. Why don't these people see sense? He must have them hidden somewhere else.'

'Where do you want to go, boss?'

Sam grimaced. 'Oh, just drop me off. I need to think about what we do now.' He really needed a magic pill and a night with the girl Tracey. No chance, now.

Helen glanced up from her book when he got home. 'Good day?' The Light Programme played in the background.

'Don't ask,' he snarled.

She picked up her book. Sam went to the drinks cabinet, poured himself a large whisky, and tried to relax in an easy chair. His brain whirred with angry thoughts.

How could a numbskull like Davy outwit him? Gradually, the whisky worked and he began to relax.

He woke up at ten to five needing a pee. A table lamp lit the room beside him, but the rest of the house was in darkness. He used the toilet and splashed cold water on his face. He needed some fresh air, put on his coat, scarf and hat, and went outside.

His father had bought an old printing works before the war, used some of it for offices and meeting rooms, and demolished the rest to build three bungalows, for himself, his eldest son Kenny, and for Sam. He'd landscaped the area, with a high fence around it, but still kept a guard on 24/7. Sam found Gav standing near the front gate. 'How's it going?'

Gav nodded. 'Fine, Mr McFadden. Nice night.'

'Yeah.' He was never going to get back to sleep now. 'Think I'll get the car round. Keep an eye out for it.'

'Will do, sir.'

Sam went back inside and called Johnny.

'Yep.' Sounded very sleepy.

'Can you bring the car round?'

'Sure. Ten minutes?'

'Fine'.

He noticed some whisky in his glass, and drank it down to perk him up a bit. He went back outside, and within a few minutes, Johnny arrived with the car.

'Where do you want to go, boss?'

'Let's go down to Bridgeton Cross and see the girls.'

'Sure. Got a problem sleeping?'

'Ach, I'm just annoyed at last night. We should have handled it better.'

Johnny parked next to the Umbrella, the large octagonal iron shelter with a clock on top. A couple of his girls stood under it. Sam got out. 'How's it going,

Sadie?' She was one of his longest serving girls. Had deft fingers and a sweet mouth, and could use them top notch.

'A quiet night, Sam. Only a few punters.'

He glanced at the young girl beside her, shivering in a light raincoat. 'Who's this?'

'This is Carol, Sam. First week.' She turned to the girl. 'This is Mr McFadden, the boss.'

The young girl smiled. 'Hello.'

Sam smiled back. 'Any punters tonight?'

She nodded. 'A couple.'

'Good.' He gave Sadie a florin. 'Go over to Carlo's and get yourselves a cup of tea and a roll and sausage or something.'

'Okay, Sam. Thanks.' The two girls walked over towards Carlo's all night café.

Jakey emerged from the shadows. Sam nodded. 'Hi Jakey. Everything okay?'

'Yeah, fine, Mr McFadden. We had a couple of outsiders try to muscle in on the pitch, and young Susie had a problem punter, but we sorted them out no problem.'

'Good, Jakey. Thanks.' He saw a news vendor with the morning papers on the steps of the Olympia cinema, and asked Johnny to get him one. Then Paulie drove up. He ran the prostitution side of the business for Sam. 'Hey Paulie, how's it going?'

'Not bad for a Wednesday, Sam. A bit quiet here and at Parkhead Cross, but everywhere else has done okay.'

'What about Glasgow Cross? Is Biggart playing ball?'

Paulie nodded. 'Yeah, he's pulled his girls back to south and west of the Cross. We're clear for the rest.'

'Good. And what about Pollokshields? How's that going? Haven't seen it for a couple of weeks, now.' Sam had rented a large detached house in the posh suburbs after he heard about Dirty Dick's brothel in Paris from an ex-Army officer in one of Kenny's night clubs. He'd spent a few bob on it, and put in Agnes, one of his long-serving girls, to manage it.

'Going great, Sam. Brilliant idea. High-quality girls. We've now got six between day shift and night shift. High prices. Super service. And it's ideal having the driveway entrance down the side street. Keeps the traffic away from the neighbours. Great business, Sam. Agnes tells me the new girl, Tracey, is *very* good. You need to get over and see them.'

'Yeah, I'll do that, Paulie. Good stuff. Thanks a lot.'

'No problem. Sam.' He turned to go back to his car.

'Oh, Paulie?'

'Yeah?'

'The wee new girl here with Sadie tonight.'

'Erm, Carol?'

'Yeah. Get her a heavy coat on me. Second hand somewhere. Sadie'll help you. She's stood there shivering. Nobody'll pick her up like that.'

'Okay, Sam. Leave it with me.' He looked around. 'Where are they?'

'In Carlo's. I sent them for a cup of tea.'

Paulie headed over towards Carlo's. Johnny strolled up with a paper. 'I think we'll get a cup of tea as well, Johnny.'

Carlo welcomed them as usual. 'Mister Sam, Mister Johnny,'

'Two teas, Carlo,' Sam said, and took a seat at the back of the café. He still felt hung over. He needed one of these pills again – to get his mind back in gear – to feel good again. How the hell could he find these pills?

Johnny sat reading the paper, 'Oh, shit.'

Sam turned to him. 'What's wrong?'

'That bugger last night. He's dead. The police are calling it possible murder.' He folded the paper over and passed it to Sam.

Sam read the article. 'Christ, we never touched him.' His brain jangled. Maybe he should get back home and snort a line to clear his head. Shit. What should he do? He needed clarity. 'I'm going to call Eddie. See what he has to say.'

He went to the counter, got Carlo's phone, and asked Eddie to join him.

Eddie arrived ten minutes later, bleary-eyed. 'Got a problem?'

'Yeah. Read this.' Sam passed him the paper.

'I take it you went there last night?'

'Yeah. But we didn't touch the bugger. We just looked for his stash of pills. He took a swing at us and overbalanced and fell into the fireplace. We just thought he'd knocked himself out and we scarpered. But it wasn't bloody murder.'

'Did you find any pills?'

'No, never found a bloody thing. He must have hidden them somewhere else.'

'Well, I'm not exactly surprised.'

'How do you mean?'

'Because this picture of Davy Wilson's not the lad I've followed for the last few weeks. That's somebody else.'

Sam's jaw dropped. He turned and glanced at Johnny and splayed his hands. 'But his was the only Wilson nameplate up the close. Isn't that right?'

Johnny nodded.

Eddie pursed his lips. 'May be. But he's not the lad with the drugs.'

'Jesus. What do we do?'

'Well, I suggest you get hold of your friend, Jack Bruce. He's on the payroll, after all. Tell him what happened, and get him to take the possible murder charge off for a start.'

'Right.' Sam rose, got Carlo's phone again, and asked for the number.

'Glasgow Police?'

'Can I speak to DI Bruce, please?'

'I'm afraid he's not available at the moment. Who's calling?'

'It's Eric.'

'Eric who?'

'Just Eric. Tell him it's urgent. It's about Arcadia.' That was the code for 'we need to meet right now'.

'Has he got your number?'

'Yeah.'

'Okay, I'll tell him.'

'Thanks.' He hung up and went back to the table. 'Right, we should see him in ten minutes. Let's get ready to go.'

***

Johnny drove them back down Dalmarnock Road into Swanston Street. He parked on a concrete area at the far end, near the river. Sam waited in silence.

A few minutes later a car pulled up alongside them. Jack Bruce got out and came across into their front passenger seat. He turned to Sam, 'What's the panic?'

'It's this.' Eddie passed the newspaper, folded at the story.

Bruce looked down at it. 'Oh, Christ. Was this you?'

Sam nodded. 'Yeah, but it wasn't murder, Jack. He took a swing at us with a crutch, overbalanced, and fell into the fireplace. We never touched him.'

Bruce pursed his lips. 'The first copper on the scene found the place ransacked and Wilson dead. He called it in as a murder in the course of a robbery. Then everyone went into panic mode.' He sighed. 'Right, leave it with me. I'll talk to the medics and see what they say. Were you gloved up?'

'Of course.'

'Okay. Why were you there?'

'Eddie's followed a drug dealer for a couple of weeks. We want to take over his business. We found out his name was Davy Wilson, and somebody that knew him gave us his address. So we went along last night to make him an offer he couldn't refuse. But he started to play silly buggers, and we had to search the place. We didn't find anything because, of course, as Eddie pointed out when he saw the paper this morning, it was the wrong guy.'

Bruce looked over at Eddie. 'So, who did you follow?'

'Davy Wilson. But not *that* Davy Wilson. Another Davy Wilson. Dark wavy hair and thick glasses.'

Bruce frowned. 'Thick glasses? Hang on a minute.' He went to his car, and came back with a briefcase. He delved into it and pulled out a photo. 'Is that him?'

Eddie nodded. 'Yeah. He's the drug dealer. A slippery bastard too. Kept losing him. Who is he?'

Sam cut in. 'More importantly, do you know where he is? I want to talk to him. I want his business.'

Bruce looked from Sam to Eddie and back again. 'Well, you can't talk to him.'

'Why not?'

'Because he's in the City Mortuary. We fished him out of the river not far from here on Saturday morning. He attempted suicide, but banged his head on the bridge and fell in the river. We've called it as an accidental death while drunk. His name's Tommy Thomson. His fingerprints are all over Davy Wilson's flat. I'd guess, from what you say, he must have used Davy Wilson's name for his drug dealing.'

Sam got irritated at Bruce's matter-of-fact attitude, and his anger rose. He took a deep breath to keep calm. 'Where does Thomson live?'

'Dalmarnock Road. Just round the corner from Wilson's place.'

'Have you searched Thomson's place?'

Bruce shrugged. 'We've had a look at it, but we'd no reason to search it.'

'Well, *I've* got a reason to search it, Jack. I want that drug stash and I want it now. Let's go and have a look.'

'Hang on a sec. We can't just go in mob handed. Let me have a look first.'

Sam looked at Eddie, who nodded. 'Okay, we'll follow you over there.'

Bruce got back into his car and drove off. Johnny followed.

Eddie turned to Sam. 'You don't look too happy. Something wrong?'

Sam grimaced. 'I think that big bastard's taking us for a ride.'

'How do you mean?'

'He says Thomson attempted suicide. How stupid can you get? There's no way a drug dealer with a successful business would commit suicide. It's ridiculous.'

'So, what do you think?'

'What if that big bastard knows about the drug business? He bumps off Thomson and calls it suicide. Once it all calms down, he picks up the stash and flogs it to one of his pals. Pockets the cash. Maybe even takes over the business himself?'

Eddie looked sceptical. 'Would he be that stupid? To upset Dan and yourself? '

'He's a sly bastard, Eddie. He's far too casual about this. His reactions aren't right. He's got his own bloody agenda here. I'm sure of it. If there's a stash in Thomson's flat, I don't want him to move it before we have a look. You go with him, Eddie. Then he can't take it out without us knowing about it.'

'Okay, we'll try that.'

They parked at the end of Woddrop Street, where the tarmac became the grass of the river bank. Bruce locked his car and came over to them. 'Just round the end of this building. It's the next building over on the main road. I'll only be a few minutes.'

Sam had his window down. 'Eddie'll come with you. Deal with any nosey-parkers.'

Bruce looked down on him for a minute. 'Don't think I need that, Sam.'

Sam smiled up at him. 'Ah, you're always better with a bit of protection. Never know what you might meet.'

Bruce glanced up as Eddie got out of the car, then shrugged. 'Okay.'

The two of them disappeared round the end of the tenement building.

Sam put his head back against the seat. He thought about Thomson and his stash of drugs. Now he knew why Thomson hadn't turned up at the Horseshoe Bar last Saturday. That was a bugger. But he still wanted to take over the business. How could he do it? How could he contact Thomson's supplier? He needed these bloody pills.

He woke up with a start as the car door opened. Eddie got in beside him and Bruce got in the front. 'I looked everywhere, Sam. There's nothing there. He must have them hidden somewhere else.'

Sam glanced at Eddie, who shrugged. Sam leaned forward. 'I need to see for myself, Jack. I want these bloody pills, or find a clue to his supplier.'

'Don't you believe me?'

'Of course I believe you. But I know what I'm looking for. You don't.'

'Come on, Sam. It's not the first time I've looked for a drug stash.'

'Yeah. But these pills are different. Give me the keys and I'll go over and have a look. Nobody's going to know. But I'm going into that flat, Jack, one way or the other. I'll jemmy the bloody door if I have to, and that wouldn't look good for you. It would give you problems you don't need. Now, give me the bloody keys and let's get on with it.'

Bruce's lips tightened. He glanced at Eddie and back to Sam again.

Sam leaned forward again. 'Johnny, get that bloody jemmy out the boot.'

Johnny opened the driver's door and moved to get out.

'Okay. Okay.' Bruce went into his coat pocket and pulled out the keys. 'But don't leave a mess like you did at Davy Wilson's place.'

'We won't.' Sam turned to Eddie. 'Right, let's go. You lead the way. Come on, Johnny.'

Bruce went back to his car. The three of them went round the end of the building, across the grass, and round the end of the next building into Dalmarnock Road. They went up the second close and stopped outside Thomson's flat. Sam turned to Eddie, 'You stay here and act like a detective on guard.' Eddie pulled his collar up a bit.

Sam and Johnny went into the flat and checked every drawer, cupboard, or hiding place they could find. Nothing. Not even a clue. Shit.

They left the flat. Sam closed the front door and pulled the storm doors closed. He turned to Eddie, shook his head and grimaced. 'Not a bloody thing.'

The door next to Thomson's flat opened and a small lady peered out.

Eddie stepped forward. 'Oh, sorry to disturb you, Mrs . . ..' he looked at the nameplate, '. . ..McGregor. We're with the police.' He pulled out his wallet and flashed it at her.

She peered up at him. 'Have you lot no finished here, yet?'

Eddie smiled. 'Just a few last-minute checks.'

She nodded. 'Oh, okay.' She went to close her door.

'Can I ask you something, Mrs McGregor?'

She opened the door again and leaned out. 'Yeah. What?'

'Have you seen anybody take anything away from Mr Thomson's flat?'

She nodded. 'Aye, that woman policeman took stuff last night.'

'Who?'

'Hold on.' Mrs McGregor disappeared for a moment, then returned and gave Eddie a card. 'Her. She got my key to check the place.'

Eddie looked at the card. 'Oh, right. Did you see what she took?'

'Aye. I heard them go downstairs and peeped out my bedroom window. She had Tommy's suitcase, and the man had a big bag of stuff. They loaded it all into their car.'

'Do you know who the man was?'

'No, but he was here with her earlier. They work together.'

'Of course. We've got our wires crossed here, Mrs McGregor. Don't worry, we'll sort it out. Thanks very much.'

'Oh, you're welcome, son.' She closed her door.

Eddie handed Sam the card. It read, 'Sandra Maxwell, Superintendent, Special Branch'

Sam looked up at Eddie. 'Jesus Christ. What's going on here?'

'Come on, let's get back to the car.'

Bruce sat in his car, head back, mouth open, fast asleep. Sam knocked the window and indicated for him to come over to their car.

Bruce rubbed his eyes. 'Sorry. Been a long night. How did you get on?'

Sam shook his head. 'Not a thing.'

'Told you. There's nothing there.'

'But I now know where the drugs have gone.'

Bruce's eyebrows lifted. 'Really? Where?'

'She's got them.' He passed the card forward.

Bruce glanced at it and passed it back. 'Shit. How do you know that?'

Sam took a big breath and tried to stay calm. 'Because the next door neighbour saw her and her partner leave Thomson's flat last night with a suitcase and a big bag of stuff. That must have been the drugs. Now, what's going on here, Jack? What haven't you told us?'

Bruce splayed his hands. 'I've told you everything I know, Sam.'

'But you never told me about her. Who the hell is she, and why's she in Thomson's flat? And she's walked away with my drugs in a bloody suitcase. How can that happen?'

Bruce shook his head. 'I don't know, Sam. I saw an empty suitcase under the bed when we checked Thomson's flat at the weekend, but we definitely didn't see a stash of pills or drugs, that's for sure.'

'Well, she found them.'

Bruce screwed up his face. 'If we're honest, Sam, we don't know what she found. It could have been clothes or some other evidence she took.'

'Clothes? Are you having a bloody laugh, Jack?'

Eddie leaned over and put his hand on Sam's arm to keep him calm. 'What *was* she looking for, Jack?' he asked.

'She's an interfering bitch. She came over yesterday to check if Thomson's death might be a target killing. I mean, it's shite. He was a depressed drunk that attempted suicide.'

Eddie leaned forward. 'Jack, I followed him, and *that's* shite. He was a sharp cookie who knew how to avoid being tailed. So, why did she think he was a target?'

'Hang on a minute. I'll check my notes.' Bruce got his briefcase from the car and thumbed through the contents. He pulled out a photo and a couple of pages of typed notes. He read the notes. 'Right. She produced a photo of this man. She thought Thomson could be a target because he had information this man wanted.'

Eddie took the picture. 'What kind of information?' Sam leaned over and took the photo. It showed an ordinary looking man with fair hair. Maybe the overall drug dealing boss?

Bruce shrugged. 'She wouldn't tell us.'

Eddie thought for a minute. 'Do you know who this chap is?'

'Yeah, hang on.' Bruce read the notes again. Sam sat quiet. This big bastard was a total waste of space when it came down to it. 'My man says the barmaid at the Boundary Bar, Peggy McLeod, told them the lad in the photo came from Amsterdam. Maxwell thinks he bumped Thomson off last Friday night and threw him in the river. She's got half the detectives in Glasgow searching for him as we speak.'

'So, what's his name?' Sam thought getting information from Bruce was like pulling teeth. Eddie had a lot more patience.

Bruce checked his notes again. 'I don't have it here. I'll get it from the barmaid.'

'So, where is she?'

Bruce thumbed through the notes again. 'Don't know. But I'll get back at lunchtime and catch her in the bar. I better go and see the medics and get last night's problem sorted.'

'And what about the drugs stash? How do we get that?'

'Look, Eddie, Sam. I can't even get into her department, far less get near her evidence vault. It's all top secret in there. Leave it with me and I'll try and find out what they've got. I'll see you back here at one o'clock.'

Bruce got out of the car, and they watched as he drove off.

Sam shook his head. 'I don't trust that big bugger any more,' he murmured.

Eddie leaned over and touched his arm. 'At the moment, you don't have any alternative, Sammy. We'll talk to Dan later and see if there's anyone else we can use.'

Sam nodded. 'Yeah, you're right, Eddie. Okay, let's live with it for now. Let's get back home, Johnny.'

***

At one o'clock they parked again at the end of Woddrop Street, and waited for Jack Bruce to appear. Sam picked up the photo of the fair haired man and glanced at Eddie beside him.

'They'll want a new distributor for Glasgow, Eddie. And I want that business. We need to find this guy. Can't wait any longer for buggerlugs. You go to the bar and see if this Peggy McLeod's on duty. Maybe find out about her – you know, kids or family – if we have to force her to talk?'

'Okay. I'll see what I can do.' Eddie got out of the car and walked down the street.

Sam sat back. Aside from the business, he also wanted Thomson's stash of pills. But this woman cop had them locked away. Why would she keep them? As evidence against whom and for what? Thomson had died, for Chrissake, so it couldn't be against him.

And it wasn't a crime to sell these pills. They weren't illegal like cocaine or heroin. Easier to take and a superior effect. That's what made them such a brilliant business.

He thought back to his day with Tracey. How could it be bad to feel that good? He could never figure it out. The vast majority of drug users never became addicted. Just like him, they could take it when they wanted and leave it when they didn't. But the whole legal palaver had been built around the small minority of stupid bastards who became addicted. Like everything else politicians touched, *they* ended up full of smug self-satisfaction, but *we* ended up with the tail wagging the bloody dog.

Ten minutes later, Eddie came back to the car. 'Yeah, she's on duty. Typical barmaid. Late twenties. Has a nine-year-old son. Lives round this way somewhere. They close at two, so she's free after that. If we go down there, we can watch for her.'

'Okay, let's do it. Still no sign of buggerlugs. Something must have happened to him. Bit bloody annoyed he didn't let me know.'

Johnny drove to Birkwood Street, and parked. They could see the pub at the end of the street at the corner with Dalmarnock Road. Just after two o'clock a few punters appeared and the doors closed.

At quarter past, a girl emerged from a side door and walked along the pavement towards them. 'That's her,' said Eddie, and opened the car door. 'I'll get her.'

Sam watched as Eddie stopped the girl and indicated the car. She looked at the car, but didn't move. Eddie spoke again, and she moved towards the car. Eddie opened the rear door and helped her in. 'This is Peggy,' he said, closed the door and came round into the front passenger seat.

Sam smiled at her. 'Hello, Peggy.'

She looked at him warily. 'What do you want?'

'I just want to talk to you for a minute. Get some information.'

'About what?'

'About this man here.' He picked up the photo of the fair-haired man. 'I understand you told the police about him, and we would like to know as well.'

She looked at the photo. 'That's Pieter.'

'Pieter who?'

'I'll need to write it for you.'

Johnny passed a pad from the front. She wrote on it and showed it to Sam.

He looked at it. 'Pieter van der Huizen.'

'And who's he?'

'He's an engineer from Amsterdam. He worked on the boilers in the power station over there for a couple of days.'

'Really?'

'Yeah.' She shrugged. 'That's what he said.'

'So, why were the police interested in him?'

She shook her head. 'I don't know.'

Sam thought he saw a glimpse of fear in her eyes as she answered. She bloody *did* know. He smiled at her. 'I hear you've got a nine-year-old boy, Peggy. I've got kids the same age. They're a constant worry, aren't they? Always getting into scrapes at school or on the street. We're scared they have an accident. Now, I don't want you to worry about your boy any more than I worry about mine, so I'd like you to tell me why the police are interested in this man. Then you don't need to worry about your boy any more.'

Tears came up in her eyes and she looked petrified. Exactly what he wanted. He waited for her to answer.

After a couple of minutes of silence, she said, 'Because they think he killed Tommy.'

'Tommy Thomson?'

She nodded. 'Yeah.'

'Why do they think that?'

She hesitated again. 'He bought a half bottle of whisky from us on Friday night, and I heard Tommy's body was full of alcohol when they found it on Saturday. He hadn't drunk much here, so I think they put two and two together and made five.'

She now talked much easier, and he believed her. 'Do you know where he stayed?'

'A hotel near Queen's Park. He didn't say the name. But he's away back to Amsterdam.'

'How do you know that?'

'Well, he said on Friday night he'd an early train to catch on Saturday, so I assume that's where he went. To be honest, I don't know where he went.'

'Well, I heard half the detectives in Glasgow were looking for him. How could that be if he's already gone?'

She shrugged. 'I'm sorry. I honestly don't know.'

Sam thought for a moment. He'd got as much as she knew. 'Okay, Peggy, thanks for that. I'll let you get on with the rest of your day.'

'Can I go now?'

'Yeah, off you go.'

She opened the door and then stopped. 'Who are you anyway?'

He smiled at her. She had her confidence back. 'Best not to know.'

'Right.' She got out of the car and walked away.

Sam sat back, looked at Eddie, and snorted. 'We've got a name, but I don't think we're much further forward.'

'Well, let's think about it. I mean, Dan's got great connections in London, and *they* must have links into Amsterdam. Let's see what we can find once we get back.'

'Okay. Let's get back to the house, Johnny. I want a word on something else, Eddie.'

***

Sam and Eddie stretched out on separate sofas in Sam's lounge. 'What do you want to talk about?' asked Eddie.

Sam outlined his thoughts about Maxwell. 'Why would she keep these pills? Think about it. It's not illegal to sell them. They can't be used in evidence against Thomson. Why would she hold on to them?'

Eddie pursed his lips. 'Fair point.'

'Do you think I should make her an offer for them?'

'Phew. From what Bruce said, she doesn't sound the type.'

'They're all the type, Eddie. Always interested in extra cash. And once you've hooked them, you've got them forever.'

Eddie grimaced. 'Mmm. I'm not sure that applies here. She's Special Branch. They're a cut above ordinary coppers. I think they deal with big issues like national security. She must have come into this from another angle, Sammy. Remember, she produced this photo from somewhere else, and said he targeted Thomson. It can't be for drugs. That's a local issue. He must have targeted Thomson for another reason. She told Bruce he wanted information. We just don't know what information.'

'So, why did she take the drugs, then?'

'Well, as Bruce says, we don't actually know she took the drugs. But, if she did, she's got to dispose of them at some stage. As you say, they're not illegal, so they can't be used as evidence of a crime. If you think about it, Thomson must have bought these drugs. So, they're his property. They'll go back to his next of kin. But that only deals with his *stash*. It doesn't get us in with the supplier. And it doesn't get us the bloody *business*, which is what we really want. How do we get that?'

Sam nodded. 'Yeah, you're right.' Made sense, he thought. It could take them weeks or months to chase through Thomson's connections, and it still wouldn't get them the business. 'So, what do you think, Eddie? Any ideas?'

They both sat in silence for a few minutes. Then Eddie said, 'You know, if Thomson sold these drugs in Glasgow, other lads must sell them in other cities. Why don't we contact Fergus in Edinburgh and see if he can find the lad over there? We could then make *him* an offer he can't refuse, and we could piggyback on Fergus, or maybe even find out how to source the drugs ourselves. Does that make sense?'

Sam smiled. 'Good thinking, Eddie. It does make sense.'

'Okay, Sam. Let me think it through, and we'll talk to Fergus tomorrow.'

'Great. Let's do it.'

The phone rang. Sam picked up the receiver. 'Hello?'

'It's me, Sam.' It was Jack Bruce. He silently mouthed over to Eddie

'Where the hell did you get to?'

'Yeah, sorry. But I've got big problems.'

'We've all got big problems. What makes yours so special?'

'I'm suspended, pending dismissal.'

'Shit. For what?'

'I don't know. They won't say until they complete an investigation.'

'I thought you had a senior-level cover?'

'Yeah, I thought so too. But he won't take my calls. They've hung me out to dry, Sam. It's something to do with that interfering bitch, but I don't know what yet.'

'So, you're now off the job?'

'Yeah.'

'Sorry to hear that. Can I just check something?'

'Yeah.'

'What did the medics say about Wilson?'

'They agreed a fall was a possibility.'

'Good. Well, sorry to hear your news. Call me as soon as you know something.'

'Will do. Thanks, Sam. Will you let Dan and Kenny know?'

'Yeah, I'll tell them. Bye.' He hung up, and outlined the conversation to Eddie.

Eddie nodded. 'Shit, that's us stuffed too, eh?'

'Yeah, the bitch.'

***

For the rest of the evening, Sam could think of nothing else. Even though he'd earlier talked about getting rid of Bruce, the fact it had now happened upset him. They'd had Bruce on the payroll for eight years now, and Dan got angry when he heard. 'How the hell could that happen? Bloody careless bastard. Who's this bitch anyway? Do we know her?'

'No, dad. She's Special Branch.'

'Shit. How could Bruce upset them? Christ, he was hard work at times, but worth having on board. Now, we'll have to start again from scratch. We don't have anybody else at that level local to us. Okay, at our meeting on Monday, let's raise this as a priority. Let's see what options we have for a replacement.'

Sam went home and got more and more angry about Bruce. Once the kids went to bed, he poured himself a large whisky. By bedtime, he'd worked himself into a fury. The bitch. What right did she have to interfere in his business? She wouldn't get away with it. He'd teach her a lesson. He pulled the card from his pocket. Bitch. He put on his coat and hat, and went out to the phone box at the end of the block. He asked the operator for the number and got straight through.

'Two-five-six-seven?'

'Watch your back, you interfering bitch.' He hung up. That was just the start. She'd pay big style for meddling in his business. Bitch.

Chapter 8. Astrid

Porritt met with his personal assistant, Sophie Silverman, at four o'clock every day. They'd started when she joined him at Admiralty Intelligence in '38, continued at Bletchley Park and then at Special Branch, and now here in Nuremberg, it was their last week together.

He'd hoped to persuade her to stay for another six months, but realised, when he found her at her desk in tears one morning two weeks ago, she'd never agree.

She had glanced through some photographs to be used in the pack that day. Specialised photography units had evidence accompanied the Allied Armies as they liberated the concentration camps. One US Army photo showed a female prisoner in her distinctive striped clothing, too weak to stand, almost skeletal, lying on the ground at the fence, with one arm raised to grip the fence higher up and lift her head off the ground, yet smiling, with her eyes wide and shining with hope.

Sophie couldn't speak through her tears, and held the picture up. Even he found it gut wrenching. That one photo told the whole story of the horror emerging from these camps.

He sat down opposite her. 'I'm going to miss you.'

She smiled. 'Thank you, sir. But Cassie will look after you. She's very good.'

He nodded. Cassie would be good, but she wasn't a Sophie. She couldn't articulate people's strengths and weaknesses in the same way. 'Okay, so you fly back Thursday?'

'Yes, sir. Sorry, but I've found it more difficult here than I thought.'

He knew she had Jewish links on her husband's side, and they must play a part. 'So, what have we got for the last three days?'

'Just to make sure everything's in order, sir. Tie up some loose ends. Gisela came to me today with a girl who, I think, could be your transport supremo.'

'Really? Tell me about her.'

Sophie checked her notes. 'She's Astrid Rhys, a Dutch national. Twenty-five. Married. Previous occupation, an events manager with Philips at Eindhoven. Has a fantastic reference from them. Speaks fluent Dutch, English, French and German. She thought she might pick up work as a translator, but I think, with her background, she could do the transport role.'

'What's she doing over here?'

'Her husband's the pool correspondent for a bunch of Dutch newspapers. He's over here for at least three months. They married in the summer, and came over here early to have a delayed honeymoon. She just wants something to occupy her while he's at work.'

'Bloody hell. Sounds good. Can we meet her?'

'Yes, sir. I thought you and Colonel Baker might want to, so I've asked her to hang on for a bit. She's with Gisela.'

'Right,' He stood up. 'Let's see if Jed's free.'

Next door, Jed crouched over paperwork. 'Sure. This can wait. Let's go.'

They introduced themselves. Astrid had long dark hair, and wore a black top and skirt. Porritt thought she looked rather plain, but with a steely confidence in her eyes. He asked her if she would consider a different, but a more urgent requirement than translation.

She nodded. 'Yes, of course.'

They all walked back to the main conference room above the front courtyard, and Porritt explained the problem. 'We have about fifty cars that arrive at the same time, morning and evening, to set down and pick up staff. And they all want to do it at the main door below us. So, the whole place just gets gridlocked. Everyone gets frustrated. We need someone to sort this out, and wondered whether you'd like to do this?'

The girl went closer to the window and looked down. 'If you had to divide the cars into groups, how many groups would you have?'

Porritt hesitated. 'Well, the logical groups would be the countries. So, there would be four; US, Britain, France and Russia, plus the local traffic, German. Five in all.'

'Uh-huh. There's a large Mercedes at the main door. Could you ask the driver to park it end on to us, facing the road, so we can get an idea of how much space we have?'

'Sure.' Gisela went to the phone and called someone. In a few moments the driver emerged and moved the car as requested.

Astrid looked from side to side along the courtyard. 'There's plenty of room for five lanes of cars plus walkways, if they're oriented end on. That would ease the congestion by a factor of five. If you wanted to ease it further you'd need to schedule the cars into the lanes.'

This girl was really bright, thought Porritt. 'How would we do that?'

'Well, you'd need to hold the cars somewhere, and then signal them into the lane when there's a space. You'd have no delays then.'

'I like it,' Porritt said, and nodded to Baker.

'The space across the road. What's that used for?' Astrid asked.

Gisela said, 'It was originally part of our complex here, but they demolished it about eight years ago. They planned to build a military barracks, but it never happened.'

'So, could we use it as a staging post, then?'

'Yeah, no reason why not.'

'We could then have someone over there and signal to them when a space came free.'

'How? By waving a flag or something?' asked Porritt.

Baker stepped forward. 'I think we could find a couple of Army HT sets – radio handsets – to make it a lot easier.'

'Sounds good,' said Porritt. 'How about in the evening, when everyone wants to leave? What do we do then?'

Astrid thought for a moment. 'They select a one-minute slot. Their car would be there at that time. If they're not, the car's moved out and they have to organise another slot.'

Porritt laughed. 'Do you think our self-important lawyers would go for that?' he asked Baker. 'They'd want the car held till *they're* ready. Then it's back to chaos again.'

Astrid turned to him. 'Are all the drivers local?'

He nodded. 'Yeah.'

'Then that's how to solve it. The drivers must obey the rules or they get fired. So, they'll obey the rules and move at the end of their one-minute slot. The lawyers will learn they have to be there at their chosen slot time, or they'll have to wait. What do you think they'll do?'

Porritt snorted. 'You're right. They'll be there.' No wonder she had a fantastic reference from Philips. 'Well, as far as I'm concerned, the job's yours. What do you think, Jed?'

He nodded. 'Yeah, I agree.'

'Good.' Porritt turned to Astrid. 'Our colleagues from France and Russia still have to endorse the decision, but we'll sort it out tomorrow. We'd also use you during the day as a translator. We're always short of resource there.'

'Oh, that would be good.'

He went on, 'So, if we agree to pay you the same rate as one of our translators or one of Gisela's managers, whichever's the greater? How does that sound?'

Her face lit up. 'That's great. Thank you so much.' She shook hands with everyone. She held Porritt's gaze for a couple of seconds too long as she shook his hand. Maybe she wasn't as plain as he'd first thought.

The girls got ready to leave. 'Gisela, could you hang back for a moment, please?'

'Yes, sir.'

Sophie said, 'I'll see Astrid out.' The two of them turned towards the door. Then Astrid stopped and turned back to Porritt.

'Just a thought about your comment earlier, sir, that everyone wants dropped or picked up from the main door. Could you put up sheltered walkways from the lanes to the door? It might take the edge off any complaints people have to walk a bit further.'

Porritt turned to Baker. 'Sounds reasonable.'

Baker nodded. 'Okay. Tell you what. Can you come back tomorrow morning?'

'Yes, of course.'

'Then ask for Bob Gonzales. He's my Head of Engineering. Tell him what you want and how you want it laid out, and he'll organise it for you. Okay?'

She smiled again. 'Thank you, sir.' She and Sophie left the room.

The three of them stood at the window. Porritt said, 'Quite a girl, eh? She should be on your team, Gisela, but we'll pick up the tab for her. Okay?'

'Thank you, sir, because I don't have a budget for her.'

'No problem. We'll sort that out.'

They watched as Astrid emerged from the building and crossed the courtyard towards the exit, her raincoat shimmering and rippling in the floodlights.

'Wonder where she got that?' Gisela murmured.

Porritt glanced at her. 'Got what?'

'Her *Kleppermantel*.'

'What's that?'

'Her grey raincoat. Klepper stopped making these in '37 or '38 and went over to military clothing. But that looks new. I'm amazed. Wonder where she got it?'

Porritt turned and smiled at the others. 'Well, you can ask her tomorrow.' He rubbed his hands. 'Another job well done, folks. Let's get back to work.'

Chapter 9. Bill

Sandra loved London. The buildings, the traffic, the shops, the people, the Underground, all just seemed to buzz with quality and excitement. As she crossed Trafalgar Square into Whitehall, on a bright Monday morning, dressed in her new smart dark-blue coat and hat, she felt the city had its sparkle back. At the Home Office, just at the Cenotaph, with its bed of poppy wreaths, she took a deep breath, entered the building and asked for Bill Franklin.

A few minutes later, he came bounding down the stairs, tall, athletic, jacket flying open, and with a big welcoming smile. 'Sandra?'

She smiled back. 'Bill, nice to meet you.' They shook hands.

'Come on, let's go up to the office.'

As they walked, they chatted about her journey, her hotel, and her views on London. In his office they sat side by side at the conference table.

'Do I detect a Scottish accent?' she asked.

He laughed. 'Yeah, everyone says when I speak to a Scot, my accent changes.'

'How long have you lived here?'

'Oh, came as a boy, nine years old. Brought up in Blantyre. Do you know it?'

She nodded.

'My father had joined the Army at the start of the First World War. Turned out to be a natural soldier. Shot up the ranks. Took a commission, and finished up a Lieutenant. He came back at the end of the war a different man, and saw Blantyre through different eyes. Within a week, we had moved lock, stock and barrel to Chislehurst, and he's never looked back.'

She thought they must be about the same age. 'What about you?'

'Oh, much less dramatic. Graduated in Classics from Cambridge. Joined the diplomatic corps, but hated pandering to the foibles of foreign despots, so transferred over to the investigations side. Did some interesting projects in Hong Kong and Istanbul, but it wasn't a job for a married man. The war loomed, travel was dodgy, so I moved to investigations in the Home Office, and got the Deputy Head job a few years ago. I've worked with Special Branch, mainly with Malcolm Craig in London, and met Commander Porritt a few times. I just met Dave Burnett for the first time last week. What about you?'

'Huh. Even less dramatic. Educated at the Girls' High in Glasgow, and joined the police as soon as I could. It's the only job I ever wanted. And I've done okay. Moved up the ranks. Took over Special Branch for the West of Scotland in June this year. And here I am.'

He laughed. 'And here we are. Got a bit of a job to do, eh? Did Dave tell you what the HS said to us after the meeting?'

'About closing this drug network down?'

'Yeah. That was unusual. He seemed very bitter. I did some probing, and found his cousin died on a rail track a few weeks ago, drug related. It might be personal, but he wants it finished. So, where do we start? Dave said you have some inside information.'

'I do. I've got a lot of info, and some ideas on how we could kill it that might give us a starting point.'

'Great. Tell me about them.'

She told him about her findings in Thomson's flat, and showed him copies of the coded pages and the documents. 'It seems to me, if the HS wants this drug operation ended, we have to take the head off to kill the brain, and take the legs off to kill the delivery network.'

He pursed his lips and nodded. 'Okay. So, how do we do it?'

'Let's look at them separately. For the legs, we have this Andrew Lyall in Hampstead, and a whole bunch of unknown people in the major cities. Now I think we could take them all out with the same approach we used to kill Aquila a few years ago. Let me tell you about it.'

She told him how Porritt had hunted down the Aquila organisation. 'Dave Burnett, Malcolm Craig, and I were all involved in it, and we could do the same again.

'However, when we nailed the Aquila legs back then, we acted under the Treachery Act, 1940. But now, the possession and distribution of these methamphetamine pills is not illegal. So, for us to act, we need emergency legislation to change that.'

'Right. I'll check with the legal eagles. But, let's proceed, assuming we *will* have a legal basis, and see where it takes us, huh?'

'Okay, I agree. We'll work with Dave and Malcolm to kill the UK operations. That's our strategy there. It's the other side, the brain side, we've got to figure out what to do. And we have to start in Amsterdam. We've got this Michael running Central Distribution. He must be closer to the brain. So, who do we know over there?'

He splayed his hands. 'Sorry. I don't know anyone, but if you give me time I can probably find someone.'

'Mmm.' She thought for a moment. 'I think Malcolm had Dutch help on a drug bust a while ago. Let's find out.' She picked up the phone and asked for the number.

'Hey, Sandra. Twice within a week? Something happening?'

'Sure is, Malcolm. I'm in London now. This drug business has mushroomed. Dave's got me on a special project with Bill Franklin, whom I think you know.'

'I do. Give him my regards.'

'Will do. We're looking for a contact in Amsterdam that could help us with our enquiries over there. Do you know anyone?'

'Yeah. Hold on a sec. We had a good chap help us with a cocaine bust a few years ago.' He paused. 'Right, I've got it. His name's Guus Mulder.' He spelled it out for her, 'and he's about the same level and has similar responsibilities to you and me. Here's his number.'

She noted it. 'That's brilliant, Malcolm. We'll give him a call.'

'Great. Anything else I can help with?'

'Well, we're just pulling our strategy together right now, but we already know, at some point, we'll kill the network across the country in much the same way Porritt did with Aquila. So, you'll have a key part, Malcolm, to deal with Lyall.'

'Oh, Jesus, Sandra. Can't wait. Listen, will you be seeing Dave today?'

'Yeah, probably. Why do you ask?'

'He's only a few doors along from me here at Scotland Yard. So, if he approves it, why don't we start on some basics? Have an early dinner. Ask Dave along too.'

'Okay, we'll see if that works. Call you later.' She turned to Bill. 'He passes on his regards.' She gave him a run down of the conversation. 'So, I think we can leave the UK side with Malcolm for the moment. Let's figure out what we say to Guus Mulder.'

'Right. I know the Dutch have a more tolerant attitude towards drugs. Helping us to kill this drug business might not help them solve any problems. So, what's in it for them?'

She thought for a moment. 'Well, their economy's probably shot to hell – even worse than ours. So, if we pay well for their help, that might relieve some pressure.

'Oh, and let's not forget these drugs fuelled the German invasion into the Low Countries. And the Germans occupied them for five years. That must have been hellish. Imagine how we'd feel with foreign soldiers telling us what to do all the time. I say we play a strong anti-German card and hope it resonates with Mulder.'

He nodded. 'Yeah, I like it. The HS has given us carte blanche within reason on this job, so we can pay well for help. Let's go for it.'

'Okay, do you want to call, or shall I do it?'

'The approach would come better from you, Sandra. Police to police.'

Within a few moments, Mulder came on the line. She introduced herself and Bill. 'We got your name from my colleague, Malcolm Craig, whom you helped with a drug bust a few years ago, and we wondered if you could do the same for us?'

'Yeah, it's possible. What are you looking for, Chief Superintendent?'

'Call me Sandra.'

'Okay, Sandra. I'm Guus.'

'Right, Guus. A company in Germany has flooded our British cities with a new drug through Amsterdam. We want to kill this business before it really gets started over here, but we need your help with the Amsterdam connection. And we're happy to pay for it too.'

'What kind of drug?'

'It's called methamphetamine. I believe the Germans used it to fuel their army's advance into your country. That must have been horrific for you.'

There was a long silence. 'You don't know the half of it, Sandra. What they did to our women – to our people – horrific doesn't begin to describe it. If I can help you get rid of this scourge, I'd do it for free. But payment would be very welcome.'

Wow, this sounded *very* personal. 'I'm sorry, Guus. I didn't mean to open old wounds.'

'Oh, I just don't think they'll ever heal. Anyway, tell me what you've got.'

'Right, Guus. The distribution centre has the telephone number Amsterdam 327491, and we have the name Michael as the contact.'

'Hold on a second, Sandra.' He talked with someone in the background. 'Right, I'm back. I've got one of my team finding out more about that number. So, carry on.'

'Each drug supplier in Britain visits the Amsterdam centre about once a month. They use a special suitcase with secret sections to take the money out and bring the drugs back. I'll send you over a photo of the suitcase so you can recognise them. We'd like as much info as you can get us on these suppliers. We also want to know more about the link upstream from Amsterdam to the manufacturing base in Germany and the brains behind it all. If you could help us identify these links, we'd really appreciate it.'

'Okay, Sandra. Here's the number for the photo.' She noted it. 'We could photograph the suppliers arriving and departing, and get their names from passport control at Schiphol, all under cover. Would that be useful?'

She thought for a moment. 'Yeah, it *would* be useful, Guus.'

'Good. What do you say then, if we put together a plan to do all of that for you and charge our resources out to you at our standard charge out rates?'

'Yeah, that's fine. Bill will confirm the arrangements from our Home Office.'

'Great. Thanks, Sandra. Oh, hold on. That telephone number you gave us is for a company called GT Pharma BV, based in Keizersgracht, not far from here. The Directors are Michael Timmermann, aged twenty eight, at the Keizersgracht address, and Gerhardt Timmermann, aged fifty six, with an address in Berlin. Neither is known to our police at this time, so we agreed they could take over the lease of this office block in June. We'll watch them and tap their phone, to get these links for you, Sandra.'

'Thanks, Guus. Berlin's now partly under British control. Give me that address and we'll check it out.' She took a note of it.

'Do you plan to come over here soon, Sandra?'

She suddenly realised she had a problem. 'Can I get back to you on that, Guus?'

'Sure. Just let me know and we'll pick you up at Schiphol.'

'Okay. Thanks for everything. We'll talk later.'

She hung up and gave Bill a summary of the conversation.

'That's brilliant, Sandra. I'll get started on the arrangements at this end. What do you have to get back to him on?'

'He's asking if we're going over.'

'So, what's the problem?'

'I've got two problems, Bill. First, I don't have a passport.'

'Not a problem. I'll fast track one for you now. You'll have it this afternoon. What's the second problem?'

'I'm terrified of flying.'

'Really? Why?'

She hesitated. 'Ten years ago, the love of my life got killed in an RAF plane crash. A maintenance error. Totally avoidable. But for years afterwards I cringed every time a plane passed. I expected it to crash at any moment. And I'm still scared of flying.'

He pursed his lips. 'Well, I don't want to trivialise your fears, Sandra, but flying's as safe as a bus or train. I mean, accidents can always happen, but aircraft today have triple systems to protect them. Crashes are very rare. And you can always cling on to me.' He laughed.

She wondered why he said that. Just light-hearted humour? She did feel comfortable with him, though. They had a warmth in their discussions, which she put down to their common aim. But let's keep it professional. She laughed in return. 'What's the alternative?'

'I'd need to check, but I think the Channel ferries still only run to Calais. So, we'd have to drive to Dover, cross the Channel, then drive north through France and Belgium to Amsterdam. It's doable, but it would take a full day as against a one hour flight.'

She knew her fear of flying was irrational. 'Okay, I'll take the flight.' She called Tom in Glasgow and asked him to send a photo of the Thomson suitcase over to Guus.

Bill called a Foreign Office contact in Berlin and asked him to check the address for Gerhardt Timmermann.

Sandra felt she could now pull a decent plan together, and arranged to meet Dave Burnett at five,

Malcolm at six and then all go to dinner. Shaping up for a good day, she thought.

***

Sandra and Bill updated Dave Burnett with their plans. She realised, for the first time, she had a boss younger than her. Only a year younger, but it told her time raced on.

She described her outline plan to take the legs off in the UK and the head off in Germany by getting the links via the Amsterdam centre. 'However, we don't yet know our legal basis, sir. We're assuming we *will* have one, but we'll need to get that from the lawyers.'

'What does the Home Office think, Bill?'

'We're seeing the HS in the morning, sir. I think he'll make it work.'

'Okay. Sounds good. What about the head?'

Sandra told him about Guus Mulder and finding out about the Timmermanns.

Bill cut in. 'My contact in Berlin has come back to me, sir. The address we had for Gerhardt Timmermann is now a heap of rubble. He asked around and found Timmermann, a qualified doctor, also runs a private clinic at a place called Bad Oeynhausen, about two hundred miles west of Berlin. "Bad" is the German word for "bath" and means it's a spa town. Apparently, it has thermal salt springs. He also runs a pharmaceutical manufacturing company there that relocated from Berlin some years ago, and we think it's where they now make these drugs.

'Now, Bad Oeynhausen is in the British Zone of Occupation, and the Military Governor of the Zone, who's effectively in charge of that part of Germany, is Sir Bernard Montgomery, aka Field Marshal

Montgomery, of El Alamein fame. He's a close friend of the HS, so we hope to get some leverage there.

'At the moment, we plan to go to Amsterdam tomorrow to meet with Mulder and his team, and then we'll get a car from the Embassy to take us over to Bad Oeynhausen on Wednesday. We'll have a meeting there with British Army staff to agree a strategy to arrest Timmermann, and close down his tablet-making operation.'

'Great. You've done well, so far. I'll do my bit when you're ready, so just let me know when and where.'

They left Burnett and joined Malcolm Craig in his office. They agreed, with the phone tap in Hampstead, they could get the network size within a week, since each of the suppliers had to call Lyall every week with their sales figures. They'd also plan to to lift Lyall and all the UK suppliers within a five seconds target, to avoid any of them alerting the network.

Dave Burnett joined them, and they all went for dinner at Malcolm's club in Pall Mall. As the host, Malcolm kept the conversation light and cheerful until the main course, when Bill raised the subject of GT Pharma, and the others outlined what lessons they could apply from their Aquila experience. In the end, they all agreed they should not underestimate the GT Pharma operation, and should treat it just like they did the Aquila enemy during the war.

After the meal, Dave Burnett and Malcolm went their separate ways, and Sandra walked with Bill across Trafalgar Square to her hotel at Charing Cross.

Bill checked his watch. 'I've just missed a train. Do you fancy a nightcap?'

She smiled. 'Sure. Why not?'

They went into the bar, found a quiet table over in the corner, and ordered drinks.

'Do you have a family, Bill?'

He looked surprised for a moment. 'A family?' He shook his head. 'No, no family.'

In an instant he'd become melancholy. 'Oh, I'm sorry, Bill. You'd mentioned earlier you were married.'

He sat in silence for a minute. 'That's true. But one night the Germans sent over a doodlebug with her name on it – and that was the end of that.'

Her jaw dropped and her eyes filled with tears. 'Oh, my God.' She put her hand on his arm. Such a gem of a man. It seemed so unfair. 'What happened?'

He sighed, shrugged, and smiled wanly. 'Oh, her sister had a three-day pass from the RAF and wanted to come up to London to visit some bar or other. Eileen didn't want to go, but she also didn't want her sister to come up alone. London was a wild place at night during the war. So, they both came up. That night, all the cross-river train and tube lines closed as usual in an air raid, We think they were headed for a shelter at Embankment Station, just round the corner from here, when bang! That was it. Life's just a lottery, really.'

She squeezed his arm. 'Oh, I'm so sorry, Bill. That's terrible.'

He glanced at her. 'Thanks. They say time heals, and – well – maybe it does. But now you'll understand why I want to get one back on the Germans, if I can. Anyway, enough about me. What about you? Are you married?'

She shook her head. 'Married to the job, Bill. That's me.'

'I just wondered, when you said you lost the love of your life ten years ago.'

She nodded. 'Yeah, well, time does heal, I suppose. But it's hard to have a social life in this job. So, I just don't bother now.'

'Yeah, I know. Me neither.' He glanced at his watch. 'Well, we've got a heavy day tomorrow, so I think I'd better get my train.'

They finished their drinks and went out into the hotel lobby. She wondered how he'd say goodbye. But let's just keep it professional, she thought. She stuck out her hand. 'Thanks for a great day, Bill.'

They shook hands. 'Yeah. See you in the morning.' He smiled and left.

She went up to her room and stretched out on the bed. A good day that had ended well. Bill was nice and genuine. But, for her, the job always came first, though in her quiet moments, she sometimes had a pang of regret that she had no one to share her life experiences. She thought about Bill and his tragic experience. Maybe. Just maybe.

But now she'd to think of tomorrow. A meeting with the Home Secretary and a flight to Amsterdam. Two big new experiences. She got ready for bed and hoped she'd sleep.

***

By the time she got off the plane at Schiphol around noon, Sandra had recovered her poise. They'd had an amazing morning. Twenty minutes with the Home Secretary, Mr Chuter Ede, a tall, thin-faced man with grey hair and moustache, and a ready smile. Bill took full control. He outlined their plans for removing the head and the legs of this drug network, and wanted help in two areas – to establish the legal basis for closing down the UK drug network, and to ask Sir Bernard Montgomery for help to close down the tablet-making facility in Germany.

Sandra was astonished at the clarity of the HS as he dictated a letter to the Lord Chief Justice, addressed as 'Dear Tom,' and to Sir Bernard, addressed as 'Dear Bernard,' both of which had to remain blank for him to hand write the greetings. As they left, he said, 'Thank you both. It's really important for the country we get a grip on this menace. When you get the tablet-making equipment, why not drop it in the Channel on the way back – accidentally, of course.' He smiled as he shook hands.

She'd enjoyed the flight in the end. Rigid with fear at take off, she'd gradually relaxed as Bill quietly convinced her to touch her surroundings, and she even looked past him out of the window as they came in to land. She now felt no qualms about the return journey.

As they came into the terminal building, she saw the sign 'CS Sandra Maxwell' held aloft. Guus Mulder, a well-built man with a square face, short fair hair and a broad smile, welcomed them. 'Hey, let's get you out to the car,' he said, and took her case.

On the way into Amsterdam, Guus chatted about the passing scene. Sandra relished the differences between Amsterdam and London. The architecture; the people, dressed differently and speaking a foreign language; the traffic on the right; the huge number of bicycles; the single-decked trams speeding along narrow streets. She found the reality of her first trip abroad very striking.

They settled around the conference table in Guus's office, joined by his assistant, Inspecteur Margreet Ursel, a tall blonde woman, who also spoke very good English.

They cleared off the admin first. Bill had brought a letter from the Home Office agreeing to the terms Guus had set out the previous day. Guus read it through and nodded. 'That's fine. Thank you very much. Now, would you like to walk us through your strategy of what you want to achieve here, and how we can help you do it?'

Sandra cleared her throat, and described the background to their visit. She went on, 'We plan, over the next four to six weeks, to identify the drug manufacturing centre in Germany and all of the suppliers in the UK. We'd very much like your help to identify and prove the links from here upstream to Germany and downstream to the UK suppliers. At some point, when we're ready, we plan to take the whole lot out in one night.'

Guus asked, 'And what about the Amsterdam centre, do you plan to take that out too?'

Sandra shook her head. 'No, we don't. Subject to your agreement, we believe this Amsterdam company probably operates legally in your country. However, if we cut off the head in Germany, that would throttle the supply of tablets through Amsterdam.'

Guus nodded. 'I agree. At the moment, we have no reason to close that company. But we're very happy to help you with the links you're looking for. I can tell you the phone tap has already shown calls from the UK – from GB04, GB07, and GB14 – to arrange visits and get more supplies of tablets. They've also had calls from France and Belgium. However, we want to know whether they distribute these drugs in *our* country. As you know, we experienced the effect of these drugs from the German army, and that's something we don't wish on anyone. I've had an informal meeting with our Minister here this morning to discuss this, and we think, depending on what emerges, we might join you in your efforts.'

Sandra glanced at Bill. 'Wow, we'd really like that, Guus.'

'Good. So, what's your plan now you're here?'

'Well, first of all we'd like to see this company, GT Pharma BV, just to get a feel for it. Then discuss the information we're looking for and the actions you've got in place to get it.'

'Okay, we can do that. We've taken over an office opposite this company on the other side of the canal, and we photograph everyone going in and out. So we'll show you that after lunch. I've organised a quick sandwich lunch here.'

'Thank you. There's something else I'd like to check, Guus.' She brought out the photograph of the fair haired man. 'We believe this man murdered another in Glasgow ten days ago. He used the name, 'Pieter van der Huizen', and said he came from Amsterdam.

'Now, we've seen a number of instances recently of crooks borrowing real people's identities to hide their own. Could you check if there's a real person with this name, and then check how this man could have borrowed that identity? It might help us catch him.

'Tomorrow we're in Germany to have a look at the pharma facility, but back here on Thursday, so we could meet again then.' She went back into her briefcase and pulled out another photo. 'Here's a copy of that man's fingerprints.'

'Okay.' Guus passed the man's photo and the name to his assistant. 'Margreet, see if one of the team can do a quick check on this, please?' Margreet left the room for a minute.

Over lunch they discussed the information Sandra and Bill wanted from the watch on GT Pharma BV. She concluded, 'If you could link the GB code number to a name, passport and photo of a UK supplier, it would give us fantastic evidence at trial.'

'Yeah, I think we can do that okay.'

'Great. And we can then get their address from passport records. Right, Bill?'

He nodded. 'Yeah, that's right. But we'd then need to verify the name and address, given what you found in Glasgow.'

Sandra thought for a moment. 'Good point. We'll need to deal with that separately.' She took a note on her pad.

As they got ready to leave, Margreet got called out. She came back moments later. 'We have some info on Pieter van der Huizen,' she said. 'We can find only one person with that name in Amsterdam. He runs a flower shop two streets away, so we can easily check it today, if you want.'

Sandra smiled. 'Yeah, let's do that.'

They left the police office and, in less than ten minutes, entered another office building beside a canal, went up to the second floor, and were admitted to a dimly lit area.

Guus said, 'We used this arrangement in another observation, and it worked well. This wooden structure's the rear of a false wall painted to look like the back wall of an office. If you look through the slits here, you'll see across the canal to the target building.'

Sandra did so. 'Wow, that's so clear.'

He laughed, then pointed upwards. 'We have these two cameras built into this wall – one a low-light camera we use early or late in the day – and both give us close-ups of those arriving or leaving the building opposite. We've built the cameras into false paintings on the other side of the wall.

'From the other side of the canal, this room looks like an ordinary office, with people working normally at their desks at the window. Let's go round the end of the wall here and you'll see it from the side.'

They moved to the end, and just as Guus had said, the painted side of the wall looked exactly like the back wall of an office. Brilliant.

Guus moved to a side table. 'We've taken these photos so far. All of them have that special suitcase in the photo you sent. We wire each photo across to the team in Schiphol, and they pick up the name and date of birth as they go through passport control. This photo is Michael Timmermann. It matches the photo ID he used when he signed the lease. We don't know the girl with him yet. So, what do you think?'

Sandra laughed. 'It's brilliant, Guus. Absolutely brilliant.'

Guus smiled. 'Yeah, we're pretty happy with it. Shall we go and see about Mr Huizen?'

Sandra glanced at Bill. 'You okay with all this, Bill?'

'Yeah, it's fantastic. Thanks so much to you all.'

Guus nodded. 'Okay, let's go.'

Ten minutes later Sandra and Guus entered the Huizen Bloemen shop in a side street just off Dam Square. Bill and Margreet waited outside. Sandra admired the variety of flowers on display. Fresh flowers were a rare commodity in wartime Britain.

A woman in her fifties came from the back of the shop. '*Hallo. Kan ik u helpen*?'

Guus showed his ID card. 'Amsterdam Police. Do you speak English?'

'*Ja*. Sorry. Yes, I do.'

'This is Chief Superintendent Sandra Maxwell from Glasgow Police in Scotland. She'd like to ask you a few questions.'

'Oh?'

Her eyes went suddenly wary, Sandra thought. 'I'd like to talk to Mr Pieter van der Huizen. Is he available?'

'I'm afraid he's not. Can I help?'

'Who are you?'

'I'm his mother, Mrs Lotte van der Huizen.' She paused, looked at the floor, then returned her gaze to Sandra. 'Is this about last night? Pieter doesn't want to report it.'

Sandra exchanged glances with Guus. 'It's not about last night, ma'am, and we respect Pieter's decision, but could you tell us what happened?'

Lotte hesitated. 'Well, two men attacked Pieter as he closed up last night. They bundled him into a car, and wanted to know about his drug-distribution business. Just crazy. Pieter didn't know what they meant. Eventually, a third man in the car pulled out a picture and said, 'It's the wrong guy.' They threw him out of the car, and warned him not to talk to the police.'

'Were they local or foreign?' Sandra asked.

'Local.'

It sounded like the local equivalent of the Dan McFadden gang in Glasgow, thought Sandra, and probably connected back to them. 'Oh, I'm sorry to hear that. How is he?'

'A bit bruised and battered. He's just relaxing today upstairs in the flat.'

Sandra nodded. 'Well, I hope he recovers okay. But that's not why we're here.' She went into her briefcase and showed Lotte the photo of the fair-haired man. 'Have you or your son ever seen this man before?'

Lotte studied the picture. 'Yes, I saw him here, maybe six weeks ago? I had come into the shop via the side door, and he was standing at our desk, taking notes. I asked him if I could help, but he said he was just noting the names of the flowers in front of him, while he waited for his wife. She was on the far side of the shop with Pieter, buying flowers. He was a pleasant man, but not local. He spoke good Dutch, but with a strong accent. I'm not sure what.'

'Had you seen him before?'

She shook her head. 'No.'

'What about his wife?'

'I'd seen her before. But not often. Pieter could tell you more about her. Let me see how he's feeling.' She went to the desk, picked up the phone and spoke, then returned to them. 'He'll come down in a minute.'

'That's good, thanks. So, can you tell me anything else about the wife?'

'Well, she had blonde hair, a very pleasant personality – in fact, a pleasant couple, really. And I remember, she wore a new *Kleppermantel.*'

'A what?'

'Oh, it's a very high quality raincoat. Klepper's the best name in Europe for rainwear. I hadn't seen a new *Klepper* in ten years, and asked her where she bought it. She'd got it at a shop four doors down – *Regendruppel* – Raindrop. Apparently, the new owners had found some boxes of *Kleppers* from the mid-thirties in a storage warehouse, and were selling them off. After the couple left, I dashed along and bought one too.'

'What makes it so special?'

'It's just such a super quality. Let me show you.' She went to the back shop and returned with a grey raincoat over her arm. She held it up. 'Here's a *Klepper.*' It reminded Sandra of the mackintosh she'd had as part of her uniform as a young cop, which she found smelly and sweaty, and rarely wore. The *Klepper* was certainly of a much higher quality, but she really couldn't get enthusiastic about clothes, far less a raincoat. Then Pieter appeared. Both his cheeks and his lower jaw were bruised and swollen, and he held his chest.

Sandra pulled a chair from the desk. 'Oh, my goodness. Sit down. Have you been checked out at the hospital?'

Pieter sat down and shook his head. 'No, I'm okay. Nothing broken. How can I help?'

Sandra introduced herself and Guus, and showed her warrant card. 'I just wanted to ask you about this man.' She showed him the photo.

'That's the same picture the man in the car showed me last night. But I've only seen him once, here. Who is he?'

'We suspect him of a serious crime in Glasgow, and want to talk to him about it. But when he visited Glasgow, he used a photo ID with his picture, but your name, address and date of birth. We're trying to find out how he got that as a step towards catching him.'

Lotte turned to the desk. 'Ah, *that's* what he was doing. After they'd gone, I noticed Pieter had left a form on the desk. It had his name, address and date of birth on it. That's where he must have got it.'

Sandra nodded. 'Okay. That explains it. Now, about his wife. Your mother says you may know more about her. Was she a regular customer?'

Pieter shook his head. 'No, not regular, but she did come in from time to time. She didn't live here – had more of an Eindhoven accent. She said she always bought her flowers from us when she was in Amsterdam. She'd admired the table arrangements at a local wedding maybe four or five years ago, a combination of pink and purple tulips, hydrangeas and ranunculus, and asked the bride who had done the flowers. That's why she always came here.'

'Do you remember that wedding?'

He shook his head. 'No, I don't.'

Lotte stepped forward. 'But we might get it from our records. We keep a note of the flowers we use for special occasions, and we haven't used that combination very often.'

'It would be great if you could. I'm away tomorrow, but back on Thursday. I could call again then, or if you find it in the meantime, let Guus know.'

Guus gave her a card. 'Call me at any time.'

Sandra asked, 'Do you know this girl's name?'

Pieter shook his head again. 'No, I'm afraid not.' He thought for a moment. 'But, about two years ago, another girl from out of town came into the shop and said a Miss Martens had recommended us. I didn't know the name, but perhaps that was her. It's the sort of thing she might have done. Maybe worth a try?'

'Okay.' Sandra took a note. 'That's very helpful. Thank you both, and I look forward to hearing from you in the next couple of days. Hope you recover soon, Pieter.'

He smiled. They all shook hands, and Sandra and Guus left the shop.

Outside, Sandra turned to Guus. 'If she comes back quickly with the wedding details, could you follow up with the bride and see if we can identify that couple's real name and address? I'd love to lift them – him for murder, her as an accessory.'

He nodded. 'Yeah, we'll see what we can do.'

'Shall we just do a quick check with the rainwear shop while we're here?'

The woman there remembered a girl, who wanted a raincoat for going to England, and bought one of the newly found *Kleppermantels*, but had no useful information about her.

Later, on their own again, Sandra agreed to have a nightcap with Bill in the bar. She flopped down on a sofa and rested her head against the tall back. He sat beside her and held his drink up. 'Cheers.'

She smiled. 'Cheers,' and clinked glasses.

'Good day?'

She turned her head towards him and nodded. 'Yeah. Good day.'

'What was the best bit of the day for you?'

'Oh, there's so many. I thought the Home Secretary was amazing. What a man.'

'Yeah, most people think he's one of the best we've had for a long time.'

'And I did enjoy the flight in the end. Thank you for your help.'

'You're welcome.'

'But I hated hearing about our Glasgow gangsters blundering around trying to find the drug distributor with the help of their Amsterdam equivalents. They've threatened me as well, you know.'

'Really? What can you do about it?'

'Ach, it's all talk and no trousers. We've put the usual precautions in place. It'll blow over in a month. What was your best bit of the day?'

He smiled. 'Working with you. Enjoyed that.'

She thought for a moment. This conversation could go in several different directions. Let's keep it going straight head. 'Thanks, but it's time for me to hit the sack. Another busy day tomorrow – and into Germany. That'll be interesting.'

'Yeah, breakfast at seven. We leave at eight, and meet Montgomery at two-thirty.'

'Great.' She rose and lifted her bag. Together they went out to the lobby to catch the lift. They had adjacent rooms and stopped outside her door.

She held out her hand. 'Thanks, Bill, for a great day.' They shook hands.

'You're welcome, Sandra. Good night.'

'Good night.' She entered her room and closed the door behind her. She leaned back against it. She'd had to force herself to stay professional, and that was new.

***

Outside Amsterdam, Sandra saw little traffic – more cycles than cars. By the border even these had disappeared. The signs for Germany – or Deutschland – also had large signs for the British Zone of Occupation, with British soldiers manning the checkpoints. In the cool morning light in Germany, she saw even less civilian traffic – almost an air of desolation. She felt relieved when they eventually reached their destination, the Control Commission for Germany – British Element, in Bad Oeynhausen.

They were shown into the Military Governor's office. Sir Bernard came round from behind his desk, welcomed them and introduced his aide, Captain Watkins, and another officer, Major Bob Conway, from the Commandos. Sandra had seen Montgomery so often in cinema newsreels with Churchill, and smiled as she shook his hand, though she thought he didn't look quite so commanding in a suit. They all sat round his conference table.

'Totally agree with the Home Secretary on this drug menace,' he said. 'Got to throttle it before it gets started. I've always thought pharmaceuticals good at relieving negatives, like physical pain, but poor at providing positives, like feeling good. Oh, I'm sure they give some initial impetus, but when it wears off, the user feels weak and dependant, and that's very bad. Saw it in North Africa. Cut off the German supply lines for their stupid pills and they all felt weak. They weren't, but that's how they felt. And how they lost. As a great man once said, 'Whether you think you can, or you think you can't, you're usually right.' Never underestimate the power of the human mind. Isn't that right, Conway?'

'Yes, sir.'

'So, Major Conway will do all he can to help you both. We've checked the legal position here. Who's that Nazi Health Leader again, Watkins?'

'Dr Leo Conti, sir.'

'That's right. Man was mad. Killed the disabled to remove the 'weak'. Used chemicals to 'cleanse' the German race. Committed suicide a couple of months ago in Nuremberg. Couldn't face trial. Tells you all you need to know about the man. But he did make these drugs illegal here. What do you call them again, Watkins?'

'Methamphetamine, sir.'

'That's it. So, let's get on with it. The HS tells me you know what you're doing. Conway will keep me informed. Good luck.' He stood up, and came round to shake hands. Meeting over. He sure didn't mess about, thought Sandra. No wonder he was such a successful military commander. She'd met the American, General Eisenhower, by chance a couple of months ago, and while he and Montgomery were very different as individuals, they both exuded authority and charisma. Just incredible men.

Conway led the way to his office. The three of them sat around the conference table, which had a series of aerial photographs on it.

Conway pointed to the first one. 'We bombed the tank factory here in March this year, and we've got an aerial recon photo taken at the time. We've blown up the section of the picture that includes the company at the address you gave us.' He lifted another photograph onto the top of the pile. 'There are three buildings on the site, all interconnected. We had a quick look this morning, and this building to the south, at the bottom of the picture, is the private clinic. It has a brass plate, 'GT Therapie GmbH'. It's surrounded on this south side by these gardens, and connected to this other building to the north, a residential mansion house with offices. And that in turn connects to this long rectangular building to the east. Its entrance, in this back street, has a brass plate, 'GT Pharma GmbH'. That building has three floors and looks like a manufacturing centre. So, the names all fit. We picked up a brochure on the clinic, and it can take up to forty patients. They specialise in behaviour problems in children and young adults. So, overall, it looks like our target. What do you think?'

Sandra and Bill examined the picture. Sandra said, 'Terrific, Major. We want to close down the manufacturing facility in this east building, and lift the head of the organisation, hopefully from the mansion house. We don't want to disturb any patients in the clinic building, if we can avoid it.'

Conway nodded. 'Right. So, at this point, we assume the manufacturing facility closes at night. We'll have a team check it tonight. When we raid, we'll isolate the mansion house, and lock it down with everyone in it. We have a photo of the head man in this brochure.' He turned the page.

Sandra looked at the target, Gerhardt Timmermann, a pleasant looking, grey-haired man with rimless glasses. The head they wanted. She passed the brochure to Bill.

Conway asked, 'When do you plan to take him down?'

'At the moment, in the early hours of Sunday, 20th January,' Sandra replied. 'The HS wants action before the end of January, but we need two things in place. First, we need to prove the link between here and the

Amsterdam distribution centre. We have a watch on that place and a tap on their phone, so I assume at some point, Amsterdam will call for more tablets from here. But I need that link proved by photographic evidence.

'Second, we plan to lift all of the UK distributors around the same time on the same night, and it'll probably take that long to identify the number involved. We also don't want to underestimate this lot. We've had experience of them before as a spy network, and so we aim to grab the key people within five seconds to avoid them alerting the network. Can you plan on doing that here too, Major?'

'Sure.' He took some notes. 'And the delay gives us a chance to find out more about this company, and get a better idea of the layout of the mansion house. At the moment we think it's offices on the ground floor, residence on the first floor, and bedrooms on the second and third floors, but I'd like to confirm that if we can. We'll also put a tail on Timmermann, so we know what he's up to.'

'Okay, great. And once we have him, we could try him here, or in the UK. We should check that with Montgomery.'

'Not a problem. I'll check with Monty. If you want, we can fly Timmermann from RAF Güttersloh, not far from here. Planes go back and forward to England all the time.'

'Good.' Sandra smiled at him, and stood up. 'Can we go and have a look at this place before it gets dark? Get a feel for it?'

They got into Conway's car and drove through the town. A pretty enough place, thought Sandra. Conway eased back as he passed the GT buildings. Sandra studied them. 'Okay, that's fine, Major.'

Back in the office, Sandra picked up the aerial photograph of the buildings. ‘It doesn’t look too easy to monitor the mansion house. Is this open parkland to the west?’

Conway nodded. ‘Yeah, it’s part of the main spa park.’

‘Mmm. We often dig up pavements and put in our people as pretend electricity board or gas board engineers to observe properties. Could you do that here?’

He thought for a moment. ‘Don’t think so. There’s a huge amount of hostility towards us from the local population. I’m on Monty’s leadership council, and we believe they have hidden hierarchies in operation, and people report everything we do. We don’t know who we can trust. We tiptoe around, trying to keep everyone onside as much as we can, but it’s not easy, since we don’t have enough German speakers.

‘And now the Allied Control Council’s about to launch a big denazification programme to clean out the swastika and Nazi influence from the German culture, economy, justiciary and politics. I mean, it sounds great, and the Americans have gone big on it, but Monty wants to push back. He sees it as just a huge bureaucratic exercise, and he hates bureaucracy.

‘They plan to assess the whole German population, and place them into one of five categories of involvement with the Nazis – Major Offenders, Offenders, Lesser Offenders, Followers and Exonerated – with reduced levels of sanctions as you go down the groups. Major Offenders could be hanged or thrown in prison with hard labour. But how the hell do you decide which group to put a person in, and then gather the evidence to support it?

'We've over twenty million Germans in the British Zone, and our initial checks show at least half of them involved with the Nazis in some capacity. But that hides the real story. In some sectors it's much more. For example, over ninety percent of lawyers and company owners and operators had direct links to the Nazis. So Monty's asking how the hell can you wipe out that lot and still have a functioning judiciary and economy? It's just nonsense.

'And London wants us to get the economy of the British Zone up to self sufficiency as fast as possible, to avoid another burden on the hard-pressed British taxpayers. So, it's difficult to balance all these conflicting goals in a way that's sensible and safe.'

Sandra thought for a moment. She'd obviously hit a nerve. 'So, does that mean you can't use local police either?'

Conway shook his head. 'No. We assume the local Germans, police or otherwise, only want to help their compatriots, not us. For this raid, I'll use Commando units from Bielefeld, about twenty miles away. We have a few Polish soldiers there who can speak German.'

Sandra nodded. 'Right, we'll leave that in your expert hands, Major. Oh, one other thing, while I remember. The Home Secretary suggested, half in fun, whole in earnest, that we drop the manufacturing equipment in the Channel on the way back to the UK. Now, we obviously don't want to drag it that far. Could we drop it into a large, deep lake near here?'

'Yeah. No problem. We'll do that okay.' He took a note.

'Good. So, we meet back here tomorrow morning for half an hour before we head back to Amsterdam?'

Bill nodded. He then discovered Conway stayed at the same hotel. 'Why don't we meet up for drinks and dinner at six?' he suggested. 'On us, of course.'

Bill kept the chat light-hearted during the meal – in full mine-host style – and encouraged Conway to tell them about some of his experiences on Commando raids.

When the conversation turned to cricket, Sandra excused herself and headed for bed. She thought about the events of the day. While it had certainly been tough to win the war, it sounded just as tough to win the peace.

***

Next morning, they met Conway again. 'How did it go last night, Bob?' Sandra asked.

Conway nodded. 'Pretty good. Because I can't use any locals, I took a REME unit with me to check on the electrics.'

Sandra frowned. 'REME? What's that?'

'Oh, sorry. They're the Royal Electrical and Mechanical Engineers. We've got several of their units at Bielefeld. They're good chaps. I wanted to check how we cut the power to the mansion house for the raid. Most houses in Germany have their utility meters in a small panel near their front door, and this one has too. We think the main isolator switch sits in a cupboard behind the panel.

'So, it means we'll have three points of entry.' He pointed to the aerial photo of the house. 'We'll have a special team go in here at the front door – we'll cut out the glass panel – and get the power off. Another team will enter via the factory pretty much the same way at its front door to neutralise the night watchman and isolate the electrics. That'll give us access to the ground floor of the house via this corridor link. We'll have our main team enter the house at first floor level from this roof garden, by cutting the glass in the French windows here. We can then quickly get to the bedroom floors, and neutralise within five seconds.

'None of the doors or locks present a problem. There's an alarm box on the outside of the mansion house, so we'll neutralise that in advance with some goo. I'm more concerned about an array of radio aerials at the north end of the house just here.' He pointed to the photo. 'You can't see them from the street, and they're not obvious in the photo, but they're this series of points here. Maybe they communicate with the network by radio? We'll check it discreetly with some Signals chaps. That's where we're at now.'

'Great,' Sandra said. 'Just to clarify. What do you mean by neutralising people?'

He laughed. 'Oh, I just mean render them useless – cuffed hands and legs, gagged and hooded – so they can't set off an alarm or communicate.'

Sandra nodded. 'Okay. Now, I need to arrest the mister big, so where do we fit in?'

'Right. We'd want to keep you two safe, so I suggest you come in behind the team through the factory. By the time you get into the house through this corridor link, we should have the whole place secure.'

Sandra took a note. 'Fine. We'll do that. It's also maybe worth noting some of the problems we met with these people when we raided them a couple of years ago,' She went on to describe how they overcame panic buttons and booby traps

Conway noted the points. 'Okay, we'll check for them.'

Sandra smiled. 'Sounds like a good operation, though.'

'Yeah, we've a bit of work to do on the details. I want every man to know exactly what he has to do on the night, so we'll organise that over the next couple of weeks. We'll keep in touch with you as we go.'

'Fine.' They exchanged phone numbers, and Sandra and Bill prepared to leave.

In the car, as they headed towards Holland, Bill turned to Sandra. 'Jesus, it's exciting. Part of a real Commando raid, huh?'

'Yeah.' She began to think of what could go wrong, but trusted Conway would deal with anything unexpected. Bill was right, though. It might not be a re-run of the famous raid on Saint Nazaire, but still a significant raid for peacetime.

***

They arrived in Amsterdam by mid-afternoon and called Guus Mulder. He invited them round to his office for an update.

'Let's clear off the easy one first,' he said. 'We've now established the pattern of visitors to the GT Pharma office at Keizersgracht. We photograph each one as they arrive and depart. They seem to spend about an hour inside. We radio telegraph the photo to Schiphol and the team there get his name and date of birth as he goes through passport control. Everyone is photographed at passport control anyway, so we end up with a record like this.' He pulled a page from his file and passed it over. It had the name and date of birth of the visitor at the top, and four photographs of him, with the date and time listed.

Sandra studied the pictures. 'That's great, Guus.'

'We don't have their GB code number at the moment. We'll get that from next week because we know from our phone tap when each code number's scheduled to visit. At the moment, GB27's the highest code number to call, so they're well established.'

Gosh, twenty-seven, thought Sandra. This could involve every regional SB unit. She needed to see Burnett quickly.

Mulder went on, 'We assume the visitors we don't see at Schiphol are local, French or Belgian, and travel by train. We'll gradually get their code numbers from next week, and we're very interested in the local ones. When do you plan to lift the brain?'

Sandra checked her notes. 'We plan to lift the head of the German operation and the head of the UK distribution network at two o'clock UK time on the morning of Sunday, 20th January. That then gives us four hours to confirm the names and addresses of the UK legs, and lift all of *them* at six o'clock. If we know any of the legs before then, we'll lift *them* at two UK time as well. Why do you ask?'

'I've had another informal update meeting with our Minister. He's happy that we've proved a link between the Keizersgracht address and the UK distributors. If we can also prove a link to the German base, and if you have a sound legal basis for the raids on the UK and German addresses, then he'd cooperate with you and sanction a raid on the Keizersgracht property at the same time, to take down the whole chain. He suggests your Minister calls him to discuss the matter.'

Sandra glanced at Bill. 'Wow. That's fantastic. What do you think, Bill?'

Bill nodded. 'I'll try to see our Minister tomorrow, but I'm sure he'll be delighted at the offer. Can you give me the contact details, Guus?'

'Yes.' He passed a one page document to Bill.

'Okay, thanks. Leave that one with me.'

Sandra picked up the photos again. The man looked like any other businessman. Nothing distinctive, except maybe for the case. What motivated him? Opportunity? Money? He wasn't breaking any law, of course. She'd have to change that to get the Dutch support. 'Can I keep this?' she asked.

Mulder nodded. 'Sure. We plan to radio telegraph all of the photos so far to you tomorrow, and then, each morning, to send the photos from the previous day. That should give you the best chance to get their addresses from passport records. Okay?'

Sandra nodded. 'Yeah, that's great.'

'Good. Let me get Margreet. She might have something for you on the flower shop front.' He got up and left the room.

Sandra glanced at Bill. 'Could we fly back tonight, Bill? I'd like to see Dave and Malcolm in the morning, and get an update on the legal front.'

'I'll phone the office and see what we can do.' He rose and left the room.

She examined the photo. Twenty-seven like that – maybe more by the time of the raid. Just like Aquila night all over again.

Guus came back into the room with Margreet. The women shook hands. Margreet came round to the same side of the table as Sandra and opened her file. 'Well, it's taken a bit of effort,' Margreet said, 'but we've got something for you. Let me take you through it.

'Lotte van der Huizen called us Tuesday evening to let us know she had two weddings – both in May 1940 – where she'd used that combination of flowers for the table arrangements. She gave us the brides' addresses, and our team found them. One of the brides remembered a guest asked her about the ranunculus. She'd never heard of it before and it stuck with her.

'The guest was a girl on her husband's guest list, a colleague at Philips. Her name's Annika Martens.' She pulled a photo from her file that showed the bridegroom with two couples to his left and one couple to his right. 'The Philips group at the wedding. Annika Martens is the girl to the right of the groom – and that's her partner on the extreme right of the picture. The bride's mother dug out the guest list and got the partner's name as Cian Connolly – spelt C-I-A-N, pronounced Kee-in. She thought he was Irish. Our photo boys have worked their magic, and we have photographs here of just the two of them.'

Sandra examined a photo of the couple – a pretty blonde girl and a good-looking young man, both with wide smiles. She pulled out the picture of the fair-haired man from her bag. The same man – a bit younger – but definitely him.

Margreet went on. 'The bride's mother had an address for her in Eindhoven, and we sent a team there. But they'd moved to Amsterdam about two years ago – she'd got promoted with Philips. Neighbours said the man travelled a lot – no one knew his job – and the girl had a great personality.

'Philips gave us her last known address in Amsterdam – she resigned from her job about four months ago to travel with her husband – though we can find no trace of a marriage. No one's seen them for weeks. Our team 'entered' their flat and had a look round. Didn't find anything of interest, except we picked up prints from them both. The man's prints exactly match the prints you gave us on Tuesday. It's the same man – a hundred percent.' She passed Sandra a copy of their prints.

Sandra smiled. 'Brilliant work. And done so quickly.'

'Thanks. None of the neighbours know where they've gone. They don't own a car, so we can't trace them from that. We have no record of them leaving the country, though they could have false papers, of course. At the moment, they've disappeared. We'll keep a watch on the flat and pick them up if they return. That's the best we can do.'

'That's great, Margreet. We really appreciate all your work. We can build on it, and hopefully work out where they've gone. Thank you all so much.'

'You're welcome.'

Bill came back into the room. 'Right, Sandra, I've changed our arrangements. We're now on the seven o'clock flight to London. We're also booked in at the Charing Cross Hotel for tonight. In the morning, I have an early slot with the HS and you have a nine o'clock slot with Dave and Malcolm. Dave's only available till ten-thirty, but I'll try and join you by nine-thirty latest.'

Sandra took a note. 'Okay, sounds fine.' They packed their bags and shook hands with Guus and Margreet. 'Thanks for everything.'

At Schiphol, she looked for the cameras at passport control, but couldn't see them. As they walked up the concourse towards the gate, she felt very comfortable with Bill. She could easily slip her arm through his. But she resisted it. Their relationship had to stay professional.

They sat in the long rows of seats at the gate. Bill leaned over to her and whispered, 'Have a look at the man in the opposite row five seats to the right.'

She let her eyes wander along the people opposite. The man looked like just another traveller, in a gabardine and hat, reading a book, but with a GT Pharma case between his feet. She leaned back in her seat with eyes half closed and watched him. She wanted to send him a thought bubble like they did in cartoons. *'Enjoy it while you can, matey, because if everything goes to plan, you'll be behind bars in six weeks'*

***

In the morning, Sandra went into the office early and called Porritt.

'I've got a photo of the couple who appeared in Glasgow and attacked Tommy Thomson, sir. Their real names are Cian Connelly, we think he's Irish, and Annika Martens, a Dutch national. It's a few years out of date, but should still help you.'

'Jesus, Sandra. That's fantastic. How did you get it?'

'It's a long story, sir. I'll tell you when I've more time. I've got to get to a meeting now.'

'No problem, Sandra. Brilliant work.'

'Thanks, sir. Talk later.'

She asked Dave's secretary to radio telephone the photo over to Porritt. Then went into Dave's office. She took Dave and Malcolm through her visits in Holland and Germany, and outlined her plans for the raids.

Burnett whistled. 'Crikey. Twenty-seven and counting? So, if we assume Bill and his team fix the legal issues, I'll go along with your outline plans, Sandra. But we need to know more about this chap in Hampstead, and validate the 'legs' around the country. We need to prove they're dealing these drugs and they're the right people. Avoid the Glasgow scenario of the false ID. So, Malcolm. What about this Hampstead chap?'

'Right. Mr Andrew Lyall, aged forty-two, married with two children, aged eight and nine, the son of Mr Roger Lyall, whom you'll remember from the Aquila bust. We've got all the usual watch works in place – tap on the phone – tail on him – photos of visitors, etc.

'He lives in a large detached property in West Hampstead, screened off with trees to the rear. We've got details of the house from an old sales brochure. Four bedrooms and a family bathroom on the upper floor. Downstairs it's a conventional layout with large lounge to the left, dining room to the right, and the other facilities to the rear.

'Known problems so far are an intruder alarm, a standard unit we can disable easily, and a large black Labrador dog, which could present more of a problem. We'll have to think how to deal with that. They may also store information in code – the same one that Aquila used, so we'll have a codebreaker as part of the team to decipher it quickly.

'Unknown problems could be potential booby traps, or unknown locks to protect their vital documents. We'll therefore have a safecracker as part of the team as well, sir.

'We've monitored the phone all this week, and it would appear, from the accents, that agents from the north of England, Scotland and Northern Ireland call in with their sales figures on a Monday, the central belt of England and Wales on a Tuesday, and London and the South of England on a Wednesday. The highest code number we've heard so far is GB27. If we use the info Sandra got in Glasgow, where the agent had a population of about a million to work with, then that would mean London could have eight agents, and then they'd have nineteen other major cities around the country with agents.

'If we assume they're the largest cities, it gives a population of about eighteen million. From the Glasgow info, that means these agents in total would have a target of eighteen thousand tablets per month, or about four thousand five hundred tablets per week.

'Now, the actual total sales from those that reported last week came to just over four thousand, from twenty five agents. We had no return from GB06, Glasgow, clearly not yet re-allocated, or from GB16, location unknown. But it still means they're well up to target, and it's a significant business in this country.

'At the moment, we only know the code number and their sales. With this info from Amsterdam, we can link the code number to a name and address, and then it's up to the regional SB heads to validate the suppliers.'

Burnett nodded. 'Good. So how do we do that, Sandra?'

'Well, sir, if they follow the pattern of Glasgow, they'll sell in up-market pubs on a Thursday, Friday and Saturday. We need to follow them and get photos of them dealing that we can present in court.'

'Right, I'll get on to all the SB regional heads and let them know what we want. Will you be in Glasgow or Germany that night, Sandra?'

'In Germany, sir. My deputy can handle things in Glasgow. He's already involved.'

Bill arrived. 'Good morning, all.' He shook hands with everyone.

Burnett said, 'We've just approved Sandra's and Malcolm's plans for the raid, which I think you know about. How did it go with the HS?'

'Very well, sir. He's really chuffed about the offer from the Dutch government, and will take them up on it. So that's good.

'On the legal side, his advisors suggest he uses . . .' he checked his notes, '. . . the Emergency Powers (Defence) (No 2) Act 1940, which has just been extended by Parliament again. It gives him powers to apprehend, try in special courts, punish and detain any person whose detention appears to him to be expedient in the interests of public safety.

'He wanted to get the Opposition on side to make the whole process easier, and met with Churchill. He explained his aim to prevent the British becoming addicted to these new pills, and told him the only losers would be the Germans, who make and sell the tablets, and a few drug dealers. Churchill agreed. 'Let's stuff the Germans again,' he'd said, with a smile.

'When Parliament's united like this, they can use all sorts of shortcuts, and so they plan to table an amendment to the Regulations, that would make methamphetamine drugs illegal in this country. It will happen on the seventh of January, their first day back, and should go through on the nod. That will then become the basis of an Order in Council, signed by the King a day or so later. And that's it. These drugs would then become illegal in this country until they repeal these powers. So, it's a short-term fix, but it allows us to act right now without a lengthy process in Parliament to change the existing drug laws.

'This also allows us to use these powers in British War Zones, so we can use it to prosecute Timmermann in Germany if we want. So, what do you think? Neat, huh?'

Burnett nodded. 'Great. Well done to our legal eagles. Okay, let's fire ahead with our plans. I need to go now, but I'd like you to give me a list of all the points I need to cover with the SB regional heads on this. Can you do that for me, please?'

Sandra and Malcolm nodded. 'Yeah, we'll do that, sir, and leave it with your secretary.'

'Good. And let's discuss it on Tuesday next, that's the eighteenth, to make sure we've captured everything we need. Talk later.' He swept out of the room.

The three of them went to Malcolm's office and developed the list for Burnett. They agreed to think about it over the weekend and finalise it on Monday by phone.

Sandra asked Malcolm's secretary to book her a seat on the one o'clock train to Glasgow, and put on her smart dark-blue coat and hat to catch a taxi to Euston. Bill came out with her and went to get into the taxi.

'You don't need to come, Bill. I'm fine.'

'Oh, I know. But we've had quite a week, and it just gives us the chance to wind up and agree our next steps.' He got in and sat beside her.

They chatted about their plans all the way to Euston. At the station, he bought a platform ticket and walked down the slope with her towards the train. They strolled past the board that announced 'Welcome to the Coronation Scot by LMS.'

'What will you do for Christmas?' he asked.

She smiled. 'Oh, mum and I go to my sister's in Ayr. Her two kids enjoy the full magic of Christmas. So it's a nice relaxed time. What about you?'

'Much the same. My parents and I go over to my brother's place. It's usually good fun. But it's not really what I want to do.'

Her heart beat faster and she felt her cheeks flush. The noises of the station all seemed louder somehow. 'Oh? What do you really want to do?'

He hesitated. 'Cards on the table?'

She stopped at her coach and glanced up at him. 'If you like.'

'I'm going to miss you, Sandra. It's been an incredible week, and we've got on so well together. I just hope it might be something we can build on. If I'm honest, I haven't felt this way for a long time. And if I'm really honest, I'd love to spend a few days with you in a lochside retreat somewhere just to see if there's something special there. Forgive me if I've gone too far, but I just think it's better to be open about it.'

Her heart thumped and she looked up into his eyes. He seemed desperate for a positive response. She was tempted, but it was still too soon for her, and her professional brain kicked in. She smiled. 'Well, thank you for being so honest, Bill, but let's wait till we complete this project, huh? Let's not complicate things. It's been a great week, though, and I look forward to seeing you again soon.' She stuck out her hand and he shook it.

She lifted her case, boarded the train, and sank into her seat. He stood on the platform, and smiled at her, until the train moved off. A bit like a little boy lost, she thought.

The door to her emotions had clanged shut the day the love of her life had died. Now, for the first time, Bill had prised it open, and it felt kind of nice.

Chapter 10. Eddie

Every morning, his three pills haunted and taunted Sam. Haunted because he didn't *have* any more, and taunted because he couldn't *get* any more. He wanted to repeat his one fantastic experience so far – to feel on top of the world, have crystal-clear thinking, and make love all night and all day to a beautiful woman. But he *had* to resist it. He didn't want to use one until he had a further supply in his hand. Maybe today, he thought, as he shaved. Maybe today.

Just after nine, Johnny came round with the car. Sam joined Eddie in the back.

'Morning. How're you today?' Eddie asked.

San nodded. 'Okay. Hope Fergus has the answer for us.'

'Well, he sounded positive last night.'

'Good.' Sam thought about Fergus. A long time friend of the family who ran the equivalent of the McFadden business in Edinburgh. He and Sam's dad had been mates from way back. They'd met regularly before the war, but only a couple of times since.

Fergus welcomed them to his home in Morningside. Dressed in an open-necked shirt, a Fair Isle pullover and grey slacks, he looked really fit, thought Sam. Johnny and Tam Dunlop, Fergus's enforcer, settled at a table in the window. Sam spread himself on a sofa, with Eddie and Fergus on other sofas, in front of the fire.

Sam leaned forward. 'You've got something for us, Fergus?'

'I have, Sam. And it's different from our usual business.'

'In what way?'

'We found the lad you wanted – eventually. We nailed him in the bar of the Balmoral Hotel a couple of nights ago, and made him an offer he couldn't refuse.

'His name's Ron Baxter. He's a quantity surveyor, whatever that is, and answered an ad in the local paper for a new business opportunity selling these tablets. A guy in London controls the whole supply network, and Ron has the franchise for Edinburgh.

'He's in with four up-market bars, but we offered to sell through our sixteen pubs and two nightclubs for a big discount, and give him protection on top. Would increase his volume by more than five times. He checked with London, and they approved it. They're obviously interested in volume, and there's lots of money in it. And it's legit. So as far as I'm concerned, it's open sesame, Sam. He'll come over later to talk to you. He's very open about the business.'

'Great, Fergus. Have you tried one of these pills yet?'

'No, I'm a bit old for that now, but Tam tried one. He says they're magic. His wife didn't know what had happened. He banged her every which way for two days. Right, Tam?'

Tam laughed. 'Yeah, right, boss.'

Mmm, brave man, thought Sam. He'd never dream of doing that with Helen.

The doorbell rang. Tam left and returned with a well-built lad in a suit and tie.

Fergus stood up. 'Come in, Ron. Let me introduce you.'

They all shook hands and Ron sat at the other end of Fergus's sofa. He looked over at Sam and Eddie. 'Good to meet you. How can I help?'

Sam sat back. He'd let Eddie answer.

Eddie glanced over at Sam and picked up the cue he should start. 'Yeah, it's good to meet you too. We're interested in handling this business for Glasgow, either through yourself, like you do with Fergus, or even on our own direct. What do you think?'

'Have you got the same type of business as Fergus – you know, pubs and nightclubs?'

'Yeah, we have nineteen pubs and three nightclubs, but we also have good connections into other up-market pubs.'

Ron grimaced. 'It's too much for me to handle on top of Fergus's business. You've got to go to Amsterdam and collect supplies. Christ, I'd be on a plane every week. But there must be someone in Glasgow, similar to me, you could work with.'

Eddie looked puzzled for a moment. 'Just a sec. You go to Amsterdam for supplies? How do you pay for them? You can't take that amount of cash out of the country.'

'Well, you can, if you do it right. You buy a special suitcase from the company that has secret sections in it. You could never tell they're there. You use them to take the cash out and bring the pills back.'

Shit, thought Sam. And that woman detective had taken Thomson's suitcase away with her. Had she figured it out?

Eddie glanced over at Sam. 'And when you bring the pills back, do you just keep them in the case, or do you store them somewhere else?' Eddie asked.

'Well, you buy a special writing bureau from the company. It has a secret compartment in it. Again, you'd never know. That's what I use.'

Sam sat stunned. He'd examined the writing bureau in Thomson's front room, and had missed this. Shit. And the bag the woman detective had taken away from

Thomson's flat could have contained the contents of the secret compartment, if she had figured that out as well. Jesus Christ. This company operated at a different level from him. He needed to up his game. He now wanted this business more than ever.

Eddie nodded. 'Sounds good. To come back to your opposite number in Glasgow, we happen to know he died in an accident a couple of weeks ago.'

'Bloody hell.' Ron looked shocked.

'So, what would happen to that business in Glasgow now?'

'Well, we have to ring Andrew every Monday – he's the boss of the UK business – and tell him our sales figures for the previous week. If you fail to do it for any reason, he will re-allocate the franchise. So, he's probably re-allocating Glasgow as we speak.'

Shit, thought Sam. He couldn't let that happen. He wanted that business. He cut in to the conversation. 'We'd like to take over that franchise, Ron. Could you phone Andrew, tell him we've met, and that we could put a team on this quickly to build up the business in Glasgow again, similar to what you're doing in Edinburgh?'

Ron nodded. 'Yeah, sure.'

Eddie leaned over towards Sam. 'Just before we do that, could we have a word?'

Sam glanced over to Fergus, who stood up. 'Aye, no problem. Use the dining room. Come on, I'll show you.' Fergus guided them across the hall.

Sam stood at the window. 'Got a problem, Eddie?'

'I don't have a problem in principle, but I'd like to clarify some details before we commit to something on the phone.'

'Okay. What details?'

'Do you plan to take this franchise in your own name?'

'Yeah.'

'Well, let's just think about it for a minute. Look at Fergus. He's piggybacking on Ron. He's got none of the risk. Ron's the one taking the risk. He travels to Amsterdam with cash and back with drugs. And you should maybe do the same. Now, it may not be much of a risk, but it's still a risk. Put the franchise in someone else's name. Use Oscar, or one of his people. Let them take the risk.'

Sam pursed his lips. Oscar ran the drug business for the family. He'd known Dan from their school days, and they were complete opposites. Where Dan was cold, down to earth and blunt, Oscar was warm, sophisticated and smooth. He was also a key figure in the Glasgow arts scene, and a member of the Citizen's Theatre. For people in these circles, he could find a cocaine supplier within an hour. Few knew he ran a ruthless drugs operation targeted on up-market areas of Glasgow. 'Hiding in plain sight' he said.

Oscar technically reported to Sam, but his long term relationship with Dan gave him real influence. Sam largely let him get on with it, with a weekly meeting to monitor figures.

'Fair point, Eddie. But I see this as a different business – different market – different users. Let's leave Oscar to do his thing. And his people are just glorified message boys. We need something better here. To me, there are two key points.

'First, Fergus doesn't have anything like our cocaine business, and that's vulnerable to this new drug. I don't want to piggyback on someone else. I want full control of it. I want to make sure I can build this new business up, but not affect our existing business.

'Second, this boss guy Andrew could re-allocate the Glasgow franchise any time. Now, I don't want to lose it because I need time to find the right one of Oscar's people to use as a front man. To me, it's time critical. Use my name today to get this business. We can always change it later if we need to.'

Eddie shrugged. 'Okay, I see your point. You're the boss.'

They went back to the lounge.

'Right, we're ready to make that call.' Sam looked at Fergus. 'Can we use your phone, please. Fergus?'

He stood up. 'Sure. Go ahead. There's an extension on this table if you want two on the line. Come on, Tam. Let's go through to the kitchen and leave them to it. Give us a shout when you're finished.' They left the room.

Ron picked up the phone and asked for the number. Sam and Eddie listened together on the extension.

'Hello?'

'Andrew. It's Ron, GB09, from Edinburgh here. How are you today?'

'I'm good. What can I do for you?'

'I'm with a couple of lads here who want to acquire the Glasgow franchise for our products. They seem pretty good – very professional – and have a similar business to Fergus here in Edinburgh that we spoke about a couple of days ago.'

'Do you know why they're interested?'

'Well, I've got them here. Ask them yourself. They're Sam and Eddie.'

'Okay. Put them on.'

'Hi Andrew, Sam here. Thanks for talking to us. As Ron says, we're interested in the Glasgow franchise. We believe we could do a great job for you.'

'I see. What makes you think the Glasgow franchise is available?'

'Well, I assume it is. The guy that ran it was a mate of my brother-in-law, and he died two weeks ago.'

'Jesus. What happened?'

'As I understand it, he broke an ankle and hobbled around on two crutches. At home one night, he overbalanced, fell into the fireplace and cracked his head open. They called an ambulance, but he was dead by the time it arrived.'

'Bloody hell. Now I know why I'm not getting a reply to my letters.'

'Well, I think he lived alone. I don't know who'd look after his mail.'

'Right. Well, each franchisee must call in every week with his sales figures, and if he fails to do that, we can re-allocate it. So, in the circumstances, I should re-allocate Glasgow. So, tell me a bit about yourself and your business.'

'Okay, I run a pretty successful business in Glasgow. We have nineteen pubs and three nightclubs, and have good connections into other up-market pubs. Hence the reason why we think we could move big volumes of these tablets quickly.'

'Have you tried the product?'

'Yeah.'

'What do you think of it?'

'Absolute bloody magic.'

Andrew laughed. 'Yeah, we think so too. How old are you?'

'Thirty-four.'

'Good. So, Ron speaks well of you, and I like what I hear. I'll agree that you can run the Glasgow franchise. Do you want me to run through the main points to make sure you're happy with them?'

Sam smiled at Eddie. 'Yeah, sure.'

'Right, what's your name and address?'

Sam gave him the information.

'Fine. Your code number is GB06. We use the code number all the time for reference. The agreement would be for Glasgow. Your target sales would be around a thousand tablets a month for that area. Once you hit this target, you get further financial incentives.

'Some people join us with very little experience of this type of business, so we offer to train them in where and how to sell, and how to look after your security. You can have a lot of cash at times, which can attract the wrong attention.

'We set prices that give you a good return. Ten pounds for a pack of five tablets. We recommend a discount structure for volume sales, which sets a minimum price, but you don't have to follow it. Most people do, but some don't.

'You need to call me every Monday with your sales figures for the previous week. That gives us a cross check on your sales and allows us to plan the business more effectively. At the moment, you order and collect new supplies from our Central Distribution in Amsterdam, but we plan to offer a similar service from London by February, fingers crossed.

'We also recommend you buy one of our GT suitcases, which has secret compartments that you can use to take cash out and bring the tablets back. We're a cash only business. We also recommend you buy a GT writing bureau, which has a secret compartment to store tablets at your home. The suitcase costs ten pounds and the bureau twenty pounds delivered.

'We offer starter packs from here now. We have three levels – two hundred tablets for a hundred and twenty pounds – five hundred tablets for two hundred and fifty pounds – and a thousand tablets for four hundred pounds. So, you generate cash very quickly, and can get between three and five times your money back. In your case, if you went for option three, it might last you through to February, and you wouldn't then have to go to Amsterdam. I think I've covered everything. You happy with that?'

'Yeah, it's fine.'

'Good. So, when do you want to start?'

'As soon as possible, really'

'Okay. Could you come down on Thursday? If you catch an early train, you'd be here by afternoon. That would give us Thursday afternoon and Friday morning if we need it.'

'Yeah, sounds fine, Andrew. Thanks very much.'

'Oh, you're welcome. Take the Bakerloo Line to West Hampstead station, and give me a call. I'm only a short walk from there.'

'Okay. Look forward to seeing you then.'

They hung up. Eddie smiled at Sam. 'Happy with that?'

'Delighted.'

Ron walked over to them. 'Congratulations. Welcome on board.'

Sam shook his hand. 'Thanks for all your help.' He put an arm round Ron's shoulders. 'Shall we go tell Fergus the good news?'

Ron laughed. 'Yeah, let's do that.' They left the room.

Outside, in the hall, Sam stopped and held Ron's arm. 'Can I ask you something?'

'Of course.'

'Do you have any of these tablets on you?'

'Sure.' Ron went into his inside pocket. 'What do you want? I've got a pack of five for a tenner, or you can have two packs for fifteen quid.'

'I'll take two packs.' Sam counted out three fivers from his wallet, and put the packs in his pocket. He smiled with relief. He now had a stock of tablets, and could arrange another sensational session with Tracey. Bloody great.

***

They found Andrew's house without problem on Thursday afternoon. A nice big detached house with big gardens. 'This guy's doing okay,' Sam murmured.

Andrew welcomed them and showed them through to his office at the back of the house. Well-built, in his late thirties, he had short hair and glasses, and had his shirt sleeves partly rolled up. Looked as though he could take care of himself, thought Sam.

They exchanged pleasantries, then Andrew said, 'We'll spend a couple of hours today, and clear the formalities, then talk about the business and security aspects. Then a couple of hours tomorrow morning to go through sales techniques, maybe do a bit of role playing so you get used to saying the words. You'll be clear by lunchtime, and that gets you back to Glasgow early evening. Okay?'

Sam nodded. 'Yeah. Sounds fine.'

'Trains get busy on a Friday, so if you want to book seats on a particular train, let us know, and my secretary can do that for you.'

Eddie said. 'Good idea. How about we book a train around one o'clock?'

'Okay, Wendy will organise that for you.' Andrew took a note on his pad. He then passed two copies of a document to Sam. 'Here's the contract, Sam. Would you read it through, and if you're happy with it, sign both copies?'

Sam read it and passed a copy to Eddie. 'What's this about a free sample?' Sam asked.

'Oh, just to remind you not to give away too many free samples. Most give a free sample to a potential new customer as a taster. But some don't. It's up to you.'

'Well, I don't think people value anything given for free. I'd probably charge half price for a taster, maybe even full price.' Sam looked at Eddie, who nodded. Sam signed both copies and passed them back to Andrew.

He signed both copies as well, and gave one to Sam. 'Welcome aboard.'

Sam laughed, and they all shook hands.

'Right,' Andrew said. 'Let's go through some aspects of the business. Now, at the moment, it's not illegal to distribute and sell these pills in this country, but we've already heard negative noises from some MPs. As usual, they believe they have a right to interfere with people's personal choice. They're a total pain in the arse. So, they may move to change the legal status of these pills, but it'll take a couple of years at best to get it through.

'Having said that, we recommend you run the business as though the pills *are* illegal to distribute and sell. In other words, be careful who you talk to, keep things hidden, and think about your personal protection. Let's talk details. First, our special GT Pharma suitcase.' He lifted a suitcase onto his desk and opened it.

'Looks like a normal suitcase?'

Sam and Eddie both nodded.

'Let me show you its secrets.' He took off the lining, eased off the leather discs, rotated the slots half a turn, and pulled out the inside layer of the case top and bottom to expose the hidden spaces. 'You can use these spaces to carry cash or pills, or whatever you want. And no one would know. I'm told the body's a leather sandwich enclosing s very fine aluminium mesh. We've tested it on one of these X-ray machines you see in some shoe shops and nothing showed up. So, we recommend you buy one – it costs ten pounds, so it's quite expensive – but now you see why.'

Sam glanced at Eddie. 'That's clever. We'll definitely have one of those.'

'Good. We also recommend you buy a GT Pharma writing bureau, which also has a secret compartment. Let me show you how this works over here.'

They walked across to the bureau against the wall on the other side of the room. Sure want to see this, Sam thought.

Andrew walked Sam through the procedure for revealing the secret compartment.

Sam gasped. 'Jesus. We'll have one of these as well.' He'd *never* have figured that out.

'Okay, we'll organise one for you. Should arrive in about a week. Let's move on to the next subject – to make sure you're not followed. We recommend you use a technique called 'last on – last off' everywhere you go. Do you know what that means?'

Sam nodded. 'I think so. But tell me anyway.'

'It means every time you get on or off public transport, you're always the last to go. That way you see immediately if someone follows you. Buses and trams are great because you can jump on and off them when they move. We recommend you practise it so it becomes second nature to you.'

'Right.' Sam now understood why Eddie had found it difficult to follow the lad Davy.

'Okay. We also think it's good practice to track your purchases and sales. It's up to you how you do it, but you could use this.' He pulled his pad over and demonstrated how he used the first two figures for the month, the next two figures for the date, the next figures for the number of tablets bought or sold, and the last two figures the price per tablet in shillings. 'It's an easy way to keep track.'

Sam nodded. 'So, the buying price per tablet comes down as the volume goes up?'

'Yeah. We also recommend you get to know the names of your customers. Use a simple code to keep them hidden. So, if I wrote this,' he wrote FFGMJ on his pad, 'who's that?'

Sam looked at the code. 'No idea. Wouldn't even know where to start.'

Eddie leaned over and shook his head. 'Don't know.'

'Well, it's actually dead easy.' He explained how each letter moved up the alphabet by its position in the word. 'So, that code is therefore EDDIE.'

Sam smiled at Eddie. 'Simple, huh?'

Andrew nodded. 'Yeah, like everything else, it's dead simple once you know the secret, but we've tested them over and over, and very very few people can detect them. So, does all this make sense?'

'Yeah. It sure does,' Sam said.

'Great. So, why don't we leave it at that for today, and pick it up again tomorrow morning. Come out here about nine. Get your case and your tablets, and get started.'

'Right, we'll do that.'

They gathered their things and left. On the tube into London, Eddie turned to Sam. 'What did you think, then?'

'The guy's a bit . . . what's the word . . . pedantic, don't you think?'

'Yeah, you're right, Sam. But maybe he has to deal with people that have never run a business before. Not like us. We know the ropes. But you've got to admit, he's got some bloody clever ideas. That case seal, for example. You turn these discs half a turn and they unlock, another half turn and they lock. But nothing clicked. How the hell does that work?'

'Yeah, and that bureau. Christ, I examined the bureau in Thomson's flat every way up and totally missed that lever. Like the man said, it's easy when you know how.' Sam paused. 'If he's got people in every major city in the country, he's got some bloody business, eh?'

'Yeah, for sure.'

Sam sat silent for a minute. 'Can I ask you something?'

'Yeah, of course, Sam.'

'Do you mind if we just do our own thing tonight?'

'No. Not at all.'

'I'll just have something in my room. Get to bed early.'

Eddie laughed. 'Something extra juicy, I suppose.'

Sam smiled. 'Yeah. Maybe.'

'No problem. I'll see you in the morning. Leave the hotel about half eight?'

'Yeah. See you then.'

***

Sam met Eddie in the hotel lobby in the morning. 'Good night?' Eddie asked.

Sam nodded. 'Yeah, very good.'

'I saw you show her out. Looked very tasty. Did you get much sleep?'

'Nah. But I'm okay. Get some on the train later.'

They made their way out to West Hampstead, and Andrew showed them into his office again. 'Any questions from yesterday?' he asked.

They shook their heads.

'Good. So, let's talk about the sales process. First, we recommend you use a false name – just to keep things hidden, as we said yesterday. If you send me the name, address, and date and place of birth of someone you know won't travel abroad, I can arrange a full ID set with a passport, for fifty quid. And don't forget your photo.'

Sam nodded. So, that's how Thomson did it.

'We also recommend you target up-market pubs and bars. These tablets sell best to men over thirty, with a bit of disposable income. We suggest you contact the bar manager and ask him to reserve a table for you at the same time every week. Offer him four pounds an hour cash up front, and let him negotiate you up to five. Most of them can never resist, and it's well worth it to get the right location at the right time, usually Thursday evenings, and Friday and Saturday lunchtime and evenings. That gives you five sessions of about three hours, and I'd expect you to sell between ten and twenty packs of five per session. So, you could reach the thousand a month target very quickly.'

Sam thought Thomson must have followed the recommendations to the letter as he developed his business.

'Generally, the pills sell themselves. Once someone's tried them, he'll want to use them again. Hence the free sample. But, from what you said yesterday, it's up to you.

'Like everything else, word of mouth's your best endorsement. We find in this business, that can happen very quickly. Hence why we suggest you go back to the same place at the same time every week.

'But, you always get objections from some punters. They'll say, for example, they don't need these pills. Or they're too expensive. Or they just want information. Or how can they trust what you say? Do you want to try some role plays, just to get the words right? We find it really helps with your credibility. I'll be the customer. You're selling.'

Sam smiled at Eddie. 'Okay. Let's try it.'

Andrew started to ask aggressive questions about the tablets, and Sam did his best to answer. If Andrew didn't like the answer, he suggested words Sam should use, and asked the question again. They did this several times until Andrew gave the thumbs up.

Sam stood up and indicated to Eddie he should try it as well.

'Well done,' said Andrew. 'I'll go get your case and tablets. How many do you want?'

Sam pursed his lips. 'We'll go for the thousand.'

'Good. So that's four hundred and thirty pounds in total.'

Sam counted out the money. Andrew left the room and came back moments later with a case wrapped in plastic and two bags of tablets. 'I've also added in two hundred small plastic bags that each hold five tablets. The red strip reseals the pack. You've probably seen these before.' He unwrapped the case. 'Do you want to load these yourself?'

'Yeah, sure.'

Andrew guided Sam and Eddie on how to open the secret compartments and lock them again. 'You're all set to go. I'll get you a taxi. It avoids a change of tube line in London.'

In the taxi to the station, Eddie turned and smiled. 'Happy with that?'

Sam nodded. 'Delighted. Can't believe I've got this business for next to nothing. I think the guy's a bit naïve. I mean, he's thinking tuppence ha'penny. I'm thinking pound notes.'

'How do you mean?'

Sam leaned over and whispered, 'He offers a two thousand pack with an eighty-five percent margin – six shillings for a tablet that sells for two pounds. Allow say twenty percent for our team, the discounts and the bung for the bar, and you're still left with a sixty-five percent profit. That's more than we make on cocaine, for Chrissake.

'He's built a business model on someone that operates on his own – like Thomson. We'll put a team in, ramp up the volumes and make some real money. We'll talk on the train.'

Eddie pursed his lips. 'Right, let's do that.'

At Euston, they walked down the ramp towards the platforms and came to the large board that announced 'Welcome to the Coronation Scot by LMS, the world's greatest transport organisation'. They showed their tickets.

'First class this end, sir. You're on the second coach about half way along.'

They made their way along the platform, past couples saying goodbye and porters with luggage, and found their seats. They had the two window seats in the compartment. There were also tickets on the two corridor seats. Sam's brain raced. He felt so clear-headed. That pill from last night still worked. He wanted to talk details with Eddie.

Ten minutes into the journey, Sam heard someone shout, 'First call for lunch'. When the white-jacketed attendant opened his door, Sam indicated, 'Two here.'

'Two, sir? Here we go.' He gave Sam two tickets. 'Next car forward, sir.'

Sam and Eddie excused themselves to the other two men in the compartment, and made their way along to the restaurant car. Sam gingerly carried his special GT Pharma suitcase. They found a table for two on the right-hand side.

Lunch comprised some carrot soup, a vegetable pie, and a kind of fruit compote. Basic, but tasty enough with a glass of wine.

Sam leaned forward. 'I've got a proposition I'd like you to think about, Eddie.'

'What's that?'

'How would you like to run this business for me? I reckon you could make two to eight times your present pay on top.'

Eddie looked surprised. 'How do you work that out?'

'Think about it. We've got nineteen pubs and three nightclubs. Not all our pubs are suitable, but we'll have about a dozen say, plus other pubs we don't own, like the Horseshoe or the bars in big hotels. So, we can see up to twenty outlets.

'Now to me, you have to concentrate on Friday and Saturday nights, and Saturday lunchtime in the pubs. That's the time people have money in their pockets. Andrew said he expected to sell between ten and twenty packs in a session. You said yourself Thomson saw ten people when you watched him, right?'

Eddie nodded. 'Yeah, at least ten.'

'And he worked on his own. I think we put a three-man team into each outlet – one at the table with the packs – one heavy three or four feet away for protection – and one that circulates and drums up business. I think you could easily get twenty sales per session. Pay them seven and a half percent off the top, which leaves headroom for an incentive.

'If you put it all together, you get between ten and twenty outlets, each selling ten to twenty packs per session, with three sessions per week, and each pack has five tablets. That gives us between fifteen hundred and six thousand tablets per week at two pounds a pop, which gives a total income of between three thousand and twelve thousand pounds a week. And if you run this business for me, I'll give you one percent off the top. That's between thirty and a hundred and twenty pounds a week, which gives you more than two to eight times your present pay. What do you say?'

'Jesus. One percent of everything?'

'Yep. That's the same deal Oscar's on, and dad would definitely pass it.'

Eddie sat and thought about the offer. Sam wondered why he hesitated. Then Eddie nodded. 'Thanks, Sam. I accept.'

'Great, Eddie.' They shook hands. 'You had me worried for a second, there.'

Eddie laughed. 'It's no problem to accept, Sam. I'm just a bit overwhelmed. But the girls now want to go to university to do medicine, and that's helluva expensive, so I needed extra cash anyway. And I agree with you, this is brilliant.'

'Good. So, when we get to Glasgow, can you call Dougan at the Horseshoe Bar, and set us up for a table tomorrow lunchtime. Let's you, me and Johnny test this to make sure we understand how it works, so we can then train teams to do it themselves. Okay?'

'Sure. No problem, Sam.'

They made their way back to their seats and Sam put his head back and closed his eyes. He felt happy and relaxed he could make the new business a big success.

He wakened with Eddie shaking his leg. 'Sam. Wake up. We're nearly in Glasgow.'

Sam rubbed his eyes, got up and gathered his things. He led the way along the corridor, and carried his special case in front of him. People streamed past as he stepped down from the train. He caught the eye of a woman who had glanced over at him. Quite tall, dark hair, round face, maybe mid-thirties, with a smart dark-blue coat and hat. Nice figure, pretty enough, but with a touch of hardness and confidence about her. She'd had a glint of recognition in her eyes. She knew him, but he didn't know her. It happened all the time, particularly in Kenny's pubs and clubs. As one of the family, everyone knew him.

He waited a second for Eddie to catch up, then joined the rest of the crowd surging down the platform towards the concourse. The woman in the dark-blue coat walked just a few yards ahead, her long shoulder bag on her left, her suitcase on her right, her bum cheeks bouncing under her coat in the middle. Bit of a sassy walk too. He liked confident, sassy women.

But he'd seen these bum cheeks before. Then he remembered her. The floor manager of the VIP area in Kenny's new nightclub that opened two weeks ago, though, then she wore a long, slinky dress. But it was the same confident, sassy walk.

Johnny met them at the barrier into the concourse, and took his case. 'Over this way, boss,' and led him towards the Hope Street exit. He glanced over again at the woman as she headed towards the Gordon Street exit. Attractive, mature, and distinctly rideable. He'd talk to Kenny about her.

Later, he caught Dan and Kenny together and told them all about the new business. They congratulated him on a job well done.

Just before Kenny left for the club, Sam asked him, 'You know the girl that's the floor manager in the VIP area of your new club? Tall, dark hair, round face, pretty, bit of a sassy walk. What's her name?'

Kenny thought for a moment. 'You mean Jen Strachan?'

'Yeah, Jen. That's her.'

'Oh, Christ, Sam. Don't tell me you've got your eyes on her now. You're really a randy bastard, you know.'

Sam laughed. 'I know. She got off the train from London. Looked pretty good.'

Kenny frowned. 'You sure? What time did your train get in?'

'Yeah, I'm sure. At least, I *think* so. About half seven?'

Kenny went over to the phone and talked for a couple of minutes. Then came back and said, 'It wasn't her, mate. Jen's been in the club since six doing staff training. Must be someone else.'

Sam grimaced. 'Shit. That's a disappointment.'

That night, as he made love to Helen, he saw these bum cheeks bouncing under the dark-blue coat, and thought how he'd love to squeeze them above him. Now, he might never find out who she was, dammit.

***

A policeman stood on patrol outside Sandra's house. 'Good evening, ma'am.'

Sandra smiled. 'Good evening, constable. All quiet?'

'Yes, ma'am.'

'Good. Thank you.'

The house felt cold, so she switched on an electric fire and went through to the kitchen. She took the photos out of her bag. It was him. Definitely. Handsome but hard-faced. With his companion, the anonymous man. She picked up the phone and asked for the number.

'Hello?'

'Tom, it's me.'

'Oh, good evening, ma'am. Good trip?'

'Yeah. I'll tell you all about it when we meet. Guess who I saw on the train up from London tonight?'

'Who?'

'Sam McFadden. And he carried a brand new GT Pharma suitcase. Somehow that bastard has wormed his way into the organisation, and taken over the business for Glasgow. And that spells trouble. He had Mister Anonymous with him, you know the man in the cat camera picture with Jack Bruce? We need to get his name.'

'Jesus. What do you want to do, ma'am?'

'Put two or three teams together. Keep them well out of sight. But I want McFadden followed from first thing tomorrow. Put a tap on his home phone, my authority. And if he's dealing, I want photographic evidence. Get on to Doc Roberts, and see if he can give you a couple of these miniature cameras he has. I want to nail McFadden good and proper.'

'Right, ma'am. Will do. Talk tomorrow.' He rang off.

She stood and looked down at McFadden's picture. 'You threatening bastard. I'm coming to get you,' she murmured.

***

Next morning, the three of them entered the Horseshoe Bar just after eleven. They wore football scarves to fit in. Sam noted the table already had a 'Reserved' sign on it. Eddie went off to see Dougan and slip him fifteen notes. He came back a few minutes later and gave Sam a thumbs up. Sam went over to the table and sat down. He put his briefcase on the shelf under the table. Johnny stood at the bar three feet away.

Within fifteen seconds, a ginger-haired lad sidled up to the table and sat down. 'Have you taken over from Davy?' he asked.

Sam nodded. 'Yeah.'

'Thank Christ for that. What happened to him?'

Sam shrugged. 'I don't know. He went off somewhere else I think.'

'You got the same gear?'

'Yeah.' Sam eased a pack out of the briefcase and showed him under the table. 'You see the symbol on one side and the letters on the other. It's the same stuff.'

The lad glanced down at it. 'Right, I'll take a pack.'

Sam slipped it over to him. 'That's a tenner.'

The lad gave Sam two fivers and relaxed back in his chair.

'Did you know Davy well?' Sam asked.

The lad nodded. 'Well, only through this. But I also saw him in the Ashton sometimes on a Thursday night.'

'Oh, right. Where's that again?'

'Up the West End, just off Byers Road. It's mostly artists and musicians go there.'

'Did Davy do okay there? Wouldn't have thought many people had money in their pocket on a Thursday.'

'Well, we don't work nine to five, Monday to Friday. We've odd hours and get paid at odd times. That's why I use these pills. I'm a session musician. Do a lot of recording work. And that can last for days on end. With these pills I can keep going when others give up. Get a lot of business that way.'

Christ, thought Sam, that's a different world. 'Do you know where else Davy went? I mean, we've just started and feeling our way a bit.'

'Yeah, he told me he did the St Enoch Hotel bar on a Friday night, and the Central Hotel bar on a Saturday night, but I don't know anywhere else. So, will you be here every Saturday lunchtime?'

'Yeah. Well, me or my mate.'

'Good. So, I'll maybe see you next week then?'

'Fine. What's your name?'

'Frank.'

'I'm Andy. Nice to meet you.'

'You too.' The lad got up and left.

Sam thought that had gone well. Lots of useful info. And the false name just flowed out. Eddie had told him on the way in that Mary shopped and collected the pensions for their next door neighbours – two brothers. He'd filched the personal details of Andy and Alex Jardine from their pension books. Sam used Andy, and Eddie used Alex.

Another older guy came to the table and sat down. 'Your mate over there tells me you've got a pill that gives you a hard on for three days. Is that right?'

Sam nodded. 'Well, let's not exaggerate. Two to three days.'

'Jesus Christ. I'd love to try that.'

'I've got them here. A tenner for five.'

'Oh, Christ. I don't want that amount. Just want to try one.'

Sam thought him very keen. 'Okay, a couple of quid for one.'

He thought for a moment. 'Okay, you're on.' He counted out two pound notes from his wallet and Sam gave him a tablet in return.

Sam said, 'I hope you don't mind if I ask, do you have a woman lined up that you can screw for a night and a day?'

The man pursed his lips. 'Well, I think so. Why?'

'Well, it's maybe not a good idea to use your wife. She'd just become suspicious you're up to something. If you want a girl that will last, call this number.' He tore off a leaf from his pad under the table and wrote the number. 'You'll get a good girl there – whatever you want.'

The man glanced at the paper and put it in his pocket. 'Thanks, mate.'

'No problem.' Cross selling opportunities as well, thought Sam. Some business this.

After an hour or so, Sam swapped places with Eddie, but found it more difficult to get people interested in the pills, and swapped back again. At half past two, they packed up, walked to the car, and headed home. They relaxed in Sam's lounge.

'So, what did we learn from that?' Eddie asked.

Sam pulled out his notebook. 'Right, we made twenty sales, some to ex-customers of Davy, who were all pleased to see us. We sold a total of ninety-six tablets, for one hundred and sixty six pounds, an average price per tablet of one pound fourteen shillings and seven pence. Each tablet cost us eight shillings, so we made a gross profit of' . . . he worked his slide rule, 'seventy-seven percent. Not too shabby.

'Now, we paid the bar fifteen pounds, and if we'd paid our staff in the way we talked about, Eddie, that would have reduced our profit to . . . just under sixty percent net.'

Sam grimaced. 'Shit, I wanted sixty-five percent net. Wait a minute. If we bought the two thousand packs, the tablets would only cost us six shillings each, which would give us a net profit of . . . there you go, sixty-five percent. And in Kenny's bars and nightclubs, we wouldn't have the bung to the bar, so that would give us a net of . . . nearly seventy-five percent. Bloody good, huh?' He smiled at Eddie. 'Now, it probably won't finish quite as much as that because, as the volumes go up, we'll maybe need to give more discounts, but it's still a good business.'

Eddie nodded. 'But I think the model's wrong, Sam.'

'How do you mean?'

'It's good for people like Thomson, who use their own money, and give discounts to attract more business. But, for us, these discounts would just allow our guys to rip us off. We could never tell if they'd given a discount to somebody or had pocketed some tablets. I think we should forget about discounts. If the team goes out with a hundred tablets, they come back with two quid for every one they sell. End of. Now, if they, as a team, want to give a discount to attract more business, that's up to them. But they pay us two quid a tablet. After all, the pub doesn't give you a discount if you buy five pints. And we need to think the same way.'

As usual, Eddie spoke a lot of sense, Sam thought. That's why he liked him around. 'You're right, Eddie. Let's do that.'

Eddie nodded.

Sam went on. 'I also learned from one of Davy's ex-customers that he used the Ashton bar in the West End on a Thursday night, the bar at the St Enoch Hotel on a Friday night, and the bar at the Central Hotel on a Saturday night. So, I think we need to go there and see if we can strike a similar deal with their bar managers. Can I leave that to you?'

Eddie nodded. 'Yeah, no problem.'

'But we need to think of the skills required in the team. I mean, I could talk at the table one-to-one with customers, but I found it difficult to break into conversations at the bar and raise the subject of the tablets. We have to work out the skills we need for these jobs and create some sort of role plays to get our people up to speed. Can you do that too, Eddie?'

'Sure. I found that bit okay, so I'll see what I can come up with.'

'Great. So. I think it's a good start. Any points from you, Johnny?'

'Ach. Just too many cops in that bar for me, I could smell them. I know they're football fans as well, but I didn't like doing business under their noses.'

Sam nodded. 'Yeah, that's understandable. But remember, it's legit. They can't touch you for it. So, don't worry. Let's just push on with the business, and to hell with them. They can't do a thing unless the politicians change the law, and *they've* too many other priorities.'

Chapter 11. Jane

The nightmares had come back. She'd had them almost every night, since Porritt told her of the Aquila link to Tommy's death. But now, a vision of Tommy struggling in the fast flow of the River Clyde had joined her two original Aquila nightmares. The three visions ran like film loops through her head.

Jane went to the British team doctor. He gave her some mild sedative tablets to help her sleep, but they left her drowsy during the day. One evening, a local mother at Stephen's football club mentioned she took a 'Hermann pill' each day to give her energy and keep her active with a young family. 'You can get them at any pharmacy. They're great. Better and cheaper than coffee. Everyone takes them around here.'

She bought some next morning. It said 'Methamphetamine' on the packet. She took one and couldn't believe the difference, now so clear-headed and full of energy. She didn't take her sleeping pill that night, and still slept like a log with no nightmares. Her 'Hermann pill' became one of the two things that steadied and stabilised her life.

The other was Andreas Schaeffer, who managed the work of all the interpreters. When he'd heard from Porritt about the threat to Jane, he'd reassured her, and told her of the actions he'd taken. They now lunched together a couple of days a week, and one Saturday, he'd turned up at Stephen's football game. 'Just passing,' he said. She thrilled at his interest, though she sensed Josef, her driver and bodyguard, didn't share that view.

The two men, about the same age, a couple of years older than her, were very different. Andreas had a much more mature and worldly approach, with his confident

Swiss manner and dry sense of humour. Against him, Josef somehow seemed boyish. Still early days, though, on the romantic front.

Since she'd come to Nuremberg, Jane had written to her grandma Weissmann in Dresden and her grandma Bilova in Prague. She'd given them her new address, and said she wanted to see them, now she lived nearer. She'd planned to visit them during the Christmas and New Year break, but for weeks had heard nothing.

Her mother desperately wanted to speak to *her* mother, grandma Bilova. They'd tried to phone her on the number they had, but it didn't connect. Jane felt relieved when, in mid-November, she received a reply from grandma Bilova that gave her new address, but no phone number. Jane wrote back that she and her mum and her two boys would visit her in Prague on Thursday, 27th December, stay two full days, and return on the Sunday.

But with still no response from Dresden. Jane agreed with Andreas she'd work extra hours so she could take Thursday and Friday, 20 and 21 December off, and planned to visit Dresden to find out what had happened to grandma Weissmann.

Hans Wolff said he could only protect her within the American Zone. His people could have problems in the Soviet Occupied Zone of Germany or Soviet Occupied Czechoslovakia, because the Russians detained Germans on the flimsiest excuses.

She spoke to Porritt about it. 'I need to go there, sir. I need to know what's happened to my family in Dresden and Prague. Something's not right, and I need to see for myself.'

He agreed, and organised a letter from Sergei to help her cross into the Soviet controlled areas. On headed paper, in Russian and German, it said.

'To Whom It May Concern,

Please grant free passage to Mrs Jane Thomson, the holder of this letter, and her party, into Soviet Occupied Territory. She is a Friend of the Soviet Union, and works with us here at the Trials in Nuremberg.

Thank you,

Colonel Sergei Bazarov, Chief of Staff, Soviet Delegation, Nuremberg'

Sergei had stamped and signed it.

But Wolff refused to budge. When Andreas heard of Wolff's response, he shook is head. 'You're not going to Dresden on your own. If Wolff's man can't go, I'll go with you.'

On the Thursday before Christmas, they met at the Nuremberg Rail Station. She'd reserved First Class seats, both ways. As they waited on the platform he asked, 'You still okay?' They spoke in German when they were together.

She nodded. 'Nervous. Don't know what I'll find.'

The train came slowly into the platform, the Stuttgart – Dresden express. It looked packed full. However, they found their seats in First Class and she tried to relax.

At Hof, where they crossed into the Soviet Occupied Zone, teams of Russian soldiers came on board to check everyone's papers. As the soldiers slowly worked their way down the coach towards them, she swallowed, and slipped her arm through his. 'I'm glad you're with me,' she whispered.

He turned and smiled, and squeezed her arm.

They handed over their passports and ID cards, and the letter from Sergei, to the Russian soldier. He looked through them, read the letter and looked impassively at her. She held his gaze. He gave them back their papers and moved on.

They saw people escorted by soldiers on the platform. Across Europe, huge numbers of people were on the move, but the authorities kept a close eye on them, she thought.

Once the train started to move again, she relaxed. 'Phew. I'm glad that's over.'

He squeezed her arm again. 'Me too.'

They got into a taxi at Dresden station and she asked for her grandma's address. The driver glanced at her. 'Are you sure?' he asked.

She nodded. 'Yeah. I'm sure.'

He shrugged and drove off.

As they drove down past the old town towards the river, Jane stared with horror at the scene. The old town, once the finest and most beautiful city she'd ever seen, was now a pile of rubble, with skeletal walls of buildings, and black holes where once there had been windows. She put her hand to her mouth and started to weep. 'Oh, my God. Oh, my God,' she sobbed. 'What happened here? What, in God's name, happened here?' She couldn't take her eyes off the horror through her tears.

The driver indicated with his free hand, pointed up and then slowly pointed down with a whistling noise. 'British bastards.' He turned along the Terrassenufer beside the river, and in a few hundred metres, pulled into a side street and stopped. 'We're here,' he said, quietly.

Andreas had put his arm round Jane, and she'd buried her head in the front of his coat. She lifted her head and looked around her, and started to sob again. Tears rolled down her face. She got out of the car and stared at the pile of rubble where the magnificent detached house had once stood, where she had played so happily as a child. She lifted her head to the sky. She could hardly breathe for her sobs, and let out a wail of anguish. Andreas held her against him, and let her cry it all out. The taxi driver smoked a cigarette.

Eventually, she pushed away and looked around. Every house in the street had gone, now just piles of rubble, with an occasional part wall still standing. The whole place resembled a desolate wasteland, yet traffic still flowed along the Terrassenufer, the river Elbe still flowed to the sea. She didn't know what to say, or do. She just stood and looked, but saw nothing.

A tall, grey-haired man came down the street towards them walking a dog. He stopped, concerned at Jane's tear stained face. He turned to Andreas. 'Can I help at all?'

Andreas sighed. 'She's looking for her grandma and grandpa. They used to live here.'

'Oh, I see. What's their name?'

'Weissmann.'

Jane glanced at the man. Maybe he had information. She stepped closer to him. 'Do you know them? Do you know what happened to them?'

The man nodded. 'I do, my dear. Mr Weissmann died that night, but I believe his wife survived. She was taken to the General Hospital, but I don't know what happened after that.'

Jane looked around. 'When did this happen?'

The man stood and stared at her, almost as though he'd gone into a trance. 'The thirteenth of February this year, just after ten o'clock at night. A wave of British bombers came over, hundreds of them, and dropped countless bombs on the old town. High-explosive bombs to blow the buildings apart, followed by incendiaries to set the whole place on fire. I was on duty, and it all just became a huge firestorm.' His voice became emotional.

'Seven thousand people attended a concert in the Altmarkt, and every single one burned to death.' The tears began to flow down his face. 'We lost over twenty thousand people that night, probably more. We'll never know how many. It was horrific. People died in front of me. I couldn't save them.' He began to sob. 'I couldn't save them. The flames sucked all the oxygen from the air. People couldn't breathe and collapsed, and then burned to death.' He sobbed steadily. 'A woman with a baby in her arms ran past me and tripped, and the baby flew in an arc into the flames.' He broke down sobbing. 'That still haunts me.

'And do you know what the bastards did then?' He couldn't talk for sobbing. 'Do you know what the fucking British bastards did then?' The sobs racked his body. 'They sent another wave of bombers over three hours later and did the same again, with the whole place full of rescuers and emergency services doing their best to help people. I don't know how I made it out of there. And then . . . and then . . . and then . . . ' he wailed and cried aloud, '. . . and then . . . I came home . . .' he pointed across the street, '. . . and it had gone . . . with my wife . . . and my family.' He sobbed his heart out.

Jane went over and hugged the man. Andreas stood totally shocked. They stood still for several minutes until the man calmed down.

He took a handkerchief and wiped his eyes and blew his nose. 'I come down here every day and talk to my wife. But there's not much to say now.' He turned to Jane. 'I'm so sorry. That's not why you came here, I know. But the pain's still so raw. Not just for me, but for everyone here. If we could meet Churchill or any of his generals, we'd happily gouge their bloody eyes out. And look at that farce in Nuremberg. A war crimes trial? It should be Churchill in the dock for what he did here. This really *was* a war crime. They made no attempt to bomb any strategic targets – the railway station, the bridges. They went only for civilians – twice on the same night. That's definitely a war crime by any standards.'

Jane stood stunned at the reference to Nuremberg. My God, what was she doing there? Was he right? Wrong? She didn't know, and would need time to process all this. She gave herself a shake and tried to think clearly.

She touched the man's arm. 'Look, we're really sorry for you. Our hearts go out to you. It's just horrific what you've suffered, but we thank you for sharing it with us. And we hope, in time, you can recover. In the meantime, you say they took Mrs Weissmann to the General Hospital? I think we need to go there and find out what happened to her.'

The man smiled wanly and shook hands with them. 'You're right. There are horror stories everywhere. And you've got to go and find out more about yours.'

They got into the taxi and asked to go to the General Hospital. There, they discovered Mrs Weissmann had been treated for a broken arm in the early hours of fourteenth February, and kept for two days because of severe trauma. She then moved to the Grand Saxony Nursing Home on the outskirts of the city.

They got a taxi from the hospital and arrived at a large manor house, with modern extensions out the back. Jane explained to the receptionist she was Mrs Weissmann's granddaughter, and confirmed the old lady's full name, address and date of birth. They were shown up a fine polished wooden staircase to the office of the Direktor, Doctor Schade, a tall woman with a warm, pleasant manner.

'Physically, your grandmother's fine for her age,' explained the doctor, 'but she has suffered a severe trauma, to the point she doesn't communicate. She takes instructions from the staff, and follows them willingly, but mentally, there's a total blank. I hope when she meets you, it may prompt a reaction that will get her mental faculties to work again. But, you should prepare yourself it may not happen. Shall we go and see her?'

They left her office, and entered a bright, airy day room, with lots of people in lots of chairs. The doctor guided them across the room to a separate area behind a glass partition. An elderly woman sat on her own and looked out of the window.

Jane realised she'd last seen her grandma Weissmann over ten years ago, when she was still a teenager, and she had changed a lot since then. But she was also shocked at how much her grandma had aged, her hair now totally white and her face heavily lined. Jane knelt in front of her, smiled, and took her hands. 'Grandma. It's Jana. Remember me?'

The old lady looked at her, but with no recognition in her eyes.

'I'm Georg's daughter. Remember your son, Georg?'

The old lady's expression didn't change.

Jane glanced over to Andreas and the doctor, then squeezed her grandma's hands again. 'Remember Georg and Willhelm and Walther, your fine sons?'

Still nothing.

She struggled for ideas. 'Remember Veronika? Walther's daughter? Remember Veronika and me? We got into trouble at your house when we tried to bake cream cakes? You gave us a row because we didn't pay attention?'

Tears welled up in her eyes. Her grandma was so precious, but was now just a shell. The brain had stalled. Jane leaned forward, hugged the old lady, and let the tears flow. Her grandma didn't respond.

A few minutes later, she felt a touch on her shoulder, and looked round. The doctor whispered, 'I think we should go, my dear. Don't torture yourself. You've done your best.'

Jane slowly pulled away from her grandma, and gave her a kiss on the cheek. She walked over to Andreas and put her arms round his neck and hugged him. She felt his arms go round her and hold her tight. Gradually, her tears stopped.

They made their way back through the day room to the doctor's office.

The doctor sat on the edge of her desk. 'We do our best for her, and as far as we can tell, she seems content. She shows no signs of distress, and seems calm all day and every day. I think you may have to accept, given the lack of response to your visit, she may remain like that for a long time. We try to stimulate her each day, and hope one day she'll react, but it's now almost a year, and I really don't hold out much promise for you. However, if you leave me your address, we'll keep in touch, and let you know if there's any change.'

Jane gave her contact details. 'Can I ask who pays for my grandmother's care?'

'We're owned by a trust fund set up many years ago by a wealthy businessman to look after elderly citizens of Dresden who had fallen on hard times. So, your grandmother certainly qualifies. The fund pays for all room, meals and the direct care costs. Any personal expenses for clothes or toiletries get paid by the guest, or his or her family. In your grandmother's case, if you just give me a second,' she went to a filing cabinet and pulled out a file, 'a lawyer, Mr Fridrik Kaufmann, pays any such expenditure. The court appointed him to look after your grandmother's estate. Here's his address.'

Jane took a note of it

The doctor went on, 'As far as I'm aware, Mr Kaufmann does not know of any surviving relatives of Mrs Weissmann, so you should maybe contact him while you're here.'

Jane glanced at her watch. 'I wonder if we could see him this afternoon.'

'Would you like me to call and check? If he's available, I can drop you in the city. I have to go in for a meeting anyway.'

'That would be great. Thank you.'

The doctor phoned and Kaufmann agreed to see Jane and Andreas as soon as they could get into the city. He explained he'd found a bank account in the Weissmanns' name, and, with the court's permission, used it for her expenses at the Nursing Home. He took a note of Jane's contact details, as the only surviving offspring of Mrs Weissmann's son, Georg, and noted the details of the other sons and their families, Willhelm, somewhere in Australia, and Walther, in Athens, though she had no address details for either of them.

That evening, Jane and Andreas ate in a small restaurant along the street from their hotel. The chef had done his best to produce tasty versions of basic dishes. Jane had now come through the trauma of the day, and they discussed the man's comments on the Nuremberg Trial and the British bombing of Dresden as a war crime.

In the end, they agreed both horrors, the bombing and the concentration camps, displayed a flawed strategy by overblown military generals, who then attempted to justify their actions with spurious claims of seeking advantage. They also thought, from what they'd seen and heard, there was a case for investigating the Dresden bombing in a similar manner to Nuremberg. But she didn't mention her brother had been a bomb-aimer with the RAF. She couldn't yet share that conflict in her mind.

They walked back to their hotel arm-in-arm. She felt very close to Andreas now, as though their shared horror at the events of the day had driven them together. They stopped outside her room.

'Are you okay?' he asked, gently. 'Will you sleep okay?'

She looked up into his eyes, then put an arm up behind his neck and kissed him on the lips. God, that felt so good, she thought. More than ever a rock for her. 'Thanks for being with me today,' she whispered.

'My privilege.' He pulled her to him and kissed her.

'I don't want you to go,' she whispered, 'but I'm not ready yet to go further.'

He smiled and held her face in his hands. 'I can wait.'

'Thanks.' She put the key in the door, blew him a kiss and entered her room.

She sat on the bed and stared at the wall. The events of the day had shattered her emotions. Life was so fragile. Her grandpa blown away by a bomb. Her grandma left a shell. She felt so numb, she couldn't even cry anymore. She needed comfort and cuddles. What stopped her? A lousy marriage? Gone. Tommy? He'd gone too. Nothing stopped her. She could start a new direction any time she wanted. And next door, a fine, strong, generous, perfect man waited for her. She stood up, left her room, and tapped on his door.

***

Next morning, she linked arms and huddled into him on the train back to Nuremberg. She'd savoured his love making and cuddles, and had a sound, dreamless sleep. She felt fully refreshed after the rigours of yesterday.

They discussed their plans for Christmas week, and when she heard he'd decided to stay in Nuremberg, rather than go back to Switzerland, she insisted he join them on Christmas Day. He also suggested, if she wanted, he'd come with her to Prague on Thursday, and she readily agreed.

They made Christmas Day as festive as possible for the boys. Andreas joined in their games, and Jane liked that lighter side of him. Her mother seemed to take to Andreas as well, and the day passed with lots of laughter and fun.

Two days later they all gathered at Nuremberg Station to catch the Munich – Prague express. The boys asked lots of questions about the train, about the passing scene, and about life in general, and Andreas answered them all with endless patience. Jane liked that. He already seemed more like a father to them than their real father had ever been.

At the Czech border, Jane and her mother became anxious at the long delay for checks by Russian soldiers, and the shunting of the train as the locomotive changed. They'd fled the country in 1935, and Jane remembered the endless discussions between her parents as her father decided to take a leap into the unknown and head for Britain. He'd thought it certain that Hitler would invade adjacent countries. The Sudetenland in Czechoslovakia had already come under threat. He saw it as fight or flight, and chose the latter.

They'd left one night without telling anyone other than her mother's parents. How right her father had been, thought Jane, and how horrific the aftermath, from the news that filtered out from Prague. Now, she felt apprehensive at their return, but was desperate to see her grandma Bilova again. She had loved her so much as a child.

As they emerged from the huge Prague Rail Station into the winter sunshine, Jane stopped and looked around. It all looked just as she remembered it. Her mother had a tear in her eye. 'What's wrong, mum?'

Her mum smiled. 'Nothing's wrong, darling. I just never thought I'd ever see it again.'

Jane gave her a hug. 'I know, mum.' She gathered them together, conscious that, while they all had some fluency in English, Andreas and the boys had no knowledge of Czech. She called to them in English, 'Come on. We don't have much luggage. Let's catch a tram.'

They made their way across to the tram stop. 'Right. Which of you boys will be the first to see a twenty-six tram?'

'There's one,' shouted Stephen.

'No, coming this way, darling.'

A few minutes later, they piled onto a tram, and the boys asked endless questions. Stephen examined the route indicator above their seat. 'Where are we going, mummy?'

'We're going to Hadovka. Can you see it?'

Stephen examined the names of the stops. 'I've got it, mummy. Where are we now?'

Jane stood up and pointed at the route guide. 'We're just here.'

'Right, mummy, I'll tell you when we get there.'

'That's good, darling.' She sat down and took Andreas' arm.

He squeezed it. 'You okay?'

She nodded. 'Just not sure what we'll find.'

The tram crossed the river and headed out towards the northwest suburbs. They got off at their stop and walked up a side street. Jane stopped at the detached house that had been her grandma and grandpa's house for as long as she could remember. A car sat outside it, and two young children played in the front garden. A woman came out of the front door and called to the children in Russian. What the hell's happened, thought Jane. Had grandma sold the house to the Russians? She knew her grandpa had died in '38, but they had a strong family network around. Surely, grandma would have got advice from them?

They walked on and turned the corner. Jane checked the house number from the slip of paper in her pocket. Number twelve. She counted the house numbers and saw number twelve ahead. An old lady stood in the garden, wrapped up against the cold, and looked towards them. Her grandma Bilova. She dropped her case and ran forward, through the gate, hugged the old lady, and wept tears of joy. Her mother rushed up and hugged them both. The three women stood for several minutes, hugging and kissing each other.

Jane glanced round. Andreas and the boys stood at the gate, with their eyes wide in wonder. She waved them over and introduced them. 'This lady is your mummy's mummy's mummy, your great grandma. Grandma, this is Stephen and George.' They shook hands and she gave them a hug. 'And my friend, Andreas.' They shook hands.

'Let's go inside,' the old lady said in Czech.

Three old ladies sat in the front room, and grandma Bilova introduced everyone. Then she led the way through to the kitchen at the back of the house.

Jane asked,'Who are these ladies, grandma? Why are you here? Is this your house now?' The questions tumbled out.

The old lady shook her head. 'No, darling. It's Mrs Hrbek's house. But three of us have been moved here to free up our houses for Russian families.'

'But that's outrageous, grandma.'

'May be, but that's the new rules, darling.'

'Says who?'

'Says the Russians. They're the ones in charge now. And there's nothing we can do about it. Our lawyer agrees.'

'Who's your lawyer?'

'Milan Prchal. He has an office at the local Dejvice Centre on the main road.'

'Well, I want to go and see him. I mean, do you still own your house?'

'Yes, I think so. But the Russians have taken it for as long as they need it.'

'But it's just wrong.'

'I know, darling. But Mr Prchal has told us if we kick up too much of a fuss, the Russians will take over the house completely, and we'll lose all rights to it. And just let me say, it used to be a great deal worse.'

'What? How could it be worse?'

'Under the German occupation, they confined me to one bedroom in my own house, and I could only use the kitchen and bathroom at set times. A German family took over the rest of the house. I hated that.'

Jane shook her head in frustration. She glanced over at Andreas and the boys, who all looked confused by the conversation in Czech. 'I'll tell you later,' she said to him in German. God, she'd had no idea that had happened. They'd had no contact during the war years. She felt helpless and angry, but realised, even if she *had* been here, she probably couldn't have done much about it. Occupation forces could do what they liked, take it or leave it.

Grandma Bilova tried to lighten the atmosphere. 'Let's have a cup of tea.' She busied herself, then knelt and talked to the boys. Jane interpreted for her.

Jane needed to think about the practicalities of their visit. She'd thought they could've stayed with her grandma, and hadn't booked a hotel.

'Is there still a hotel at the Dejvice Centre?' she asked.

Her grandma nodded.

'Right. Andreas and I will go and book rooms. We'll leave the boys here. Okay?'

Her mother said, 'Yes, it's fine. Off you go.'

Jane and Andreas walked back to the main road and crossed to the main shopping and commercial centre for the area. At the hotel, they booked two rooms for three nights. Each room contained a double and a single bed. She presumed, if her mother agreed, she and Andreas would share one room, with her mother and the boys in the other.

As they strolled round the Centre, they passed the office of Milan Prchal, Legal Advisor. Jane decided she wanted to talk to him, to establish where her grandma stood legally with respect to her property.

He had a very pleasant and concerned manner. He confirmed her grandma still owned the property, but the Russians had moved lots of staff into Prague, and passed local laws to maximise the use of property by moving single owners together.

'Do they pay for the use of her property?' Jane asked.

'Well, they *should* pay her a hundred *Koruna* per week, less than half its value, but no one's been paid yet. It's stupid. It just stokes up even more resentment. But they're not bothered. It's the same all over, and there's nothing we can do about it. They're in control now. We Czechs don't matter any more.'

Jane and Andreas went to a tea room and chatted about the situation. They concluded, in the circumstances, they shouldn't create waves about it. There already seemed plenty of local resentment that had to run its course.

They talked about what they'd do for the next two days. Grandma had said Aunt Eva, her mother's sister, would host a lunch for the extended family at her place on Saturday. Jane had picked up a local newspaper, and checked the forecast. The dry, cool weather would continue for the next few days. She suggested they take the boys to Prague Zoo. The boys had never been to a zoo, and Prague had one of the finest in the world. She'd loved to visit it as a child. Andreas thought it a great idea.

That night, they had a drink in the bar next to the hotel after her mother took the boys up to bed. They eventually headed up to their room.

She put an arm up around his neck and kissed him. 'Thank you for being with me today,' she whispered.

He smiled. 'It's my pleasure.'

***

Next morning, Jane, Andreas and the boys caught a tram and bus up to Podbaba, and then the ferry across the Vltava river to the zoo. Inside, she spread a map of the zoo across a table. 'Right, boys. It's a huge place, and we won't see it all today. What top three things do each of you want to see?'

The boys studied the map and asked questions. After a few minutes Stephen said, 'I want to see the gorillas, the lions and the elephants.' George piped up, 'I want to see the giraffes, the kangaroos and the penguins.'

'Good. We'll see them and lots of other things too.'

Andreas worked out the best route to follow and to capture the feeding times, and they set off, with the boys full of excitement.

By late afternoon, on the way back on the ferry, Jane savoured the day. For the first time ever, she'd felt part of a proper family outing, walking arm-in-arm with her man, watching the wonder in the boys' eyes, and answering their interminable questions. She had a tear in her eye. She wanted this, permanently.

That evening, her mother said she'd look after the boys if Jane and Andreas wanted to go into the city. They took her up on her offer and caught a tram down to the Old Town.

Jane showed Andreas the sights of her home city. They wandered the cobblestoned streets of the Old Town, admired the fine architecture, the unique Astronomical Clock, the Powder Tower; strolled round Wenceslas Square; popped into a couple of bars along the way for warming drinks, and ended up at the magnificent Charles Bridge, with its fine statues along each side, and Prague Castle looming above them. Her favourite spot in the city.

'God, such a perfect day,' she said. She put her arm up around his neck. 'Thank you,' and kissed him. 'Love you so much.'

'Yeah, it's been great with you and the boys. Just great. Love you too.'

She began to shiver in the cold winter air. 'Let's get back, shall we?'

They strolled back towards the Old Town and joined the small crowd at a tram stop. Two women, about her age and a bit tipsy, joined the crowd and stood in front of them. The women cackled together. Up to now, Jane hadn't heard laughter in the streets. There had been some laughter at the zoo, particularly at the penguin parade, and in the bars, with some raucous men, but people didn't seem to laugh much in Prague now. Maybe, with the occupation, there wasn't much to laugh about, she thought.

Then, she recognised one of the tipsy girls as her best friend, Valentina, from her teenage years. They'd lived two houses apart, and were forever in each other's houses, playing music and admiring magazines. She hesitated a moment, then leaned forward and touched the girl's shoulder. 'Val?'

The girl turned, with a puzzled expression, her eyes glazed.

Jane smiled and held out her hands. 'Val, it's Jana. Jana Weissmann. How are you? It's great to see you.'

The girl examined Jane's face, and slowly recognised her. Then her expression suddenly changed and she sneered. 'Hah, you're back, then?' She waved to her friend and the other people at the tram stop. 'Look at this selfish bitch. Ran away with her family to England ten years ago. Never a goodbye. Never a letter. And now she's back, with her fancy hairstyle and her fancy clothes and her fancy boyfriend, to take pity on all us poor Czechs that had to suffer under the Germans and now with the Russians. Selfish bitch.'

Jane stared in horror. Why did she say such thing? Andreas had come closer and held her tight. 'That's not true,' she said to the girl. 'It's just not true.' She felt tears well in her eyes.

The girl snarled, 'It *is* true. You bloody selfish bitch.'

Jane turned to Andreas. 'Let's get out of here,' she said, in German.

'Oh, that makes it even better,' the girl shouted. 'Her boyfriend's bloody German. Can you believe it? A bloody German, for Chrissake. Selfish bloody bitch traitor!'

Jane grabbed Andreas' arm and hurried away from the tram stop. They turned up a side street and came to a taxi rank. 'Let's get a taxi,' she said, jumped into the first one, and gave the name of the hotel. The taxi drove off.

Andreas leaned over. 'What happened?' he asked, in German.

She glanced at the driver, who seemed to be listening to them. 'I'll tell you later.' She sat back and fumed. She now regretted talking to the girl. The sneers and calls of 'selfish bitch' echoed through her head.

She realised the taxi had arrived at the hotel, and Andreas seemed to be arguing with the driver. She tuned into them. The driver spoke in fractured German, and said, under council rules, he had to double the fare if the journey took more than four kilometres. Sorry, it had nothing to do with him. That's the rule.

Jane put her arm out in front of Andreas, leaned forward, and snarled in Czech, 'Don't try to con me. There's no such rule.' The meter indicated 3.85. She counted out four *Koruna* from her purse. 'That's all you're getting. And you're lucky to get anything at all. I should report you to the authorities.'

'Oh, I'm sorry. I didn't realise you're local.' He took the money. 'Don't say anything, please. Life's tough, and I've got a wife and children.'

She got out of the taxi and slammed the door. At least the notorious rip-off tactics of Prague taxi drivers towards foreigners seemed to have survived the war.

Andreas suggested they go to the bar, and over a drink, she told him what had happened. They talked it through, and he encouraged her to try to forget the incident, but she couldn't forget Val's sneer and snarl. Worst of all, it had spoiled such a perfect day.

That night, she cuddled into him, but it took her a long time to get to sleep.

***

Next morning, Jane took her mother aside and told her about the incident with Valentina. Her mother wasn't surprised. She'd spent the previous day with grandma Bilova, who had mentioned at one point, that some of the extended family had refused to come to the lunch because of lingering resentment at them going abroad. Grandma advised, if they talked about life in England, they should stick to facts, and not crow about it.

In the light of this, Jane thought the lunch passed off reasonably well. Aunt Eva did her best to inject a happy note, and Jane thought most of the questions and discussions about life in Britain had been polite and interested, rather than accusatory. But it hadn't been the warm welcome she'd expected.

On the train back to Nuremberg on the Sunday morning, Jane and Andreas discussed the visit. Jane said, 'I'm glad we went, but if I'm honest, I'm glad it's over. I loved seeing grandma Bilova again, and hopefully we can talk with her on the phone now, but I'm not bothered if I don't see Prague again.'

Andreas smiled. 'Yeah, I think it's difficult to go back to your roots, once you've been away for a while. If you've been successful, some people will resent you. If you've not, they'll gloat. Either way, it's not pleasant. That's why I don't go back to Basel too often.'

The next day, New Year's Eve, Andreas came round and joined them for their evening meal. Jane and her mother had become devotees of Hogmanay traditions from their time in Scotland, and so, they cleaned the house from top to bottom, cleared the rubbish out at ten minutes to midnight, and sent Andreas out just before midnight to come back in as their 'first foot' just after twelve. He carried a piece of coal, to represent heat; a box of shortbread, to represent food; and a small bottle of whisky, to represent drink. Jane had brought the latter two with her from Scotland. The fact Andreas was tall, dark and handsome, would bring them extra good luck in the new year. They opened a window to let the old year out and the new year in. Jane relished these traditions in her new location.

The three of them toasted the new year with a tot of whisky, and went through to the boys' room, where they toasted them, and wished their sleeping heads every success and happiness in 1946. Jane's mother went to bed shortly after, and left Jane and Andreas by themselves in front of the fire. They cuddled together on the sofa, and clinked glasses. 'Happy new 1946,' she whispered. 'Hope it's a good one for you,' and kissed him.

'Hope it's a good one for us all,' he said, and returned her kiss.

'Wonder what this year will bring,' she murmured.

'Well, I wanted to talk to you about that.'

She turned and smiled at him. 'Really? What in particular?'

He cleared his throat. 'I'm leaving Nuremberg in a few months.'

She eased away from him and frowned. She didn't want to lose him. 'Oh, no.' She put her hand to her mouth. 'Nooo.'

'But I want you to come with me . . . as my wife.'

Her eyes widened, and she bit her finger. 'Oh, my God. Yes. Yes. Yes.' She threw her arms around his neck, hugged him tight and started to cry. 'To where? When?'

He smiled. 'Thank you. I hoped you'd agree.'

She hugged him again. 'Of course, I agree. I don't want to live without you.'

He nodded. 'I feel the same.'

'So, where are you going?'

'Geneva, in Switzerland. Once my contract runs out here at the end of April.'

'To do what?'

'There's a new organisation just started a couple of months ago. It's called the United Nations, and its aims are to get all the countries of the world to work together to maintain international peace and security, and to protect human rights. They've already got fifty countries signed up for it, and hope to include all the others in time.

'They'll need huge translation and interpretation services, and they've been very impressed with how we use the new simultaneous interpretation here in Nuremberg. They want to use it at all their meetings and conferences, and offered me the job of Global Head of Interpretation Services, based in Geneva. Their letter came when we were in Prague. I couldn't pass up the opportunity, and accepted, and hoped you'd come with me.'

She laughed. 'It sounds fantastic. Of course I'll come with you.'

'And I'd like you to head up the German / English group as well.'

'Oh, my God.' She laughed and cried at the same time. 'That's fantastic. And I accept. But what about *my* contract. That's not up till the end of August.'

'I know. Let's just see how it develops. If we can't change it, we'll live with it. We're in this for the long term.'

She cuddled into him. 'What's Geneva like?'

'It's a beautiful city on the shores of Lake Geneva. It's in the French-speaking part of Switzerland, but it's a truly international city. There's a great international school there for the boys. I think they'll love it. And the UN pays very well, so we might even afford an apartment near the lake.'

She lifted her head and kissed him. 'It sounds fabulous, darling.'

They huddled and cuddled until the fire began to die.

She kissed him again. 'Shall we go to bed?' she whispered.

His love making was so gentle and tender and loving and satisfying, all the things her ex-husband's wham-bam style was not, and she gloried and relished it. Life looked rosy. 1946 would be a good year.

***

Jane thrilled that they spent New Year's Day as a family, games with the boys in the morning, out to a play park in the afternoon. She told her mother about Andreas' proposal, and that she'd accepted. Her mother seemed pleased.

Then, on the Wednesday, back to work after the holiday. Josef picked her up as usual at eight twenty. 'They've changed the traffic arrangements at the Palace to avoid gridlock. All the drivers got briefed on Friday. There's a note for everyone when they get in this morning.'

'Oh? So what have they done?'

'In the morning, you can't drive straight into the courtyard. You've got to go to a staging area across the street, and wait to get called over. The courtyard now has five lanes facing the building – France, UK, Russia, USA and Local/Others – and you can only go over when your lane has a space. Our car ID is UK08,' He held up a large white card with the ID in large black letters.

'Well, at least they're now doing something.'

'In the evening, you have to call the transport office and book a slot for your car to arrive. Each slot is for one minute, and if you're not there on time, the car moves out, and you have to rebook another slot.'

She laughed. 'You're kidding me. Who thought that one up?'

He shrugged. 'I don't know, ma'am, but it's a woman called Astrid in charge, and Porritt and Baker and the others all signed off on it.'

She wondered how all the self-important lawyers and judges would handle it, but if Porritt had signed it off, he must have confidence it would work.

They pulled into the staging area, and Josef put the ID card on the right hand side of the windscreen. A few cars waited with US and RU cards.

He wound his window down. 'Morning, Marta.'

'Morning.' She spoke into a large handheld radio. 'UK08 arrived.' She listened for a moment. 'Okay, go straight across.' She waved two waiting cars to move also.

Josef drove across into the courtyard, turned sharp left and then right into the second lane marked with the UK flag above it. Jane got out of the car. 'I'll see you later once I know my slot,' she laughed.

He smiled. 'Yes, ma'am. See you later.' He drove off.

Jane walked under a temporary shelter down a walkway to the front door. A woman walked up and down, with an eye on the lanes, and talked into her handheld radio, She wore a long grey *Kleppermantel.* My God, thought Jane, when had she last seen one of them? Her mother used to wear a raincoat like that years ago. She presumed that was Astrid. Well, she had to admit, the traffic arrangements had worked for her. And the cars flowed through, dropped their passengers, and moved off freely. It sure as hell had got rid of the gridlock. Full marks to Astrid. Let's hope it flowed as well in the evening.

Jane took her usual seat in the courtroom, and greeted her colleagues beside her who did the French to English and Russian to English translations. 'Happy New Year.' She put on her headphones. The American senior judge opened the session, so she didn't have to translate. She picked up the evidence pack for the day and thumbed through it to see any problem documents. Tables of information were particularly difficult as she had to listen to what the lawyer or witness said in German, interpret it into English, and try to follow the columns and rows in the table they referred to. But, at first glance, today looked okay. Then the French judge started to talk, and she passed the microphone and evidence pack to her colleague.

After her usual Wednesday lunch with Porritt, she pondered whether she should tell him about Andreas' proposal and long-term plans, but decided against it. She didn't want to raise any questions about her contract too early. Porritt announced that, from the end of January, he'd move to a fifty/fifty split between his duties in Nuremberg, and a new communications control service for the UK. Everyone wished him well.

In the evening, the court usually finished just before five. Jane had read the note from Gisela with instructions on the new traffic arrangements, and when she got back to the interpreters' room, called the transport office number. 'UK08 at five twelve, please.'

'That's confirmed,' came the reply.

She left the building on time, stood in the UK shelter, and sure enough her car came down the lane right on time. She got in and said to Josef, 'Well, that seemed to work okay. Looks like they've solved the gridlock problem at last.'

By the end of the week, everyone had got used to the new arrangements, and the whole sequence of cars arriving and departing worked smoothly. During the day, the girl, Astrid, helped out in the translation department with her fluent English, French and German.

She sometimes also joined the interpreter girls for lunch, and Jane discovered she'd recently married, and had come over to Nuremberg for three months with her husband, as part of the international press corps.

On the Saturday after New Year, after they attended Stephen's football game, Jane, Andreas and the boys went into town. They'd told the boys the previous evening they planned to get married, and the boys seemed content.

Andreas wanted to buy her an engagement ring, and so they visited a number of jewellery shops. Jane chose a beautiful, straight five diamond ring, and when Andreas slipped it on her finger, her heart leaped and she kissed him there and then in the shop. 'Euch,' said Stephen, echoed a second later by George.

They went to a tea room and Stephen glanced at the ring. 'Does that mean we should call you 'Daddy' now?' he asked.

Jane wondered how Andreas would answer that one.

He glanced at her and then leaned over towards Stephen. 'Only if you want to. But I'd be *very* honoured if you called me 'Daddy'.'

Stephen nodded seriously. 'Okay, then. I'll call you 'Daddy'.'

George piped up. 'Me too.'

Jane leaned over towards the boys. 'That's a really nice thing to do, boys. And it's very much appreciated by both of us.'

Stephen glanced over at her. 'That's okay, mummy. Alvin in my class at school says second daddies are *much* better than first daddies.'

Jane wondered what would come next. 'Why's that?'

'Because second daddies give you lots more dollars and presents than first daddies.'

Jane put her two hands up to hide her mouth and try to stop herself laughing. She glanced over at Andreas, who raised an eyebrow as though to say, 'That's boys for you.'

At work the following week, her female colleagues cooed over her ring and screamed with delight. Marie said, 'Oh, my God. Lucky, lucky you. He's such a catch.'

Porritt gave her his warmest congratulations. 'That's brilliant news. All the very best to both of you.'

Jane settled into her work pattern. She'd now largely forgotten about her 'Hermann pill' each day. And apart from the constant reminder of Josef, she'd forgotten about the invisible police presence that followed her and her children.

She found the Thursday, two weeks after New Year, a particularly tough day. The court heard evidence from inmates of the concentration camps, and she was 'on mic' for almost the whole day. Their stories were heartrending, and at times she had to swallow some water just to keep her voice steady. She felt relieved when the day ended, and she could book her car slot. 'UK08 at five fourteen, please.' She just wanted to get home.

'That's confirmed, Jane.' By now, all the transport people knew who was in each car.

She walked out to the UK shelter, and waited in the fresh air. Astrid came over in her *Kleppermantel*. 'I hear you had a tough day in court, Jane. You okay?'

'Yeah, I'm fine, thanks.'

Astrid smiled at her and checked her board. 'Oh, Josef called me twenty minutes ago. He's had a family emergency. Something about his father being rushed to hospital. He's got his colleague, Kurt, to collect you tonight, but he'll pick you up as usual in the morning.'

'Okay, that's fine. Thanks.' Just then, her car pulled up, and she got in, sighed, and put her head against thc back of her seat.

'Tough day, ma'am?'

She nodded and wiped her eyes. 'Yeah, tough day.'

Several cars waited to get out to the street. The driver said, 'I'm working with the Americans, ma'am. I've got some cans of orange juice here, straight from Florida. It's so sweet, it's unbelievable. Do you have children, ma'am?'

'Yeah, two.'

'I could get you a couple of cans for tomorrow. They're three marks each. I'll pass them on to Josef and you can pay him. Would you like to taste it? It's delicious.'

'Okay.'

He poured some juice from a tin into a plastic cup, and handed it back to her.

She'd heard a black market flourished on the American side, and tasted the juice. It was utterly delicious. Wow, her boys would love this. She snuggled into the comfortable seat. It had been a hell of a day. She put her head back and closed her eyes. Home in twenty minutes. Andreas would come over later. She needed a cuddle from him. She dreamed the car stopped briefly, and the girl Astrid got in, her *Kleppermantel* swishing as she settled herself in the front passenger seat, but that couldn't be. She loved her ring.

***

Porritt reread the letter from London, and grimaced. Shit, he really needed to get back there and take control of this communications project.

After the Aquila incident, Churchill grumbled that the British authorities had missed radio signals to and from abroad that had allowed Aquila to flourish. He'd asked Porritt and Sir John Halton, Porritt's ex-boss, to recommend what he should do about it.

They had examined the situation, talked to experts, and recommended the government should set up a specialist organisation, called Government Comunications Headquarters (GCHQ), with three broad aims. First, to gather information from all incoming and outgoing radio traffic with foreign countries; second, to secure the integrity of Britain's internal communications network; and third, since much of the data was coded, to extend the breadth and depth of the Code and Cypher Service at Bletchley Park, and integrate it with the new organisation. All of this would require a significant upgrade to existing capabilities.

Churchill had approved their recommendations, and asked them to draw up a plan on how to create such an organisation. Their initial assessment included the use of a Ministry of Defence site at Eastcote in North-West

London, and they developed plans on how best to use the site for their purposes.

Churchill had lost the General Election in July 1945, but in his hand over to Attlee, had emphasised the importance of the communications work. Attlee had supported it, but information on the plans had seeped out, and now it seemed every sofa strategist, academic and left-wing intellectual wanted to be part of it.

Porritt had blocked all of them in favour of experienced operations people who could bring a project to fruition, rather than those cerebral time-wasters, whose idea of action was to set up a sub-committee. But he now faced pressure from Whitehall mandarins, who had accrued influence, but little ability, to include some of these talking-shop veterans.

Fortunately, he didn't need to spend as much time now in Nuremberg, and could devote more time to the new project. But the letter indicated it might take more than he expected.

His phone rang. 'Hello?'

'Mister Porritt, this is the mother of Jane Thomson.' He recognised her voice and limited English. 'Jane is not home now, but did not phone. I'm worried.'

He glanced at his watch, ten to six. 'Let me check, Mrs Wiseman. She may still be here at a VIP reception.'

'Thank you.'

He called Gisela. 'Is Jane Thomson on duty at a reception tonight?'

'No, sir. It's just a small local reception. We didn't need a translator.'

'Well, she hasn't arrived home and didn't phone, so her mother's worried.'

'Okay, I'll call the transport office and find out when she left.'

'I'll see you down there.' He packed his papers and headed for the main door.

Gisela said, 'She asked for a five fourteen slot and got picked up then, sir.'

'Then something must have happened on the way home. Check with the ambulance service and see if there have been any accidents with one of our cars? I'll call the police.'

'Yes, sir.' She picked up the phone and talked rapidly in German.

Porritt called Hans Wolff. 'Hans, we seem to have lost Jane Thomson. She got picked up at five fourteen, but hasn't arrived home. Could you check with the tailing car?'

'Yeah, will do. Did Josef pick her up?'

'I assume so.' Just then, Josef appeared. 'No, he didn't. He's just walked into the office.'

'Let me speak to him.'

Josef talked rapidly in German and eventually handed the phone back to Porritt.

'Jonathan, the transport office told Josef to pick up Jane from a reception in the Garden Room at six. When she didn't appear, he went in to find her, but she hadn't been there. He then came round to the transport office to find out what happened.'

'Exactly who told him that?'

'Put him on the line again.'

Again, Josef talked rapidly in German, then handed the phone to Porritt.

'He says Marta, in the staging area, told him, but he thinks Astrid told her. Let me make a couple of phone calls from here, and I'll then come over to you.'

'Okay, I'll try to find Astrid.'

Gisela came off the phone. 'The ambulance service says there's been no road accidents in the last hour that would fit.'

Porritt felt his heart beat faster. 'Okay, Gisela, could you find Astrid, please?'

Gisela talked to the man in the transport office in German, then turned to Porritt. 'Astrid left about half an hour ago to go home.'

'See if you can phone her at home, please.'

Gisela got the number from the man, and phoned. 'No reply.' She hung up.

Porritt thought for a moment. 'She's married to someone in the press corps. Can you remember his name?'

Gisela thought. 'Erm. Rhys?'

'See if he's still here. These chaps file their stories, so they're always late leaving.'

Gisela picked up the phone again. 'All lines are engaged, sir. I'll go and find him.'

'Thanks.' Porritt took a big breath. What else could he do? It was a bugger that he couldn't speak or understand German.

A few minutes later Gisela returned with a man in his forties. 'This is Geert Rhys, sir.'

Porritt shook his hand. 'Do you speak English?'

'*Ja*. Of course.'

'Do you know where your wife is?'

Rhys looked puzzled. 'Yeah, she's at home.'

'There's no reply at the number we have. Can you check, please?'

He shrugged. 'Yeah, if you like.'

He picked up the phone and talked in German. In a few moments he said, 'Hi Astrid, it's me. Hang on a minute.' He looked at Porritt. 'What is it you want to ask her?'

Porritt thought for a moment. ‘I want to know why she told Josef here to go and collect Jane Thomson at the Garden Room.’

Rhys looked blank. ‘That doesn’t make sense.’

‘Why not?’

‘Well, why would she talk to him?’ he asked, and pointed at Josef.

‘Because she’s in charge of transport here, and he’s one of the drivers.’ He knew as he said it what was coming, and a pit developed in his stomach.

‘But she’s at home in Amsterdam.’

Porritt dropped his head. Shit. Shit. Shit. He’d been duped by these people again. Yet the girl had used Rhys’s wife’s name, Astrid. She must have met him to know that. He held up a finger. ‘Hold it. Please stay here. I’ll be back in a moment.’

He left the office and ran back up to his own office, searched through his filing cabinet, and found the photo of the couple Sandra had sent over weeks ago. He grabbed two copies and headed back downstairs.

‘Have a look at this. Have you ever met this couple before?’

Rhys studied the picture and shook his head. ‘Don’t think so.’

Porritt looked at the picture. Why wouldn’t he recognise the girl. Then it hit him. Astrid had jet black hair, but the girl in the photo was blonde. He took a pencil and blacked in her hair. ‘Do you recognise her now?’

Rhys glanced at the picture. ‘Sure. I met her and her husband at a hotel here before Christmas. But I’m not sure it’s this lad. He had dark hair and a moustache.’

Porritt got the pencil again and darkened the man’s hair, and drew a moustache.

Rhys nodded. ‘Yeah, that’s them.’

Porritt took a deep breath and exhaled. Jane had been kidnapped. Again. Now what should he do? First of all, deal with the family. 'Can you get me Andreas on the phone, please, Gisela?'

'Of course.' In a moment she handed the phone to Porritt.

'Andreas, it's Jonathan Porritt here.'

'Yes, sir.'

'Something's happened to Jane. She's disappeared for the moment. Could you get round to her family, please. They'll need some support.'

'Oh, my God. What's happened?'

'Remember we talked before Christmas about her being a target? Well, it looks like they've managed to get her. They switched her car this evening. Now, there's another police car on her tail for just this possibility, but we haven't heard from them yet.'

'My God. What else can I do?'

'If you could keep her mother and children calm, that would be a great help. I'll let you know more when I can, though it may be tomorrow.'

'Okay, I'll get round to her mother now.'

'Thanks. Tell her we're doing all we can to find Jane and bring her back safe. I still believe she's not in any danger.' He hung up, and hoped his words were true. Then Hans Wolff arrived.

'What's happening?' he asked. 'Any progress?'

Porritt quickly updated him. 'What about the tailing car? Have you heard from them?'

'We haven't, Jonathan. All our car phones are down. We don't know why.'

Wolff turned to Josef and asked him a couple of questions. Then turned and talked to Gisela. She gave him the piece of paper with Astrid's phone number, and dashed out of the room. Wolff picked up the phone and issued instructions to someone.

Porritt felt impotent, with all the discussions going on in German, and waited for Wolff to clear his phone call. Gisela rushed back into the room and handed Wolff another piece of paper. He talked on the phone, then hung up and turned to Porritt.

'Right, Jonathan. This girl, Astrid, instructed Josef to go to the North Door to get him out of the way. She's then organised a similar car to pick up Jane, and must have given her a plausible story so she wasn't suspicious, even though Josef wasn't the driver. So, we're on the lookout for a black Mercedes 170.

'Unfortunately, we don't know the reg number of the car. I've sent a team to the address we've got for Astrid to see if we can pick up any info on the car or on them. I assume the driver's her husband or boyfriend. I've also issued instructions to all our police colleagues in adjacent states, to stop all Mercedes 170 cars and verify the occupants. But there are lots of them, so it's a bit of a long shot.'

He turned to Rhys, who looked bewildered.

'Now, sir,' he said, in English. 'You met this couple some weeks ago. Can you tell me how you met and anything about them?'

'I met them in the Hotel Royale bar. That's where a lot of the press corps stays. I had ordered some drinks at the bar, and I guess she heard the Dutch accent. She said, 'It's a long way from Amsterdam,' or something like that. I took the drinks to my party and came back to the bar to chat with them, just to be polite, really. Very pleasant couple. He's an engineer for boiler controls in power stations, and works for a Dutch company. Just after the war, they got a contract for a power station in Dortmund. They then saw a big opportunity, and phoned other power stations in Germany. They picked up a lot of business that way.

'He was allocated this job in Nuremberg, and they decided to take a delayed honeymoon in the Black Forest. He's not Dutch, though he spoke the language well. They asked about Nuremberg, about the trial, and how we reported the stories. The total conversation was maybe fifteen minutes, twenty tops. And that's it. Never saw them again.'

'Didn't you see her here? She organised he transport office, I believe.'

He shook his head. 'The press pack use the East Door, so we're never round this side.'

'I see, sir. What I'd now like you to do is to keep very quiet about this. Please don't talk about it to anyone. Would you do that for me, please?'

He nodded. 'Sure, though it sounds like a good story.'

Wolff turned to Porritt and waved for him to say something.

'Mr Rhys. I'm Commander Porritt, Head of the British Delegation here. We would really appreciate it if you kept this very quiet. If you agree to do so, I promise, at some point in the future, when it's all done and dusted, I'll give you an exclusive insight into *some* aspects of the story that you can publish. Do you agree?'

Rhys pursed his lips and nodded. 'I agree.'

'Thank you,' Porritt said, and shook his hand. 'I'll let you get back to work.'

Rhys left the room.

The phone rang. Gisela picked it up, listened, and passed the phone to Wolff.

Wolff listened, asked a few questions, and then hung up. He turned to Porritt. 'Well, now we know why our car phones went down. The cable to the aerial up on the hilltop was cut with an axe. Someone planned this *very* carefully.'

Porritt shook his head. Shit, these people sure were serious. He just hoped Jane would be safe. He glanced at his watch. Quarter to seven. It would be a long night.

The phone rang again. Gisela passed it to Wolff. He listened, asked a few questions again, then hung up. He looked grim. 'The car on Jane's tail has just called in from a town called Würzburg, about a hundred kilometres away. They lost them. They had to stop for fuel before they got stranded. They say the crooks could have continued on the A3 westward to Frankfurt, or taken the A7 north to Hanover. We've asked the relevant police to set up road blocks on both these roads, but there's a hundred side roads they could take. To be honest, Jonathan, I think we're stuck until we hear from them.'

Chapter 12. Friday 18 January

Jane woke in a strange room. A comfortable bed, though. She still wore her outdoor clothes under a thick warm blanket. She let her eyes roam round the room. A mirror and dressing table at the foot of the bed; a wardrobe beside it; a table with two chairs at the window; a small chest of drawers beside the bed, with her handbag on it; an open door beyond that; a bookcase on the back wall; all in the same beige colour. Kind of like a hospital, she thought.

She swung her legs off the bed and sat up, but still felt woozy. Her shoes lay neatly beside the bed, adjacent to some fluffy slippers. She struggled to her feet. The open door led to a bathroom. She staggered in and had a pee. She closed her eyes and tried to think what had happened. She'd drank some delicious orange juice in the car. 'Straight from Florida,' the driver said. Laced with sleeping draught, she now realised.

Jesus, it had happened again. The last time she'd been kidnapped, she'd been fully aware of it. This time, she couldn't remember a thing. She tried to think back to her discussion with Porritt. He didn't think she'd be in danger. They'd merely want to ask her what happened to the spy, Brenner, he'd said.

But why all the cloak and dagger stuff? Why couldn't they just come and ask? Her head cleared a bit. Because, Porritt had said, they wanted to use her to flush out the top decision maker who'd wrecked their precious Aquila organisation. And that was him. She was the bait to get him to break cover.

Now she'd gone through the logic again, she felt more confident she could handle whatever would come. But oh, how she wished she had Andreas at her side right now. She kissed her ring, and wondered about her family. What information would they have, and would Porritt have organised a search?

She flushed the toilet, slunged cold water on her face, and looked at herself in the mirror. 'Come on, girl. You can do this,' she whispered. 'You've done it before, and you can do it again.' She brushed her hair, washed her hands, and got ready to face Aquila. She'd make her approach interested, rather than frightened, though frankly, she felt closer to the latter.

She glanced at her watch – ten fifteen – and went back through to the bedroom to draw the curtains. Just some roofs and some trees beyond, a church in the distance. Could be anywhere. There was a knock at the door. 'Come in,' she shouted.

The door unlocked and a young girl came in dressed in a maid's uniform. A big man in a white jacket and black trousers loomed in the doorway.

'Can I get you a light breakfast, ma'am?' the maid asked, in German. 'Maybe some tea and a croissant? Doctor G has invited you to lunch with him at twelve thirty, ma'am.'

'Who's Doctor G?'

'He's our boss, ma'am.'

'Boss of what?'

'Just the boss, ma'am.'

She wouldn't get anything further. 'Tea and a croissant will be fine, thank you.'

'I'll just be a few minutes, ma'am.' The girl left the room and the door locked behind her. Oh well, at least she'd meet the boss soon.

***

Dave Burnett got into the office early. Today, his Aquila plans would all come together, hopefully. Three years ago, Porritt had pulled off a real coup with his Aquila raids. Now, this was *his* first big nationwide job since he'd taken over Special Branch last June. He thought of it as Aquila Two, and needed it to go at least as well as Porritt's.

He'd read all of Porritt's notes, talked to him a couple of times on the phone to clarify details, and now planned to follow a similar approach. He had the advantage of having led the raid on the spymaster's house in Yorkshire last time, and could clearly remember the three keys to success then – immobilise the targets within five seconds to prevent them using a panic button – beware of booby traps that could destroy key data, so have a good safecracker on the raid team – and have a good codebreaker available, to decode the data.

When Porritt had taken over Special Branch in the early years of the war, he had reorganised it into eighteen regions. When *he* had taken over six months ago, he'd integrated some of the more remote areas that had been strategic in wartime, but were now not so important, and had reduced the number of regions to eleven. He still kept the big four – London; the North West; the North East; and the West Midlands – which together covered about two-thirds of the UK population. He then had seven other regions that covered the rest. It was now much more manageable, and during the handover, Porritt had given him excellent advice on his top people, so he now had the best eleven of his team as regional heads.

He'd talked to each of them during the week, and explained the plan in detail. From the phone taps and films at the two Aquila bases, in Amsterdam and West

Hampstead, they had gradually compiled details of each of the twenty-seven drug distributors in the UK, with names and addresses, and photographs. He'd passed on the details to each regional head. Some had only one distributor to deal with, but others had several. London had eight.

He planned to raid all known suppliers at two o'clock in the morning on Sunday, and immobilise them within the five-second target. At the same time, Malcolm Craig would raid the main distributor in West Hampstead, and capture the names and addresses of each target. These would then be checked against the current master list at Scotland Yard, and any anomalies advised to the relevant regional head, who would then take appropriate action. As far as he knew, they had identified and resolved any false IDs, but could only confirm that once the lists were compared.

At the same time as the raids on the 'legs' in the UK, raids would also be made on the 'head' of the organisation in Germany, and on the 'body' in Amsterdam, under the leadership of Sandra Maxwell.

All the raids, with the exception of Amsterdam, would be made under the amendment to the Emergency Powers (Defence) (No 2) Act 1940, which had come into force on 9th of January, and published by the Government as normal. It effectively brought drugs such as methamphetamine under the same category as cocaine and heroin, and hence illegal to possess or supply in the UK.

He'd prepared well, and awaited the arrival of his team, Malcolm Craig and Sandra Maxwell, with Bill Franklin, who had done such great work lubricating the Home Office machine. They were shown into his office at half past nine.

Burnett welcomed them and shook hands. 'Morning, everyone. Well, I trust? Looking forward to an interesting weekend? Right, let's get started. Malcolm, you first.'

'Right, sir. West Hampstead. We're pretty much ready now. We'll approach the property from the trees at the rear, and we've figured out a way we can deal with the dog and the alarm, immobilise Lyall, and get in fast. We've used something similar before, and we've tested it at the police driving centre.' He went on to give them details of the plan.

'We'll go in with a team of sixteen. Each one knows exactly what they've got to do. We have female officers for the children, and a handler for the dog.

'We don't know if they'll have a booby trap to protect their data, but we now have a good safecracker on the team – the same one I used before. And we also have a codebreaker lined up from Bletchley Park to help us decode. So we're all set there.

'In terms of the London region, we have eight suppliers that we'll raid at the same time. Brian Walker's in charge of that lot, and each raid will be led by a CI or above. Each team leader has done a recce on their target, and has a plan to meet our five-second objective. We reviewed each plan on Wednesday. We think, based on what Sandra found in Glasgow, the suppliers will use the writing bureau and / or the special suitcase to hide drugs and money. We've given each team leader Sandra's note on how to get into them. We did another review with each team leader yesterday, and everyone seemed happy.

'On the wider front, our phone taps show the suppliers moved a total of over six thousand tablets last week. That's a fifty percent increase in a month, a hell of a rate of growth. Oh, and there was a call from a GB29. So, that means we need to find two more. Hopefully, we'll get that information on Sunday. Alison will still match the lists, sir?'

'Yeah. She did a great job last time. Couldn't go past her for this.'

'Good, so that's it from me, sir.'

'Right, Sandra, what about you?'

'Okay. First, let me give you some info on the Glasgow supplier. By chance, I saw a well-known Glasgow criminal carrying a GT Pharma suitcase off a train, just before Christmas. That means organised crime has muscled their way into this business. And they've poured resources into it. We've got photos of them doing business in several Glasgow pubs and nightclubs. Malcolm's also got pictures of them at West Hampstead, picking up more supplies. So, I just hope it's the crime family boss who's on the new Glasgow contract. I'd love to put him away. But they're well organised, and keep IDs well hidden, so let's not underestimate the problems once organised crime gets involved.'

Burnett nodded. 'Yeah, well said, Sandra. Sounds like we're not a moment too soon.'

'Right. Now Amsterdam, sir. I talked to Guus Mulder yesterday, and he's all set to raid the GT Pharma premises at three a.m. local time on Sunday. He's got clearance from the Dutch equivalent of the Home Secretary. So, that's good.'

'It's great. Well done, to you both.'

'Now, to Germany, sir. I talk to Major Conway pretty much every day. He has several covert teams trying to find out more about this GT Pharma company. We can't tap their phones without alerting the German telephone company, which would just alert the GT company, so Conway's tailed their vans. They have a weekly delivery run to Amsterdam, and we've got the evidence to prove it in court. They also have twice weekly runs to the major cities of North, West and South Germany. That's a lot of tablets on the move.

'However, just after New Year, they followed a car south to a town called Marburg in the American Zone. It offloaded at a factory identical to the one at base. It also had a plate on the wall, GT Pharma GmbH, so it looks like a duplicate factory for making these pills. Vans from there deliver to the cities of East Germany and to Prague, which seems to be the equivalent of Amsterdam for servicing eastern bloc countries.

'Without giving anything away, Conway got one of Monty's senior people to contact his American equivalent, and ask him if they'd ever close the Marburg factory, as it made illegal products. The word came back they wouldn't, because Marburg needs every job it can get. They aim to get the American Zone up to self sufficiency as soon as possible. That means, sadly, if we close our factory, it won't be the end of these tablets in Europe.'

Burnett had listened patiently to Sandra. He pursed his lips. 'Shit. That's a bit of a blow, huh? But it doesn't stop us doing the job the HS wants done. To stop these drugs in this country. That's our objective. Once we've killed the business here, it'll be a lot more difficult to start up again, particularly when it's illegal. What else have you got, Sandra?'

'Right, we still have to decide if we try the head of the GT Pharma group here?'

Bill cut in. 'I've now got the answer to that, Sandra. All the trials in the UK will take place in special courts, almost like court martials, with no public present. The HS has talked to Monty about it, and they feel, if we put the head man on trial in Germany, it would become a distraction. They want him tried here out of the limelight.'

'Fine. We'll bring him back here, then. That's it from me, sir. We're off to Germany now. The plans look good, and all being well, we should see you here on Monday.'

'Brilliant. Thanks, Sandra. Anything from you, Bill?'

'No, I'm clear, sir. But I'd just like to add something a colleague told me last week. Ignorance of the law doesn't excuse the crime.'

Burnett laughed. 'Well said, Bill. I wish you two a safe trip to Germany, and look forward to a successful outcome over the weekend. Let's make it happen.'

***

Sam came round from behind his desk and sat against the front edge. Johnny placed a single chair about six feet in front of him, and stood behind it. Eddie sat over at the conference table. Sam buzzed his secretary. 'Ask Cammy to come in.'

The office door opened, and a thin-faced man in his thirties peeped round it.

Sam waved him in. 'Come in, Cammy. Take a seat.' He indicated the single chair.

Cammy looked around nervously, and shambled across to the chair.

Sam looked down at him. 'We've known each other a long time, Cammy, and so I was disappointed when Eddie told me you were twenty quid short at the Ashton last night, with no reason. Do you want to tell me about it?'

Cammy sat with his hands clutched in front of him, and looked at the floor.

After a few minutes silence, Sam lifted his index fingers a fraction, and nodded. Johnny hauled the man to his feet. Sam took a couple of paces forward and punched the man hard in the stomach. The man collapsed on the floor, moaning. Johnny hauled him back onto the chair. He sat with his head bowed, holding his stomach.

'Now, Cammy. Can you hear me?' The man nodded. 'Don't annoy me. We don't need this. But you stole twenty quid from me last night, and I want to know why.'

Sam waited. Still no response. He looked at Johnny and briefly nodded. Johnny hauled the man up again, and Sam punched him even harder in the stomach. The man cried out, and collapsed again on the floor. Johnny hauled him back onto the seat again, and he sat doubled over, moaning, and holding his stomach.

Sam sat back on the edge of his desk. 'Cammy, we've already spoken to Barry and Fraser this morning. Barry says you went out to the toilet at one point, and asked *him* to take over the table for a minute. But you were away for over ten minutes. What happened?'

Cammy muttered something.

'Come again, Cammy? I didn't catch it.'

'I got robbed.'

'Oh.' Sam exchanged glances with Eddie. 'Really? At the urinals or the sinks?'

'In the cubicle.'

Sam's mouth fell open. This guy, Cammy, must be a bloody shirtlifter. Why didn't he know that? Yet he's married with a family. Jesus Christ, no wonder he didn't want to talk about it. 'So, he robbed you with your trousers round your ankles? Is that it?'

Cammy nodded.

Sam sighed. 'You know, Cammy? I don't give a shit what you do in your own time. You can play with as many willies as you want. But when you work for me, I want your mind on the job. I've got to have people I can rely on. And you're not one of them.'

Cammy looked up. 'It's a one off, Sam. I'll pay it back.'

'Oh, that you definitely will. By tomorrow night. Leave an envelope with my secretary. And if you don't, we'll come after you. You're fired. Get him out of here.'

Johnny hauled him to his feet again and ushered him out the door.

Sam looked over at Eddie and shook his head. 'Can you believe it? Do these guys play with every willy they see? Jesus Christ, I don't get it.' He sighed. 'Can you get someone else to handle the Ashton?'

Eddie nodded. 'Yeah, leave it with me. I'd better get our blokes out for the lunchtime meets. He pulled his case up onto the table, opened it and pulled out his notebook. The teams came into the room, one by one, and signed for the number of tablets they asked for.

Sam just sat and watched the procession. Eddie sure had this business well organised

***

Jane tried to keep calm. After all, she had nothing to hide. Just be frank and honest.

She leafed through a book about Paris. Maybe some day she'd go there with Andreas. She kissed her ring. She felt him beside her, strong, sensible, with that great smile. With his help, she'd get through this okay. There was a knock at the door.

'Come in.'

The same maid appeared. 'Doctor G's ready for you now, ma'am.'

Jane took a big sigh. Keep it simple. Nothing to hide. She lifted her handbag, followed the girl along a thickly carpeted corridor, downstairs to the floor below, and entered a dining room. It had a long table set with two places at the far end, and a sideboard along the end wall. Behind the chair at the head of the table stood an elderly man, of medium height, with grey hair, rimless glasses, and a pleasant smile.

'Come in, my dear. It's a pleasure to meet you,' he said, in German. 'First, let me apologise for the means of bringing you here, but you were well protected in Nuremberg, so we didn't have much choice. I'm Doctor G. Just call me G. May I call you Jane?'

She pursed her lips. He seemed pleasant enough. But, don't smile back at him. It's not a pleasure being here, no matter how comfortable he makes it. 'If you like.'

'Thank you. Will you please join me?' He indicated the place setting on the long side of the table to his left. As she stepped forward, a butler came from behind her somewhere and dashed forward to pull out her chair. He pushed it into place as she sat down, then went and stood at the sideboard behind G.

'We have smoked salmon from Norway as a starter. Would you like that, Jane?'

Bloody hell, she thought. Nothing but the best. 'That would be very nice, thank you.'

The butler brought two plates over from the sideboard, serving her first. It certainly looked delicious, she thought. He then brought her small slices of buttered brown bread and placed two of them on her side plate.

G splayed his hands, palms upwards. 'Please, enjoy.' He lifted the small knife and fork from the outside of the place setting, cut off a piece of the salmon, and swallowed it, followed by a taste of the bread.

She did the same. The salmon tasted delicious. She'd never had it before.

'I understand you're a translator at the trial in Nuremberg. How's that going?'

She thought for a moment. 'Harrowing at times.'

'Yes, I can imagine it must be difficult. What do you translate from and to?'

'German to English.'

'And which are you, German or English?'

'Neither. I'm Czech. Born in Prague. But my father was German, originally from Dresden, so I spoke German from a young age. We then moved as a family to England in 1935. Hence, I'm fluent in both languages.'

'Ah, I see. Why did you move to England?'

'My uncle in Dresden got hassle from the Hitler Youth. Someone alleged we had a Jewish ancestor, though none of us knew anything about him. Total rubbish, but mud sticks. My father also thought Hitler would invade Czechoslovakia, and didn't fancy that, so the two families left and went to England. The men were master tailors, and made successful businesses over there. We settled in Glasgow, Scotland.'

'Ah, Scotland. I visited there in '37 I think. Stayed in a cold castle somewhere up north, but it had wonderful grouse shooting. Beautiful country.' He turned and waved the butler over to the table. 'We have lamb or fish for the main course. Which would you prefer?'

'Lamb, please..'

'Make that two, Otto, thanks.'

The butler removed the starter plates and pressed a button on the wall above the sideboard. The maid arrived, the butler gave her instructions, and she left. Jane casually glanced round the room. On the right hand side of the sideboard stood an array of photographs, and she was stunned to see the one on the extreme right had

G posing beside Hitler. She put her hand to her mouth. My God.

He noticed her look, and glanced round. 'Ah, yes, the Fuhrer. We had mutual friends, you know. I met him several times. That was taken at Nuremberg, incidentally. At the big rally in '38. The high point of it all. The Rally of Greater Germany, we called it. We had just annexed Austria, and thought the world was our oyster. But sadly, most of Europe and the world didn't agree with our *Neuordnung* vision, and put a stop to it. A hard pill to swallow.'

The maid came back, pushing a trolley, and the butler served two plates covered with cloches. He lifted the cloches to reveal two thick slices of lamb steaming on each plate. When had she last seen slices of meat that thick? He then served potatoes, carrots and peas. She had heard the Germans were on starvation rations, but not here. One law for the rich, she thought. The maid departed with the trolley, and the butler returned to his stance at the sideboard.

'*Guten Appetit*,' G said, and lifted his knife and fork.

She cut some lamb and tasted it. God, it was perfect. G sure had a great cook.

'However, that brings us to the subject of our discussion, my dear. It's about a man, whom you probably knew as Karl Brenner. Do you remember him?'

She pursed her lips and glanced at him. 'Oh, yes, I remember him. He kidnapped me and threatened to rape me. I'm not likely to forget him.'

'Yes, I'm sorry about that. Please accept my personal apologies. Brenner was far too impetuous. I instructed Kay to release you as soon as possible, but he had to remain covert, and we also had to get Brenner back here quickly. In the end, we agreed, when Brenner got on the plane in Ireland, we'd leave you behind. We were sure you didn't know Kay's location, and by the time you contacted the British authorities, Brenner would be long gone, and Kay would have moved and changed identity.

'But, of course, Brenner never arrived at the plane. We had no idea what happened to him. We tried to call Kay, but couldn't get him. We tried others, with no result. Our whole organisation had just been wiped out overnight. How could that happen?

'It took us a long time to work our way back up the chain from Ireland, into Northern Ireland, and eventually we found Sergeant Brown in prison in England. I'm sure you also remember him. We had tasked him with your protection until Brenner got on the plane.

'However, he told us with regret, he'd accepted a bribe from Brenner to let him be alone with you on the ferry. And that's when something went seriously wrong for us. I'd very much like to know what happened. Could you tell me, please?'

She finished a mouthful of the delicious food. 'Well, I can tell you what happened to Brenner, and I know Commander Porritt captured all the Aquila people that night, but I don't know the details. You'd need to ask him.'

'Ah, Commander Porritt, you say.' He took a note on the pad at his side. 'Okay, let's first talk about Brenner. His mother grieves for him, and needs closure. I promised to find out what happened to him. Hence the subterfuge to get you here.'

She glanced at him, and snapped, 'Including killing my ex-husband along the way.'

He stared at her for a few moments, then dropped his gaze. 'Yes, that was very unfortunate. But for my man, it was kill or be killed. Your ex-husband attacked him with a gun, because he asked questions about you.'

Her jaw dropped. Tommy? A gun? He could be stupid and aggressive at times, but why would he have a gun? 'I don't believe that.'

He showed surprise. 'Well, I questioned my man at length about it, and I do believe him. They had a fierce fight down by the river, the gun fell in the water, they struggled on the bank, and your ex-husband slipped into the river.'

'Couldn't your man have caught him?'

'Of course, he could. But why should he? Your ex-husband was trying to kill him. And I should add your ex-husband did *not* reveal where you were. My man worked out you were in Nuremberg from hints he got from others there.'

She suddenly felt a pang for Tommy. If what this man said was true, he'd done his best to protect her, and paid the ultimate price. Maybe he'd had some love and respect for her after all, though she'd rarely seen it. Poor Tommy.

G broke the silence. 'So, I'm sorry that happened, my dear. Can we go on?'

It was the only way she'd get out of this. She nodded.

'Thank you. Going back to Brenner. You say he threatened to rape you. How did you know that? Did he attack you?'

'No. He was very lovey-dovey. Too much so. He tried to convince me we had a future together. Talked about a wonderful life in Germany after the war. Bit mad really. I went along with it because it was my only chance to get free. But I overheard him one night ask Elizabeth Kay for the key to my room. He wanted to make love to me to keep me compliant. She refused, and told him that was just rape. They had a furious row. But she took my side. In fact, she slipped me a knife for protection. One of those where the blade springs out.'

'A stiletto?'

'That's right.'

'*Mein Gott*. And would you have used it?'

'Of course. I got ready to use it when he took me out on deck. We had never been alone before, and he went all lovey-dovey again. But he held me too tight in a very dark corner. I thought he planned to attack me and then throw me overboard. But he suddenly felt sea sick, and stood on the rail to lean out and retch. He leaned out further, just as the boat wobbled in the heavy sea, and fell overboard.'

'*Mein Gott*. Couldn't you have caught him?'

'Of course, I could. But he was trying to kill me.' She stopped, stunned at the parallels with what he'd just said about Tommy's death. Was she right to say that? But it's what happened. Don't say any more.

He stared at her. 'Then what happened?'

'I dashed up to the ship's bridge, and asked the captain for help. There were police on board, and they arrested Brown and Henry.'

'And what about Brenner?'

'They recovered his body the following day. I identified it at the mortuary in Belfast. I don't know what happened to it afterwards. I think Porritt arranged the burial.'

'And then?'

'Porritt arrested everyone in the UK connected with Aquila that same night.'

He stared at his plate for several minutes.

'I think I'd like to talk to Mr,' he looked at his notes, 'Sorry, Commander Porritt. Where is he? In London?'

'No, he's in Nuremberg. He's the head of the British delegation there.'

'I see.' He thought for a moment. 'Is that why you were so well protected?'

She shrugged. 'Not really. When Porritt heard the Glasgow police had put my ex-husband's death down to suicide, he became suspicious, and started an investigation to see if my ex-husband had been targeted by the Aquila organisation as a step to find me. Porritt thought they'd want to know what had happened to Brenner, and I was the only one who knew. The investigation showed he *had* been targeted, and so Porritt arranged for extra security for me from Hans Wolff of the Nuremberg police.'

'Ah, Hans Wolff, I've met him. A good man.' He paused. 'So, the Glasgow police put your ex-husband's death down to suicide, but Porritt's investigation changed that?'

She nodded. 'That's how I understand it.'

'That's very interesting. And Porritt expected we would want to talk to you?'

She nodded. 'Yes. Hence the extra security.'

He sat and pondered for several minutes. 'Would Commander Porritt talk to me?'

She shrugged. 'I don't know. Why don't you ask him?'

'Does he speak German?'

'No.'

'Well, I don't have good enough English. Could you ask him for me?'

'Yes, I could do that.'

'Thank you. But first, let's finish lunch.' He waved the butler over to the table. 'We have a very fine dessert from Italy called tiramisu. It's coffee flavoured, and I find it utterly delicious. Would you like some?'

'Yes, thank you, I'll try that.' Might as well enjoy it, she thought.

***

Porritt watched Cassie leave the room. He banged his fist on the table. 'Shit. Shit.'

Hans Wolff turned from the window. 'What's wrong?'

Porritt shook his head. 'Oh, nothing.' He paused. 'Well, everything, actually. She's my new assistant, and she's very good. But I have to spell everything out. The last girl could almost read my mind. She'll eventually tune in to me, but it just adds to the frustration.

'And I've got a bunch of useless intellectual pilloocks who want to muscle in on my latest project. I really need to get to London to swat them off. And then, of course, there's Jane. It's nearly twenty two hours since she disappeared, and not a word. Shit!'

He shook his head again. 'I can't believe we got duped so easily, Hans. I mean, this girl Astrid, real name Annika, fooled me good and proper. You've got to hand it to them. They're clever and cunning. We knew that from the last time, but it still hurts.'

Wolff snorted. 'I know. Josef blames himself. And we've had nothing from the road blocks. How're the family doing?'

'Oh, they're just worried out their minds. Andreas, her fiancé, has done his best to keep them calm, but it's not easy. The kids ask all sorts of questions. It's tough for them.'

Then the phone rang. Wolff came over to the desk and waited till Porritt lifted the receiver. Wolff lifted the ear piece extension to listen in. 'Porritt.'

'Sir, it's me, Jane.'

'Jane! Thank God. Are you okay? Where are you?'

'I'm fine, sir. I don't know where I am, but I'm with a man called Doctor G. He's the head of the Aquila organisation, and would like to speak to you. But he doesn't speak good English, and has asked me to translate.'

Porritt glanced up at Wolff. 'Okay.' He heard Jane talk in German, and the man talk back to her. She then translated his words as he spoke.

'Commander Porritt, thank you for agreeing to speak with me. For some years now, unknown to both of us, we've been adversaries. Sometimes we won. Sometimes you won. But, in the end, you were the victor. I've now learned you wiped out our entire organisation in Britain in one night. I acknowledge that as a formidable feat. I hope, though, you consider us a worthy adversary, as I do you.'

Porritt nodded. 'Indeed I do. You didn't make it easy.' He heard G chuckle.

'Thank you. For reasons I won't go into, I don't have much time left, but I'd very much like to meet you face to face, to get closure for the family of the man you knew as Karl Brenner, and perhaps learn of our mistakes. Not that we would, or could, ever do it again. I'm afraid these days are well and truly over. But it would close a chapter for me that was, in some ways, perhaps, unique in human history. I'd like to invite you to join me for dinner tomorrow evening. I'll send a car for you in Nuremberg tomorrow morning. It's a six hour journey up to here, but that would give you time to relax before dinner. I can assure you it will be a superb meal by any standards. You can then stay overnight – we're very comfortable here – and the car will take you and Jane back to Nuremberg on Sunday. What do you think?'

Porritt looked up at Wolff, who indicated to him they needed to speak before he answered. 'Could you hold on a moment, please?' Porritt put his hand over the phone and held it down at his side.

Wolff leaned over and whispered. 'You can't go there on your own, Jonathan. That's the lion's den. You don't know what's waiting for you. He was your enemy, for Chrissake. I'll come with you, armed.'

Porritt heard Jane call on the line. 'Hello, sir? Hello, sir?'

He held the phone to his ear. 'Yes, Jane.'

'Doctor G wants to say something.'

'Okay.'

'Commander Porritt, you may be concerned about your personal security while you're here. I can assure you that you'll be perfectly safe. I've too much respect for you to play tricks. But I understand from Jane that Direktor Wolff organised her security, and probably organises yours. I know him from the past. He's a good man. And if you'd feel more comfortable, I'm happy for him to accompany you. In fact, I'll give you an even better guarantee of your safety. I'll send my son, Manfred, down with the car, and you can lock him in a cell somewhere as security until you return. It won't do him any harm, and it may give you extra reassurance.'

'Hold on again, please.' Porritt again held the phone at his side.

Wolff leaned over. 'I don't know this man, Jonathan. But we were always on security duty for VIPs at the big Nazi rallies here, so he's presumably one of those. Ask him how we'll know it's his son.'

Porritt lifted the phone and asked the question.

'He'll carry photographic evidence Wolff will recognise.'

Wolff indicated it sounded okay.

'All right, Doctor G. I'll accept your invitation, but I would like Direktor Wolff with me, and your son here as extra security.'

'That's fine, Commander. Thank you so much. The car will arrive at police HQ around nine-thirty tomorrow.'

'Yes, fine.'

'Good. Look forward to seeing you tomorrow, then.'

'Yes. See you tomorrow, And you too, Jane.'

Porritt hung up and smiled at Wolff. 'More or less what we expected, but with a twist.'

'That's for sure. Roll on tomorrow.'

***

Amid flurries of light snow, Sandra dashed across the tarmac to Conway's car. She'd just flown in to RAF Güttersloh on an RAF Transport plane that ran a shuttle service from RAF Hendon for senior staff. It had been her worst journey ever. Nearly two hours in a noisy aircraft, on uncomfortable padded canvas seats, knee to knee with the man on the other side of the plane, she was glad it was over. She turned to Bill, next to her in the rear seat, 'I'll never complain about a commercial flight ever again.'

He laughed. 'Well, at least it got you here quicker.'

The three of them settled around the conference table in Conway's office, at the huge British army base in Bielefeld. Conway started the meeting. 'Right, Sandra, it's your show. We're here to help you in whatever way we can. This afternoon, we'll make sure we've thought of everything; tomorrow morning, we have a final meeting with my team leaders; and then tomorrow afternoon, I'd like you to brief the whole team. We can then relax before we leave here just after midnight.'

'What have you told the team so far, Bob?'

'We've given them only limited information to avoid leaks. We've merely said the Home Secretary has authorised the arrest of a German citizen in the interests of public safety, and to maintain public order, in the UK. These were the words you gave us.'

She glanced over at Bill, and he nodded. 'That's fine.' She had talked with Conway almost every day about aspects of the raid, but now, as they faced the reality of it, they needed to tie up loose ends and get everyone on side. 'Yeah, it all sounds good.'

'Great. So, let's first go through how we've organised the raid.'

She nodded. 'Do we have any more info on the mansion house?'

'No. We still can't use any local resources. We think there are twelve bedrooms, and we have to assume all of them *could* be occupied, and operate accordingly. We'll have twelve two-man teams, one for each bedroom, and they'll stick a number to their bedroom door for reference – one through six on the second floor – seven through twelve on the upper floor. They'll enter the house through the French windows at the roof garden level.

'We'll enter all bedrooms at three a.m. precisely, and immobilise the occupants within five seconds. So far, we've detected no signal activity from the radio aerials, so we assume they're dormant or only used in an emergency.

'We'll cuff each occupant, wrists and ankles, and gag and hood them, to minimise communication, until you're ready to talk to them. All of our teams have been warned about the possibility of booby traps to destroy information. We want to capture this man,' he held up a picture, 'Gerhardt Timmermann, to allow you to arrest him. As far as we're concerned, all others will remain incommunicado until you're satisfied they're not required as part of your case. We'll then release them.

'As per your instructions, Timmermann, and any other relevant persons, will go to Hendon on a special flight on Sunday morning, and you and Bill will accompany them.

'Our REME colleagues will dismantle the manufacturing equipment and, together with any production material and finished products, dispose of it all in a nearby deep lake as per the Home Secretary's instructions. I'll personally oversee that operation.

'In addition to the twenty four, we'll have a team of four – two from us, two from REME – enter the house by the front door to switch off the electrics and guard the link to the clinic. We'll also have a similar team enter at the rear factory entrance, switch off the electrics there, and guard the link between the factory and the house. We'll also have a team of two to guard the main entrances from the road, both front and back. So, that's thirty six in total.'

He checked his notes. 'In addition to those, we'll have eight female staff from the regular Army base, to deal with female occupants. We'll also have four translators available, one with you, one with me, and the other two on the bedroom floors. The teams have all been taught to shout 'Britische Polizei' as they enter. One of my team leaders raised a question on the legal status of them saying that. So, can you clarify, please? We also have Captain Paige of the Military Police, and Captain Whyte, one of our medics, available to discuss any support you need from them.'

Sandra glanced over at Bill, who looked impressed. 'Thanks, Bob. That's brilliant. I really appreciate all your support. Let's take these points in reverse order. I definitely want a medical team with us, just in case. It's always good to have them on the spot. And I'd like to talk with Captain Paige right now, so if you can get him in here, that would be helpful.'

Conway picked up the phone and called Paige.

Sandra went on. 'As far as the legal side goes, Bill and I discussed this at Hendon this morning. We've checked with the Home Office, and they advise we swear in all persons involved in the raid as Special Constables, for the duration of the exercise. So, I can do that tomorrow when we have everyone together. Okay?'

Conway nodded. 'That's fine, thanks.'

Paige arrived and, after introductions, asked, 'How can I help, ma'am?'

Sandra thought for a moment. 'I don't know who and what I'm going to find when I get in there. So, I'd like to cover the obvious problems. Do you have a crime lab here, Captain?'

'We do, ma'am. It's not Scotland Yard, of course, but we can cover most routine scene of crime issues – like fingerprints, material or liquid analysis, autopsies in conjunction with our medical staff, ballistics, photography, and so on.'

'Great. I think we're most likely to get ID problems – you know, who's who and what are they doing there? I take it you can telegraph pictures from here to London?'

Paige nodded. 'We can, ma'am.'

'So I think if you could come with a fingerprint expert, a photographer, and a good all-round analyst, it would be really helpful.'

Paige took notes. 'No problem, ma'am.'

‘Great. So, we’ll see you and your team tomorrow for the final briefing?’

‘Yes, ma’am. Look forward to it.’ Paige left the room.

Sandra looked over at Conway and nodded. ‘Sounds good. Roll on tomorrow.’

Chapter 13. Saturday 19 January

Porritt and Wolff stood behind the reception window and watched the young man walk from the car into the police station. He carried a small case and a briefcase.

'I know that lad,' said Wolff. 'I've met him before.'

They walked out and introduced themselves.

'Let's go into this meeting room,' said Wolff.

The young man opened his briefcase, and pulled out a couple of photos. 'My father wanted me to show you these,' he said.

The first showed Wolff standing beside four men, one of whom was the young man opposite, taken some years ago.

Wolff nodded. 'I remember now. The Nuremberg Rally of '38. That's you, your brother, and your father. And here,' he turned to Porritt, 'we have the Personal Secretary to Hitler, Martin Bormann. I did security for the Bormann party throughout that rally.'

The young man passed over the second photo. 'My father said you'd be interested in this one, Commander.'

Porritt stared at the picture. It showed five men at a swimming pool, laughing and raising glasses of beer and champagne. Porritt had unmasked the man on the left as the head of the Aquila spy group in the UK, who had been tried and executed as a result. Bastard.

Wolff leaned over to see it. 'Does that mean something to you, Jonathan?'

Porritt nodded. 'Yeah.' He looked up at the young man. 'I know the man on the left. Who are the others?'

'That's my father, my grandfather, and my Uncle Ernst, with Martin Bormann.'

Porritt turned the picture over. 'BO 09/36'. That bastard had consorted with senior Nazis as far back as

1936. And no one knew. Porritt had moved on from his Special Branch days, and no longer had power of arrest, but he just *had* to find out more about this.

The young man said, 'My father asks you to bring these pictures with you.'

Porritt nodded. 'Okay.' He turned to Wolff. 'Shall we go?'

Wolff stood up. 'Right, Manfred. Come with me and we'll make you as comfortable as possible until we get back.' He and the young man left the room.

***

Sandra scanned the faces from the platform of the briefing room. She'd never led such a big group, and her throat felt dry. Fine men and women all. Put their lives on the line for their country. Grossly underrated in her view.

Conway had done a great job. At the final briefing with team leaders that morning, he'd gone through each plan, and discussed the role and actions of each person, to make sure they fully supported Sandra and Bill's objectives.

The team leaders had then gone through the plans with their teams, and now they had this final briefing for the entire group. Conway summarised the raid, so each person knew their role in relation to everyone else. 'And now, as I've said, it's *not* our usual Commando raid. It's a Police raid led by Special Branch, and I'd like to introduce Chief Superintendent Maxwell to conclude the briefing.'

Sandra stood up. 'Thank you, Major. Good afternoon, everyone.' She scanned the faces. 'I've been involved in many raids in my time, but never one as important as this, in terms of its benefits to our country, and never one with such an impressive team. It's been a pleasure to meet you, and get to know the important work you're doing here.

'As Major Conway said, it's a Police raid. I understand you usually attack and take control of enemy assets in a military sense. In this raid, we'll do something similar.'

She held up a photo of Gerhardt Timmermann. 'We aim to arrest this man. He's the leader of a group that has set out to undermine public safety in our country. At the same time as we go in tonight, we'll have around thirty similar raids across the UK.' Sandra gave the group time to murmur among themselves. 'So, this raid's just one part of a much wider attack, authorised by the Home Secretary, and under the command of my boss, Commander Burnett, in Scotland Yard.' She paused again. 'We want to take control of the assets of this group, its material and equipment, and its people.

'Now, I'd like to add, in Special Branch, we bumped up against this lot a few years ago, during the war. At that time, they ran a spy network across the UK, and they were very clever in what they did. They'd set up alarm systems to warn others, and clever ways to protect their information and secretly dispose of it.

'So, we need to be on our guard. All of us. We need to immobilise people within five seconds, so they can't trigger any alarms. We need to watch out for booby traps that protect filing cabinets or safes. And don't let anyone we capture, and I mean *anyone*, go to their toilet, no matter how desperate. If someone appears in distress, then contact me, and we'll arrange for them to visit a toilet on a different floor, where they'll be stripped and supervised at all times. Their dignity's not as important as our mission.

'So, remember, information is evidence, and that includes identity data. Let's make sure we protect all ID info we find. We'll hold people in their bedrooms until we're happy we know who they are and why they're there. Then we'll take appropriate action. Clear?'

Everyone nodded.

'Now, finally, we were asked by one of your team leaders, the legal basis for this raid. We're advised you all need sworn in as Special Constables for the duration. So, would you all please stand, hold up your left hand, and repeat after me.' She waited until they all stood. 'I hereby do solemnly, sincerely, and truly declare and affirm that I will faithfully discharge the duties of Special Constable until the satisfactory completion of this mission.' She stated it in phrases, and everyone repeated the words.

'For the purposes of this mission, the duties of a Special Constable are those already detailed to you by Major Conway and your team leaders.

'Thank you for your attention and let's hope our raid goes to plan.'

She returned to her seat. Conway stood up and concluded the meeting. As she prepared to leave, Bill leaned over and whispered, 'Great job.'

***

As Porritt entered the dining room, he checked Wolff was with him. An elderly man stood at the head of the table, with Jane to his left. A butler stood behind the man at a sideboard against the far wall. Four places were set at the table, two on the long side to the man's left and one to the man's right. The man splayed his hands. 'Welcome, Commander, Direktor. I'm Doctor G. It's a pleasure to meet you. Come.' He indicated Porritt should sit on his right, and Wolff should take the second place on his left. Jane sat at the first place on his left. Porritt shook hands with G and sat down. He studied the man. Late fifties, maybe. Seemed pleasant enough, but didn't look at all well. He had dark shadows under his eyes.

Porritt glanced at the butler. Did he have a gun? Just try to relax, he told himself. Wolff would protect him. Better be sociable. 'Thank you for the invitation. We meet at last.'

G turned to Jane, who translated Porritt's words. G smiled, and responded in German, 'We do indeed.' Jane translated as he spoke. 'I believe it's important we understand each other's point of view. Not to learn lessons. That's all over. But for me at least, to get closure. You see, I have a cancer that's incurable, and don't have much time left. I'd like to tie up some loose ends before I go. But first, let's eat. We have some delicious smoked salmon from Norway for starters. Okay?'

Everyone nodded, and G turned and waved for the butler to serve.

'For mains, we have lamb or fish. Which would you prefer?'They each gave their preference. 'Sounds like lamb all round, please, Otto.'

Porritt tasted the salmon. It had been years since he'd had such a perfect starter. But G seemed so sanguine about his illness. It must be hellish to live with a known death sentence. He didn't know how he'd have coped with it.

'So, to the first of my loose ends,' G went on. 'The man you knew as Karl Brenner, I knew as Brendan Connolly, his real name. Jane has told me how he died, and said you arranged his burial. His father worked with me as a senior engineer for many years. I've promised his mother, I'd try to find him, so she and her family can get closure. Do you have that information, Commander?'

Porritt lifted the envelope he'd placed on the table at his side, and drew out a typed page. He passed the page to G. 'If the family contacts CS Alan McGowan, and gives the code words 'Emerald Three', he will accompany them to the burial ground near Belfast, and help them recover Brenner's body. I hope that's helpful.'

G nodded. 'It is, Commander. Thank you. I'll pass this on. Now, may I turn to Aquila? Do you have the photos I sent with Manfred?'

Porritt passed him the envelope and he extracted the photo of the five men at the pool.

'We took this photo at our outdoor pool here on the day we launched Aquila in 1936. You know the man on the left?' G asked, showing the photo to Porritt.

'I do. He was Sir James Dunsmore.'

'With myself, my father, my brother, Ernst, and my cousin, Martin Bormann.'

Porritt interrupted. 'Do you know what happened to your cousin?'

G shook his head. 'I know you're looking for him, but I honestly don't know. I last spoke to him at the end of April last year. He called to tell me Hitler had committed suicide that day. He also told me his wife Gerda and their children had fled to Italy. He said the game was now over. He planned to escape Berlin via the U-Bahn tunnels. Oh, he's been sighted in various places, of course. But I think if he'd survived, he'd have contacted Gerda by now, and she's heard nothing. I'm pretty sure he didn't make it out of Berlin.'

Porritt nodded. 'Okay, thanks. Sorry to interrupt. Back to your story.'

G held up the photo again. 'We all thought Dunsmore a greedy, pompous bore, but Martin thought him a useful contact. That day, Dunsmore told us he'd been appointed to some influential Whitehall committee, and it gave Martin an idea.

'At the time, Martin was Private Secretary to Hitler, and controlled access to him, so he had an incredibly powerful seat among Hitler's inner circle. Hitler also confided in Martin on where he might take the whole Nazi movement.

'Hitler aimed to take over Europe as a starter, but his long-term ambitions went much further. To take over the world, or at least a large part of it. He wanted to take over Britain, and get control of the British Empire, which stretched from Australia and New Zealand, through India, South Africa, West Africa, to Canada, with lots of places in between.

'But he didn't fully trust Canaris, head of Abwehr, the military intelligence service, to get accurate reports on British interests. Himmler, head of the SS, told him the British had turned Abwehr agents in Britain, and they were now sending deceptive reports. Canaris denied this, but Hitler thought there might be a grain of truth in it. He never quite believed Canaris really supported the cause.

'Hitler always wanted inside information to play his senior officers off against each other, and on that evening, here, everything came together for Martin, and he seized the opportunity. Once Dunsmore and my father had retired to bed, the three of us talked about Dunsmore, and how we could use him to feed us inside info that Martin could then use to impress Hitler, and strengthen his own position. I don't know whether you know, but Dunsmore was a homosexual, quite blatant in Berlin, where they tolerated that behaviour, to an extent unacceptable – and illegal – in England.

'So, we devised a two-pronged strategy to trap Dunsmore in a homosexual liaison, and then reward him with financial and other benefits for valuable reports. Martin had access to huge funds within the Nazi party. We planned to increase the pressure on Dunsmore, so as we approached the time to invade Britain, we would know more clearly the extent of British capabilities. In the event, we didn't have to apply much pressure. Dunsmore was a willing party. He expected a senior position in any new regime.'

G paused while the butler served the main course. Porritt wondered about G being so open about the past. Perhaps it didn't matter to him any more.

'Now, as we talked that night, we realised Dunsmore could feed us good strategic info from Whitehall, but to invade Britain, we'd need to know much more about their operations on the ground. We thought Dunsmore couldn't give us that, and we couldn't rely on Abwehr agents. So, my brother, Ernst, proposed a solution.

He ran huge mining operations in South West Africa and South Africa, and also ran the local Abwehr group there on the side. A couple of English businessmen, sympathetic to the cause, had impressed him, and when he heard they planned to relocate to England, persuaded them to set up a spy network, which became the Aquila group. Lyall relocated first, followed by Kay. Ernst trained them on surveillance and detection avoidance techniques, and they became top class operators, who provided incredibly useful information, alongside that from Dunsmore, which Martin fed Hitler. Martin asked me to lead this organisation to keep it separate from Abwehr, and hidden from Himmler.

'We were very careful, and used what we thought were undetectable radio links, yet I now know from Jane, you wiped out that entire operation in one night,

Commander. We must have had a weak spot. But where? I've worried over that. Could you enlighten me now?'

Porritt thought for a moment. How the hell should he answer? He pursed his lips. Might as well be open about it now. 'We all have the same weak spot in our organisations, Doctor. The people. You had a great format, well managed and effective, but people aren't like robots. They don't have the discipline to follow the correct procedure a hundred percent of the time. Three people let you down.

'The first was Brenner. He took a shine to Jane, and then took her with him when he escaped. Big mistake. He couldn't have had an easy life as a spy, of course, and maybe he took pills or something to make him feel better, that also made him more reckless. But, if he hadn't done that, we would never have caught him. Yet, even with Jane dragged along, he could still have got away with it, if the second person hadn't made a tiny error.

'Your agent in Glasgow. She had a rock-solid cover. Totally credible. Went from house to house with a flyer and a free offer, without suspicion. Yet, after the key house, where she took her photos in secret, she rushed away. That alerted our team. If she hadn't done that, we'd never have caught her. We carefully followed her, and picked up the address to which she sent the photos. So, for us, the odds had improved, but were still not guaranteed, until the third error.

'I understand from Jane that Brown took a bribe to allow Brenner to be alone with her, and you know what happened then. It allowed us to identify them, even though they were disguised, and as a result, we arrested Brown and Henry.

'We'd got the link between your key men from phone taps. When we raided their houses, we decoded the names and addresses of all your agents around the country, and arrested them four hours later. We also caught Dunsmore by dogged detective work.

'So, now you know. That's how we closed down Aquila in a single night. Our teams were good, but they could never have done it without these errors by your people.'

G smiled wanly, and dropped his eyes to the table. He sat for several minutes, then looked up at Porritt. 'Thank you, Commander. You've put my mind at rest now. Please, excuse me, I have to get to bed. Feel free to remain here and finish your meal. We have an excellent tiramisu for dessert. Relax and finish your wine, or if you want a nightcap, just ask Otto. He'll look after you, and see you back to your rooms.' He stood up to shake hands. 'Good night, Commander. It's been a pleasure to meet you. Direktor Wolff, good to see you again. And Jane,' he lifted her hand and kissed it, 'I'm sorry for all the problems you've had. I hope it will not have a lasting effect on you or your family. I won't see you in the morning. The car will be available at nine o'clock to take you back to Nuremberg. Have a safe journey.' He lifted the envelope and left the room.

Porritt topped up their glasses with the remains of the bottle of Sancerre. It sure had been a memorable evening.

Wolff leaned forward. 'Quite a story from both of you. It's funny how success or failure sometimes hinges on tiny actions or errors. I've learned a few lessons tonight. What about you, Jane?'

She looked at them in turn. 'I'm amazed at his insight into the Nazi high command. I wonder if his hero Hitler,' she pointed to the photograph on the sideboard, 'also failed because of a few minor errors. Otherwise, we'd be in a very different place tonight.'

Porritt lifted his glass. 'I'll drink to that.' He leaned forward and clinked glasses with the others. 'Here's to peace for all of us.'

***

G hobbled into his bedroom and laid the envelope on the table. His wife, already in bed, put her book down and took her glasses off.

'How did it go?' she asked.

'Oh, as well as could be expected, I think. Porritt's a remarkable man. A worthy adversary. We didn't miss by much, you know. But we still missed. Just because of a lack of discipline in our people at crucial moments.

'He gave me some interesting insights, though. Maybe our magic pills weren't as magical as we thought. I know Brendan swore by them. Wouldn't it be ironic if they were the root cause of Aquila's demise? But, that's life, I guess. Unpredictable.

'I did get closure for Kathleen Connolly. The instructions to retrieve Brendan's body are in the envelope. Could you give them to Cian in the morning, please?'

He changed into his pyjamas, went into the bathroom to brush his teeth and have a pee, then sat on the side of the bed.

'It's time now, my love,' he said, quietly.

Her eyes filled with tears. 'Really? Must you?'

He nodded. 'Yeah, I must. The pain's now unbearable, even with the morphine. And it'll get worse in the next few days. I don't want you to see me like that.'

'What about the boys?'

'I said goodbye to them last weekend.'

He went to his safe, and lifted out a vacuum flask. He poured some of the contents into a glass, then got into bed and drank it down. He snuggled under the bedclothes.

'Good night, my darling. Goodbye, my love.'

She leaned over, cuddled him, and wept. 'I don't want you to go. But I don't want you to stay like this. Thank you for a wonderful life, my darling. Thank you so much. I love you.'

'Love you too.'

Chapter 14. Sunday 20 January

Eddie glanced at his watch. Almost ten to two. Late tonight, he thought. Business had been good, though. At that last club, the lads usually stopped around midnight, but they still had a demand. And then he'd to reconcile the cash and tablets. It all took time. He peered through the gloom of Glasgow Green, as Gordy drove slowly past the People's Palace. Up ahead, two large black cars moved even slower.

'Just ease back a bit, Gordy. Let's see where these guys go.'

At the junction with James Street, the two cars turned left and then right into Greenhead Street. That's the way he should go too. To his home.

'Just go straight across, Gordy. Take it easy.'

'Okay, boss.'

Eddie watched the two cars, separated now from the Green carriageway by a strip of grass and a row of trees. One stopped just before his house, the other stopped just beyond it. Too much of a coincidence, he thought.

'Go down Main Street, and back round again, Gordy.'

Next time round, Eddie saw dim silhouettes of tall, dark figures opposite his house.

'Go back round again, Gordy.'

Next time, the figures had gone, but his front door lay open. Shit. A police raid? But why? The tablets were legal. Maybe it had to do with that big bastard, Jack Bruce. Had that come back to haunt him?

'Go round past Shawfield, Gordy, and stop at the first phone box you see.'

'Right, boss.'

If he'd to run, how much money did he have? He quickly estimated – six bars and three nightclubs – he had over two thousand pounds in cash in the secret compartments of his case, plus packs of tablets as well. Nearly ten years salary for some people. So he could get by for a while. And he also carried a passport and ID card in the name of Alex Jardine. Would the police know that? Probably not. He'd never used them. Gordy pulled up at a phone box.

Eddie asked for Sam's number. It rang out. *Very* odd. Had it to do with the tablets after all? He checked his notebook and asked for Andrew's number in Hampstead. No reply. Shit. This looked bad. He asked for Ron Baxter's number in Edinburgh. Again, no reply. Time to run. He asked for a number in Belfast. She'd said to call anytime, day or night.

'Hello?'

'Anne-Marie?'

'Yeah, who's this?'

'It's Eddie Frame. I work with Dan McFadden. Remember, we met a few months ago?'

'Oh, yeah. Eddie. I remember. What can I do for you?'

'I need to get out the country fast. Can you help me?'

'Of course I can.'

'What are the options again?'

'Basic, we get you over the border. Fifty quid. Second level, we get you over the border to Dublin with a new passport and ID card. A hundred quid. Third level, we get you all of that plus book your flights from Dublin, open a bank account that you can access in Spain, and give you a contact number in Belfast for friends and family. A hundred and fifty quid. Cash up front. Which do you want?'

'I'll take the third option, Anne-Marie.'

'Okay, where are you?'

'I'm still in Glasgow.'

'Right, get yourself down to Stranraer. Call me from there and let ne know what ferry you're on. There's an Ulster Information kiosk at Stranraer. Buy a bus ticket from Larne to Belfast. If anybody asks about your onward journey, show them the ticket. It makes you look like a regular. I'll have a car meet you at Larne. The driver will carry a board with the name Jon Kelly, the first name spelt J-O-N. Give him the money. We'll fly you out Monday. In the meantime, don't call family or friends. Just disappear. All right?'

'Fine. Sounds like a well-oiled machine.'

'Yeah, we do it two or three times a week. No problem. I won't see you, Eddie, but you'll be in a safe house, and the team will look after you. Okay?'

'Thanks, Anne-Marie.'

Eddie got into the back of the car. 'Gordy, could you do me a favour, please? Could you take me down to Stranraer? In your own car?'

'No problem, boss.' He started the engine and drove off.

'I don't want you to tell anybody you've done this, though. Not even Mary. If anybody asks, just say you dropped me at my house at quarter to two. You saw me walk towards the door, but didn't see me go in. You went off to join your mates for a few hours. Okay?'

'Sure, boss. I often play cards on a Saturday night. They'll back me up.'

'That's great, Gordy. How about fifty quid for this?'

'Oh, Jesus, boss. That's too much.'

'Well, it's worth it to me.'

Eddie sat back and thought about Anne-Marie. She'd taken over the family business when her father, Charlie

Flynn, had been killed in prison three years ago. Charlie and Dan had been old mates. Charlie had four sons and a daughter. Each boy thought he'd take over the business, but the fiery, red-haired Anne-Marie had more brains than the boys put together, and they soon had to work for her. Quite a girl. Who now held his future in her hands as he headed for Spain.

***

Malcolm Craig crouched under the trees at the back of Lyall's garden, his team alongside, all dressed in black. They'd devised a strategy that hopefully would get round the problem of the dog and the burglar alarm. He glanced at his watch. One minute to two.

He heard the car come down the street and then the loud bang as it smashed into the lamp-post outside Lyall's house. The dog barked, and the group ran across the garden, half going down each side of the house.

Craig peeped round the corner and saw his two amateur dramatists, John and Sally, emerge from the car, John dressed in a dinner suit with bow tie and silk scarf; Sally in a pale yellow ball gown. They'd worn harnesses to protect them from the impact.

The front bedroom window opened above them. 'Are you okay?' a voice called.

John looked up, and in a very pukka accent, said, 'Sorry to disturb you, old boy. The bally steering's just gone, dammit. Any chance I could use your phone?'

'Yeah, sure. I'll be right down.'

The two groups skunked along the front of the house. Craig had a judo expert as the lead man on the other side. He'd immobilise Lyall as they entered. Craig held his breath as John and Sally walked towards the door.

John said, ‘I really appreciate this, old boy. I’ll get my brother to come and collect us. Shouldn’t take long.’

‘That’s okay. As long as you’re all right. In you come.’

‘Thanks, old boy.’ They entered the house.

The two teams crashed into the house behind them. The lead man shouted, ‘Armed Police,’ tossed Lyall to the floor, cuffed his wrists and ankles, and gagged him. The others spread through the house to follow their instructions.

Craig knelt on Lyall’s back. ‘Mr Andrew Lyall, you’re under arrest for breaches of amendments to the Emergency Powers (Defence) (No 2) Act 1940, for the possession and distribution of methamphetamine tablets in the UK. You have the right to remain silent, but anything you do say will be taken down and may be used in evidence. Do you understand?’

Lyall grunted. Craig searched Lyall’s dressing gown pockets and found a bunch of keys. These could come in handy, he thought. The dog had stopped barking. He asked John and Sally to turn Lyall over and lean him against the wall, then went upstairs.

Two female officers stood in front of the doors to the back bedrooms. They wore tabards with ‘POLICE’ on them. All quiet in the children’s rooms.

Craig entered the front bedroom. Two female officers had Mrs Lyall cuffed and gagged on the floor. One said, ‘This room’s clear, sir. No sign of a panic button.’

Craig knelt beside her. ‘Mrs Lyall, I’m Chief Superintendent Craig of the Special Branch. We’ve arrested your husband for possessing and distributing methamphetamine tablets, which is against the law. We’ll release you as soon as we can. Your children don’t seem disturbed so far. If they wake, we have specially trained officers to deal with them.'

He went next door to the office. His team had already emptied drawers and cupboards, and checked the contents. The team leader said, 'We've got a problem with this filing cabinet, sir. It's locked, and we haven't found the keys.'

'I've got keys here,' Craig said. Then the phone rang. Craig turned to the desk. 'Don't answer it.' He didn't want to alert anyone to their presence. He found the right key and unlocked the cabinet, but the drawers didn't pull out. Then he noticed a metal frame around the back of the cabinet, attached to the wall. He called the safecracker over. 'How the hell do we get into these drawers? Do you think there's a booby trap here?'

The safecracker examined the filing cabinet. 'Well, it's not like the last time, sir. No sign of any cables or switches. What are these discs down each side of the frame?'

That rang a bell for Craig. 'Hold on a second. I might have the answer in my car.'

He dashed downstairs, got his briefcase from the car, now at the front door, and pulled out the instructions Sandra had written on the secret compartments in the special suitcase.

He and the safecracker pored over them. 'As I remember it, these discs cover magnetic switches. So, can we get these off?'

The safecracker gently pulled the discs off. Each revealed a circle a couple of inches in diameter with a slot in it.

'Right,' Craig said, 'these instructions say if you turn the slot 180 degrees, it switches the magnetic lock off. Let's try with the top drawer.'

The safecracker turned the slots on either side of the drawer. 'Try that.'

Craig pulled the drawer open. He smiled at the safecracker. 'Clever, eh?'

The safecracker scratched his head. 'How the hell does that work?'

'Well, you can look up the details later. Let's get the other drawers freed first.'

In the top drawer, Craig found a series of files marked GB01 to GB29. Each had a copy of the GT Pharma Distributor agreement with the name and address of the distributor. Exactly what he wanted, and even better, not in code. He lifted the phone, called Alison, and gave her the names and addresses of all twenty-nine distributors. He gave the team the thumbs up. 'Great job, team. Let's box all this up and get back to HQ.'

He went to the front bedroom, and got the cuffs and gag removed from Mrs Lyall. She rubbed her wrists and ankles. 'You're a monster. You know that?'

Craig shrugged. 'Well, I've a job to do, ma'am, to uphold the law. Lots of people don't like me for it, usually the ones that break the law. We'll take your husband to Hampstead Police Station, where he'll be charged and detained until his court appearance, probably tomorrow. He can use the duty solicitor, or appoint his own. If it's the latter, ask him to contact the duty officer at Hampstead for access.

'In the meantime, this house is a crime scene. That means you and the children must leave until we complete our enquiries. Do you have somewhere you can go?'

She nodded. 'My mother's.'

'That's fine. I'll leave you in the hands of these officers. Thank you, team.'

Craig went downstairs, and found his team leader. 'Rob, take two officers and get Lyall dressed.' Lyall still lay in the hall. 'Okay, take the gag off.'

Lyall snarled at him. 'I'll have you for wrongful arrest.'

'Really? Why?'

'Because we're not doing anything illegal.'

'That's where you're wrong, Mr Lyall. The possession, selling and distribution of methamphetamine tablets were made illegal in this country ten days ago.'

'Well, I didn't know that.'

'Too bad. Ignorance of the law's not a defence, I'm afraid. Take him away.'

***

Tom Hamilton sat in the passenger seat of the lead car as it passed through the grim grimy Glasgow landscape towards the east end. No police officer had ever bagged a McFadden, or any senior member of the Glasgow crime family. The targets had always wriggled off the hook from advanced inside knowledge, unbreakable alibis, or the use of very sharp lawyers. Now, he had his chance to make history.

He'd examined the McFadden compound from every angle under the guise of the 'Electricity Board' checking underground cables in Reid Street and Colvend Street. Inside its gates to the right stood the remains of the original print works, which contained offices and meeting rooms, and where the night watchman sat. Behind that, a large storage unit occupied the far right corner, and backed onto the alleyways along the rear and along the river bank.

To the left of the gates stood Dan's bungalow, which backed onto Colvend Street, with Kenny's bungalow beyond. Sam's bungalow stood almost opposite the gates, and backed on to the rear alleyway. The bungalows each had separate addresses in Reid Street. A seven-foot-high wire fence surrounded the property. Three-storey tenement buildings overlooked the compound in Reid Street and Colvend Street.

Tom checked his pocket, yet again, for the search warrant, signed by a Sheriff at the last minute to avoid leaks. He'd filmed activity in the compound on previous nights from a tenement flat in Reid Street, occupied by two of his young detectives, who played the part of newlyweds Ian and Jessie McIvor.

He'd also taken over an empty factory unit at Shieldhall, and recreated parts of the compound inside it, to rehearse and perfect his raid strategy. He hand picked his team with no one from the Eastern Division. Most of them still didn't know the target. He'd done all he could think of, but knew he couldn't afford any cracks in the evidence, otherwise the lawyers would widen them to unbridgeable crevasses. Fingers crossed.

The cars dropped them in Main Street at the alleyway beside Rutherglen Bridge, and the team scuttled a hundred yards along the alley until they reached the compound. They had switched off the street light there the previous night, leaving the area adjacent to the offices and storage unit in darkness. The team, dressed entirely in black, blended into the shadows, pretty much hidden from the overlooking tenement blocks.

Tom watched as his team sprung into action. They each had a job to do and had rehearsed it several times. The lead entry man took his wire cutters and cut the fence open to let the team through. They stood against the office block and storage block. The locksmith went to the back door of the office block, and within fifteen seconds had the door open. The two lead 'heavies', both ex-commandos, entered the building to immobilise the guard. They reappeared within half a minute and gave the thumbs-up.

Tom and the team leaders had studied the film of the guard at night as he patrolled the compound, typically every hour or so. He wore a heavy, hooded jacket, heavy gloves, dark trousers and heavy boots. On one film the guard had rung Sam's doorbell. Within a few moments, the curtains twitched, and Sam opened the door. The key to achieving the five-second target, thought Tom. He studied the way the guard walked with a slight limp, the way he stamped his feet and beat his gloves to stay warm as he stood at Sam's door, and had his substitute guard learn the exact same movements.

The team scuttled around the back of the compound and spread down both sides of Sam's bungalow. They could now potentially be seen from the tenements, so they had to move quickly now. Tom watched as his substitute guard did his rounds and rang the doorbell at Sam's house. The guard stamped his feet and beat his gloves. Tom could imagine the curtains twitch and then heard the door open. A voice said, 'Yes, Gav. What is it?' before the two lead 'heavies' shouted 'armed police' and bundled him back through the door.

Tom had a cameraman at his shoulder, to film him as he entered the property. Sam McFadden lay face down on the hall carpet, wrists and ankles cuffed, and a gag in his mouth. Tom reckoned he'd hit the five-second target okay. He knelt on Sam's back. 'Mr Sam McFadden, you're under arrest for breaches of amendments to the Emergency Powers (Defence) (No 2) Act 1940, for possessing, distributing and selling methamphetamine tablets. You have the right to remain silent, but anything you do say will be taken down and may be used in evidence. Do you understand?'

McFadden wriggled and grunted. Tom checked the cameraman still followed him, and moved through to the lounge. He needed the film in one take without a break, so lawyers could not argue it had been tampered with.

Tom saw the GT Pharma writing bureau in the far corner and headed for it. He had already seen Sandra Maxwell find the secret compartment in the bureau in Thomon's flat, and had memorised the instructions she'd left. He talked to the camera, opened the bureau, and revealed the secret compartment. It contained two packs of 500 tablets, some bundles of cash, and a passport and ID card in the name of Andrew Jardine. He lifted the bags of tablets to give the camera a close-up view, and then showed the pages of the passport and the ID card to the camera as well. He indicated to the cameraman to cut the film at that point.

The team searched in silence. Tom hoped the other half of his team had the same success in the office and storage blocks. The phone rang. He indicated to his team not to answer it. Then he noticed the female officers at the hallway through to the bedrooms held a woman in a dressing gown. The woman looked angry.

Then another team member came to him. 'There's a man at the front door here wants to talk to you, sir. He says he's the owner of the property.'

Tom went outside to the compound. A tall, grim-faced man, in a Crombie coat over his pyjamas stood and watched him as he emerged. It was Dan McFadden. Tom had seen pictures of him over the years. But Tom still had the initiative, and wanted to keep it.

'You in charge?' the man demanded.

'I am, sir. Chief Inspector Hamilton of the Special Branch.' He showed his warrant card.

'Special Branch, huh? So, what the hell's going on?'

'I'm sorry, sir. But who are you?'

The man's lips tightened, clearly angry. 'I'm Dan McFadden. I own this property. And you've got my son trussed up in there. So, what's going on? Do you have a warrant?'

'I do, sir.' He went into his pocket and passed over the warrant.

The man studied it. His lips got even tighter. 'Where will you take him?'

'Our HQ in St Andrew's Square, sir.'

The man pursed his lips. 'It's not illegal to sell these tablets.'

'I'm afraid it is, sir. The law changed ten days ago.'

The man looked Tom up and down. 'Ten days ago?' He pursed his lips again. 'Ten days ago? Well, you won't hold him long, Chief Inspector. My lawyer will see you shortly.' He turned and walked off towards his bungalow.

Tom watched him go. That meant he could expect a visit from Vince Pastrano within the hour. The smartest and most expensive criminal lawyer in Scotland, the top choice of the criminal classes, he thought. He'd better get Sam into custody quickly.

He went back into the bungalow and told his team leader to get Sam dressed and take him to HQ. The senior female officer came over and told him she'd advised Sam's wife to get the children and leave the property. The wife had called her mother-in-law, and they'd go over there until the police released the house.

Tom reckoned he could leave his team to complete their search. He put the contents of the secret compartment into an evidence bag, and went out to his car, which had now appeared in the compound. He picked up the radio phone and asked for Neil Ross, who led the team tasked with arresting Eddie Frame.

As he waited for Neil to come on the line, he thought about Frame. It had taken them weeks to get his name and address. He'd been Mr Anonymous, until they got a steer from a retired Inspector who had dealt with cases against the McFaddens in the thirties.

Neil came on the line. 'Hi Tom. We've got a problem this end. Frame hasn't turned up at home. The tailing car got blocked in at Tony's night club. They saw Frame's car move off, but by the time they got clear, he'd disappeared. We're still at Greenhead Street. We've put out an alert on the car, but it's a case of sit and wait for the moment, sir.

'Okay, keep me posted, Neil. I'm headed back to HQ with Sam McFadden. Looks like they already have the lawyers on the job. Talk to you later.'

Pity about Frame, thought Tom. They'd worked out he probably organised the teams in pubs and night clubs, and collected the cash, but they'd no verifiable evidence so far. They needed to catch him with the GT Pharma suitcase, with tablets and cash in the secret compartments, to make the charge stick. Otherwise, they only had circumstantial evidence. Dammit, a loose end, and he hated loose ends.

***

Sandra Maxwell crouched against the wall at the entrance to the manufacturing plant, and waited for the signal to move. She held her satchel case tight against her, and glanced round at Bill Franklin behind her. He gave her a nod. They'd dressed like everyone else, in black, top to toe, with torches strapped to their forehead. They were part of a group of six, that comprised

Captains Paige and Whyte, and a translator, led by Barney – Sergeant Barnes. Sandra had the impression Barney felt he'd drawn the short straw. He had to look after a bunch of unfit senior staff, rather than lead the charge, but he hid it well.

Barney hissed, 'Torches on. Let's move.' Sandra switched on her head torch and followed Barney across to the door. Two commandos on guard helped her through the gap where they'd removed a glass panel. Barney moved down a dark corridor, then through a door to his left into the factory area.

A commando at a door on the far side of the factory waved at them to indicate they should move round to their left. Barney led the way, scurried along painted walkways, round several right angles, and headed for the far door.

Suddenly, Sandra heard a bump and a thump. The group stopped. Bill had bumped into a metal conveyor at a corner, and knocked a box onto the floor. The box had burst and spilled some of its contents. Sandra saw the plastic packs with the red sealing strip, each with five tablets, and realised she should take a few as evidence.

'Give me five packs, Bill. I need evidence.'

He put the five packs into her satchel. 'Right, you get on. I'll tidy this and catch you up.'

Barney nodded. 'Okay, through that door, along the corridor and then up the stairs at the far end.' He set off with the other four in his wake.

On the first floor, Conway met them in the corridor. The doors had 'CLEAR' signs stuck to them. 'In here,' he indicated.

Sandra entered a large ornate dining room. There were two rows of six white cards on the table, some blank, some with numbers, and some with numbers upside down.

‘Just the final two to come,’ he said. ‘Numbers this way mean clear, secure and occupied. Numbers upside down mean clear and secure, but unoccupied.’

A commando came into the room. ‘Number twelve clear and secure, sir. Occupied.’

Conway turned the card over to show the number.

Another commando entered. ‘Number one clear and secure, sir. Occupied.’

Conway turned the card over. ‘Right, we have four rooms occupied on the second floor, one, two, three and four; and four rooms occupied on the third floor, seven, eight, nine and twelve.’ He turned the upside-down numbers to blanks, and said to one of his team. ‘Get the power on, please, sergeant.’ The man left the room.

‘Excuse me, sir.’ The last commando to enter walked over to Conway and whispered in his ear. Conway looked shocked and glanced over to Sandra.

They came over to her. ‘The sergeant says the target is deceased, ma’am.’

Sandra’s jaw dropped. ‘Do we know what happened?’

The sergeant shook his head. ‘We don’t, ma’am. His wife tried to tell us, but we don’t understand German.’

Sandra turned to Doc Whyte, Paige and the translator. ‘Right, let’s all go and see.’ Then turned to Conway and the sergeant. ‘Can you lead the way, please?’

The group left the dining room, went up to the next floor, and entered the bedroom with the number one card on the door. The lights came on. An elderly woman sat cuffed in a chair, a female soldier at her side. The man on the other side of the bed certainly looked dead, thought Sandra. The doctor went over to check. ‘He’s gone, I’m afraid.’

Sandra had a sense of anti-climax, but knelt down beside the woman and waved the translator over. She held the woman's hands. 'I'm so sorry for your loss,' she said. The translator repeated the words in German. 'Can you tell me what happened?'

The woman responded. 'My husband had cancer. It had gone into the lymph system. There's no cure, and unbearable pain.' She glanced over at the vacuum flask on the bedside table. 'He wanted release, and drank from the glass.'

The doctor picked it up, smelled it and passed it to Paige. They did the same with the vacuum flask. Paige said, 'We'll check this out, ma'am.'

Sandra nodded. 'Thanks.' She turned to the woman again. 'Would you like us to move your husband's body to another room, ma'am?'

The woman watched the translator as he spoke, then turned back to Sandra and nodded.

Sandra said, 'Would you take care of that, please, sergeant? Put him in room six.'

'Yes, ma'am. Will do.'

She turned to the woman again. 'We need to ask you to move out of this room while we check it. Can we help you move somewhere until we're finished?'

The woman nodded, and pointed to her husband. 'I'll stay with him.'

The female soldier said, 'I'll look after her ma'am until we're clear.'

Sandra stood up. 'That's good. Thank you.' She looked over at Conway. 'Right, Major, let's see who else we have here.'

They went out into the corridor, and Bill joined them. Sandra explained the target had taken his own life because of severe cancer. 'Shit,' he said. 'All that effort too.'

Conway went into the next three bedrooms and asked the senior person to join them.

Sandra said, 'Right, room two. Who do we have?'

The commando said, 'Female, ma'am. British passport in the name, Jane Thomson.'

Sandra's jaw dropped again. 'Let me see the passport, please.' It was definitely Jane. What the hell was she doing here? Was she part of the conspiracy? Had she always been part of the conspiracy? 'What about room three?'

The commando stood to attention. 'Male, ma'am. British passport in the name of Jonathan Porritt.' He passed it to Sandra.

Jesus Christ, thought Sandra. What's going on here? She turned to Conway. 'Were these bedrooms locked, Major?'

Conway looked at his men. 'No, ma'am,' the commandos said in unison.

Sandra thought for a moment. So, they weren't held under duress then? Otherwise, they could have walked out. So, why are they here?

Bill asked. 'Is it *our* Jonathan Porritt?'

She nodded.

'There must be some mistake. He's one of our good blokes. I've known him for years. We've got to free him, surely.'

Sandra looked at him. 'Could I have a minute, Bill.' She turned to Conway. 'Back in a moment.' She walked Bill down the corridor ten yards, and said to him, very quietly, 'Look, we're all tense, but I'd like you to keep your opinions to yourself, Bill. They're not helpful. I'll decide who's good and who's bad on the basis of evidence, not opinions. I've seen too many senior people unmasked as bad guys. So, please keep quiet.'

'Sorry. I didn't mean to interfere. I'm just shocked.'

They went back to the group. 'And what about bedroom four?' she asked.

The commando said, 'Male. German national. Name of Hans Wolff, ma'am. Address in Nuremberg. Has a warrant card for the Nuremberg Police. He's also armed, ma'am, with a shoulder holster.'

'Really? Well, well.' She wondered how she should handle this. In these group situations, she always started with the least professional and most vulnerable. In this case, it had to be Jane. 'Let's go talk to the girl.'

She and Conway and the commando from that room went into bedroom two. A female sat on the floor, with a blanket round her, wrists and ankles cuffed, and a hood over her head. A female soldier stood to attention. The contents of a handbag lay on the bed in a neat pile. 'Apart from a few clothes, that's all she has with her, ma'am,' said the soldier.

Sandra glanced at the pile. She saw a small tin tube and picked it up. Methamphetamine. She opened it and compared the tablets to the ones in her bag. They were identical. Jesus, was Jane addicted to these tablets? Where had she got them? Yet another surprise in a night of surprises. 'Take the hood and cuffs off, please.' The soldier did so, and Sandra saw the gag. 'And the gag as well, please.'

Jane looked up at her. 'Sandra! How good to see you. Are you here to rescue us?'

Sandra helped her to a chair. 'Not really. I'm here on another matter. But I'd like to know why *you're* here.'

'They kidnapped me on Thursday.'

'Oh?. Could you tell me what happened?'

Jane told how Astrid had duped her to take the wrong car, and then how she drank the laced orange juice that knocked her out. Then about her lunch on Friday with Doctor G, the head of Aquila, who had asked her about Karl Brenner. She'd told him what she knew, but only Porritt knew where Brenner was buried. Doctor G wanted to know that to give closure to Brenner's family. She'd challenged Doctor G about her ex-husband's death, but Tommy had attacked his man with a gun. It was kill or be killed, he'd said.

Sandra stopped her, and thought about what she'd said. This Doctor G, her target, had been the head of Aquila? Of course, he had. She just hadn't made the connection. She'd focused on the tablets. But that's where the spy business and the drug business came together – at the top. Jesus. Jane's story sounded plausible. But was it rehearsed? She needed evidence, and turned to Conway, 'Could you ask Paige to come in here, please, Major?'

'Yes, ma'am.' He left the room and in a few moments came back with Paige.

Sandra took Paige by the arm and went out into the corridor with him and Conway. 'The girl says she got knocked out by drinking laced orange juice in the car. Could you check whether that car's still here – I noticed a garage on the way in – and if there's a container with orange juice that we can test for drugs? I'd just like some independent evidence her story's true. As soon as you can, please.'

'Yes, ma'am.' They headed off together, and Sandra went back into the bedroom.

'Sorry about that,' she said. 'Please continue, Jane.'

Jane went on to tell her about the phone call to Porritt, and the invite to come here last night for dinner. As security, Doctor G had left his son in custody in Nuremberg, but Porritt had also brought along Direktor Wolff of the Nuremberg detectives for extra security. She told Sandra about the dinner, when Porritt handed over details of Brenner's burial, and then the insights into the Nazi regime. She also said, after her lunch on Friday, Doctor G had allowed her to phone her fiancé, and let him know she was safe and well, and would return on Sunday. That had been a big moment for her.

Sandra smiled. 'Congratulations.' She admired the ring. 'Tell me about him.'

Jane told her about Andreas, and about their experiences and their plans. Sandra wanted her to feel comfortable now.

'One last point, Jane, I noticed on the bed there, you've got methamphetamine tablets. Could you tell me about them, please?'

Jane glanced at the bed. 'Oh, I've had them for a while now. When all this carry-on broke about Tommy's death, I had nightmares, and the company doctor gave me some sleeping tablets. But they made me feel drowsy. A neighbour told me about these tablets. She said everyone uses them over here to give them energy and help them through the day. More effective and cheaper than coffee, she said. I haven't used them since I met Andreas.'

'Did you know they're illegal here?'

'What? They can't be, Sandra. They're openly on sale in every pharmacy.'

'How much did you pay for them?'

Jane thought for a moment. 'The equivalent of five shillings.'

Jesus, Sandra thought. These tablets, sold undercover for two pounds each in the UK, were available openly over here in Germany for sixpence each? What the hell was going on? Had they got it wrong? There had to be *some* difference between the tablets. 'Could I have one of your tablets, please. I just want to check something.'

'You can have the lot. I don't need them any more.'

Sandra put the tin in her satchel bag. ‘Thanks. Now, we’ll leave you to get washed and dressed, or go back to sleep if you want. But can I ask you not to leave the room until we give you the all clear. We’ve still to check the rest of the house.’

‘Okay. No problem.’

Sandra asked the female soldier to stand outside the room until she got the all clear, and entered bedroom four. Let’s get Wolff’s story before she saw the boss.

She went through the same procedure with Wolff, and his story confirmed Jane’s. She now believed she was being told the truth. Before she left the room, she asked the senior commando to check Wolff’s gun.

He checked it. ‘Fully loaded, ma’am.’

‘Take the bullets out and return them to Direktor Wolff when he leaves the building.’

‘Yes, ma’am. Will do.’

She went into bedroom three, and ordered the hood, gag and cuffs removed. Porritt looked up at her. ‘I should have known you’d be behind this somewhere along the line, Sandra. Very efficient team, I must say. But not easy to be on the receiving end.’

‘Sorry it’s taken so long to get to you, sir. But we’ve had a few problems. Our target was Doctor Gerhardt Timmermann, whom you knew as Doctor G. The Home Secretary had authorised us to arrest him and dismantle his drug distribution business in the UK. And we’re part of that operation. Very similar to the Aquila raids you led a few years ago.’

‘I see. And have you been successful?’

‘Well, not really. Doctor G took his own life last night.’

‘What? My God. How sad.’

'His wife said the pain from the cancer had become unbearable, and he drank a prepared liquid to get release. We've confirmed it with our medics here, sir.'

Porritt pursed his lips. 'Well, I hope last night's dinner gave him some closure. We discussed a lot about Aquila from both sides.' He went on to give her a summary.

'On that subject, sir, I understand from Jane you gave Doctor G the details of Brenner's burial. What form was it in?'

'A typed sheet in a large white envelope.'

'I'll need to find it. After all, it's one of the driving forces behind this whole exercise, and I want to make sure it's completed. In the meantime, you're free to get washed and dressed or go back to bed, as you wish. But I'd ask you not to leave your room until we give you the all clear. Okay?'

He smiled. 'Of course. You know I always follow orders, Superintendent.'

She smiled back. 'CS now, sir.'

'Congratulations. You'll make Commander yet.'

'Thank you, sir.' She left the room and found Conway and Paige in the corridor.

Paige said, 'We found a plastic container in a cup holder in the back of the car, ma'am. Initial tests show it's orange juice with a powerful sedative added. We can give you more details once we get it back to the lab.'

'Excellent, Captain. Just what I need for the moment.' That evidence confirmed Jane's story, and verified why Porritt and Wolff were there. Good news.

She went in to bedroom one. The senior commando had a box filled with papers. She asked him, 'Did you find a large white envelope here?'

'We did, ma'am.' He delved into the box and pulled the envelope out.

She opened it and read the note on how to contact Alan McGowan to recover the body of Karl Brenner, and signed by Porritt. 'Thanks, I'll hold on to this.'

She went out to the corridor, found her translator, and went in to bedroom six to speak to Doctor G's wife. She was sat in a chair at the dressing table, and had calmed down.

Sandra pulled over the other chair and sat beside her. 'May I ask you something, ma'am?' The translator spoke in German.

The woman nodded.

'Your husband got this note at dinner last night. It tells how to retrieve the body of Karl Brenner. Can you tell me what he planned to do with it?'

'He asked me to give it to Cian this morning.'

Sandra thought, Cian? Where had she heard that name before? 'Who is Cian?'

'He's the brother of Brendan Connolly, one of our couriers who disappeared in England. Brendan used the name, Karl Brenner, when undercover as a German. He also used the name, Tim Convery, when he was in England. Cian is his brother.'

'And where's Cian now?'

'He's upstairs with his wife at the moment. They plan to go to New Zealand, and start a new life there.'

Like hell they do, thought Sandra. She now remembered Margreet in Amsterdam had told her Cian Connolly was the real name of Pieter van der Huizen, who Sandra reckoned had killed Tommy Thomson. Wow. That would be a win among all this disappointment.

She thanked the woman, left the room and found Conway and Paige in the corridor. She said, 'Let's go upstairs now. I'm told there's a couple in one of the bedrooms, and I'm very keen to talk to them.' She turned to Paige. 'But I'd like you to first take their fingerprints, and compare them to these sets here.' She went into her bag and pulled out the sets of prints Margreet had given her.

'Right, ma'am. Will do.' He went off to find his fingerprint expert.

Sandra and Conway, with the translator, headed upstairs. Bill tagged along behind. Conway got his senior people from each bedroom to tell them who they had.

'Room seven, ma'am. Male, with German ID in the name of Otto Fuchs. Would appear to be living here. Could be an employee of the house, ma'am.'

'Room eight, ma'am. Female, with German ID in the name of Gudrun Eckhart. Again, would appear to be living here. Could be an employee of the house.'

'Room nine, ma'am. Male, with German ID in the name of Marius Lemmel. As for the others, ma'am, appears to be living here, and could be an employee of the house.'

'Room twelve, ma'am. Couple. Both with multiple IDs. Male has a British passport and ID card in the name Aidan Connor; Irish passport in the name Cian Connolly; German passport in the name Kurt Reinhard; and Dutch passports in the names, Pieter van der Huizen and Geert Rhys. The female has Dutch passports in the names of Annika Martens. Lotte van der Huizen, and Astrid Rhys. There's no evidence they're married, ma'am.'

Jesus, thought Sandra. Big win indeed. Paige and his fingerprint expert appeared. 'Your couple's in room twelve, Captain.'

She took Conway and the translator into the other bedrooms in turn. It became clear they were a butler, maid and footman in the house, and were not part of any conspiracy. Sandra asked Conway to relocate them to the clinic until she'd given the all clear.

She met Paige and the fingerprint expert in the corridor. 'Their fingerprints match the ones you gave us a hundred percent, ma'am. There's no doubt they're the same people.'

'Thank you.' She turned to Conway. 'Right, we'll start with the girl. Bring her into room eleven. Let's keep them separate from now on. And keep the wrist cuffs on.'

Sandra and Bill went into room eleven. Conway and the senior commando brought the girl in and sat her in the chair beside the table. She wore a dressing gown over her nightclothes, and looked warily at Sandra and Bill.

Sandra pulled out the photograph of the couple at the wedding. Same girl. Pretty blonde. 'Do you speak English?' Sandra asked.

'No comment.'

Oh, Christ, thought Sandra. Not one of those 'no comment' interviews. Well, she wouldn't waste her time.

'What's your name?'

'No comment.'

'What are you doing here?'

'No comment.'

That's enough, Sandra thought. 'We've identified you from your fingerprints as a Dutch national named Annika Martens, who, among other things, visited Glasgow, Scotland, between Wednesday, 28th November and Saturday, 1st December last year. I'm Chief Superintendent Maxwell of the British Police Special Branch, based in Glasgow, and I hereby arrest you as an accomplice in the murder of Thomas Thomson, on or around Friday, 30th November, 1945, contrary to common law. You have the right to remain silent, but anything you do say will be taken down and may be used in evidence. Do you understand?'

The girl blanched, and looked at Sandra in horror.

'You'll be taken to Glasgow later today, charged and tried in court for that offence. In the meantime, you'll remain in this room, and will not be allowed contact with anyone until you reach Glasgow. Have you anything to say?'

The girl shook her head.

Sandra turned to Conway. 'Right, let's go next door and see what *he* has to say for himself.' They left and entered room twelve.

The male sat on the floor, hooded and fully cuffed.

'Take the hood and gag off, please, sergeant,' Sandra asked the senior commando. 'Let's sit him on this chair.'

Sandra sat opposite him. The same man in the photos she'd got from Lincoln and from Margreet, even though he now had darker hair and a moustache. No doubt about it.

'I'm Chief Superintendent Maxwell of the British Police Special Branch. Would you give me your name, please?'

'No comment.'

She went through the same palaver as with the girl next door, and then arrested him for the murder of Thomas Thomson, and told him he'd be taken to Glasgow later that day.

'You can't do that,' he said.

'Oh, really? Why not?'

'Because we're in Germany. You don't have powers of arrest over here.'

'Well, that's where you're wrong, Mr Connolly. There *is* no Germany. You're currently in British

Occupied Territory, which is the same as being in Britain, and I certainly *do* have powers of arrest here.'

The man bit his lip, but said nothing.

'Just before I go,' Sandra pulled the white envelope from her bag. 'Here's the information you've searched for, and killed for. It's the instructions on how to recover your brother's body in Belfast. You could just have asked us for it and we would have told you. You didn't need to kill or kidnap, or cause all this hassle.'

As she left the room, she noticed a long grey woman's raincoat on the hook behind the door. She checked the label. '*Klepper.*' So, this must be the *Kleppermantel* the girl had bought in Amsterdam. Well, well, it had all come together nicely.

She talked to Conway in the corridor. 'Give the all clear now, Major. Box everything related to the couple, and address it to me at Glasgow Police HQ. Box everything else related to GT Pharma, and address it to Commander Burnett at Scotland Yard. Okay?'

'Yes, ma'am. No problem.'

'A superb job by your team, Major. Please pass on my congratulations to them all.'

'I certainly will, ma'am. And they'll be much appreciated. The REME boys have now started to dismantle the factory, so we should have that clear in a couple of days. I'll give you a call when it's complete.'

'Good. We need a couple of female soldiers and a couple of male soldiers to escort the couple to Glasgow. How about, if you have any Glaswegians in your team, give them a quick visit to Glasgow? On me?'

He laughed. 'Leave it with me, ma'am.'

One more thing to do, she thought. She went downstairs and found Hans Wolff. 'We have the people upstairs who kidnapped Jane,' she said. 'I've arrested them for a murder in Glasgow, but it's probably a fifty

fifty case. Do you want to arrest them now for the kidnap, and I'll arrange to have them escorted to you in Nuremberg, once the Glasgow case concludes, one way or the other?'

He thought for a moment. 'Yeah, let's do that.'

They went upstairs, and Wolff arrested the couple in their real names for the kidnap and detention of Mrs Jane Thomson on Thursday, 17th January, 1946. The girl held her head in her hands as they left.

Sandra knocked and went into Porritt's room.

'That's us finished, sir. We're headed back from RAF Güttersloh at nine.' She updated him on the arrest of the couple upstairs.

'Great. Well done,' he said.

'Hope you have a safe journey back to Nuremberg, sir.'

'Thank you. I'm not there for much longer. Got another project.'

'Oh? What now, sir?'

'Well, we think the world's had enough of military might for a while. Power will rest with those who hold secure information, so we'll set up the UK to be one of the leaders in that field. Fingers crossed.'

She smiled at him. 'Best of luck, sir.'

'You too, Sandra. Great job, here. Meet again soon, I hope.'

'I hope so too, sir.'

She left and popped in to see Jane.

'That's us on the way now, Jane. Hope everything works out for you in Geneva.'

'Thank you, Sandra. We'll maybe meet again sometime.'

Sandra went off to phone Burnett.

***

Dave Burnett paced up and down beside Alison's desk. He had a complete picture of the raids in the UK. They'd picked up Andrew Lyall in Hampstead, and all twenty-nine named distributors as planned, though they still had three ID questions to resolve. They'd also aimed to pick up another seven people involved in the drug business, but one of them, in Glasgow, seemed to have gone on the run.

Guus Mulder had called to say the Amsterdam raid had gone well. But Dave hadn't yet heard from Sandra, and couldn't relax until she called. Then his phone rang.

'Sandra,' he barked. 'Did everything go alright?'

'It went fine, sir.' She explained the loss of Doctor G to suicide before they turned up, and the arrest of the couple who had killed Tommy Thomson in Glasgow. She also told him about Jane Thomson's kidnap, and Porritt's visit to meet Doctor G to discuss Aquila. 'In the end, we didn't get the target, sir, but we've closed down the operation. And that's what we wanted to do. I'm on my way back, sir, so I'll see you tomorrow.'

'Well done, Sandra. Great news. I'll let the HS know. Safe journey.'

'Thank you, sir.'

Chapter 15. Aftermath

Sandra Maxwell worked alongside Malcolm Craig and Bill Franklin to examine the evidence in each individual case developed by the SB Regional Heads. They met with Dave Burnett twice a week to review progress.

The Home Secretary had taken the option to use Special Courts, held in camera, and had issued sentencing guidelines to the judges. For local distributors, he recommended one to three years. With evidence of organised crime, these sentences should double to send a message. For regional distributors, he recommended four to six years.

They had resolved all the initial ID problems with the named distributors, and Sandra had decided on the other six people arrested in the initial sweep. Of these, she only had strong enough evidence in three cases, and she added them into the pack for the prosecutors.

Only Glasgow had direct organised-crime involvement, but she couldn't prove it, because the named distributor had no record of criminal history. Edinburgh and Leeds thought they might have organised crime involved, but had no verifiable evidence to support it. Sandra reckoned they had closed the business just in the nick of time.

The team faced delays to their proposed timetable, because lawyers for the Glasgow distributor claimed the legislation flawed and unfair, as it didn't give legitimate businesses enough warning the law had changed before police took action. However, the House of Lords ruled the government had followed procedure, and the police had acted properly.

By the end of March, all the cases had cleared through the Special Courts, with guilty verdicts. Sam

McFadden received three years. Sandra made a point of going to court that day, and became intrigued at the way McFadden looked at her. She couldn't work out whether he admired or hated her.

However, in retrospect, she still worried about the overall strategy of the case. She'd asked Doc Roberts to analyse two tablets, one from Jane's tin, and one from a pack she had taken from the factory as evidence. They were identical.

She concluded Andrew Lyall, who had good connections to Doctor G through his father from the Aquila days, had seized an opportunity with Michael Timmermann, to market these methamphetamine tablets, unknown in the UK, at a huge profit margin, on the basis of their ability to deliver increased sexual stamina. Unfortunately, their other effect of huge euphoria, sometimes led to deaths, and the Home Secretary, faced with a family tragedy caused by these tablets, had taken action, as only he could, to kill the business in the UK.

On the evening the last case cleared, Sandra sat with Bill in 'their' corner of the bar at the Charing Cross Hotel.

'What will you do now?' he asked.

She leaned her head back against the cushion. 'Sleep for a week, I think.'

He smiled. 'Me too. How would you feel about doing it together?'

She glanced at him, not sure about him coming on to her so quickly. She certainly felt very comfortable with him, and liked his friendly and relaxed style. But would that translate over into her personal life? Then she remembered the phrase he'd used at Euston Station, months ago. 'Cards on the table?'

He nodded. 'Yeah, of course,'

'If I marry, I'd probably have to leave the police. If I have children, I'd *definitely* have to leave the police. And I don't want to leave my job.'

He pursed his lips. 'I can live with that.'

'Really?'

'Sure. I've worked with you now for over three months. I've come to admire you more than any woman I've ever known. I don't want it to stop. I've fallen in love with you, and I'd happily live with you without a wedding ring or kids. I think the two of us could have a great life together. Satisfying jobs, with travel to exotic places, good friends and happy times. Why not give it a try? You've nothing to lose, and maybe lots to gain.'

She smiled. 'By doing what?'

'Give it a test run in that loch-side cottage I mentioned. I could fly up to Glasgow on a Friday. We have the weekend away, and back home on Monday. At least we would then have some idea if it would work.'

Sometimes she felt she'd like a companion – more than a companion – on her off-work time, particularly at weekends. Maybe she should give it a try. She found him easy-going and attractive, and as good a chance as she'd get, without joining the dating scene, heaven forbid. And it just might develop into something deeper. She smiled at him. 'Okay, let's try it. See if it works. When?'

'Jesus. That's fantastic.' He checked his diary. 'I'm clear any weekend next month.'

'Okay. My cousin has a cottage on Loch Lomond. I'll see if it's available.'

'That would be great.' He smiled at her. 'Kiss to seal it?'

She nodded, leaned towards him, and kissed him full on the lips. Her body responded in a way she hadn't felt for years. 'Thank you.'

'Oh, thank *you*, my darling.'

***

Sandra sat with her Chief Inspector, Tom Hamilton, and senior prosecutor, Jim Hannah, and discussed the options on the trial of Cian Connolly, for the murder of Tommy Thomson. A final decision had to be made one way or the other.

Hannah shook his head. 'There's no evidence of intent, Sandra. A murder charge on Connolly won't succeed. The best we can go for is culpable homicide, and I think even that's dodgy. Connolly will almost certainly plead self defence. And you'll have to disclose Thomson had a gun. I don't think any jury would convict on that evidence. But we *could* try to prove, once the gun fell in the river, Connolly went on and drowned Thomson. After all, we're not the judge, and we're not the jury.'

She pursed her lips and thought. 'Okay, let's run with culpable homicide as you suggest, and let the jury decide.'

'And the girl?'

'Well, if he walks, she walks. And we then cart them off to Nuremberg.'

***

Sandra stood with bated breath, and watched the Arrival doors at Renfrew Airport, desperate to catch her first glimpse of him. Then she saw him and gave him a wave. Tall, handsome, with a big smile, in blazer and flannels, open-necked shirt, and with a sports bag and coat. He came over to her. She looked up at him and smiled, 'Hi. Welcome to Glasgow.' They kissed.

'Hi. Great to see you.' He stepped back and admired her. 'You look fantastic.'

She laughed. 'Thank you. You're not so bad yourself.' She took his arm as they headed for the exit. 'Good flight?'

'Yeah, fine.'

He threw his bag and coat in the boot, and she drove off west towards the Erskine Ferry. The cottage lay on the shore of Loch Lomond, just north of Luss village, near a hotel. They stopped in Balloch to get some provisions.

As they drove north from Balloch, the loch opened up. Bill gasped, 'Bloody hell, it's beautiful here. What a view.'

'Yeah, superb, isn't it?'

At Luss, she gave him the directions to read out, so they'd catch the access road on their right. The cottage was semi-detached, and her cousin had told her the neighbours would have the key, or if they were out, they'd leave it under a flower pot at the door. A car stood outside the cottage to the right. Sandra parked to the left, and they got out. She headed for the next door cottage, and Bill stretched. 'What a place. And such clean, fresh air.'

An elderly lady came to the door. 'Hello. We're Viv and Matt. Here's the key. Just let us know if we can help.'

Sandra smiled.'Will do. I'm Sandra. That's Bill. Thanks for the key.'

She opened up their cottage. A large lounge led through to a kitchen and dining area along the back, which in turn led out to a patio that overlooked the loch. Two bedrooms and a bathroom led off the lounge to the left. They stood in the lounge and embraced.

'This do you for a couple of days?' she asked, with a smile.

'Perfect,' he said, and looked around. 'Just perfect.'

The doorbell rang. Viv said, 'I'm sorry to bother you, Sandra, but we've got a hospital appointment, and our car won't start. Do either of you know about cars?'

Bill came over. 'I'll have a look,' he said, took off his blazer and hung it over the end of the sofa, rolled his shirt sleeves up, and then left with Viv to check their car.

Sandra went over to the bedrooms to check which had the longest bed, then thought she'd better bring their bags in from the car. She headed for the door, but bumped the sofa. His blazer slipped off onto the floor. She bent down to pick it up, and froze.

The two inside pockets showed. The one on the left as she looked down at it held his wallet, but in the one on the right, a thin plastic bag with a red sealing strip peeped out. She felt as though someone had punched her in the stomach. She glanced out the widow. He still had his head under the bonnet of the car. She opened her handbag, took out a pair of tweezers, and eased the plastic bag from the pocket. It was the same as the ones she'd seen in the dark factory when he'd knocked the box over. She had a flashback of him with his head torch, looking up and saying, 'You go on. I'll tidy this,' and felt sick. She rushed over to the sink and boaked as the bile hit her throat.

She came back to the sofa, where she'd dropped the tweezers and the plastic bag. It had once contained five tablets. It now contained three. She stood and stared at them. The surge of anger made her dizzy.

He came in and walked over to the sink to wash his hands. 'All done,' he said, brightly. 'Just a loose wire. They're away now.' He looked over at her and frowned. 'Are you okay?'

She tried to stay calm, but her voice wavered. 'What do you think you're doing?'

He looked puzzled and glanced down. 'Drying my hands.'

'I meant with this.' She held up the tweezers and the plastic bag. 'It fell out your pocket.'

He blushed and looked away.

Her lips tightened with anger. 'We've just spent weeks, removing them from circulation, and now I find you've got them. And used them. Have you already taken one today?'

He stood and shuffled from one foot to the other. 'I just wanted to make this weekend special for you.'

'Special? Special? Oh, I feel special, all right. I'm so special my man doesn't really fancy me unless he pops a pill. That's *really* special'

'But it's not like that, Sandra. I want to make you feel good.'

'No, you don't. You want to make *you* feel good. You just see me as someone you can use to satisfy yourself.'

'That's absolutely not true. I love you.'

'It *is* true. You just see this as some sort of coupling. Pop a pill. Get a stiffy for a couple of days. Brilliant. No problems there. But don't I have a say in this? Where's the emotional togetherness? Where's the love you talk about? Nowhere. And that's not good enough.'

'You've got it all wrong, Sandra.'

'Oh, no, I haven't. And you know what makes it even worse? You *stole* these tablets. What went through your mind when you saw that box burst open? I'll just snaffle a few packs of these, huh? I've a good mind to arrest you for theft.'

'Come on, Sandra. That's just ridiculous.'

'You don't get it, do you? No woman wants to feel she's just a tool for her man's pleasure, unless she's a whore. And I'm *definitely* not a whore. I want a relationship of equals. A soulmate and a lover. And you're not it. Get out.' She picked up his blazer from the floor and threw it over to him. 'Get out!'

'But we've got to work together.'

'No, we don't. I want you to resign your position on this job within four weeks, and recommend a replacement. Make up whatever excuse you like. But do it.'

'But where will I go?'

'I don't give a bugger. But I want you off this job. If I ever speak to you again, it'll only be because you're required as a witness, and strictly professional. If you don't get off the job, I'll charge you with theft.' She held up the tweezers and the plastic bag. 'I've no doubt your prints are all over this, and that's all I need. So, get out. I don't want to see you again.'

He shuffled out the door, with his head bowed.

She picked up her handbag, dropped the tweezers and plastic bag in it, had a look around, and left the cottage. She locked the front door and dropped the key in the neighbour's letter box. Then went to her car, and dropped his bag and coat on the ground She got into the car and started the engine.

'You can't just leave me here,' he shouted. 'How do I get back?'

'That's your problem,' she shouted, and drove off.

She ground her teeth. Such a fool. How had she fallen for it? Bastard. Now the door to her emotions had well and truly slammed shut again. Bastard.

She pulled onto the main road and pushed her foot to the floor. The engine raced and the car swerved. A car going the other way sounded a horn. Shit. She shouldn't drive like this, a danger to herself and other road users. She eased off and cruised into Luss village. She saw the sign for the car park, pulled into it, and parked in the far corner, near the pier.

She sat and stared at the loch and the mountains, but saw nothing. She hit the steering wheel with the heel of her hand. 'Shit!' Then repeated it. 'Shit! Shit! Shit! Shit! Shit!'

A woman walking her dog looked at her curiously as she passed.

She couldn't work out whether she was angry at him, or at herself for getting into this situation in the first place. Shit!

Her brain had frozen. The whole scenario at the cottage kept rerunning in her head, mixed with the flashback of him in the factory. Her hands gripped the steering wheel. She leaned forward and rested her head on them.

She didn't know how long she'd stayed like that, when she heard a tap on her window. She lifted her head and looked round. The woman with the dog she'd seen earlier mouthed, 'Are you okay?'

Sandra could read her lips, but couldn't hear her. She looked concerned. Sandra wound down the window.

'Are you okay?' the woman asked.

Sandra nodded. She tried to speak, but the words wouldn't come.

'Let me make you a cup of tea, my dear. My cottage is just here. It'll help.'

Sandra looked at the woman – in her fifties, maybe, grey hair, glasses, obviously concerned – and nodded.

She wound the window up, grabbed her handbag and locked the car. She let the woman guide her into the house.

'That's the loo there, if you need it.'

Sandra suddenly felt the need to pee and dashed into the loo. As she washed her hands afterwards, she splashed cold water on her face to try to get her brain to work again. She made her way out into the hall and heard the woman shout, 'In here,' and followed the voice into a comfortable sitting room.

'Come and sit here, my dear,' the woman said, and indicated a sofa

Sandra sat down.

'I've made some tea. How would you like it? Milk? Sugar?

Sandra shook her head. She still couldn't get her words out.

The woman sat down beside her, put a hand on her arm, and smiled. 'My name's Lizzie Steele. I'm the local doctor here. Everyone calls me Doctor Liz. Now, I don't know who you are – I don't want to know who you are – but I do want to help you, my dear. Will you let me help you, please?'

Sandra felt tears well up in her eyes. She hadn't wept for ten years. And she still couldn't speak. She just nodded.

'Now, take a drink of tea.'

She drank from the cup. God, it tasted good. She took another sip.

'Now, is the problem with a man?'

Sandra nodded.

'Did he attack you?'

Sandra looked at her in surprise, and shook her head. 'No.' The word came out a croak.

'That's good. Has he broken your trust, then?'

Sandra thought that's exactly what he'd done. She nodded.

Lizzie paused. 'Ah. Too bad. Is there anything he could do to rebuild that trust?'

Sandra glanced at her. God, this woman asked all the right questions, and she wanted to answer, but she still couldn't speak. She shook her head.

The woman patted Sandra's arm. 'Mmm. Trust is the main building block – the foundation – of relationships, my dear. Without it, there's nothing. And if it's broken beyond repair, you may just have to accept it and move on, even though you may not want to.'

God, thought Sandra, was her trust broken beyond repair? She saw his face in her mind – heard his words, 'I wanted to make it special for you.' But he'd *stolen* these pills. Her trust *had* shattered, and he could do *nothing* to rebuild it. She'd agreed to the holiday too early. She hadn't been ready. This woman was right. It was now over. She had to move on.

She began to calm down, and took another drink. She smiled at the woman and found her voice. 'Thank you. I needed that.' The tears welled up in her eyes again. 'Thank you.'

'Oh, you're welcome, my dear. Relationships are tough right now. The war's caused untold damage to people's lives. Sometimes I wonder if we'll ever get over it. But please remember, number one, you need to look after yourself. If you're not content within yourself, it's very difficult to love and live with someone else. And I can tell you from experience, it's more difficult to rebuild trust than to just walk away, even though that's hard. So, look after yourself, my dear. There are probably others that need you more than the man who broke your trust. Focus on *them*, and you'll come through it okay.'

Sandra now felt calm and clear-headed. Her analytical brain worked again. This woman had taken her gently though the trauma and brought her out the other side safe and well.

'Thank you so much, Doctor Liz.' She gathered her handbag. 'I'm ready to drive again.'

The doctor smiled at her. 'That's good. And if you ever want to talk to me again, just give me a call.' She gave Sandra a card from her mantelpiece. 'Best of luck, my dear.'

Sandra left and got into her car. She gave a big sigh. That had been tough, but how lucky had she been to meet Doctor Liz? Such a wise and truly remarkable woman.

***

A week later, she got a letter from him. A copy of an internal note circulated within the Home Office, with a handwritten note attached.

'Sandra,

Planned to tell you this at Loch L, but other things got in the way.

Sorry about that. You'll never know how much. Will never forget you.

Best wishes, Bill.'

The Home Office note read,

'Internal Memo No 46/019/3218

The Home Secretary is pleased to announce that William James Franklin, Deputy Head, Investigations, London, will transfer to the Foreign Office on 1st June to join our Embassy in Washington DC, USA, as Commercial Attache.

We wish Bill every success in his new position, and thank him for his contribution to our continued success over the last eight years

Bill will be succeeded by Charles Mungall, currently . . . '

She didn't read any more, and threw it in the bin. He must have known about this for weeks. It couldn't just happen over a couple of days. Yet he hadn't mentioned it. Just another black mark against a weak, stupid man. Thank Christ, she'd avoided that one.

***

Jane and Andreas stood arm in arm on the balcony of their modern four-bedroom apartment just north of he city centre, and admired the view over Lake Geneva, with the snow-capped mountains still just visible in the distance. She snuggled into him.

'Happy?' he asked.

'Oh, more than that. Delirious.'

She loved Geneva. The fabulous Old Town, the iconic Jet d'Eau fountain. So clean. So organised. After Glasgow, Nuremberg, Dresden and Prague, Geneva seemed in a different world. All these other cities had problems caused by the war, but Geneva had sailed through it all untouched. Neutral Switzerland had remained pristine while the countries around it had crumbled. Now she'd seen this place, she didn't want to live anywhere else. And, of course, at the United Nations, she now played a small part in making the world a safer place.

The wedding had gone off like a dream that morning in the Mayor's parlour. She had her mother and the boys, Andreas had his parents and brother from Basel. All of them had enjoyed a superb wedding breakfast at a top restaurant, then back to the apartment for nibbles and drinks. Now, all the visitors had gone. The boys were asleep. Her mother had gone to bed. Just the two of them now, savouring a perfect day. The phone rang.

'I'll get it,' she said, and went back indoors. 'Hello?'

'Jane. It's Doctor Koehl here. Thought I'd just catch you before I went home. Your test results are positive. Congratulations.'

She put her hand to her mouth, and tears welled in her eyes. 'Oh, my God. That's wonderful. Thank you so much, Doctor.'

'Oh, you're welcome, Jane. I should call you Mrs Schaeffer now, huh?'

'That's right. You've made it a perfect end to a perfect day.'

'Well, I'll see you soon. Take care.'

She walked back out onto the balcony, and put her arms up around Andreas's neck. 'That was Doctor Koehl. Congratulations, you're going to be a dad.'

He stared at her, and laughed and cried at the same time. 'Oh, Christ. That's fantastic. You need to sit down and rest.'

'Darling, I'm pregnant. I'm not ill.'

'A perfect end to a perfect day.'

'That's what I told him.'

A Note from James Hume

Thank you so much for reading Chasing Aquila. I hope you enjoyed it. If you have a moment, please leave an honest review at Amazon. Even if it's only a line or two, it would be *very* much appreciated.

I welcome contact from my readers. If you'd like to hear about new releases in advance, send a brief email to james@jameshumeauthor.com

I won't share your email with anyone else, and I won't clutter your inbox. I'll only contact you to respond or when a new release is imminent.

James Hume

Further Reading

Hunting Aquila (An intriguing WW2 spy drama, with a twist)

During World War 2, Churchill stumbles across a leak of vital information from the UK to the enemy and calls in Commander Jonathan Porritt to catch the mole. Porritt has no leads until Jane, a young British translator, unwittingly gets caught up with a German spy trying to flee the country. Can Porritt use his Special Branch teams in Glasgow, Yorkshire, London and Belfast to rescue Jane and smash the undercover spy organisation before Churchill's invasion plans get leaked?

This deftly plotted, action-packed thriller is full of twists and turns, and provides powerful and intriguing lessons that still apply in today's changing world.

'A proper page-turner full of well-plotted twists and turns. I loved the story, which rattles along at a cracking pace. The attention to detail with impressive research meant the whole book stayed with me long after I'd finished reading.' (Kerry Barrett, Author / Editor)

'Well written spy novel. Grabs you from the beginning to the end. A great cast of characters, both good and bad.' (Kindle customer)

'A brilliant story. I couldn't put this book down and read it in less than a day to the exclusion of everything else.' (Kindle customer)

Available – on Amazon now

Killing the Captain (A Sandra Maxwell thriller)

Just after World War 2, when partly deaf Adam Bryson lip reads a conversation between two businessmen planning an assassination in the UK, it sets off a series of events that involve Sandra Maxwell, Head of Special Branch in the West of Scotland. Can she identify the target, capture the crooks and deal with the aftermath before anyone gets killed?

This deftly plotted, action-packed thriller is full of twists and turns. Carefully weaving fact and fiction, it provides powerful and intriguing lessons that still apply in today's changing world.

Available – Mid 2020